Framed

Also by Leslie Jones

Framed

Deep Cover

Bait

Night Hush

Framed

Duty & Honor Book Four

LESLIE JONES

WITNESS
IMPULSE
An Imprint of HarperCollins*Publishers*

This is a work of fiction. Names, characters, places, and incidents are products of the author's imagination or are used fictitiously and are not to be construed as real. Any resemblance to actual events, locales, organizations, or persons, living or dead, is entirely coincidental.

Digital Edition JANUARY 2018 ISBN: 978-0-06-249947-9
Print Edition ISBN: 978-0-06-249948-6

FIRST EDITION

18 19 20 21 22 LSC 10 9 8 7 6 5 4 3 2 1

To Scott. You are my greatest joy and proudest achievement. You're what keeps me going when things fall apart. Yes, you'll always be my baby, but I'm so excited to watch all the amazing things you'll do in the future. I have and will always believe in you.

Acknowledgments

This book would not have been possible without the all-encompassing support and patience of Nicole Fischer, my incredible editor. Thank you for working with me through all my false starts and hiccups, and for believing that I could finally finish this most difficult book. I appreciate you so much!

I'd also like to recognize the expertise and care of Tracy Wilson, copyeditor extraordinaire, and the Witness cover art team for designing this fantastic book cover—it, and you, are amazing.

And to Sarah E. Younger, your know-how continues to guide me through my writing career, and your humor always cheers me up. I promise there will be a dog or cat in the next book!

I would like to express special gratitude to Scott Jones, whose great suggestion to revise my battle scene improved it tremendously and made it credible.

And finally, nobody has been more supportive of me than my family. Kim and Scott, your love and belief in me brings me joy in good times and sustains me in difficult times. I love you both!

Acknowledgments

[illegible]

[illegible]

[illegible]

Framed

Chapter 1

Sunday, January 29. 8:00 p.m.
Lyubinsk, Russia.

"AN HOUR OUTSIDE a metropolis of twelve million people, and we end up in the middle of nowhere."

Fatianova hated leaving Moscow for any reason. Moscow provided excitement. The metro and the Bolshoi. The Danilovsky Market and Café Pushkin. Gorky Park and the White Garden spa.

Lyubinsk stank of fish and onions.

They passed through the sprawling farms, empty of workers this time of the evening; then skirted the fisheries, with their long docks, floating cages interconnected with netting, and rank stench. She tried to cover her nose with her sleeve. It helped a bit.

Pavel turned down an unpaved road. He slowed to thirty kilometers an hour.

"It's about eight kilometers to the facility," Fyodor Petrov said. "We've passed the worst of it."

Until we go back, she thought.

The sun had set an hour ago. Lyubinsk after dark became downright eerie. The snow flurries didn't help. The slushy track seemed threatening in the jouncing headlights. The windshield wipers barely worked, forcing Pavel to lean forward to see. He slowed again.

The facility came into sight. The ugly cement building rose three stories, smack in the center of an icy mess of mud and gravel. A second, much smaller building sat behind it, also unadorned cement. The trees had been cut back, preventing anyone from approaching unobserved, and a ten-foot-high barbed wire fence surrounded the complex. Pavel hopped out and propped open the deliberately unlocked gate, then drove the van straight up to the small building, parking in front of it like he had every right to be there.

Fyodor opened his laptop and typed in a few commands. A grid showing nine views of the facility and its surroundings popped up, then went black as he pressed a few buttons. "The codes I got are good. The exterior cameras are disabled. Working on the interior ones now."

"Hurry up." Fatianova tapped her long nails on her trousers, leaning away from Konstantin. He smelled almost as bad as the rotting fish.

Fyodor closed the laptop. "Cameras inside this building are down. We have maybe fifteen minutes before they bother to come check."

They all exited the van. Fatianova turned up her fur collar against the cold as Pavel walked to the door and tried the handle.

"It's unlocked." He pulled it open, peering in before gesturing to Konstantin, who drew a submachine gun from under his long coat.

Fatianova shivered. She hated guns; had since the GRU stormed her family home and killed her parents right in front of her eyes. They hadn't been dissidents, as the KGB claimed. Just poor factory floor workers committing the occasional petty theft to make ends meet.

The door opened into some sort of tunnel. Age and calcium pitted the cement walls. The low ceiling seemed to be half wooden beams, half exposed cabling. Every ten feet, an oxidized steel door barred entry into whatever was hidden there. About halfway down the tunnel, one of these doors stood ajar.

"The guard should be on a smoke break," Fyodor said. The tunnel echoed his words.

"Shut up," Fatianova whispered. "We don't know who else might be here."

"No one's here," the man insisted. "Just like the gate guard conveniently went to take a piss. None of the guards here have been paid in five months. It was easy to bribe them."

"No one better show up," Konstantin said. "Or they're dead."

Her group made its way down to the reddish steel security door and the men hauled it further open. When Fatianova stepped over the threshold, she nearly stumbled and fell before scrambling over rubble and pipes that had fallen onto the floor, or been abandoned there.

"Here," Konstantin said. He turned left, stepping over a black tarp and crowbar to a banded wooden shipping crate. Pavel picked up the crowbar. At a nod from Fatianova, he pried the top open and shoved the lid back.

She looked down at the oversized red-and-silver suitcase nestled on a bed of industrial packing material. Excellent. Fingering the clasps before pulling them open, she eased the lid up, calculating and recalculating in her head how rich this simple suitcase would make her.

"Hurry, Fatya," Fyodor said.

"I'll take all the time I want; do you hear me? This isn't a box of marbles. And don't call me that." She shot him a glare before inspecting the contents meticulously. "Everything looks good."

Fyodor gave a sharp nod and gestured to Pavel. "Go get the cart. Quick, now."

He was gone and back in less than five minutes with a heavy-duty padded cargo dolly. Fatianova snapped the suitcase closed. Konstantin closed the crate and the three men lifted it onto the dolly.

"Slowly," she hissed. "Be careful. Very, very careful."

They obeyed. She was, after all, the expert. The only one who knew how to handle the dangerous contents of the suitcase.

"It's got to be worth millions of rubles," Konstantin said. "While you're only paying us a couple thousand."

Closer to a billion rubles. Fatianova kept silent.

Fyodor sneered. "I'm paying you six thousand rubles to steal something you couldn't possibly understand or sell. Count yourself lucky."

"What are you going to do with it? Use it?"

"None of your business. But if it'll shut up your yapping, I intend to take it to America and sell it. They're rolling in money there. They can afford to pay."

"How do you plan to get it across the border? You can't exactly check it at the airport as though it were a regular suitcase."

Fyodor cast him an impatient look. "We're taking it to Kamchatka. I have someone who can get us into Canada, and from there to Massachusetts. Are you done asking stupid questions?"

Konstantin shrugged. "Sure. Whatever you say. You're the boss."

I'm the boss. She had no choice, for the moment, but to let Fyodor think he was the one in charge. She needed his contacts. Soon enough, though, he would cease to be useful to her. Fatianova locked down the safety straps on the dolly, double-and triple-checking to ensure the container wouldn't shift even a little bit.

"Lift it over the rubble," she ordered. "Keep it smooth and slow. Steady, you clods!"

She watched them like a hawk. She had no desire to die. The group inched its way back to the van, where she supervised loading the suitcase, dolly and all, and secured the whole thing inside.

The snow had stopped while they were inside the building, leaving the landscape dark and bleak. Her heart began to thud and her breath came in excited spurts as Konstantin snapped the doors closed. She had it!

"If you tell anyone about tonight, I'll hunt you both down and carve your hearts out," she said. "Tell me you understand."

"Yeah, sure," Konstantin said. "Give us our six thousand, and we're gone."

"Fyodor, give them what they're owed," she ordered.

The muffled report of a silenced gun caused her to flinch. She turned in time to see Pavel collapse. Fyodor turned the weapon onto Konstantin, who froze in the process of unslinging his submachine gun.

"What the fuck are you doing?" he snarled.

Fatianova knew she should just let Fyodor shoot him, but why shouldn't she have a little fun after the anxiety of transporting the suitcase?

Slipping her knife from under her long coat, she moved well

into his personal space, smiling into his eyes. A cat-with-a-canary, you're-an-idiot kind of smile.

"I'm killing you, you dimwit."

Uncertainty touched his eyes, which then widened as she slipped her knife between his ribs and twisted.

Chapter 2

Tuesday, February 14. 10:00 a.m.
FBI Field Office. Boston, Massachusetts.

Hadley Larkspur entered the bulletproof cage turnstile and finger-waved at the security guard on duty. After a wait that always seemed eternal to her, the mechanism disengaged and allowed her into the lobby of the FBI's Boston field office.

"Morning, Hoyt."

Hoyt flipped closed the magazine he was reading and shoved it out of sight. "Morning, Lark."

She glanced up at the bank of monitors bolted to a bar near the ceiling. Three faced toward her and three faced the security desk. All showed views from the sixteen cameras at the building's entrance, in the lobby, and in the hallway outside of the field office itself.

"You know they can see you reading *Penthouse*, right?" she said. She leaned against the reception desk, large enough that it covered a quarter of the lobby space.

Hoyt flushed. "It's *Men's Health*. My wife wants me to join a gym."

She took in the gut overhanging his uniform pants and his growing double chin. "Probably she just wants you to live longer. Heart health, you know?"

"I guess," he said, voice sullen. "By the way, Melvin's been on a tear this morning. He's been out here half a dozen times looking for you."

"Ugh." She loved her new job and everything about it. Everything, that is, except for her boss. "I guess I'll go get my ass-chewing out of the way. Then I can enjoy my coffee in peace."

"What did you do?"

"Does it matter? He'll find something."

Hoyt managed a half smile. "True. I like the new hair, by the way. What happened to the blond?"

Lark fingered the ends of her bright pink hair. "Got bored."

"You get bored easy?"

"Yeah, you could say that." She walked to the second set of turnstiles and slapped her badge on the reader. The light turned green, and she pushed through. She had to badge in again to gain access to the cube farm. Before she even made it to her cubby, Melvin bore down on her like a freight train.

"You're late again, Larkspur. What the hell is it with you? Don't you own an alarm clock?"

She tried a sunny smile, which only made him glower more. "Crash on the highway. It took half an hour to go two miles."

Special Agent Melvin Dewey, Cyber Crime supervisor in Boston, was built like an NFL linebacker. His receding hairline offset the belligerent thrust of his chin, and his dark blue suit sat awkwardly on his beefy six-foot-four-inch frame. Today he wore a chartreuse tie with some sort of insipid pattern she thought was particularly ugly.

"Leave earlier, then," he snapped. "And what's with the hair? This is a professional organization. If you can't manage to look and behave like a professional, then maybe you don't belong here."

Her eyes slitted as irritation flooded her. Before she blew her top, though, a cheery voice interrupted them.

"Good morning, you two."

They both turned to face Doug Huckabee, the Special Agent in Charge of the FBI's Boston field office, and Melvin's boss.

"Good morning, sir," Melvin said.

"Morning, Doug," Lark said. "How's your wife? Gone into labor yet?"

Doug's face grew dreamy. "Not yet. The doc says any day now. I can't wait to hold my daughter."

"I can't wait to see the pics. I bet she'll be cute as a button." Lark punched him on the arm as Melvin stared at her in horror. Maybe she was breaching some sort of protocol, but she liked Doug. And he was certainly more laid back than her uptight boss. As she expected, he laughed.

"God help her if she looks like me. Hey, I have something I'd like you to take a look at. Our computer scans detected some malware on one of the virtual desktop servers."

Melvin's mouth turned down in displeasure as he stepped forward to partially conceal Lark from his boss. "Sir, I already assigned her a task. Maybe a more senior computer scientist?"

"What are you working on, Lark?"

"A complaint from a woman who claims her internet service provider called and said her router had a virus. The usual scam. He said he could remove it for a fee. She paid it using her debit card. He emptied her bank account. I'm pretty much done with it. I just need to write up the report."

"Good, good. I think this one will be right up your alley. We've isolated the server, but we need to know what the malware is designed to do. Interested?"

"Sir, I'll handle it personally. She's not ready—"

"Absolutely! Deconstructing malware is my specialty." Sort of. She was more familiar with creating it, but if something could be created, it could also be dissected.

"Sir, Ms. Larkspur's very new to this office, and she's only been with the FBI a few months. I don't think she has the experience for that."

Doug slapped him on the back. "You'll supervise, naturally. Give the kid a chance. Let's see what she can do."

Melvin's brows knit and he narrowed his eyes, but in the end forced a nod. "Of course, sir."

"Good man. Lark, the server's in the SCIF. Jocelyn will show you which one." He pronounced the acronym "skiff"—the Sensitive Compartmented Information Facility, a secure data facility where the most sensitive systems, programs, and information could be discussed, cached, and handled.

After Doug left, Melvin scowled down at Lark. "I'll expect that report on my desk before you even look at that server. Got me?"

Lark couldn't help herself. "Of course, sir," she mocked.

He looked daggers at her, stepping closer. She guessed she was supposed to faint in terror. Instead, she gave him a saucy grin and walked away. She needed coffee to wash away the taste of Melvin's bullying.

Jocelyn Katsaros popped her head into the break room as Lark poured herself a cup. "Morning, sunshine."

"I know, I know. I'm late again." She added six sugars and some half-and-half, stirred it, and slugged back a gulp. It wasn't too godawful.

Jocelyn came inside and went straight to the vending machine. Coins clinked and a Snickers bar dropped into the tray. She tore open the wrapper and took a bite before sitting at one of the laminate tables. "Who cares? You get more done in the time you're here than the rest of us combined. You're making us look bad."

Lark sat opposite her, taking another drink before setting the Styrofoam cup on the table. "That's because Melvin keeps assigning me rinky-dink little jobs."

Jocelyn rested her elbows on the table. "That's because you're the newbie."

"I know, I know. At least this server malware thing will let me spread my wings a little bit."

Her friend finished the last bite of the candy bar and rose, dropping the wrapper into the trash can. Her smooth chestnut hair rippled in waves halfway down her back; her exotic face and curvy body screamed sex appeal. Men were drawn to her like moths to wildfire. Lark couldn't bring herself to feel any jealousy, though. Most men weren't worth the time.

"It's not fair you can eat whatever you want and never gain a pound," Lark said.

"Sunshine, I've seen you eat." Jocelyn tore off a paper towel and blotted her full red lips. "I ain't got nothing on you."

"Huh. Whatevs."

"Anyway, I work it all off in karate. You should really come with me some time. You'd enjoy it."

"Sure, maybe. Someday."

Jocelyn chuckled. "Your sister's wedding's coming up soon, isn't it? This Saturday?"

Lark felt her face soften. "Yeah. You should come to the bachelorette party Friday night."

"I just might. Come on. I'll show you which server has the infection."

Lark drained her cup and threw it away, then followed Jocelyn to the other end of the building to the SCIF. They signed in with the security guard, dropped their cell phones into the small lockboxes, and pocketed the keys. Jocelyn entered the access code into the keypad that let them into the data center.

The windowless room had rows of tables sporting two, three, or four monitors, as well as individual workstations. An area set aside for group collaboration had a triple row of monitors on the wall, as well as individual screens for four or more analysts. Jocelyn led her to a workstation on the right wall, pushed her into the chair, and sat next to her. A tower server rested to the left of the double monitors.

"It's a Unix sever running Solaris. Standard user interface. The malware is quarantined on bay three." Jocelyn clicked through to the right folder. "No one's touched it since it came in here."

Lark turned the server to see the back. Three fans cooling seven hot-swap bays. "Where was it?"

"In the server room catty-corner from you. It runs about a hundred virtual machines. I've run scans, and the code isn't replicated anywhere else on our network. Whatever it's doing, it's stopped cold. I can help if you get stuck. Where do you think you'll start?"

"With the logs."

"Good idea. That alone will take you a while. Ping me if you run into any snags. I've got ten years on you; I can help."

"Thanks." She barely noticed when Jocelyn left. Before she did anything else, she needed to create a backup of the quarantined folder. While it copied, she brought up her case report and finished the write-up. She felt the familiar burn of anger toward unscrupulous asshats who preyed on the unsuspecting. This woman lost only a few thousand dollars, but she'd read about cases where entire life savings had been lost to scam artists.

She sent the report to Melvin, then opened a text file to document everything she did with the malware, in case criminal charges were ever filed against the idiot who'd written the program.

Lark brought up a command line and tapped the keys. A list of partitions on the drive appeared. She poked around, seeing if anything jumped out at her.

Huh. That's weird. The clock time was off.

She checked the server time against the access logs. A certain amount of time drift was not uncommon. However, the secure Network Time Protocol corrected that by having a server's clock check in with the NTP at regular intervals. Why hadn't that happened here?

Digging deeper, she found a program inserted where it had no business being. Reading through each line of code would take too long, so she copied it into a safe folder and executed it.

"What are you doing?"

Lark started, her concentration broken. Craning her neck around to see Melvin, she suddenly realized how stiff her muscles were. She sat back, shaking out her hands.

"What time is it?"

Melvin turned to rest his buttocks against the table. "Two o'clock."

Wow. She'd lost track of time, totally immersed in the mystery of the malware.

"It's been hours. Have you managed to come up with anything at all?"

She swiveled her chair to face him more fully. "Well, I know what it's not. It's not a virus, and it's not ransomware."

"Are you sure? I still think Doug's making a mistake assigning this to you. Have you ever worked on a project like this before?"

Lark took a deep breath before answering. "Yes, I'm sure. I have more experience than you seem to think."

"Huh."

"I did come across a weird anomaly in the clocking system. According to this server, the time is thirty minutes into the future. I'm curious why."

Melvin crossed his arms over his chest. "Odds are it's just time drift. Focus on the job at hand, Larkspur. Don't go down rabbit trails."

"But what if it's connected—"

"It's not," he snapped. "But if you're going to get so wound up about something so simple, I'll tell Jocelyn to take a look at it. Will that get you back on track?"

"Sure thing." Her fists clenched and unclenched. Why the hell did he dislike her so much?

Melvin didn't linger, which was good. Lark stretched and went in search of more coffee. SCIF rules even forbade caffeine machines, in case someone tried to mount a camera inside. Regular sweeps for bugs didn't alter that unwelcome reality.

Jocelyn was eating lunch when Lark came into the break room, surrounded by two other computer scientists and one analyst—all male—who hung on her every word. Lark's stomach growled.

Oh, yeah. She'd better eat, too. She grabbed her brown bag from the refrigerator and sat at the other table. Jocelyn immediately excused herself to come sit with her.

"How's it going?"

"Slowly." Lark couldn't discuss specifics outside the SCIF, but her friend wouldn't expect her to. "But steam is shooting out of Melvin's nose, like a pissed-off bull about to charge."

Jocelyn smiled. "His boss assigned you directly to a project; of course he's pissed-off. He's territorial, in case you hadn't noticed. But his huge ego outweighs his actual talent."

"He's a bully." Damn it. She'd forgotten her coffee. Rising, she made a beeline for the coffee machine, poured herself a cup, mixed it the way she wanted, and returned to her seat. "I really need to bring in my own mug. These Styrofoam cups hold like two drops. Also, your admirers left. Why do you encourage them?"

Jocelyn shrugged. "A girl's got to have a hobby. Haven't you ever dated a coworker? Been in love? Gotten your heart broken?"

"Well, that escalated fast." She balled up her sandwich wrapper. "Would you believe I was engaged once?"

Jocelyn's eyes sparked with curiosity. "Who? When?"

Lark sighed. "Short version? Ralph Pearson. Eldest son of a rich family. Both our families wanted us to get engaged, so we did. I thought he was like me, rebelling against his parents' edicts. Turns out his father ordered him to date me."

Leaving out a lot of details made her feel less foolish. They'd made a pact to be true to themselves, whatever their parents wanted. Each changed their name in rebellion against their parents' manipulations, her to Lark and him to Pierce. A few months later, Ralph-now-Pierce left for Princeton, where he'd been successfully molded into a stuffy, pretentious boob who tried to rein her in at every turn. When she told her parents she intended to end things, her father threatened to pull strings to get her kicked out of Carnegie Mellon unless she went through with the marriage. Unwilling to be trapped into a meaningless role as a society miss, she broke off the engagement anyway. Her father made good on his threat, forcing her to transfer to CalTech on scholarship, and she refused to speak to him for eight months.

"Well, this has been fun," Lark said. "But it's time for me to get back to work."

"Chicken. Someday I want to hear the rest of the story."

"Maybe. Someday."

Chapter 3

Friday, February 17. 12:24 p.m.
Viktor Sokolov's Home. Boston, Massachusetts.

ELLIOTT WEBER TRIED to rub the grit out of his eyes as he trudged down the hallway to his doom. He scrubbed his palms over his bright blue hair, short on the sides and longer up top, then scraped his fingers through the gelled tuft at the front, artfully styled to look messy. He didn't know why he bothered; his uncle hated the hairstyle, hated the color, and, frankly, didn't care much for Elliott, either. He'd been called useless, stupid, and irresponsible.

A juvenile delinquent, through and through.

He'd own up to that one. Even before his father—and then his mother—died, he'd become expert at sneaking out of the house, meeting his friends to drink beer and smoke weed. When he was sixteen, his mother finally succeeded in overdosing on oxycodone, and his uncle became his guardian. Elliott graduated from misdemeanor joyriding to felony larceny of luxury motor vehicles, until he'd been caught and arrested. Sure, his uncle had pulled strings. Probation and community service for what should have been six years in prison and a fifteen-thousand-dollar fine. It's not that he wasn't grateful, really, just that sometimes he thought prison might have been more fun.

That screw-up had cost him a beating and confinement to the townhouse. What would be the penalty for this one?

He knocked, then pushed through the door into the Inner Sanctum, his heart thumping painfully before beating in triple time. He winced at the sunlight pouring through the tall windows, head pounding with hangover and anxiety. As usual, his uncle held court from behind his obnoxiously enormous walnut desk, custom-made for him by the Amish so he could say he supported independent craftsmen. As usual, Palachka sat off to his right in a brown wingback chair, staring down at a newspaper open on his lap. It fooled no one; everyone knew he listened to and catalogued every word said in this room.

And as usual, Palachka raised his head to stare at him, eyes flat and nearly inhuman. Elliott twisted up one side of his mouth in a smirk and made kissy noises at him. His uncle's chief enforcer didn't so much as twitch in reaction, returning his gaze to the newsprint. As brutal as he knew Palachka to be, Elliot wasn't afraid of him. His uncle kept a tight hold on his leash. Palachka wouldn't hurt him unless his uncle ordered it.

His uncle, on the other hand, terrified him.

"All right, gentlemen," he said, rising from his throne. He buttoned his suit coat and came around to shake hands with his three guests. "Send me the cost projections on Monday. I'll let you know if I need anything else from you."

"No problem, Mr. Sokolov."

"We'll get right on that, Mr. Sokolov."

"Thank you, Mr. Sokolov."

Palachka rose, escorted the men from the room, and closed the door firmly behind them before returning to his seat. This time, he set the newspaper aside and focused on Elliott.

"New criminal enterprise?" Elliott asked. Apparently even fear of dismemberment couldn't curb his smartass impulses.

His uncle cast him an impatient look. "I'm expanding one of my nightclubs. Roman, ask Mikhail Kerghakov to meet me here Tuesday morning. Nine sharp."

Palachka dipped his chin once and rose, pulling his cell phone out and moving to a corner to make the call.

His uncle's gaze ran down Elliott's body. "Ripped jeans, ratty shoes, and that ridiculous hair. You're a disgrace."

In contrast, everything about him was meticulously groomed. Gray hair neatly clipped and brushed back. Nails trimmed. Tie precisely knotted. His wool suit had been custom-tailored, and his shoes alone had probably set him back two grand.

"Since you clearly haven't come here for fashion advice, what do you want, Elliott? I'm a very busy man."

Now that the moment of truth had arrived, he couldn't seem to push words past his dry throat. His fingers twisted together of their own volition. Clenching his teeth, he shoved them into the front pockets of his jeans. *Show no fear, remember?*

"Well?" his uncle barked.

Elliott's gaze jerked up to meet his. Inside his pockets, his nails dug into his palms. He'd really porked the pooch on this one.

"There's a problem with the cyber business account," he finally said. His uncle insisted on hearing bad news up front. "There was an unauthorized withdrawal."

Dead silence. When his uncle spoke, his voice had dropped an octave.

"Explain."

Elliott couldn't help the convulsive swallow. "I get texts on my phone whenever there's a withdrawal. Usually it's me moving money around, so it's no big deal. This morning, someone took money out."

"Who?"

"I found a name. SPURious. That's who transferred the money out." Elliott tightened his shoulders.

Uncle Viktor's brows snapped down, storm clouds gathering in his eyes. "What the fuck does that mean, Elliott? Is that a person?"

Wishing he had the nerve to sit, he muttered, "It's a hacker handle."

"And? Who is it?"

"Well, I don't know. Yet," he added hastily. "I need to—"

"How much?"

Elliott cleared his throat. "All of it."

His uncle's brows shot toward his hairline. "Excuse me?"

"Yeah. They drained the account. Fifty million dollars."

His uncle moved close enough that Elliott could smell his aftershave and see the anger in the flecks of his eyes. "This is the money I set aside for the auction. How could you let this happen?"

"I . . . I'm not sure. I mean, I didn't. I don't know what happened."

"When?" he snarled. "When did you lose my fifty million dollars?"

Palachka walked to the built-in bar, opened a triangular crystal decanter, and splashed two fingers of Scotch into a glass. He brought it to his boss, who tossed it back and thrust the glass back into his hand.

Elliott's stomach knotted as he suppressed a hard swallow. "Early this morning. Around four thirty."

His uncle's eyes slitted. "And you're just bringing it to me now? Eight hours later? What the fuck have you been doing?"

Moron. Half-wit. His uncle's scorn rippled over his skin, but he was used to it. He reminded his uncle of his father, the waste of air he was virtually certain Palachka had killed.

"I just woke up. When I saw the text, I came to you right away."

It really was too much to hope that his uncle wouldn't catch on. Sure enough, anger morphed into pure rage. "In other words, you frittered away your night with those losers you hang out with online? Fooling around with some moronic game where you play a half-dressed woman with big tits?"

"Uncle Vik—"

"Now is not the time to remind me we're related," his uncle screamed into his face, and drove his fist into Elliot's stomach. As he doubled over, agony clawing through him, his uncle back-handed him across the face. He felt his uncle's ring tear his cheek as he collapsed onto the carpet. Another scar to add to his collection. Funny, the carpet really did feel as soft as it looked. He rubbed his sore cheek into it as he curled into a fetal position, hoping the blood smearing his face would stain the fibers.

Hard hands clamped onto his biceps, and he was dragged upright. Palachka showed no expression—no animosity, no pleasure, and certainly no sympathy—as he steadied Elliott.

"Dolt. Why did I ever trust you with the cyber business? You don't have the sense God gave a jackass."

Elliott rubbed his cheek, then wiped the blood down one leg

of his jeans. "Because I make you a fuckton of money, Uncle Vik. That's why. Skimming PINs and selling credit card numbers is big business. And me and my *losers* are damned good at it."

"Insolence will not serve you well right now, Elliott." His uncle turned abruptly and went to sit on one of the leather sofas grouped around the coffee table, built by the same Amish artisan who'd designed his desk. He picked up a file folder and opened it, effectively dismissing Elliott. "You have until the auction to find my money."

"What if I can't?" he blurted out.

His formidable uncle didn't look up from the papers in hands. "Then I unleash Palachka on you, and you'll wish you were dead."

Chapter 4

Friday, February 17. 11:45 p.m.
The Promenade. Boston, Massachusetts.

"I'M GETTING MARRIED in the morning!"

Lark grinned. "Yes, you are, baby sister. You're glowing so much I can't see anything else."

"Tomorrow I'll be Mrs. Kaley Newman." Kaley's bright eyes glazed as the Jell-O shots caught up with her. "Mrs. Kayyy . . ."

Lark deftly scooped the last shot off the table and handed it to Dana. Kaley pouted as her friend downed it.

"Time for another round," she said. "Your turn, Lark."

Lark shrugged and wandered toward the bar. Even a hangover wouldn't dim her sister's beauty one iota the next day. If Kaley wanted to celebrate, who was she to deny her?

"Another round," she shouted over the din. This time of evening, the nightclub was packed with partiers. The music alone deafened her, and she felt a headache burning deep into her skull.

The bartender brought over a small tray with six Jell-O shots. She dug into her pocket for some cash.

Someone jostled her elbow, causing her to drop the folded bills. Muttering a curse, she bent down to snag them before someone stepped on them. A sweaty hand gripped her shoulder.

"Tha's it, baby," a male voice slurred. She looked up and realized the man who'd bumped her had moved closer, so her head was close to his junk. She jerked away and stood.

"Fucking asshole," she said. "Go away."

The idiot moved well into her personal space. "But you'd be so good, baby. Come on. Let's go into the alley."

Charming. She pushed his chest. "You go right ahead."

Confusion flitted across his florid face. "You coming?"

"Not in a million years." She shoved the bills at the bartender, who grinned and moved on to the next customer. Grabbing the tray of drinks, Lark started back toward their crowded little table.

She'd almost made it back when someone touched her shoulder. Swearing, she whirled around. The shot glasses clacked together. "I'm not going to blow you, jackass."

Her mouth snapped shut. Instead of the drunken idiot, another man stood behind her. A really hot man. Six feet and three inches of hard muscle straining against a black T-shirt tucked neatly into black cargo pants, which were, in turn, bloused over black combat boots. But she wasn't looking at his clothes. She was staring at gorgeous cheekbones and a square jaw. At gunmetal blue eyes and grooves running down his cheeks like long dimples. At the five o'clock shadow darkening his jaw and his perfect, perfect lips.

Which stretched into an amused smile. "Why don' you wait till you're asked?"

Holy shit. She couldn't for the life of her form a single coherent word. The man was hot. And that accent . . . !

"Uh."

"I take it you were expect' your drunken admirer? I suggested to him—rather strongly—dat he go elsewhere." His words, smooth and rich as molasses, rolled lazily off his tongue. New Orleans, she thought.

"Ugh. You saw that? Jerk."

The smile widened. "Him or me?"

Lark found herself grinning up at him. "Him, of course. Unless you're a jerk. Are you a jerk?"

"Depend' who you ask. My teammates tell me I can be a class-A jerk."

She cocked her head. "What sport? I'm guessing you're a swimmer."

For some reason, that made him laugh. "I do swim, yes."

Lark turned her head to glance at her table. No one had noticed her. Her sister's four best friends were admiring her engagement ring again as Kaley wiggled her fingers to make it sparkle. "I'd better—"

"Dance with me? I agree completely."

He took the tray from her and carried it to her table, sliding it in front of Kaley with a megawatt smile. "Congratulations, *chér'*. You'll make a lovely bride."

Leaving the five ladies with their mouths hanging open, he laced his fingers into hers and tugged her toward the dance floor. Lark found herself following him, admiring his broad back and tight butt. Dancing with a stranger hadn't been on tonight's agenda. Why not, though? She loved to dance, and the DJ knew his stuff.

He towered over her own five-foot-five, but she didn't mind as she raised her arms, already swaying to the music. She gyrated slowly, letting her body absorb the beat, hips swiveling and toes sliding. He joined her, his rhythm smooth and easy. Of course he would be an excellent dancer. He was perfect.

Which meant he probably would turn out to be a jerk. Or a serial killer. Right now, though, she didn't care. His gaze slid down her body and she put in an extra shimmy just for him. Heat flared and he locked eyes with her, moving closer. His extralarge hands settled onto her hips as the music softened and grew dreamy. Looping her arms around his neck, she closed the gap. Her hormones rejoiced. Being in his arms felt more right than anything had in a long time.

"You're a terrific dancer," he said.

She smiled up at him. "I don't even know your name."

"Call me Mace. Everyone does."

She tilted her head to look up at him. "What's that? Some sort of call sign? Like Maverick or Goose?"

Surprise flickered through his eyes. "Something like that, yeah."

She ran her eyes down his body. "You look all army-like."

He liked her gaze on him. She could tell by the way his eyes warmed and softened. "You look like a fairy princess."

She'd heard variants of that her whole life. When he said it, though, her insides melted.

"A damned sexy fairy princess." One hand left her hip to touch her throat. His finger traced the top of the lacy minidress as it dropped to her breasts, following the material as it curved around to zip in the back. "You take my breath away."

The faint touch of his fingers caused her to shiver. "You're not so hard on the eyes, either."

Amusement touched his eyes. Women probably threw themselves at him all the time. "So what do I call you?"

"I'm Lark."

"Like the bird?"

"Something like that, yeah." She grinned as she repeated his words.

He returned her smile. "Do larks have pink hair?"

"Pretty sure they do."

"Pretty sure they're brown."

"That's ordinary."

He chuckled. "No way anyone would call you ordinary."

"Better not." She scowled. "Ordinary is for losers."

She'd had her hair trimmed into a messy pixie cut and brightened the color for the wedding. Thank God Kaley accepted her as she was, and hadn't begged her to tone down her look as her parents had. She loved them, but found their conservative attitudes tiring.

Somehow she'd moved closer to him. Or he'd moved. Either way, her body approved.

"Where are you from? New Orleans?"

"Almos'. Born in de Louisiana bayou. Cajun down to my bones."

Lark couldn't help her grin. "I bet you could melt stone with that accent."

"I admit my accent peaks when I flir'." He shifted closer. "Am I melting you?"

Yes. Yes, he was. She let out a puff of air and didn't answer.

"So when's the wedding?"

She switched gears effortlessly. "Tomorrow. I'll be glad as hell when all this shit is over. Weddings are a pain in the ass."

He locked eyes with her again. "I don't know. They can be great with the right person."

Lark laughed. "Are you inviting yourself to my sister's wedding?"

"Why not? I already know I wan' to see you again."

That silenced her. Men hit on her all the time. She'd learned to shut them down; either nicely, or as she had the drunk at the bar.

"Tell me you're not dying to see me again."

She wrinkled her nose. Conceited prick. "I'm not sleeping with you."

Again, amusement twinkled in his eyes. "Did I ask?"

She cocked her head. "Sounded like it to me. Sneaking into a closet at a wedding is a time-honored tradition."

"No. *This* is me asking." His hands urged her toward him as his head dipped. He captured her lips, demanding entry, his tongue dueling with hers. He deepened the kiss into an all-out, tonsil-touching, I-want-to-screw-you-right-now onslaught. When he pulled back, both of them were panting.

"See the difference?"

She started laughing. "Are you always this sure of yourself?"

A grin tugged at his mouth. "Usually. Not this time."

The music changed again. "I should get back to my friends," she said reluctantly. "They're pretty wasted, and I'm the designated babysitter."

"Designated driver?"

"Yeah. I'm the only one with a car here, so I get to pour them into the back seat and hope no one pukes. So . . . gotta go."

"I'm sure they'll be fine for another dance."

"Nope. Sorry."

"*Co faire?* Why?"

Because she didn't want to move from the warm circle of his arms. Because her body had lit up like a firecracker waiting to go off. Because Kaley needed her right now more than Lark needed a quick romp in the hay. "It's my sister's night."

The rough pads of his fingers caught against the lace as he briefly tightened them, then released her. "Thanks for the dance, *chérie.*"

It was harder than it should have been to turn and walk back to her table.

All five women stared as she slid into her seat. The grilling started immediately.

"Who was that hot piece of—"

"What's his name?"

"Did you give him your number?"

Lark pulled her Sprite to her and sucked down a long drink. "His name or call sign or whatever is Mace. No, I didn't give him my number. He didn't ask."

Dana frowned. "You should have given it to him anyway."

"I'm not looking for a hook-up. That's all he wanted." She frowned down at the tabletop, tempted to search for him.

"But he's so hot!" Dana said. "Maybe you need a hook-up."

"I abdicate as designated driver," Lark said, snagging Dana's beer. "I'm going to get drunk instead of jumping the bones of some stranger I met at a bar."

"We're about to call it a night," Kaley said. "Ish after midnight, and I have to be up at sheven o'clock."

"Rats." Lark pushed the beer away. "So much for getting drunk."

Kaley slanted her sister a sly look. "Why don't you stay? Dance with some stranger you met at a bar. It could be romantic."

"It could be tawdry. You see romance everywhere because you're getting married."

Kaley laughed. "And why not? I'm happy. I want you to be happy, too. Whash wrong with that?"

"Nothing. But I'm not going to find true love from a hook-up at a bar." She rose with the others and snagged her purse from under the table. As she followed them toward the nightclub's entrance, she glanced back. Despite the crowds, she easily found Mace sitting with a group of men, and he was watching her. He mouthed a word.

Stay.

Tempted, she nevertheless lifted her hand and wiggled her fingers in farewell. She had matured past drunken one-night stands, no matter how drool-worthy he seemed.

"We can take a taxi back to the hotel," Kaley said. "You don't need to drive ush. You can stay a bit longer, if you want."

"Because I might decide to jump Mr. Hottypants after all?"

"Would that be so bad? He ish completely jumpable," Kaley said, words slurring together. "For you, I mean. Peter ish my one and only."

Lark looked from Kaley to her bridesmaids. "Kaley's wasted. Any of you sober?"

Evelyn nodded. "I hardly drank anything. Dana kept stealing my shots."

Dana gave a cry of protest. "Did not! They just sort of ended up in front of me, is all."

Kaley snorted. "You stole mine, too."

Lark laughed. "I have to go to the bathroom. Wait for me by the door, okay?"

She headed toward the restrooms. The line stretched out of the door and halfway down the hall. Ugh. Should she wait, or just hold it? In the end, nature's call decided the matter for her, and she watched the line get shorter, shifting from foot to foot. Finally, she darted into a stall, then washed her hands and headed for the front door.

Her phone chirped, letting her know she had a text from Kaley.

Go dance w/Hottypants. Ill CU at 8am, k?

Uh-oh.

Did u leave?

Yep. He he he.

Lark rolled her eyes.

But b back by 8

12 crocs couldn't keep me away

Her sister meant well, but Lark had already decided to go back to the hotel alone.

Was Mace still there?

Don't look, she told herself. But of course she did anyway. He still sat with his friends. He lifted a beer bottle and took a long drink. Lark experienced a pang of regret for her decision, but squared her shoulders and headed for the front door, nearly running headlong into two men. Like Mace, they wore black pants and boots. Probably more of his friends, arriving late to the party.

One did a double take, staring at her hard enough that Lark gave him a look brimming with *back off, jackass.* He reached out as though to seize her shoulder, but she jerked back. No one had the right to grab at her.

"Hey, are you—" he started.

"Shut up," the other man snapped, shooting his friend a warning look. He glanced around pointedly. "Not the time."

They both stepped aside, allowing her to exit the building.

Weird.

Chapter 5

Saturday, February 18. 12:05 a.m.
The Promenade. Boston, Massachusetts.

THOMAS "MACE" BECKETT tried to focus on the story Alex was telling, but his thoughts kept returning to the sprite he'd danced with all too briefly. She sparked all sorts of fires in his belly. Lust for life poured from her like a rainbow, and he found he wanted to immerse himself in it. Wrap her energy around him like an electric blanket. His teammates laughed. He joined in without ever really hearing the punchline.

A waitress came over with a new round of pilsners. He slugged some back.

"You shoulda seen how fast Mace moved," Alex said to Heather Langstrom-Reed, who rested her chin on the back of her hand as she listened. "You'd'a thought someone lit his ass on fire."

"That's because I didn't wan' to get shot conducting a fucking exercise."

Their Delta Force team had relocated to Boston, awaiting corroborating intelligence on rumors that Russian agents might be trying to smuggle major ordnance into Massachusetts. To relieve their boredom, their commander had arranged for them to be part of the opposing force during a counterterrorism exercise at Natick Labs. Mace and his team had been assigned to rob the bank, taking hostages and negotiating with SWAT. After a few hours, they were supposed to start killing hostages, forcing SWAT to storm the building. The actors involved already wore eerily real-looking "wounds" under their jackets, which first responders would triage and treat.

The first part of the exercise had gone smoothly. Mace and his team stormed the bank, stole money from the registers, and herded the hostages into the center of the room. After initial negotiations with SWAT, though, everything had gone to hell. Unbeknownst to them, a newly assigned—and armed—military police corporal had driven onto the Natick Labs complex just before the gates had been locked, and, instead of reporting in to her command, had gone straight to the credit union to cash a check. When she drew her revolver and demanded that his team surrender, Mace had been forced to take her down hard, very nearly dislocating her shoulder as he disarmed her.

"I didn't want to get shot," Mace said again. "She got a well-deserve' ass-chewing from the MP company commander. If she'd bothered to check reciprocity laws, she'd have know' Massachusetts doesn't recognize a Texas conceal' carry permit."

The entire exercise had been terminated because of her. The installation commander was pissed. The first responders were pissed. Mace was pissed.

He glanced over at Lark's table, and saw the group gathering up coats, preparing to leave. *Look back,* he urged silently.

As though hearing him, she turned her head, meeting his eyes.

"Stay." Had he said it aloud, or only thought it?

She gave a lopsided smile and waggled her fingers, turning away to hug and kiss her sister before heading toward the bathrooms.

Maybe after, she'd decide to stay and would approach him. Maybe he should waylay her and get her number before she slipped away forever. Instead, he lifted his beer and chugged it.

He couldn't seem to stop himself from looking, though. She had reappeared and was now headed straight for the front.

"Be righ' back," he shouted, pushing back his chair. The others nodded or lifted their beer bottles in acknowledgment, barely glancing his way as he got up and threaded his way through the throngs.

Two men in black army pants blocked Lark's way. One made as though to seize her arm, but pulled back when she jerked away, finally stepping aside to let her pass. As soon as her back was turned, the two exchanged a look, turning to follow her out the door. Mace's instincts shot into overdrive as alarm rippled along his spine. They had nothing good on their minds.

He ducked out the front door, past the bouncer who controlled the line of partiers waiting to get inside. Lark meandered down the sidewalk, apparently heading toward the parking lot behind the nightclub, arms wrapped around her torso despite her long coat.

Oblivious to the men.

Mace sprinted down the sidewalk, ignoring the frigid February air and the slushy walk. She'd made it halfway down the building, but the men stalked after her, closing in fast. Mace glanced back at the line of people; nobody paid any attention. He was just another partier leaving the nightclub.

Lark came even with an idling taxi, unaware of the danger as the two men stopped on either side of her. She half turned, surprise and then alarm filling her face as she finally noticed them. A puff of white escaped her open mouth. She wrenched open the door of the taxi to escape, but one of the men yanked her away, pulling a Colt M1911 and pressing it into her stomach.

Mace came in fast and low, catching the second man around the waist as he, too, drew a weapon, riding him down hard enough that the man's head smacked against the pavement. Mace tore the semiautomatic from his hand, already rising and turning to the man holding Lark. The taxi driver yelled something Mace couldn't hear and burned rubber as he raced away from the violence. *Fucking coward.*

He forced himself to ignore the blind panic on Lark's face, instead focusing on the threat.

"What the fuck?" said the gunman. "Who the hell are you?"

Mace felt his expression go cold. "I'm the man who's going to kill you if you don' let her go."

The man's eyes narrowed and his grip on Lark tightened. The two gunmen—Dumb and Dumber—wore clothing almost identical to his own. Black jackets over T-shirts, military pants, and black boots.

Dumb frowned as he looked Mace up and down. "Did Palachka send you? We got this covered, man. Get lost."

"Let her go. Now."

Dumb shook his head, anger growing in the depths of his eyes. "I got my orders. Palachka wants to have a chat with her, so I ain't going to hurt her none."

Damned straight he wasn't. These men were muscle, just following orders. Palachka's orders.

Who the hell was Palachka?

He glanced at the crowd. A small group watched them, grinning and nudging one another. As long as they thought theirs was simply a drunken brawl, no one would bother to call the police.

Lark hadn't so much as twitched a muscle, but the whites of her eyes showed and he could feel her terror. She, too, looked at the line outside the nightclub.

He took a risk with a bald-faced lie. "Palachka tol' me to take over. He said to tell you to head back and leave her to me. I'm the one's goan to chat with her."

Dumber picked himself up off the pavement and staggered over to his partner. "Lying prick. He'd've called us. And I don't know you."

"Best you don' know me. I'm who Palachka calls when fucks like you bungle it." Mace snorted. "What, you think he don't have nothing better to do than deal with the likes of you? He's waiting for you, though. Don't want him pissed, do you?"

Both blanched. Mace walked casually over and tugged on Lark's arm. Dumb hesitated, looked into Mace's icy eyes, and finally loosened his grip. Mace lifted the Colt he'd taken from Dumber, pointing the barrel at the sky.

"This registered anywhere?"

Dumber felt the back of his head for the lump that must be forming. His fingers came away red with blood. "Nah, man. It's clean. Why'd you wallop me, man? You could'a just told me Palachka sent you."

"Get out of here. We're attracting attention." He stared pointedly at the line of people outside the Promenade. "I'll check in with Palachka when I'm done with her."

Mace settled the matter by tightening his grip on Lark and

dragging her toward the parking lot. Dumb and Dumber followed, exchanging a look.

"I'd better check in with him," Dumb called. "Make sure you're on the level."

Mace forced an uncaring shrug. "Your funeral."

They reached the edge of the deserted lot. Mace paused, raising his eyes pointedly. The two men hesitated, then shrugged and started in the opposite direction.

Stupid fucks.

Lark wrenched her arm so abruptly he lost his grip, and she took off like a rabbit back toward the nightclub. How could she even run in those ridiculously high heels? He caught her in three strides. Sure, she'd be safe inside—for now. But what happened when the two gunmen realized Mace had clowned them? They'd be back, and they would be furious.

"Wait," he said. He pulled her to a stop.

She swung her huge purse like a brick. He pulled back just in time to avoid being clocked in the head. She dug into her bag, scrabbling around inside. Maybe she really did have a brick in there.

"Come on. We have to get away from here. It won't take those idiots long to figure out I'm not one of them." He risked a glance behind.

When he turned back a second later, she had dropped her purse and now pointed a Smith & Wesson .38 Special at him, backing off several steps to gain distance. Her hands shook so badly he feared she'd drop it. He looked hard at it, then had to bite the inside of his cheek to stop the laughter that threatened.

The cylinders were empty; the revolver wasn't even loaded.

Clearly, she was no criminal mastermind. So why were those men after her?

He needed to get her somewhere safe. Then he could get the answers he wanted. Pulling his cell phone from his pocket, he punched in the code to unlock it.

"Put it down!" she nearly shrieked. "Put down the goddamned phone. Drop it right now!"

Of course. He was the idiot. She now thought he worked for the same man who'd sent thugs after her. Interestingly enough, she'd demanded he drop the phone, but not the pistol he still carried. He bent down and set both on the muddy slush of the asphalt, stepping away from them and raising his arms from his sides to show her he meant her no harm.

"Look, that was just—"

"Shut up," she snapped, narrowing her eyes. He guessed she was trying to cow him, but she seemed as threatening as a baby kitten. "If you don't do what I say, I'll . . . I'll shoot you."

Chapter 6

Saturday, February 18. 12:35 a.m.
The Promenade. Boston, Massachusetts.

LARK TIGHTENED HER grip on the gun, her mind a blank. Her life had been threatened. Why? And what the hell was she supposed to do now?

"I'm calling the police." She tried to reach her right front pocket with her left hand, but it shook so badly she couldn't manage it.

"No."

"What?" She stopped fumbling with her phone out and stared at him.

"No. I can't allow you to call the police. Either I'll have to vacate the area, or you'll tell them I tried to kidnap you and they'll arrest me. Either way, I can't protect you."

He seemed so calm. Did he know she wouldn't shoot him? The gun Kaley had loaned her, had insisted she carry, felt heavy in her hand. Lark often worked late at night, when Chelsea was dark, deserted, and dangerous, and her sister worried about her. The box of bullets in the bottom of her purse made it worse than useless, but she'd barely had time to register for a class in how to use the gun, let alone load it. Not that she'd admit such a thing to him.

His words finally penetrated her panicked mind. "You should be arrested. Attacking defenseless women on the street? Kidnapping? You should be in jail."

"I did none of those things." Mace nodded toward the nightclub. "This is too public. Someone is going to come into the parking lot soon. Someone will have called the police by now. We need to get out of here."

She snorted. "So you can *protect* me?"

"Yes." He remained maddeningly calm.

"Bullshit." Call the police, her rational mind told her. Let them handle it. It was their job, after all. But some buried instinct agreed with him. In her experience, the police were the enemy. *You're not a hacker any more. You're legit. You work for the FBI. You have nothing to fear.*

Except maybe being arrested for carrying a gun in her purse without a permit. She'd worry about that little detail later.

But old habits died hard. If Mace were arrested, the odds that the cops would share information with her were minimal, and she would still be in the dark. And it pissed her off that her big brain couldn't find a logical solution to her current dilemma. "We're going to walk to my car. If the police show up, so be it. You become their problem. Get your hands up higher, and walk in front of me."

Common sense dictated she force him to leave. To get into her car and drive away. To call 911 and hope for the best. But she'd still know nothing. Mace was clearly working with those other men with guns, and she needed him to tell her what was going on. That meant keeping him with her. Not her smartest idea ever, since he'd been sent to kill her. But what choice did she have?

She'd make him spill the beans. Somehow.

Right now, she needed to get out of this neighborhood before any more black-clad thugs came within grabbing distance of her.

"Move," she said, deepening her voice and snapping off the words. Hopefully he couldn't see the tremors in her hands. Thankfully he obeyed, strolling down the line of cars as though she didn't have a gun trained on him. She scooped up her purse and followed.

"Go to the left. Down this row. There . . . no, stop. The orange Jeep Liberty."

He paused beside her car. "Good God. You actually drive this thing?"

It had been her first purchase after getting her master's degree, even before the FBI hired her. She'd been so relieved to ditch her junker and drive a newish car, and she'd gotten a smoking deal on it. Her hackles rose, and for a moment, she forgot to be terrified.

"It's a sweet ride. What do you know?"

He grinned at her. "Whatever you say."

For a moment, she wished she'd gone through agent training with the FBI, instead of as a computer scientist. She'd know, for instance, how to shoot her shiny new gun. Computer scientists received training at Quantico, sure. But in reverse engineering of malware, digital forensics, and intrusion detection. Administrative processes. She'd received no training in firearms, tactics, or taking kissably hot men prisoner.

Who else could she call for advice? Trevor's mobile was number five on her phone's favorites tab. It would be, what? Nine in the morning in London. He'd be available, assuming he wasn't on assignment. She put a hand to her head. Her gun hand, she realized, as the barrel thumped her temple. "Goddamn hairy ass wrinkly old man balls!"

Mace laughed. "You don' mess around, do you? Dat was an impressive bit of cussing."

"Gee, thanks."

"Lark, I'm serious. It won' take those yahoos long to come back. We need to be long gone by then. Please trust me."

First thing first. Before her innards melted from his honeyed Cajun drawl, she switched the revolver to her left hand, keeping it trained on him as she fished her phone out.

"Please don't call the cops," he said again. "Say they show up. You tell them what happen'. I tell them what happen'. Maybe they take me down to the station, maybe they just put me in a squad car while they check me out. Either way, the cops will release me. But while all the fuss is going on, you might decide to just walk away. Bad people are gunning for you. Keep me with you."

She shot him a warning glare and pressed Trevor's number. It went straight to voice mail. Now what?

She swung her bag forward so she could scrabble inside for her keys. Damn it! She risked a quick look inside her purse and spotted them. Hooking the ring out with a finger, she tossed the whole thing to him. He caught it one handed.

"Get into the driver's seat," she commanded.

He obeyed, squashing his extra-large frame into the driver's seat. "Gawd damn. This t'ing built for a child."

He reached down and pulled the seat lever, sighing in relief as the seat moved back. He stretched his legs, reaching across to unlock the passenger door for her. She dropped her bag at her feet before easing inside, keeping the gun trained on him. He glanced at her and away. She could have sworn he hid a smile.

"Now what?" he asked.

She had no earthly clue. Putting a hand to her aching head, she made a sound of pure frustration. Only he could provide the information she needed.

She couldn't take him to her home; that would be insane.

Would it?

It would have to be her room at the Hyatt Regency Cambridge. Kaley had insisted the entire wedding party stay at the hotel the night before the wedding.

"A hotel."

"Good choice. I know one down by—"

"No," she said. "I'm not going anywhere anyone knows you, or can find you."

"All right. You're calling the shots."

Why did he seem so calm? She'd threatened to shoot him.

"Get on the freeway."

He put the car into gear and drove on surface streets till he got to the highway, then took the entry ramp and merged with traffic. They headed northwest.

"Take this exit."

"Why this one?"

"Just do it!" She couldn't help the way her voice rose. "Turn left."

Mace made a soothing motion with one hand, then returned it to the wheel. "Look, I know what I said back there. I played along to get them away from you. I'm not trying to hurt you."

"Yeah, you're just trying to kill me." Anger replaced her fear. She lifted the gun and pressed it against his head. "Turn in here, asshole."

Mace slowed and turned into the parking garage for the Hyatt

Regency Cambridge. Lark cringed, already regretting her choice to bring him back here.

"What now?"

In for a penny, in for a pound. That sounded like something Trevor would have said. Remembering his cool competence steadied her. She squared her shoulders. "Park it."

Mace did so. "Now what?"

Lark felt like tearing her hair out in frustration. How could she get him up to her room without him just walking away? "Now you tell me what's going on. Now you tell me who the fuck Palachka is, and why he wants me dead."

Surprise lifted his brows. "You don't know?"

"Aagh!" She thunked her head against the headrest. "Fuck. Fuck fuck fuck. All right. This is what we're going to do. You're going to open your door and come out with your hands where I can see them. Is that clear?"

"Yes, ma'am."

What would she do if he attacked her here, in the quiet, dark parking lot? He'd already caught her once because of her high heels. She could threaten all she liked, but, ultimately, she had no control over him.

"Stand by the hood and don't move."

When he'd complied, she dug frantically in her purse for the box of bullets. Kaley had shown her how to open the cylinder thingy so she could put the bullets into the holes, but she hadn't bothered to do it. Pulling the box into her lap, she fumbled it open, spilling most of the bullets down her leg and onto the floor mat. Swearing and sneaking looks at Mace to ensure he hadn't moved, she pressed the button to swing the cylinder open, and got it on the third try. Shoving some bullets into the holes, she pushed the cylinder closed again. According to Kaley, all she had to do now was pull the trigger. She reached down and scooped as many bullets as she could find back into her purse.

Time to face the music. Or the firing squad.

Opening her door and stepping out without lowering the now-loaded revolver proved to be harder than it looked, but she managed. She came around the hood, keeping it pointed at him. So far, so good.

Mace looked at the hand gripping the revolver and frowned. "Curiosity ends when the gun gets loaded."

"What's that supposed to mean?"

"It means," he said, voice hard, "that I have no interest in getting shot."

Her mouth dropped open, shivers racing through her. "You knew it wasn't loaded?"

"Yeah. I saw your situation and acted. You know I could take that from you, right?"

She backed up several steps, heart racing. Was it true? It certainly explained his cavalier attitude until now. He dwarfed her small-boned frame. She'd been counting on the gun to keep him at bay. "That's an idle threat. All I have to do is pull the trigger." She hoped. Maybe she could distract him. "Isn't your boss going to wonder why you haven't checked in? Aren't you on some sort of leash?"

Mace tipped his wrist and looked at his big fancy wristwatch, having evidently decided to ignore the threat of the revolver. "It's almost one thirty in the morning. Yeah, my boss will be waiting to hear from me. But it's sure as shit not who you think."

"Uh-huh. Sure. Right." Now would be the perfect time to end this ridiculous scenario. She could just get into her car and drive away. He didn't know she was staying here, and in the time it took him to call his boss or a friend, she could be long gone.

But then she'd be back at square one. Not any the wiser about the awful things happening to her. She sighed, rubbing her temples, where her headache had grown worse.

"I'd be worried you'd have me arrested for kidnapping if you weren't a criminal."

"I'm not."

"Whatever. Walk to the hotel."

She pressed the gun into his side as they walked into the hotel lobby, welcoming the sudden warmth. The heat in the building didn't come close to the heat pouring off her captive, though. Nobody seemed to be on duty this late. She prodded Mace toward the elevators.

Why was he cooperating, especially now that he knew her little gun had bullets in it? Shame rippled through her. Violence was not in her nature. Someone would worry when he didn't show up. Palachka? A family? A wife and kids? He'd been at the nightclub tonight to kill her, that much was clear. So everything he'd said to her had been a lie.

Asshole.

She shifted from foot to foot as the elevator took just short of forever to open. Finally, though, she prodded him inside. He seemed even larger in the enclosed space. Her fingers tightened on the revolver. He glanced down at it and frowned.

"Please take your finger out of the trigger guard till you actually mean to pull the trigger. Accidents happen when nervous little birds don't know basic gun safety."

"I'm not nervous," she said, nevertheless pulling her finger free and wrapping it around the handle instead. "I'm pissed, and . . . and dangerous. Room five oh two. Three doors down to the left."

"Hand me your key."

She did so, then backed up almost to the opposite wall as he slid the key card into the lock and pushed the door open. And Lark realized her latest in the comical series of mistakes she'd made tonight.

One bed. She had only one bed.

Her latent hormones perked up, and she squashed them with an irritated breath. *Not* the time. Focus. With a criminal in the room with her, she wasn't likely to sleep anyway. She prodded Mace forward with the barrel of her gun, shutting the door behind them and flipping the security bar into place out of habit. Realizing what she'd done, she pulled it free again. If she lost control of the situation and had to run, moving the bar might be the difference between escape and capture.

Mace came to an abrupt stop just past the door to the bathroom. A long, slow whistle emerged. "Your room's been tossed."

"Tossed? Like, searched?"

"Yes. What were they looking for? Can you tell what's missing?" He positioned himself at the side of the bed to give her room. She looked around, puzzled.

"I don't think so. Nothing looks out of place."

He twisted to stare at her, eyebrows climbing toward his hairline. "Are you shittin' me? Everything's out of place!"

She tried to see her room through his eyes. Huh. Maybe she should put her clothes in one place? Or hang them up? Take the shoe off the desk, and another one off the windowsill? Red color burned its way up the column of her throat to her cheeks.

Mace put his hands on his hips, a slow grin tugging at his

mouth. "Do you honestly mean to tell me your room looked like this when you left?"

"Maybe." She squinted at the clearly unmade king-sized bed. "I might have taken a nap this afternoon. And then I couldn't decide what to wear tonight."

He threw back his head and laughed.

"So I'm not Martha Stewart. Big fucking deal," she said, annoyed. "Kaley made me stay here so I wouldn't have to drive all the way back from Danvers in the morning. Something about me always being late."

Mace strolled over to one of the armchairs. He scooped two dresses, a couple of pairs of hose, and some silky underwear into his arms and deposited them on the bed, then settled into the chair. "This place could swallow you whole, like the Sarlaac in *Star Wars*."

Lark tipped her head to one side, humor lighting her eyes. "'You will find new definitions of pain as you are slowly digested over a thousand years.'"

He didn't miss a beat. "'On second thought, I'll pass on that.'"

She laughed before she could stop herself. Not only was Mace gorgeous and a great dancer, but he was a *Star Wars* fan, as well. The whole killer thing kind of put a damper on any future relationship, though.

She would have to search him. It hadn't even occurred to her until just now, and she kicked herself for being an idiot. For all she knew, he still had a cell phone or gun on him. She raised her revolver and pointed it at him. "Stand up."

He sighed, scratching his forehead before pushing himself to his feet. The sudden motion had her backing away fast, heart thundering. Bringing him here had been one completely stupid, harebrained idea.

"Slowly!" she squeaked. He stopped. Dropping her bag onto the bed, she bent to grab one of her colorful winter scarfs off the floor. "Now turn around."

He eyed the scarf, then her. "How about we just talk?"

Lark almost stamped her foot. "We're going to talk, asshole. Now turn the fuck around. Put your hands behind your back."

"That's not a good idea," he said, nodding toward the scarf. "We don't know if those men can track you using the GPS on your phone, or even if we were followed here. I didn't see a tail, but why take chances?"

A tail had never even occurred to her. Tears of impotence and fury burned behind her eyes. Nothing could have prepared her for this, but it pissed her off that she couldn't figure out what to do. She'd have some time to think, though, after her prisoner was as helpless as she felt. She took four steps forward and pressed the gun to his chest, glaring up at him.

"Do it!"

He shrugged and turned, crossing his wrists behind his back. Ready to leap away if he moved, she tucked the gun under an arm and wrapped the scarf over and around his wrists. Tying it tightly made her simultaneously feel safer and ashamed. She'd never in her life assaulted anyone. When she finished, she put a hand between his shoulder blades and nudged him forward.

"Sit down."

He looked like he wanted to argue, but settled himself back into the armchair. "This isn't a good idea," he said again.

"Yeah, well, it's the best I can come up with at the moment. Put your feet together."

Sorting through the rest of her clothes frustrated her. The only other scarf she could lay her hands on was rainbow-colored and silky. Maybe a pair of nylons would be better? No; too stretchy. She set the gun on the carpet and twined the silky fabric around his clunky boots, relieved once his ankles were tied. After slipping off her long coat, she dropped it onto the carpet and stepped over it. "I have to search you."

"Be gentle."

Was he laughing at her? She couldn't tell. Setting the gun on the carpet beside the chair, she gingerly patted his shoulders. Wait. If he had a weapon, it would be at his waist, right? She moved her hands down his shirt to his ribs. He twisted away from her questing fingers.

"That tickles!"

She growled her frustration, pressing more firmly around his waist. No gun, thank God. She felt the thrill of fear as she belatedly realized that if he'd had one, he could have simply drawn it and shot her while driving.

Sitting on the edge of the bed, she set the gun onto the bedspread beside her and pressed her fingers to her temples, where an insistent throbbing made her grit her teeth.

"All right. Now we talk."

Chapter 7

Saturday, February 18. 1:00 a.m.
Ebony Point Hotel & Conference Center. Boston, Massachusetts.

FATIANOVA DROPPED HER handbag onto the king-sized bed and dug out a couple of dollar bills to tip the bellboy. Compared to colorful rubles, American currency seemed dull to her. The man deposited her two copper spinner cases by the door, thanked her, and left. Fourteen hours in the air, long lines through Customs, and a trip on a minibus left her exhausted to the point she saw double. She barely had the energy to look around.

Still, the Boston hotel seemed huge after the cramped rooms in Moscow. As the head of one of the larger research and development teams at The Kuznetsov Institute of Applied Nuclear Physics—and the only woman—she merited a room to herself. She'd had to push hard to be included on this trip; neither her supervisor nor the administrator appreciated her work in predictive analysis for core meltdowns. In case of catastrophe, the first thing they would want is the scope of damage—radiation levels, speed of spread, effects on the population. But since no core had melted down, her research went unvalued.

Soon enough, she wouldn't need the Institute's paltry salary. Living the pampered life she craved floated so near her grasp she felt it. As soon as she sold her prize, she would be set for life.

A huge yawn caught her by surprise just as someone knocked at her hotel room door. She frowned, displeased. Maybe if she ignored it, whoever it was would go away. But the knock came again. Sighing, she pulled the door open.

Fyodor Petrov grinned at her, holding aloft a bottle of vodka. "Look what I snagged at the duty-free."

He stepped forward as though to come in, but she held her ground. "Not tonight, okay, Fyodor? It's late and I'm tired."

He slipped around her anyway, walking all the way to the center of the room before heading for the ice bucket and glasses by the television. Pouring several fingers of vodka into each glass, he brought them to her and handed her one. She took it automatically.

He dropped his gaze to her breasts, still covered by her trench coat with its sable fur collar. "Jesus Christ, Fatya. Take off your coat."

"Don't call me that. You have no right."

He downed his vodka in one gulp. "We work together. Why can't we be friends, too? Chill out and have a drink."

Fyodor disgusted her. His receding hairline merged into a thin ponytail, which always looked greasy to her. Add his constantly scruffy chin, squinty eyes, and big lips, and he seemed downright seedy.

Sighing, she slipped the coat off and hung it in the closet. The trouble was, she needed him to bring her precious cargo into the United States. He had contacts among the Armenians she lacked.

Once she had it, though . . . she enjoyed her mental image of ramming her shiv into his heart.

True to form, his gaze slid down her body. He'd seen her outfit at the airport and on the plane; she wore a stylish gray wool-and-silk dress with sleeves ending at her wrists and a skirt that caressed her knees. It fit her trim body like a glove, with the faux belt nipping in her waist. She disliked looking unkempt. After so many hours, though, strands of hair hung around her face and she felt grimy. All she wanted was a hot shower and bed.

Fyodor splashed more liquor into his glass and unbuttoned his brown wool sport coat. His shirt, creased from the long flight, gaped open halfway down his hairy chest. He wore a gold cross that nestled against it. Sitting on the edge of the bed without invitation, he grinned and gestured to her untouched glass. "It'll help you relax, Fatya. You're too uptight."

"If it'll get you out of my room so I can sleep, fine." She drained the glass, not even blinking at the burn crawling down her throat. "Okay. Good night."

"Hang on, hang on," he said, getting up to refill his glass. He brought the bottle to her, but she covered the top of the glass with her hand. "We have something important to discuss. I thought maybe you'd want to fortify yourself, but it's up to you."

"Can't it wait until tomorrow?"

"Nyet."

His tone alarmed her. "What is it, then?"

He moistened his lips. "Our package is stalled in the Yukon."

"What?" A chill crawled through her gut. "What happened?"

"My Armenian friend hasn't heard from his courier," Fyodor admitted, grimacing. "The plane made it to Whitehorse, Canada. The pilot was supposed to make contact with someone reliable to smuggle it across the border. But neither of us has heard a thing from either of them. The pilot isn't returning my calls. Maybe the Mounties caught and arrested him. Maybe the smuggler stole it. Hell, for all I know the plane crashed."

Fury exploded through her. She slapped Fyodor with every bit of force she could muster. He staggered back, shocked.

"You had one job, you utter moron," she hissed. "One. Single. Job."

He rubbed his cheek sullenly. "It's not my fault."

"Of course it's your fault. Why I ever thought you could—"

"It'll be fine," he insisted. "I'll call tomorrow. You'll see. Everything will work out."

"It better." Fatianova curled her fingers into fists. "I've spent too much time and money on this to fail now."

Fyodor tilted the bottle toward her, brows raised in question. She snatched it and poured three fingers into her glass, tossing the whole thing back in one swallow. He'd been right; fortifying herself did help.

"The auction is in a week, Fyodor. If I miss this chance because of your incompetence . . ." She let her voice trail away in tacit threat.

Fyodor came close to her, so close she felt his rank breath against her cheek. "I know you, Fatya. I know how you think. I saw how you handled Konstantin."

"And?"

"If you try to cross me, you'll wish you'd never been born. Understand?"

When she killed Fyodor, she intended to carve him up piece by piece. She walked to the door and jerked it open. "Get out."

"Pleasant dreams, my sweet."

Chapter 8

Saturday, February 18. 1:30 a.m.
Hyatt Regency. Cambridge, Massachusetts.

Mace worked his fingers around the woolen scarf. She'd done a decent job of securing him—if he were a normal man. For a trained Delta Force special operator, he could free himself in just a few minutes. He didn't try. Whoever Lark was, she needed his protection. He couldn't help himself. He'd seen her terror when those men attacked her. He'd looked into her eyes and seen intelligence, determination, and grit. But past the danger, past the fear, past the now-loaded revolver, he'd seen the purity of her spirit. She wasn't naïve, but she was an innocent in the truest sense of the word. And that innocence was afraid. That purity was under threat. His need to protect and defend blocked out all else.

Except their mission. His unit remained in limbo, awaiting critical intel on the exact location of the nuclear bomb. As soon as that came through, the mission superseded everything.

Lark had bounced from her perch on the bed and now paced around the room, muttering curses under her breath, clearly working herself up to something. He could make an educated guess.

She intended to interrogate him.

He almost smiled, but caught himself in time. Her search for weapons had entirely missed the knife in his boot. Anyway, he didn't need hands, feet, or the knife to take her out, if he wanted to.

Instead, he waited to see what she would do next. Maybe he'd get some answers.

"So now you're going to talk," she said, coming to a stop in front of him. "Who are you, anyway? Not your call sign or whatever. Your real name."

"Thomas Beckett."

She laughed, but not like she found it funny. "Yeah, right. You were named after the Archbishop of Canterbury? Feed me another line of bull."

"I'm pretty sure he's not the only Thomas Beckett in the history of the world. But yes, in this case, *ma mère* named us all after saints. She was a devou' Catholic."

She cocked her pink-topped head at him. He couldn't remember when he'd found pink hair so adorable. "Which ones?"

He felt his face soften. "My older sister, Susanna. My brother is Solomon, and Bonnie is the youngest. Not sure about that one. Maybe it's a nickname for Saint Elizabeth."

"Who is Palaki?" She fired the question at him, perhaps to throw him off guard.

"Palachka."

"Whatever. Your boss. Who is he?"

"I don't have any clue, *chér'*. He's not my boss. I just said that to get those men to leave."

She scowled. "Sure. That's why you said *Palachka* told you to *take care of me.* Kill me, right? Why?"

The last was almost a wail.

Mace shook his head. "Their orders were to bring you to him. Don' you know why? Think, *chér'*. You must have some idea who this man is."

Her arms shook. She crossed them and glared down at him. "If I knew that, I wouldn't need you to tell me. Now stop pretending."

"Look. One of us has to trust the other. I'll go first." He needed her to calm down. At the rate she was going, she would hyperventilate and pass out. "My name is Staff Sergeant Thomas Beckett, United States Army. Check my wallet. You'll find my driver's license and military ID card. Go on. See for yourself."

She approached him slowly, wariness in her eyes. Circling to the back of the armchair, she slid her fingers into his right rear pocket and tugged the wallet free. Returning to sit on the edge of the bed, she opened it and began to rifle through it. License, Army ID card, a bank debit card, and his concealed carry permit. Her eyes widened at that one before she set it aside. Three plain white cards with his first and last name and a telephone number. Seventy-four dollars in cash, and two condoms. She turned a cute shade of pink.

"I am who I say I am. A soldier. I don' know why someone would be after you. I met you for the firs' time tonight when we danced. A ver' pleasurable dance."

She met his warm look with narrowed eyes and made a scoffing sound. "Targeted me, you mean."

"Naw, *chér'*. I'm telling the truth. Now it's your turn. What's your real name, Lark?"

"You probably know already. Hadley Larkspur."

"Okay, good. Thank you. What do you do for a living, Hadley?" Calm her down, get her talking about anything. Hell, at this point he'd settle for a weather report.

She groaned, fisting her hands in her hair. "Lark. Just Lark. We're going to have an issue here if you call me Hadley."

"Noted. Lark. Where do you live? Pixieland?" He dropped his voice, making his tone soft and teasing. Hoping to regain some of the connection they'd shared at the Promenade.

She made a noise that was half growl, half moan. "You're hilarious."

Mace grinned. "You have to trus' me, Lark. I can help you."

She started pacing again. "Help me do what? What is happening?"

"I don' know. Untie me, and we can figure it out together."

She laughed in his face.

"Or not. But I can still help you."

"Then come clean with me." Her words came out as a soft plea. "The Army can't have sent you to kill me. That's so illegal. I can't even wrap my head around it. What, are you part of some rogue unit whose mission is to go around beating up innocent women?"

He laughed. "Not hardly. I protect and defend."

"Are you some sort of supersoldier?" she asked, voice hopeful. "Leap tall buildings and stuff?"

"I'm in logistics," he said, not even batting an eyelash as he lied. "Resupply to troops overseas. Beans and bullets. That sort of thing."

"Oh."

Did she look disappointed? No matter how much he wanted to reassure her he was one of the good guys, he couldn't divulge the true nature of his job. Not to anyone outside of the SpecOps community.

She came to stand before him again. "Enough fooling around. Tell me the truth, or I'll . . . I'll beat it out of you."

Would she really? He doubted she would hurt a fly. "I can't tell you what I don't know. I saw a woman in trouble and I stepped in to help. You've got this backward. I didn't attack you. I saved you."

She balled up a tiny fist. When she drew back her arm, his brows shot up. Was she really going to . . . ?

The fist shot forward. At the last second, she hesitated, opening her fingers so that she slapped him instead. He barely felt it. She looked horrified, putting that same fist to her mouth.

"OhmyGodohmyGod."

"Steady there," he murmured. "Relax, Lark. You didn't hurt me."

Relief washed over her face, followed quickly by a forced glare. "That was just a warning."

He really needed to contact his team. By now, they would be wondering where the hell he was. Too bad he'd left his phone in the parking lot. They'd find it, and assume the worst.

"Who is Palachka?"

"I don' know." He shook his head. "I could find out, though. I have friends—"

Lark laughed in his face. "Yeah, right. Let me guess. I need to untie you so you can call them."

"I just need your phone. You can hold it up to my ear."

She ran her fingers through her hair, yanking the strands before releasing them. "So you can tell them where I am? No way."

He sobered. "You're in way over your head, Lark."

Lark almost screamed her frustration. That might be the biggest understatement since mammoths roamed the earth. "I wouldn't be if you'd just tell. Me. What's. Going. On."

Mace blew out an annoyed breath. "Can't tell you what I don't know. For the last time, I save' you. I mean you no harm."

This conversation would go in circles, just like the last one had. Lark swore. "Fine. Be that way. I'm leaving. You can stay here. Someone will be by in the morning to clean the room, so you'll be free then. Go back to whatever hole you crawled out of and leave me the hell alone."

Mace sighed. "You're not thinking clearly. You're safe here for a couple more hours. Why don' you get some sleep? You'll feel better for it."

"Sure. And you'll get free and strangle me in my sleep."

"I won't."

"If you won't tell me anything useful, I'm safer without you. You won't know where I've gone."

He looked down at his lap, then back at her. Was that regret in his eyes? "*Chér*', listen. I have—"

"Don't call me that!"

"Fine. Lark. I'm not after you. The Army isn't after you. No one I know is after you. I know I have no right to ask, but I'm asking you to trus' me."

She growled, stopping herself from stamping a foot in frustration as she'd done as a child. "Why are you so calm?"

His steady look unnerved her. "Because you won' hurt me. And I won' hurt you, Lark."

"Yeah, right." She forced a laugh. "Because you were just pretending you were going to kill me."

"Yes. Think about it logically. If this Palachka tried to kidnap you, why not just let him do it? He could kill you just as easily once he had you. Why send someone else to kill you before he'd talked to you? That make' no sense."

No, it didn't. Lark frowned, pressing her fingers to her temples, wishing she'd watched more spy movies. Learned interrogation techniques. Maybe even learned karate, like her friend Jocelyn Katsaros. "He changed his mind?"

Mace gave her a disappointed look. "Anyone powerful enough to hire goons like that isn't going to kill someone until he learn' what they know, at the very least. And, unlike you, he won't pull his punches."

She couldn't argue that logic. For the first time, she considered the possibility that he might be telling the truth. "I'm sorry I tied you up. I'm sorry I hit you."

He smiled. "You hit like a girl. And under the right circumstances, you can tie me up any time you want."

Her mouth opened, but no sound emerged. After everything she'd done, he still flirted with her? An image of him tied up in her bed caused a rush of dampness at her core. If he hadn't been sent to kill her, if he had, indeed, saved her from Palachka's thugs . . .

It might still be a ploy, though. She couldn't afford just to take him at his word.

"Tell you what," he said. "I'm starving. I haven't eaten since breakfast. If you feed me, I'll be in a much better frame of mind to submit to your interrogation."

Her eyes widened, thrown off balance. "No way. As soon as I leave, you'll find a bent nail or a sharp piece of wood and cut yourself free."

"I promise I won't."

"Uh-huh." She threw her hands up, her multiple bracelets jingling. "I'm in *The Twilight Zone*. Things like this just don't happen to me. Maybe I'm asleep."

Mace tilted his head to look up at her, giving her a warm, slow smile. "Naw, no way. If this were a dream, we'd be together on that bed."

She sucked in a breath. Yes. Yes, they would. No, wait. She'd walked away from him at the nightclub, and she could do it again now.

"I'd've strewn rose petals over the pillows."

Lark beseeched her inner lust to show some sense and dissipate. "Stop saying things like that!"

"I saw a restaurant down the road when we came in. It looks like it's open all night. Probably caters to the college kids up the road at MIT," he said, giving her a pitiful look and a hopeful smile. "They'll probably do up a decent omelet. Bacon and extra cheese, please."

"All right! Stop it! I'll get you some damned food. But if you try to escape, I'll . . . I'll shoot you."

With a revolver she didn't know how to use. She'd finally loaded it, though. If she did go out and was attacked again, having it might make all the difference. She moved around him, pushing between his shoulder blades to see his wrists. He bent forward agreeably, then slouched back while she checked his ankles.

"I'll be here when you get back, *chér*."

"Stop calling me that!" she snapped. "That means *dear*, right? Stop it."

"Whatever you say."

She glared at him one more time before picking up the key card, dumping the revolver in her purse, and stomping to the door.

Chapter 9

Saturday, February 18. 1:57 a.m.

Hyatt Regency. Cambridge, Massachusetts.

As soon as the door clicked shut behind her, he began working the wool scarf loose. Lark would be gone for at least a half an hour. More than enough time.

Four minutes later, he sat down at the desk, nudged her laptop aside, and snagged the telephone. Jace answered on the first ring.

"It's me."

"Where the hell you at, asshole?"

Mace chuckled. "Nice. I'm feeling the love."

"You're going to feel my boot up your ass while you scrub latrines all weekend. Why did we find your cell in the parking lot next to a gun?"

Mace blew out a breath. "It's a little complicated. I saved a woman tonight from being taken against her will. She—"

Jace broke in with a disgusted snort. "And she was so grateful you're now snuggled up nice and tight? Jesus, Mace."

"Naw, it's not like that," he said quickly. As concisely as he could, he filled Jace in. "These guys were thugs. But if I hadn't been there, they would have taken her."

"Is this some sort of prank? Because after scouring the area for an hour trying to find you, I'm not amused."

Mace winced. "Swear on my mother's grave. I wish this were some big joke. I'm calling from the Hyatt Regency in Cambridge. I convinced the girl to go grab us some grub. She thinks I'm tied up."

Jace laughed. "Are you serious? Let me guess. She's blonde with big—"

"She's scared." Mace spoke over him. "The attack tonight was a total surprise to her. I'd stake my life on it."

"You are," he pointed out. "She loaded her peashooter."

"True. But if she shoots me, it'd be the worst case of pure dumb luck I've ever come across. Trust me. She's no criminal. She's a total innocent. And she does need my help."

His team leader remained uncharacteristically silent.

"Jace?"

He blew an annoyed breath down the line. "Christ. You're doing your Saint George slaying the dragon thing again, aren't you? Rescuing a damsel in distress."

Mace didn't know what to say to that. His teammates knew him better than anyone else on earth. They knew he couldn't help himself. As he had for the young boy being bullied at school in Goldsboro, as he had for the Guatemalan woman beaten nearly to death by her abusive husband, his need to defend victims from predators defined him.

"All right, Saint George. I'll give you some latitude here."

"Thanks, man." His apprehension eased. Jace had his back.

He could almost feel Jace's resigned shrug down the telephone wire. "What do you need?"

He expelled a relieved breath. "Need a weapon, first off. Maybe two or three. Stephanie Tams to work her keyboard magic to figure out who Palachka is and why he's after Lark. A safe house while we figure things out—"

"Whoa. Slow your roll, soldier. I'll send Alex to your hotel room to pick up your piece, and obviously we'll help you for whatever time we have left here. But as for the rest, I'm not going to reroute regimental resources on what is probably nothing more than a case of mistaken identity. I get that you want—need—to help her, but I gotta ask. Are you sure you're thinking with the right part of your body?"

Mace hesitated. No, he wasn't sure. But the fierce, fearless pixie brought every protective instinct he possessed roaring to the forefront.

Jace sighed. "Sergeant Tams is a no-go. She's working two missions and training the new kid. Archangel's almost as good, though, and he's not mission-ready until his ankle heals."

"That'll teach him to miss the landing zone on such a simple night jump. Broken ankles are a pain."

"True dat."

"Thanks, Jace."

He exhaled a laugh. "Don't thank me just yet. The minute we get the intel we're waiting on, we all muster. Including you. Understood?"

"Loud and clear, sir." He hung up, feeling his muscles relax. Now all he had to do was figure out how to get Lark to trust him.

Chapter 10

Saturday, February 18. 2:00 a.m.
Viktor Sokolov's Home. Boston, Massachusetts.

"HAVE YOU FOUND my money yet?"

Elliott dropped his video game controller, ripping off his headset as he lunged to his feet. What the hell? Uncle Viktor never came into his bedroom. "What are you doing here?"

His uncle cast a sour look over the mess in his room. "It's my house, or have you forgotten?"

Elliott glanced around, forcing himself not to leap to pick up the pizza boxes and empty beer cans littering every surface, nor scrape his dirty clothes off the floor. This was his sanctuary, damn it, and his uncle had no right to barge in without so much as a knock.

"I can fix it so both of us will be happy."

His uncle shook his head, seating himself uninvited on the wicker love seat. "I promised my goddamned sister I'd take care of you after your useless dud of a father died. And then she had to go and overdose, and I got stuck with you."

"That was nine years ago, Uncle Vik. I'm twenty-five now. I think you've done your duty."

To his surprise, his uncle's face slackened in what he could only interpret as apprehension. "She'd come back to haunt me, I know she would. No, you're staying put."

Seriously? His cool-as-a-cucumber, vicious uncle was afraid of ghosts? Elliott bit his tongue to keep anything stupid from coming out of his mouth.

He plopped back onto his DXRacer, the best gaming chair money could buy. Through the headphones on his desk, he could hear his friends complaining that he'd abandoned them at a critical point in their mission. He nudged the headphones farther away.

"Where's my money? Why are you wasting your precious time playing . . . whatever the hell that is?"

Overwatch, but his uncle wouldn't care less. "I'm still looking for the money, but I found the hacker."

"Who?"

"It's really tough to link just a handle to a person," Elliott said. "Hackers are really cagy. Although this one's not real good. Left her fingerprints all over the theft. That's why I found her so fast."

"Fast? It's been, what, fourteen hours?"

Elliott rubbed the back of his head. "That is fast."

"And?"

"Her name is Hadley Nia Larkspur. Turns out she lives right here in Boston."

His uncle nodded, but didn't seem surprised. Then again, he didn't show much of a reaction to anything. "Why didn't you tell me right away when you found her?"

"Uh."

"Still, now that you've found her," he continued, saving Elliott from having to answer, "what do you think my next move should be?"

Uncle Vik was asking his opinion? Pleased, Elliott straightened from his slouch. "I think you should have Palachka's goon squad go pick her up. See what she has to say for herself."

His uncle nodded slowly. "That's a good idea. A very good idea. Here's the thing, though, Elliott. Palachka tells me a couple guys were already dispatched to grab her."

Oh, shit. Elliott shrank against the back of the chair.

"Funnily enough, though, Palachka didn't send them. The two idiots failed at such a simple task as to find one fucking woman. They finally crawled their moronic asses up to him to try to explain their inadequacy."

"Okay," Elliott said, raising his hands. "Okay. I did that. I tracked the GPS on her phone, so I knew where she was. I figured I'd, uh, take the initiative and get her to return your money."

"And how did that work out for you, Elliott?"

His uncle still seemed eerily calm. Elliott rubbed his palms against his thighs. "I can fix this, Uncle Vik. I'll go myself. Talk to her. Convince her to—"

"Since when has thinking gotten you anywhere, you incompetent deadbeat?" his uncle snarled, lunging from the wicker seat. He grabbed Elliott's collar and yanked him to his feet. "Your job is to find my money. Where's my fucking money?"

Elliott grabbed his uncle's wrists and pulled, but couldn't break his grip. "I'm trying, I swear to God I am."

"By playing video games?" His uncle's voice splintered with chilly impatience, but he released Elliott's collar and moved to the center of the bedroom. Elliott collapsed back into his chair. "Those two fools you sent out. Don't you play video games with them?"

Foreboding swept through him. "No. I mean, sometimes, but—"

"Sure you do. That's why you picked them. No one else would believe Palachka sent *you* with a message."

Yes, that's exactly why he'd chosen them. Elliott shoved his hands into his pockets. How could he get out of this?

"Your two playmates won't be joining you tonight. Nor any other night. They're decomposing in a landfill somewhere. I'm still trying to decide if you should join them."

"I have three algorithms running," Elliott said, feeling a trickle of sweat sliding down his temple. "I'm backtracking along the hack to find the IP address where the theft originated. I'll find the money."

"When, Elliot."

Behind him, one of his monitors signaled. *Tink tink tink tink.* Taken aback, Elliott spun around in his chair and leaned close to the dark terminal window, where lines of search information had ceased to scroll. A single line at the bottom flashed.

"I'll be damned," he said. "I got it. The originating IP address."

He typed in a quick command to back-trace the address, then stared, mouth dropping open. "Huh?"

"Talk to me, Elliott," his uncle barked.

He shook his head to clear it, pressing the heels of his hands into his eyes. No way. No fucking way. This must be some sort of joke. He brought up a public IP tracker in a browser window, and repeated the trace.

"Elliott. Now."

"Uh," he managed, turning back. "So this IP address—"

"Explain it in English, not geek-talk."

Elliott scratched his chin, unwelcome shivers tripping along his spine. "Okay. Okay. So I followed the trail back to a . . . a unique combinations of numbers that tells me what network the hack came from."

"And?"

"I ran it twice. It's one of the standard networks used by . . . by the FBI. Why on earth would the FBI want to steal your money, Uncle Vik? What's going on?"

His uncle crossed his arms, gripping his biceps on either side. It was an even worse sign than the temper in his eyes. "I don't know. Does Larkspur work for the FBI? I want to know everything about her, Elliott. Every fucking thing. Get me that information. Understood?"

Elliott fisted his hands under his thighs. "I will, Uncle Vik."

"You better. No one steals from me and lives."

Chapter 11

Saturday, February 18. 2:12 a.m.
Clover Food Lab. Cambridge, Massachusetts.

STUPID, STUPID, STUPID! Why had she let her prisoner convince her to leave him all by himself while she waited endlessly for their meals to be prepared? He must be laughing his ass off about her gullibility. But she'd really, *really* needed a few minutes to process. To think rationally, without Mace's distracting presence.

By now, he'd probably freed himself and was lying in wait for her. She couldn't risk going back to the hotel. Her safest option would be to get into her Jeep and drive home. Better yet, she could go upstairs to Kaley's suite and sleep on the couch. Her dress and shoes were up there already.

Nothing, not even a gorgeous assassin, would keep her from her sister's wedding.

Lark couldn't leave without her laptop, though. She'd modified the standard FBI-issued one, and needed those special programs to help her decipher the code from her current project. That meant returning to her hotel room. Or, she thought, she could come back the next day, after housekeeping found and released her prisoner.

But what if Mace didn't leave, just patiently waited for her to return? Or Palachka's men staked out the hotel? At least if she went back now, there was a chance Mace would still be tied up.

She paid cash for the food and bundled it and herself into her car. The best option was still to go back and talk to him. It would serve her right if he escaped, after how she'd treated him. She'd never struck another human being in her life. Shame burned in her gut. True, she'd hesitated at the last minute. Now he had to know she wasn't equipped to beat the truth out of him. Assuming he hadn't yet freed himself, how would she get any answers? Maybe he'd take pity on her.

Parking the car in front of the hotel, she unloaded the bags, rode the elevator up, and approached her door warily. She pressed her ear against it, but heard nothing. Well, what had she expected? If he planned to attack her, he certainly wouldn't be playing the radio or singing. Biting her lip, she slid the card into the reader with fingers that shook, then eased the door open by degrees, ready to run at the first suspicious noise.

"Finally," came a deep voice. "I'm starving."

Lark released her breath in a rush. Her prisoner still sat in the armchair, just where she'd left him, arms behind his back and boots strapped together with her filmy scarf. She set the bags on the desk, her glance flicking to him and away.

"Did you think I'd get free and plan your demise?"

"It occurred to me, yes," she admitted. "I don't think Donna Karan had this in mind when she designed that scarf, though."

Mace laughed. "Hey, it brings out the blue in my eyes."

"Huh." She glared at his feet. His eyes, like the rest of him, were gorgeous. "I didn't notice. It's time to tell the truth, Thomas Beckett."

His stomach growled, loudly enough for her to hear it. "Could we eat before the interrogation? Pretty please?"

She wished he would stop giving her the melting gazes and amiable smiles. Why wasn't he angry? Fuming? Spewing threats? He did have beautiful eyes, though. And smile. And . . . she cut her thoughts off.

"I guess so. I need to eat, too."

"Great," he said with enthusiasm. "You'll need to feed me, though."

What? Aw, hell. She groaned as she realized she hadn't thought this through. She either needed to cut him loose . . . or hand-feed him. "No way. You'll bite me."

His eyes gleamed. "Only if you want me to, *chér*."

"No. No no no. God." She pulled two Styrofoam boxes from the bag and a couple of bottles of water, then dragged the desk chair close to him. His large frame dwarfed the armchair. The grooves along his mouth deepened as he watched her fidget with the box. Shit. Get on with it, she ordered herself. *And while you're at it, quit looking at his perfect lips.* He ran his tongue across his full lower lip, the corners tipping up very slightly.

"Fine. Open up." Flipping up the lid on his omelet, she grabbed a plastic fork and jabbed it into the eggs. She scooped out a bite and thrust it at him. The egg fell off the fork and into his lap.

He grinned. "I guess tha's better than egg on my face."

Lark's cheeks reddened. She glanced at the glob and away again.

"Can you get it off? It's hot. I'm getting burned here." The look on his face suggested he was enjoying her predicament too much.

No way was she touching him, there or anywhere else. She thought for a minute, then reached down and flicked it off with the fork, scooping the mess into a napkin and pitching it into the trash can.

"Thanks."

She refused to meet his eyes, glaring instead into the food. This was stupid. Why didn't she just untie him? She no longer felt afraid of him, exactly. But being so close to him caused her traitorous body to perk up. Her next offering made it to his mouth. He chewed and swallowed.

"Not bad." He opened his mouth, inviting another forkful, eyes drooping with a pleasure she suspected didn't come from the eggs. In this strangely intimate way, she fed him the omelet bite by bite until all that remained was the empty Styrofoam.

"Thank Christ." Sighing in relief, she threw it into the trash can.

He exhaled a small laugh. "That wasn't so bad, was it? But I t'ink I have cheese on my chin."

Lark glanced at him and away. "No, you don't."

"I feel it. Won't you wipe my mouth for me? It's only polite." He kept a straight face, but Lark could tell he was baiting her. She ignored him, digging into her corned beef sandwich. He watched her eat with lazy eyes.

"Stop watching me."

He chuckled. "*Chér*', you're the most interesting thing in this room."

She set her sandwich down and found the remote, clicking through the channels until she found CNN. "There."

He barely glanced at the screen. "No contest."

Even as Lark narrowed her eyes in warning, she couldn't help the purely feminine thrill at his unabashed interest. Either that, or he'd been playing her from the start with the dance that seemed a lifetime ago already. "Two hours."

"Closer to three."

Her eyebrows shot up. "What?"

"You were calculating how long ago we met, right? It's been close to three hours now."

She stared at him in astonishment. "Nobody follows my train of thought. People say I babble nonsense."

"Then they're not listening." He focused on the television screen for a moment. "More drama in Washington. It's out of control."

"I think someone else got fired. Or quit." Lark clamped her mouth shut. She didn't want to know him, and she certainly didn't want him to know her. He was her prisoner; nothing more. She looked at her half-eaten sandwich, no longer hungry. "Are you ready to talk?"

"Sure."

"You said before I was safe here for now. Why do you think so?"

"Because I'm with you." He shifted in the chair, stretching his shoulders as well as he could while bound. "Those knuckleheads went after you at the nightclub. Attacking you here in your hotel room would have been safer and less conspicuous, so I have to assume that they don't know where you're staying. Yet. That will change, but they won't move again until they've talked to Palachka, and that probably won't happen until tomorrow if I'm reading them right. They won't want to admit they got played, so they'll wait as long as they can."

Lark shivered. Tonight had been a close call. If not for Mace . . .

Shoving the food aside, she opened her laptop and brought up a browser window. "Palachka," she said, typing the word into

Google. "*Palach.* Russian word meaning *executioner.* Jesus. Okay. Palachka Skopek, died 1866. Woman named Palachka on Instagram. Oh, here we go."

"Whatcha got?" Mace asked.

"I found an article in the *Boston Globe* from last year, talking about Roman Vetrov, nicknamed Palachka, on trial for racketeering and fraud. I remember hearing about it at the time. One of the witnesses recanted after another one disappeared."

"What kind of fraud?"

"Um. . . ." Lark scanned the article. "Doesn't specify what kind of fraud. Part of Sokolov crime family, operates in New England, yada yada. He's apparently the chief enforcer for the mob. The mob? Really? The actual mob?"

"Are you telling me you have no idea why the mob is after you?"

She sat back, laughing a little, relieved. "They can't be. They must've mistaken me for someone else who was at the nightclub tonight."

"Is there a photo? Do you recognize him?"

"Yes, and no." She spun the laptop around to show him a picture of a balding, thickset man, glaring at the camera from under heavy eyebrows. "He looks scary as shit. I can't wrap my head around this. This has to be just some huge mistake."

"Might or might not be a mistake. But I believe you believe it is."

She yawned, fatigue pulling at her. In truth, she could barely keep her eyes open.

"It's adrenaline letdown," Mace said. "Perfectly normal. Lark, you need some rest. We'll figure all this out, I promise. But later."

"All right," she said, giving in. None of this seemed quite real.

"Fine. I'll lie down for an hour or two. If you're really just an Army soldier, you won't try to get free to hurt me."

He gave her a gentle smile. "Good."

"I feel bad, but you'll have to stay tied up."

"I've slept in worse. I'll be fine." He pointed his chin at the bed. "Go on, now. Get some sleep."

Chapter 12

Saturday, February 18. 4:00 a.m.
Hyatt Regency. Cambridge, Massachusetts.

MACE WAITED UNTIL her breathing deepened and evened out. Once again, he worked himself loose from the scarves. Padding across the room, he retrieved her revolver and cell phone. Slipping them into the back of his pants, he eyed Lark. She hadn't so much as twitched.

He pulled one of the condoms from his wallet and wedged it between the door jamb and the lock as he left the room. His teammates waited in a rental vehicle near the main lobby. Alex reversed the truck and pulled in next to him. Gabe rode shotgun, his crutches stowed next to his seat. Tag pushed open the door, and Mace climbed into the back.

"You're the only person I know who could get himself into a situation like this," Tag said. "Dumb shit."

Mace felt himself grow defensive. "What was I supposed to do? Let those assholes drag her away?"

Tag glowered. "No, because you have to be fucking Sir Galahad. Fucking awesome."

Alex linked his hands under his chin and batted his eyes.

"Knucklehead." Mace punched him in the arm.

"Ow!"

Mace ignored him. "They were paramilitary, by the looks of them. And yeah, you might be right that this is just a case of mistaken identity. I sure hope so. But if not, we—I—need to figure out what the hell's happening to Lark."

Alex winked at him. "Is she your type? I haven't noticed that you have a type. You seem to like anything with—"

Mace shot him a warning glare, then spread it around to all of them. "This isn't about getting into her pants. This girl's in trouble. She's smart, she's tough, she's got courage in spades. But she's never experienced anything like this. She needs my help. None of you have to be here."

Alex raised his hands in mock surrender, though childish glee radiated from him. "Chill, dude. We're here to help."

Mace sat back. "Yeah, sorry. I know that."

"So." Gabe rubbed his hands together. "Your lady's involved with the mob."

Mace scrubbed a hand down his face. "I know. What I don't know is why."

"You want me to dig into Lark's background?" Gabe asked.

He hesitated, then nodded. "Yeah. She claims she doesn't know what's happening or why, and I believe her. But . . . yeah. Dig around. Her full name's Hadley Larkspur."

Alex laughed. "Seriously? What kind of name is that? It sounds made up."

Mace worked his shoulders to loosen the tension there. "Maybe it is."

"Okay," Tag said. "Here's what we're going to do. You'll stay with Lark. Alex and I will pull twelve-hour rotating guard shifts, unless Jace'll give us more bodies. Gabe can focus on research. Sound good?"

Mace nodded, throat tight. "Hey, I really appre—"

"Fuck you," Tag said casually. "You'd do the same for us."

That pulled a reluctant smile from Mace as the tension drained from his body. "Truth."

"Here," Tag said, handing him his Browning Hi-Power. "I got your piece and three boxes of ammo."

Mace accepted the semiautomatic handgun, sliding his belt free to thread the pancake holster through it. He pulled his T-shirt out to hide the bulge, then dropped the boxes of ammunition into the cargo pockets of his pants. Next, he pulled Lark's cell phone from his pocket. "Crap. She's got it password-protected. Any ideas?"

Gabe shook his head. "You want me to try to crack it?"

"Nah. I mostly just wanted to give you her number, just in case."

"Speaking of which." Tag fished in his pocket and pulled out Mace's phone. "Jace said to get this back to you, and to lecture you on leaving it lying around."

"Consider me lectured." He slid the phone into his right front pocket.

Tag chuckled, transforming his usual glowering expression into something rascally. "I'll tell Jace you cried like a baby. I'll take first watch."

Mace let himself back into the hotel room, padding silently across the floor to look down at Lark. She'd turned over onto her side in the time he'd been gone, but her eyes still scrunched tightly together, and her breathing said she still slept.

"Lark."

He put out a hand and touched her shoulder. Nothing. He shook her arm gently. She didn't so much as stir. Squashing the urge to lie down next to her and pull her head onto his chest, he returned to the armchair and settled into it. Knowing Tag kept watch outside allowed him to relax, stretch out, and doze.

Sometime later, he lifted his eyelids, already fully alert as Lark shifted her head on the pillow and raised a hand to her head. She uttered a noise somewhere between a moan and a growl. The position of the sun told him what his watch confirmed—it was approaching nine o'clock. Stretching muscles stiff from sleeping in the armchair, he considered wrapping the scarves back on, but rejected the idea. She needed to know he meant her no harm.

Lark groaned and lugged the covers over her head to block out the lackluster February light brightening the expensive sheers.

"Good morning."

She mumbled something he couldn't hear.

"Probably best if we get moving," he said. "Your *sweet ride* is pretty distinctive. We don't want those boneheads from yesterday finding you by accident."

She grabbed a pillow and put it over her face, grunting something that sounded like a curse.

"It's a quarter of nine, Lark. I know you only got a few hours' sleep, but we need to get moving."

Lark shot upright. "Holy fuck, holy fuck!" She scrambled out from beneath the covers, bouncing the pillows onto the floor. "I'm late! Shit shit shit. Kaley's going to kill me!"

The sister's wedding. Mace had forgotten all about it. "Where do you need to be?"

She focused bleary eyes on him, then stumbled toward the bathroom. "Anywhere there's coffee. Then upstairs to her suite. She has my dress."

Mace waited for her to finish. When she emerged, her entire head was wet, as though she'd dunked her head under the water faucet. But her eyes, the color of new spring grass, finally focused. Alarm flashed across her elfin features as she saw his fingers casually laced behind his head. She darted toward the bedside table, saw it was empty, and flung the blankets around, digging through the pile with a frantic hand.

"Relax," he said. "I have it."

She whirled to face him, hands out in a defensive pose as though expecting him to shoot at any moment.

"You're the deepest sleeper I ever met in my life. I don't think you'd've woken up if a troop of howler monkeys came in."

She didn't answer, frozen in her defensive posture.

"Relax," he said again. "While you were sleeping, I called a couple of my buddies. They're going to help us figure this whole thing out. But right now, you need to focus on your sister. Why don't you shower?"

She didn't move.

"Come on, Lar'," he cajoled, deliberately deepening his Cajun accent. In his experience, women responded favorably to it. "Surely you realize I could have either hurt you, kidnap' you, or killed you las' night if that had been my intention."

"Fine," she said, eyes and voice suspicious. "So great. You're free to leave, so leave."

"Nuh-uh. You'll stumble your way into danger. I'll be your date for the wedding. We can talk more after."

"Just like that, huh?" She narrowed her eyes. "I don't think so, Romeo. Closet sex is definitely off the menu."

He threw back his head and laughed. Damned if her spunk didn't tickle him. "Noted. No closet sex. But I'm goan wid you, whether or not I'm your date."

She waggled her head back and forth even as resignation touched her eyes. "Do you even own a suit?"

He grinned. "I happen to have a suit with me. Just in case I met a beautiful woman."

"Or you can just not go. Just leave. Go back to your life. I see now this was a big mistake. A ridiculous stunt on my part. I was stupid and . . . and . . . I'm really sorry about the way I treated you." Her shoulders hunched, as though expecting him to lambast her.

His mouth pulled into a lopsided grin. "Hey, I tol' you I was dying to see you again. See how cleverly I arrange' to go to the wedding with you? Minus the closet sex," he added hastily.

"I need to call Kaley." She dug around in her purse. He pulled her cell phone from his pocket and rose, walking across the room to hand it to her. She took it reflexively, storm clouds forming in her eyes. "You stole my phone?"

Mace nodded, unapologetic. "If for no other reason than to pass your number on to my friends, just in case. But I had no clue what your passcode might be."

She humphed, turning her back on him as she unlocked the phone and dialed. "Kaley?"

"Oh, my God, Lark! Where have you *been*?" Kaley's screech came through so loudly Mace could hear it from three feet away.

Lark winced. "Pipe down, Kay. I haven't had any coffee yet."

"But where *are* you? You were supposed to be here an hour ago!"

"I know. Something came up. I'm on my way up now, though."

"Something came *up*?" If anything, Kaley's voice grew louder. "What could be more important than being here for your sister's wedding? I need you here, Lark."

Lark sighed loudly. "You're being dramatic. I'll *be* there. I just need to shower and inhale caffeine. Dana and the others are there, right?"

Kaley must have calmed down, because Mace could no longer hear her. After a few more words, Lark hung up and turned back to Mace. "I need to shower. I'll lock up behind you." She walked to the door and stood beside it, clearly waiting for him to leave.

No way. Whatever she thought, Mace knew the danger to her was real. Until and unless this whole situation turned out to be just a misunderstanding, he would stick to her like white on rice. "I'll shower first. That way, I know you won't run off on me. Gotta be powder-fresh for your sister's big day."

Her eyes narrowed and her mouth flattened. "Look, just because it seems like you actually might have saved me from those other men after all doesn't mean I want a guard dog sniffing around 24/7. Your being there would raise some eyebrows. And I'd get bombarded with a lot of questions I don't want to answer."

He cocked his head to the side, hands tucked into his belt loop. "So let me get this straight. You don't want to take me to the wedding because people would talk?"

She took in a lot of air and blew it out with an annoyed sound. "Yes, if you must know. And not just talk. Interrogate. Where do you come from? What do you do? Did your family come over on the *Mayflower*, because otherwise you're not good enough for their precious little girl? I was hoping to avoid them today, but my mother's like a bloodhound when it comes to acceptable husband material."

He couldn't help the belly laugh that burst from him. "How about we slow things down just a little? I said I wanted to see you again, not that I want to marry you tomorrow."

Her brows pulled together. She pressed the heels of her hands into her eyes and rubbed. "Duh. Let's just say my parents are a bit on the conservative side. And they still have this delusion that they have a say in how I live my life. Today's not the day to have a knock-down, drag-out. It's Kaley's day, and I won't let anything spoil that. Ergo, you can't come."

He would be there, one way or another. Having her cooperation would help, though. "Won't your folks be on their best behavior? For Kaley?"

She chewed her lip. "Maybe. Why do you want to come so bad, anyway?"

He closed the distance between them, easing a finger under her chin and lifting her face so he could see her eyes. "Easy question. I don't want to let you out of my sight. I have the strangest feeling that if I do, you'll vanish without a trace and I'll never see you again. You're a fascinating package of dynamite, and I want to get to know you a whole lot better. Minus the closet."

That drew a smile from her, which she quickly turned into a scowl. "Fine. Be that way, if it's so important to you. Then go shower, because I'm late."

Mace didn't hesitate. He was in and out of the shower in less than ten minutes. While Lark bathed, he dialed Tag. "I need my suit. Lark's sister is getting married, and I intend to make sure nothing interferes with that."

"Gotcha. I'll bring it to you, and we can scout out the venue."

"Thanks." He rattled off the address of the hotel.

Lark took considerably longer in the shower, emerging with a towel wrapped around her head and wearing woolen slacks and a sweater. He, on the other hand, looked wrinkled.

"My buddies are bringing my suit here," he said.

She gave a long-suffering sigh as she pulled the towel off and rubbed her hair briskly. "Fine. You can change in here."

She ran her fingers through her hair, trying to tame the tangles. It stuck up in all directions. "I need coffee."

He followed her down to the lobby.

"Starbucks!" Lark crowed in triumph. The small coffee bar had been tucked into a corner. She cut across the reception area. "Thank Christ."

Three people waited in front of her. "Come on come on come on," she said, moaning a little.

Mace's lips twitched as he tried to control his grin. He'd been in situations where caffeine had been the only thing keeping him going, but apparently Lark needed the jolt just to function. He dug out his wallet as they approached the counter.

"What can I start for . . ."

"Venti quad shot cinnamon dolce latte, please," she hollered. "Extra hot, no foam, light whip."

"Short Caffè Americano for me, please," he said, sharing a quick grin with the barista.

"Wuss. And two breakfast sandwiches, please."

Mace handed the barista his credit card, then followed Lark to the pickup counter. She rocked from foot to foot until her coffee came, then took a long swallow. “Ow. Ahh.”

Why did she order the drink extra hot, if it burned her throat?

She passed his drink and the sandwiches to him, then took another slug of her coffee before she walked away. “So. These buddies you called while I was asleep. Who are they?”

Chapter 13

Saturday, February 18. 9:40 a.m.
Hyatt Regency. Cambridge, Massachusetts.

THE BURN OF the too-hot coffee jumpstarted Lark's brain. She should have asked the question before leaving the room, but her sleep-muddled state hadn't leant itself to coherent thought.

Mace looked unsurprised at the question. "Couple of my teammates. They've agreed to help keep you safe while we figure this out."

"Your swim team?" Maybe she needed more coffee. She upended the cup and drained it. "You said you swim."

"I work with these guys," Mace said. "Gabe's pretty handy with a computer. Tag and Alex are useful in other ways."

Her brows wrinkled as she absorbed this. "Unless he's Zane Quimby, I should probably use my laptop. I'm a little more than 'handy' with computers."

"Is this Zane a friend of yours?"

She laughed. "Kind of. He's only one of the best hackers of

all time. Now he's a white hat. Went from being one of the FBI's most wanted to consulting for them. He's actually a pretty cool guy."

"You work for the FBI?"

The ultra-casual question didn't fool her for an instant. Still, it wouldn't hurt anything to tell him. "Yeah, I do. Not as an agent or anything. I'm a computer scientist."

"Sounds pretty technical."

"Yeah, but it's interesting, though. Right now I'm analyzing some malware to figure out what it does. Like reverse-engineering it, which is wicked cool."

Mace tilted his head down to look at her. "So how did you wind up reverse-engineering malware for the FBI? Seems pretty specialized."

Self-preservation made her skip over her years in the hacking community. "Uh, got a degree in cybersecurity and digital forensics. Purdue. My bullshit degree was in computer science from CalTech."

"Bullshit degree?"

She smiled, heading back to the elevators. "Bachelor of Science. BS."

His eyes twinkled with amusement. "Nice. So this project you're working on. How far have you gotten?"

"Why should I tell you that? Don't think for one second I actually trust you. Much. How about instead of interrogating me, you answer some questions?" She stopped in front of the elevators, but didn't push the button.

"Why not? Fire away."

"Well, how long have you been a soldier?"

He answered without hesitation. "Eight years."

"Do you like it? Did you get sent to Afghanistan? Are you married? Wait, don't answer that last one."

Mace chuckled. "Yes, yes, and no."

She wrinkled her nose up to hide her embarrassment. Why had she let her curiosity get personal? "Details, Staff Sergeant Thomas Beckett. I want details. How long were you stationed in Afghanistan? People get stationed there, right?"

"They do, but I generally only go when I'm needed. I couldn't give you a firm count unless I thought hard about it. But yeah, I love what I do."

"You said before you, like, supplied beans and bullets? What does that even mean?" A picture formed in her mind of a uniformed Mace standing between a tripod holding a huge swinging pot and a waist-high bucket of bullets, ladling oatmeal with one hand and spoonsful of shotgun shells with the other. The absurdity made her laugh.

"What's so funny?"

She shook her head. "I couldn't even begin to explain. Just tell me what logistics people in the Army do."

"At its core, it's basically just receiving equipment and materials and making sure it all gets where it's needed." He fiddled with his coffee, sounding bored.

She had a few minutes before she really, truly needed to be up in Kaley's suite. Leading the way to a padded bench, she tucked a leg under her and settled back. "Like putting boxes of food and medical supplies onto trucks, like the Red Cross did last month for that town in Syria?"

"Sure, dat." Mace joined her. "But also delivering tools, furniture, gasoline. Bombs. Tanks. The stuff an army needs to operate. And paperclips. Lots and lots of paperclips for the brass."

"If it's boring, why do you like it?"

He stayed silent long enough that she glanced at him in surprise. "Did I hit a nerve? I'm sorry if I did. It's just you don't sound like you love it. And even just listening to it is making me yawn."

"Because I also get to swim with my buddies."

His evasive answer raised her brows and the hairs on the back of her neck. Why prevaricate about such a mundane job? Was he embarrassed about what he did?

His phone buzzed, and he glanced at it and relaxed. "My buddies are here."

"Okay. Here." She handed him her room key. "Go get changed. I'm heading up to the Presidential Suite."

"All right. I'll meet you up there?"

"No, the wedding is in a church a few blocks over. Big, fancy, room for all the guests and paparazzi. You can meet us there."

He caught her by the arm, skimming his hand down to her wrist. "Wait a minute."

She tossed him an impatient look. What now? "Kaley's going to be freaking out."

"I need you to promise me you won't go anywhere without me. I can't protect you if we're not together."

Remembering how he'd disabled one of her attackers and then finessed his way out without further violence, Lark found herself nodding. "But you're not coming in with me if I have to tinkle."

"Agreed." He grinned, letting her wrist slip free as she skipped into the elevator, turning to watch him as the doors closed. He raised a hand in farewell; she found herself grinning foolishly.

The elevator rose smoothly, depositing her at the top of the hotel. Kaley's room door stood open, excited chattering emanating from it. As soon as she entered, Kaley leaped at her.

"You're here! Finally," she squealed, silk and satin rustling as she dashed to Lark. "Where have you *been*?"

Her mother scooped up the train, holding it out of the way as Kaley enveloped her sister in a perfume-scented hug.

"You're late, as usual," her mother said. "Hurry up, now."

Lark felt the familiar weight of her mother's disapproval. Today, though, she refused to let it spoil her good mood. Despite the lack of sleep, she felt great. Better than great. Her gorgeous baby sister was about to marry the love of her life. Plus, she could dance again with Mace, who had rescued her outside the nightclub and wasn't trying to kill her. Two points in his favor. And she could probably resolve this case of mistaken identity easily enough. Maybe she could just contact Palachka the Mobster and explain she wasn't the one they wanted. Could it be that easy? Or Palachka would figure it out all on his own. Even better.

She suffered in silence for an hour as the makeup and hair stylist fussed and brushed and squirted and gelled, then dressed under her mother's impatiently tapping foot.

"Everyone ready?" Isla asked. "Let's head downstairs."

Chapter 14

Saturday, February 18. 12:30 p.m.
Hyatt Regency. Cambridge, Massachusetts.

THE BRIDAL PARTY minced across the lobby like royalty, led by an older woman who could only be Lark's mother. He nearly swallowed his tongue at the sight of Lark; she looked magnificent, graceful from head to toe. She glanced to where he waited near the doors at the far end, hesitated, then came toward him, aping the mincing steps of the older woman, amusement curling her lips. Mace nearly laughed aloud. No, the Lark he'd seen to date did not fit in with these primping ladies—and yet, she did. He met her in the middle, offering his arm and ignoring the curious looks.

Lark tightened her fingers around his forearm. "Mother, this is Thomas Beckett."

No mention of the attack, nor of the danger she could be facing. The look she shot him, though, held warning. Nothing would interfere with Kaley's wedding.

Got it.

Did that mean she trusted him to keep her safe? Lark had courage in spades, but she was so far out of her depth she might as well be a kitten in a cage full of leopards.

"It's nice to mee' you, Mrs. Larkspur," he said, stepping forward and extending his hand.

"A pleasure." She gave him one of those limp fish handshakes he despised, then looked around and briskly clapped her hands. "The limousines are waiting, ladies. Dana and Evelyn, you'll ride with Kaley and myself. The rest of you, and Mr. Beckett, will travel in the second limousine."

"I'm Yvette, one of the bridesmaids," the lady across from him said, once they'd settled into their seats. "That's Grace."

"A pleasure, ladies."

"This trip will take like five minutes," Yvette said. "The church is really close. What kind of name is Mace? English? Norse?"

He chuckled. "It's jus' a nickname."

Lark seemed disappointed by his lack of an answer. Well, what could it hurt to tell them?

"I'm pretty good with improvised weapons," he said. "I was in a fight once, a long time ago, and I was losing. I picked up a piece of fencepost with a chunk of wood a' the top. It kind of looked like a cross. I won the fight. Someone said it looked like I was swinging a mace from God. The name stuck."

"Who were you fighting?"

"Where were you?"

"Was it a bar fight?"

He answered Lark's question. "No, it wasn't a bar fight. Just something that happened." A something that had happened in a mountain jungle in Columbia, but he wouldn't tell her that.

"You want to hear a Lark story?" Yvette asked, wiggling her eyebrows.

"No," Lark said. "Please no."

"Yes, absolutely." He grinned at her as she groaned and closed her eyes.

"Okay," Yvette said with relish. "This is a funny one. Once upon a time, Lark rode dressage. She made it to states, but instead of riding into the ring in proper attire—a top hat and tails, mind you—she comes out wearing a jockey's outfit and proceeds to do trick riding acts around the ring like she's in a circus or something."

Mace burst out laughing. Yes, that sounded like something Lark would do. "What happened?"

"The judges tossed me out of the competition," Lark said in satisfaction.

"How old were you?" he asked.

"Twelve." Color rose in her cheeks. "I wanted to be a jockey."

"That would definitely make a point," he agreed. "Did you get to be a jockey?"

Lark scowled. "No. I got grounded for a month instead. But at least I never had to ride dressage again."

Grace peered out the window as the limousine slowed. "We're here."

The driver turned onto the long drive of a shining silver church. He bypassed the main parking lot, which was choked with cars, more arriving every minute. Couples and groups chatted as they moved inside. Reporters clogged the drive, snapping photos of the guests and doing quick interviews with the presumably important ones. Apparently, Peter and Kaley's wedding was big news. For the first time, Mace wondered just how wealthy Lark's family was.

How far did her rebellion go, now that she was an adult? She drove a used Jeep rather than a fancy car, so she seemed pretty determined to make it on her own.

The driver maneuvered through a police barricade to a side entrance, pulling in behind the other limo. Mace exited first, turning to offer a hand to the ladies.

"You'll need to join the others in the pews," Mrs. Larkspur told him, not unkindly. "Obviously you're not part of the bridal party."

"Of course," he said, shifting his shoulders to stretch them. His suit weighed in at seven pounds. It, and the undershirt he wore against his skin, had been custom made for him. Both were bullet resistant, lined with special lightweight ballistic material that would also keep him safe from knife attacks. The undershirt, with its concealed gun pocket, kept his Browning Hi-Power snugged under his arm. His right front pants pocket had been torn open to allow easy access to the Asp baton strapped to this thigh. Even his dress shoes had been fitted with special soles for grip. Every member of his team who worked executive protection details possessed the same specialized attire.

The truth was, he loved weddings. Watching two people dedicating themselves to one another warmed his insides. Sure, fifty percent of them would hire lawyers and split their belongings later on, but here, now, at the beginning, the future seemed bright and hopeful. He felt the familiar tug in his gut, the sense of aloneness weddings also evoked.

Someday.

The image of Lark, dressed to kill at the nightclub, flashed through his mind. The feel of her in his arms as they danced. The taste of her mouth as he kissed her. He suppressed the soppy grin that threatened.

Isla Larkspur entered the building, gesturing for the others to follow before disappearing inside. Mace trotted to the nearest corner, angling himself so he had maximum range of vision.

A blue panel van eased around the news vans and crawled toward the barricade. One of the off duty cops stepped forward, arm raised in a clear order to stop. Instead, the driver stomped on the gas pedal. The van jumped forward, ramming the barricade. The cop dove out of the way, no doubt eating gravel as he rolled several times.

Mace drew his Asp baton and launched into an all-out run. What the hell? No way was this just some overzealous news crew. The van careened close to the entrance, screeching to a halt near the bridesmaids, who had all stopped to stare in astonishment.

"Scatter," he shouted. "Get inside!"

Clearly they didn't hear him as three men piled out of the van, because they cried out in fear and clustered together as one of the men shouted and waved a MAC-10. The other two cut Lark out of the herd and dragged her, kicking and screaming, to the blue van.

Mace kicked it harder. Goddammit! He'd moved too far away from her. His stupid, amateur mistake would cost her.

The driver saw Mace barreling closer and yelled, pointing his way. The one with the machine pistol turned and fired, spraying rounds indiscriminately in his direction. He flung himself past the shrubs fronting the church, bounced against the wall, and used his own momentum to push off and get back on the sidewalk.

One of the two who had grabbed Lark climbed into the back of the van, holding her wrists and trying to pull her bodily inside. The second tried unsuccessfully to grab her legs, but, brave woman that she was, she kicked and shouted and twisted. Kaley darted forward, clawing and scratching, trying to pull him away from Lark. He raised the back of his hand and slapped her across the face. She stumbled and fell to her hands and knees, tearing her wedding gown. Dana cried out and ran to her side, helping her up and away.

"Let her go," Kaley screamed, holding her bleeding cheek. "You let her go right now!"

He'd nearly closed the distance. Without hesitation, Mace hurled the closed baton at the shooter's head. The man flinched as the baton ricocheted off his shoulder and clattered to the sidewalk. With a snarl, he swung the MAC-10 back toward Mace and fired it full auto. Mace dove sideways, bouncing on the concrete. The shooter sprayed another burst of rounds. The first bullet slammed into his upper right chest, pushing him onto his back. The second shot skidded along his ribs. He ignored the instant burn, turning his head to search for Lark.

The men had succeeded in wrestling her into the back of the van, but she continued to punch and kick, trying to crawl to the doors. The driver stomped on the gas pedal, causing the van to slew around on the gravel before it gained purchase. The doors swung crazily.

Ordering his body to move, he struggled to his hands and knees as liquid fire seared along his scalp. But blood obscured his vision, and he fell as the darkness pulled him under.

Chapter 15

Saturday, February 18. 12:30 p.m.
Rooftop Bar, Ebony Point Hotel. Boston, Massachusetts.

THE LURE OF the ocean drew Fatianova to the floor-to-ceiling windows. Most of the boats in the harbor rested in their slips, but a three-story yacht cruised in lazily. She could make out a group of people milling around on the ship's roof, shivering in the bitter February cold, watching the guests on her rooftop bar, just as she watched them.

An amber glow bathed the entire enclosed bar area. Lighting had been carefully planned to reflect off the eggshell tiles and brass railings. Guests filled almost every seat, every table, every lounging area, and lined the bar two deep. She drained her fancy crystal goblet as she admired the sun shimmering off the buildings of downtown Boston.

The yacht gave her an idea.

A tanned wrist settled onto the window sill. She glanced over. The man leaning beside her wore a soft cashmere coat that had easily cost him three thousand dollars. The suit underneath had been custom-tailored, she felt certain. The man himself looked distinguished, from his full head of gray hair, assessing eyes, and strong chin. She smiled.

"Magnificent view, isn't it?" he said.

"*Da.* As beautiful as Moscow's skyline. Still, nothing I've seen can rival the Kremlin when it's lit at twilight."

"You're Russian," he said, gazing warmly into her eyes. "*Zdrast vwee tye.*"

Fatianova laughed. "Hello to you, too. Clearly you do not speak Russian."

"Did I pronounce it wrong?" He chuckled, a warm, masculine sound. "No, I'm embarrassed to say that I'm one of those Americans who never mastered another tongue."

"No?" She fluttered her lashes and made her eyes sparkle. "Tongues are not the only way to communicate."

"True." He shifted closer so that their arms brushed. "You take my breath away. You're easily the most stunning woman I've ever seen."

She ducked her chin, feigning modesty. "Thank you."

"May I buy you a drink? Or better yet, join me for lunch."

She set her empty glass on the edge of one of the curved metal planters. "Unfortunately, I'm meeting someone. Who is late, as usual."

"A . . . friend?" Was it her imagination, or did he sound disappointed?

"A co-worker. We need to discuss a matter, but it shouldn't take long." Would he wait, or prowl after another companion? She hoped he would be patient. A recreational romp in the hay seemed just the thing to relieve her stress.

"Then lunch it is." He smiled wryly at her. "I'm sorry. That was presumptive of me, wasn't it?"

She brushed a hand over the sleeve of his cashmere coat. "I like a man who takes charge."

He immediately moved closer. "Then, after your meeting, meet me at the bar."

She touched the tip of her tongue to her upper lip, then smiled coyly. "All right. I will."

"It's a date. Don't take too long." He straightened and walked away, heading to the bar. She watched as a seat magically opened up as he approached. He unbuttoned his coat as he sat, then swiveled around to look back at her, raising a hand and smiling.

A group of ladies gathered up their belongings and headed to the door. Fatianova appropriated their table before anyone else could, thoughts flickering back to her earlier idea. The fees to enter into the bidding to purchase her stolen nuclear bomb would more than cover the cost to rent a fancy yacht and a pilot for an evening.

Pulling her smart phone from her trouser pocket, she opened her email. The window had closed an hour ago; eighteen people had responded to her invitation. A goodly number. She added the last three to her master list, then composed a short message.

> Applications have now closed. Wire the nonrefundable $10,000 entry fee to this account number. Details to follow.

The waiter brought her drink, which wasn't at all bad for an American attempt at a classic Russian drink.

"Get me one of those, too, would you?" Fyodor said, settling into the adjoining wicker chair.

"You're late."

"I took the wrong Metro. Damned confusing maps."

"What can I get for you, sir?" The waiter hovered by Fyodor's chair, his English momentarily jarring to her ears.

"Bring him the same," she answered, lifting her glass. Fyodor's English barely passed muster. If he could even ask directions to the toilet, she'd be surprised.

"Make sure he uses Stolichnaya Elit, not some cheap vodka."

Fatianova conveyed his order. The man jotted it on a pad and left.

"Have you gotten through to your smuggler?" she asked.

"*Da*. He had to lie low for a few hours."

"What happened?" Fatianova didn't really care. As long as she got what she wanted, nothing else mattered.

"He didn't tell me, but he says he can't risk crossing the border for a few weeks, at least."

She tried to quash her growing frustration. "Did you offer to pay more?"

"Of course. He wouldn't budge. At first, I thought he might be trying to steal our package and sell it on his own, but I'm convinced he doesn't know what it is."

Be nice to him, she reminded herself, drinking half of her cocktail in one long swallow. She forced a smile. "I'm assuming you've thought of a solution?"

"I didn't need to. He gave me the name of a group he says might help."

"Who?"

He shrugged, but Fatianova sensed his tension. He wasn't nearly as confident as he sounded. "They call themselves the Citizens for a Free America. They're neo-Nazis, like the National Socialist Party."

"And they'll agree to go to Canada to retrieve my package?"

"Our package. Don't forget for one minute that you need me, Fatianova." He dropped his eyes along her body. It didn't matter what she wore; he always acted as though he could see her naked.

She gritted her teeth. He disgusted her, but she would do whatever it took to secure a comfortable life for herself.

She forced herself to smile as she raised her tumbler in a quasi-salute. "Of course I need you, Fyodor. We're partners, aren't we?"

The waiter approached with Fyodor's drink. She'd never been served so fast before. She, like most Russians, was used to waiting in long lines.

He sipped suspiciously, then took a deeper drink. "I didn't know Americans knew how to make a good Russian drink."

"When will you call them?"

"As soon as I leave here. These people always need money for their guns and drugs. I'll let you know what they say."

After he left, Fatianova stared into her glass, the activity and noise around her fading into nothingness. She couldn't bring herself to feel sorry that Fyodor had to die. If he scored an American contact, he could live until his usefulness ran out. If he failed, she would kill him just for the sheer pleasure of it.

Rising, she headed to the bar to find Cashmere Man.

Chapter 16

Saturday, February 18. 1:05 p.m.
Viktor Sokolov's Home. Boston, Massachusetts.

LARK GROANED AS the panel van jolted against another pothole. The zip ties securing her wrists behind her and the cotton bag over her head prevented her from anticipating the rough ride. She could see dim light through the bag, but no concrete shapes. Her hysterical tears had finally subsided, but she still snuffled and hiccupped her grief through the gag.

Mace was dead. She'd seen him shot, seen him fall and not move again.

It was all her fault.

If she'd never taken him to her hotel, if she'd believed him when he claimed not to be her enemy, maybe he'd still be alive. If she'd never gone to the Promenade with Kaley and her friends. If she'd never danced with him. If, if, if. She could drown in the ifs.

Right now, she needed to concentrate on the whens. When the van stopped, she needed to be ready. When the two men in the back of the van tried to take her, she needed to fight. And when none of that freed her, she needed to be prepared for whatever came next.

A cell phone from the front of the van jangled out one of those retro home-phone rings she hated. Loud, unnecessary, jarring noise. "Iggy. Yeah, boss. Headed there now."

Where? Where were they headed? Hearing the brief conversation slammed home the danger of her current situation. Shivers of fear replaced her grief. Logic said she was about to meet Palachka. Would he hang her from a meat hook in an abandoned warehouse? Shove needles under her fingernails? Cut off her ear?

With her whole glorious life spreading before her in high definition, being shot execution-style, a single bullet to the back of the head, seemed abrupt and grossly unfair. In the movies, mobsters tortured their victims to get information out of them, then killed them. The mobster wouldn't believe her if she claimed innocence. He would continue the torture until he got the answer he wanted.

What was the question?

The van turned onto a smoother road. Its suspension sucked, but at least the jolting eased. After a few miles, they merged onto a highway. The van rattled from the increased speed, and she heard other cars around them.

They got off the highway and onto surface streets, stopping at several red lights. Would anyone hear her if she started screaming? Not through the gag. When the van finally stopped and the engine died, her fear came roaring back. She tried to steel herself for what was coming, but already knew she wouldn't hold up under torture. She had no tolerance for pain.

The doors opened, and one of the men grabbed her arm. She fought for her freedom, fought against the hands hurting her, kicked as strongly as she could. One heel connected with flesh.

"Fucking bitch." One of the men twisted her arm up behind her, forcing a gasp of pain from her. Momentarily stunned, she was helpless as he simply lifted her down as though she were a bag of flour. One man took each arm and pulled her forward. Something blocked the sunlight. A building?

A door opened, and the men dragged her inside.

"Stairs," Iggy said. "Go down. Come on. Do it."

She fumbled to find the first step. They yanked her down, causing her to stumble. She fell the last few stairs, grunting as she hit concrete. The men went back up the stairs and shut the door.

Struggling to sit up, she listened for any sound. Nothing. No light penetrated the bag over her head. Wherever she was smelled musty, and the floor chilled her bottom. She worked her tongue around the gag, finally managing to push it out of her mouth. It hung around her neck. At least now she could take a deep breath.

How could she get herself free? She stretched out on the concrete, laying her head along the ground, and tried to use the faint roughness of the floor to help drag the cotton bag off her head. After a few minutes, she realized she wasn't making any progress. Knowing she would bump into something eventually, she stood, taking tiny, tentative steps.

Her stomach hit some sort of plastic bin. She stepped sideways, grunting as her ribs connected with something solid. Turning around, she felt along it with her bound hands, eventually finding the corner of what seemed to be some sort of workbench. She slid into a squat, trying to catch the bag on the corner. After the third attempt, she succeeded in shifting the bag to the top of her head, and wasted no time in shaking it off.

She was in a basement. Sunlight trickled in from a horizontal window near the ceiling. Even if she could get her hands free, she'd never fit through the window.

She spent the next hour exploring her prison, but found nothing she could use to get herself free. In fact, it looked to her as though this basement had been designed for this very purpose. Finally, she sat down on the bottom stair, defeated.

If Mace were here, he'd have no trouble getting himself free. Tears trickled down her cheeks. The thought of his strength, his humor, his fierceness all snuffed out in an instant choked her, and she began to sob.

Eventually drained, she curled onto her side. Waiting like this made it all so much worse. When would Palachka finally come for her? And what would happen when he did? The light coming through the window shifted around to the west, then faded entirely.

She fell asleep.

The door at the top of the stairs banged open, jerking her to wakefulness. Iggy and the other man stomped down and lifted her unceremoniously to her feet, pushing and shoving her upward. She stepped into a kitchen.

"He's waiting." A woman, her voice pitched low and hurried, made shooing motions. "Go up right away."

Iggy lifted a knife in her direction. She backed away, heart thumping, but hit a wall. He spun her around and flattened her against it with a hand between her shoulder blades. She squeaked in dread, but relaxed as the zip tie around her wrists tightened, then fell away.

Iggy pulled her out of the kitchen and through a foyer. She caught sight of herself in a round mirror above a console table, and couldn't stop the slightly hysterical titter that bubbled up. Her careful makeup had smeared, her hair stuck out in all directions, and her bridesmaid dress was ruined. The lace had torn at her shoulder and above her right breast, and part of the hem of the skirt hung down to her knee. She'd lost an earring.

She looked like she had at eight, when she'd run away from her parents' summer home in Nantucket. Her younger self had evaded search parties for three days before hunger forced her to take refuge in their caretaker's cottage. For that, her mother grounded her for two weeks, causing her to miss the scheduled class trip to the zoo. She refused to speak to her mother the entire time. She'd been dying to feed a giraffe.

"Where are we?" she asked.

"Shut up," one of the men growled.

Lark shut up. She didn't want to get kicked or punched, and annoying her captors wouldn't accomplish anything. The true threat lay with whoever had ordered her kidnapping. Instead, she looked around. To her right, a cozy sofa sat in front of a gas fireplace. Some sort of metal table was tucked up against the sofa's back. The area opened up beyond that, the wood floors gleaming. A mahogany conference table and six chairs sat on a rectangular carpet. Smooth wooden stairs on the other wall rose to the second floor, which is where her guards prodded her.

She took her time on the steps, gripping the polished brass handrail, wishing she dared take her high heels off. "Where are we going?"

"You'll see. Turn right at the top."

She did as commanded, her heart starting to pound again. Whatever was going to happen was near. Part of her was relieved. The anticipation made it hard to breathe. She walked past the Plexiglas half wall, which prevented anyone from falling to the first floor, past an enormous abstract painting in blood reds and deep blues, to a door standing wide open. A guard put a hand between her shoulder blades and pushed her through the door, stepping in behind her.

"She's here, Mr. Sokolov," he said respectfully.

A broad-shouldered man in his late fifties rose from behind a dark bean-shaped desk and came toward her. "Thank you, Iggy. Wait outside, please."

"Yes, sir." Her guard closed the door behind him as he left.

Mr. Sokolov wore an impeccable three-piece suit that had obviously been custom-tailored for him. Despite the dark circles underneath, sharp intelligence gleamed from his eyes. His nose had clearly been broken more than once. He smoothed a hand over his already neat salt-and-pepper hair.

"My name is Viktor Sokolov," he said. His gaze met hers, as though looking for a reaction, then roved over her, taking in her torn dress, mussed hair, and red eyes. "I've heard a great deal about you, Ms. Larkspur."

Two other people occupied the room. A slim man about her own age sat alone on a sofa ringed by three other chairs. His blue hair was tousled and spiky in the front and shaved on the sides. A gray T-shirt with a green logo on the front hung loose over jeans torn at the knees. The other, a heavyset man, sat in one of the chairs in front of Sokolov's desk. She took in his thinning hair, bulbous nose, and heavy eyebrows, recognizing Palachka. He met her gaze with frigid, flat eyes that filled her with fear. This man would hurt her without hesitation or mercy.

Still, Lark couldn't help the fury and grief that flooded her.

"I've never even heard of you at all," she said, voice shrill. "But your sacks of boar shit killed my friend. Just shot him dead when all he was trying to do was stop you from kidnapping me."

Mr. Sokolov's brows snapped down. He looked over at Palachka, who rose and moved behind her. She twisted around to glare at him. He crossed his arms, feet planted solidly on the carpet. His face betrayed no emotion whatsoever.

"The man interfered." His voice sounded as cold as the winter in his eyes.

Sokolov nodded and shrugged. "Then Iggy had no choice. Your friend should have stayed out of it."

"Stayed out of it?" Rage swamped her. "You deserve a special place in hell, you murdering bastard!"

He slapped her. Searing pain ripped through her face and she cried out, falling hard onto her shoulder. Jesus God, that hurt! Even after the spots stopped dancing in front of her eyes, her cheek still throbbed like a motherfucker. When her vision returned, she found herself staring at a sideways set of navy pants and dress shoes. Hard hands dragged her upright and held her still while Sokolov grabbed her jaw in rigid fingers.

"Nobody talks to me like that, you stupid little bitch. Am I making myself clear, or do you need another demonstration?"

She'd never been struck in her life. The shock of it robbed her of breath.

His grasp tightened painfully. "Do you understand?"

She clamped her lips over the words that wanted to escape. *Murderer. Monster.*

A soft knock on the door caused Sokolov to step back and drop his arm. Palachka, still gripping her arms, pushed her over to a chair and thrust her into it. She put a hand to her cheek and discovered it was already swelling.

A young, attractive maid entered. She brought a coffee tray to the desk without a single glance around and poured hot liquid into a cup, adding some cream from a tiny pitcher.

"Don't piss him off."

She barely heard the urgent whisper. Lark rolled her eyes toward the young man on the sofa. "What?"

"You don't know him. This is him being nice."

She dropped her hand from her puffy cheek and pointed it at his bruised face. "Did he hit you, too?"

He nodded, casting a furtive look at Sokolov. "And I'm related to him."

The maid picked up her tray. "Did you need anything else, sir?"

"No."

Sokolov returned to his seat behind the desk and picked up the cup, inhaling deeply before sipping. He jerked his chin at Palachka, who went back to his seat, as well.

"Mr. Sokolov, I'm pretty sure there's been a mistake here." She couldn't help the wobble in her voice. The truth was, even through her anger she felt so frightened her knees knocked together.

His brows rose. "Do you?"

Lark took another deep breath. "I think you have me confused with someone else. Someone else who was at the Promenade the other night?"

He bared his teeth in what was probably supposed to be a smile. "Hadley Nia Larkspur of the Nantucket Larkspurs, eldest daughter of Chauncey and Isla Larkspur. One younger sister. Formerly engaged to Ralph Pearson, but currently unattached."

She felt her eyes widen. "You're kidnapping me for ransom? Is that it? You want my parents to pay a ransom?"

He chuckled, but the sound lacked any real humor. "No. That's not why you're here. You currently work for the Federal Bureau of Investigation in their Cyber Crime division."

She sucked in a breath. "I'm not spying for you. No way."

"No? Too bad. That might make me feel less like killing you. But that's not why you're here, either."

Palachka produced a knife from somewhere and used it to clean under his fingernails. As far as Lark could tell, they were immaculate. It was another attempt to cow her. She could have told them not to bother. She already felt cowed.

Sokolov leaned back in his chair, resting his elbows on the arms. "You say you don't know who I am. So, what am I supposed to believe? That you didn't know who you were stealing from? Is that it?"

"What? Stole?" She knew she sounded dumb, but she couldn't think of anything more clever to say.

Mr. Sokolov's mouth flattened in displeasure. "I don't have a lot of patience today, Hadley."

Don't call me Hadley. "I don't steal."

He inhaled through his nose and let it out in a slow stream through his mouth. "Take my word for it—if you keep making bullshit denials, this conversation will go south fast. Let's try this again. You stole fifty million dollars from me. I want that money back. Now."

Lark sucked in a sharp breath and leaned forward, hands braced on her thighs. "Fifty million dollars? Fifty *million*?"

"Are you deaf? That's what I said."

Lark's brain froze. What the hell was going on here? "I didn't steal any money," she said faintly. "And I truly don't know who you are."

He jerked his chin toward the young man on the sofa. "Elliott?"

Elliott sauntered over to Sokolov's desk and sat on a corner, one leg dangling. He either didn't see or ignored Sokolov's glare.

"You're the hacker goes by the handle SPURious," he said. "You're the one hacked the MIT mainframe while you were at CalTech. You hacked a nuclear power plant and made a zebra's ass the first thing users saw when they logged on. You wear a black badge at DefCon for winning Capture the Flag two years in a row."

By the time he'd finished, Lark's mouth hung open. "Oh, my God. How do you even *know* any of that?"

"Let's just say Elliott is very motivated to find my money."

Lark glanced at the young man's bruised face. She needed to be more careful. "I don't do any of that any more. I'm legit now. And I never did any damage. I found vulnerabilities in their systems that could be exploited by unscrupulous black hats."

Elliott shrugged. "I don't give a shit about that. I found your signature all over the hack."

Back in the day, Lark took gleeful credit for her successes. It pissed her off that someone was using her handle against her. She fisted her hands in her hair, feeling like tearing it out by the roots. "That's not even possible," she almost wailed. "Only a few people know about my past. Sure, I got a rep after the MIT thing. I never told anyone about the nuclear plant, though. The only—"

She snapped her mouth shut.

"The only other person who knew was your partner?" Elliott guessed, eyes shrewd.

"Um, yeah," she mumbled. She had to be the dumbest person on the planet. Elliott couldn't possibly know about ChaosCowboy, who had been her mentor and partner for many years. He'd severed all ties with her after his arrest, not wanting to drag her down with him. She missed him still.

Lark moved to leap out of her chair so she could pace, but a swift glare from Palachka made her reconsider. "I didn't do that.

Okay, yeah, I used to poke around in other people's systems. I don't, anymore. I have immunity as long as I don't."

Sokolov tipped his head, pinning her with his deep-set eyes. His brows furrowed. Finally, he sat forward again, arms on the desk and hands clasped loosely together. "Interesting. I've gotten real good over the years at telling when people are lying to me. And damned if I don't think you're telling the truth."

Air whooshed out of Lark as she felt herself go limp. "I am."

He shrugged. "That means shit to me. Either I'm wrong and you did it, or you know who did, or you can find out who did."

Lark's fear turned to a slow burn of anger. Hackers had a code. Someone had violated the code, taken her hacker handle, and used it to steal money from the scary man. "Who would do that to me?"

She didn't realize she'd spoken aloud until Sokolov answered her. "You better figure it out real fast. I'll give you forty-eight hours to find my money and return it to me."

She gaped at him. "Two days? That's impossible!"

"Make it possible."

"I need more time. It's going to be like trying to find the golden needle in a pile of silver needles. You still have to dig through all the needles."

"I'm a reasonable man." He sneered at her, then banged the cup onto his desk hard enough that it cracked. "I need that cash available to me in seven days. I'll give you six of those days to get my money back. Not one second more."

She wrung her hands together. "Mr. Sokolov, I get why you're angry. I'm angry, too. Someone broke our code. Even among black hats, the code is sacrosanct. But tracking down a hacker is a tricky thing. Without some sort of signature, we're virtually invisible. He'll have covered his tracks; I doubt I can even find him."

Sokolov nodded to Palachka. Before she could register what was happening, Palachka yanked her bodily to her feet and smashed her into Sokolov's desk, bending her over it. Elliott scrambled to get out of the way as the breath crashed out of her lungs and her abdomen spasmed in agony. Dread clawed its way up her throat as she tried to twist away, terrified tears springing to her eyes.

"Oh my God, oh my God, please! Stop, please stop," she gasped through the pain.

Palachka slammed the side of her face into the wood of the desk, stretching her right arm forward and pinning it into place as he leaned over her, knife poised to strike.

"Do you see how serious I am? No? Palachka, cut her finger off."

"No! No!" she shrieked, yanking futilely to free her hand, weeping hysterically, tears and snot running down her face. "Stop! Please stop!"

Palachka brought the knife down, slicing through her pinkie fingernail. "More?"

Lark closed her eyes, heart beating frantically as she sobbed. "No. Please no. Don't. Just please stop."

The weight against her back disappeared, and suddenly she was free. She slid off the desk and crumpled to the carpet, cradling her hand to her chest, examining it frantically. Palachka's knife had trimmed her nail and sliced the top layer of skin from the tip of her finger. It hardly bled at all. Lark found herself bizarrely grateful for his precision with the knife.

"You'll get my money back. Or I'll give you to Palachka."

She found herself nodding over and over. "Yes. I will. I'll find it. I will."

"Good. I'm glad you understand me."

Palachka's hard hand bit into her bicep as he hauled her to her feet. She shrank away from him, batting at his grip. He ignored her, holding her until her shaking legs strengthened and she stood on her own. Elliott came and put an arm around her back, supporting her as he guided her to the door.

"It's over," he muttered. "You survived it."

Lark leaned against him, grateful for the assistance, her whole body trembling in the aftermath of the assault. She tried to gulp back her tears, wanting nothing more than to get the hell out of this nightmare and go back to a world she understood.

Elliott opened the door, slid his hand down her arm, and pressed a small thumb drive into her palm. She closed her fingers around it reflexively. "It's our bank account information and the code used in the hack. Check out your own nine-to-five, if you're smart. The originating IP address is on this USB stick. Use it to find the thief."

"You have that money back to me in six days," Sokolov called after her. "After that, Palachka will find you and make an example of you."

Chapter 17

Saturday, February 18. 2:15 p.m.
Cutler Army Hospital. Fort Devens, Massachusetts.

NINE SECONDS.

That's all it had taken him to fail. Nine seconds.

Mace shifted impatiently as the doctor peered through a magnifying lamp, probing gently into his scalp. The crease hurt like a bitch even with the local anesthetic to dim the pain. He deserved it.

"Please try to sit still," she said. She used the forceps to remove a fragment of cement, dropping it into a small glass jar. "I see three more particles."

"And then we're done," he growled. Self-condemnation burned a hole in his gut. He needed to get out there; needed to find Lark. God knew what she was going through at this very moment, because he'd let her out of his sight.

"And then you let the doctor look at your ribs," Jace said firmly. Nods from Tag, Alex, and Gabe had him gritting his teeth.

"Saw you get hit, dude," Alex said. "If not for your suit, you'd be dead."

Tag stuck his finger through the two holes in the suit jacket and lifted the garment with his forefinger. He made it sway.

"Point taken," Mace said. In truth, his shoulder and ribs hurt like a twin pair of bitches. And head wounds always stung, even if only caused by flying concrete shrapnel from a missed shot from the MAC-10.

The doctor dropped the last fragment into the jar. "You don't need stitches. I'm going to apply a topical antibiotic." She wiped down the area, spread the ointment, and taped a bandage over the cut.

"Strip," Jace ordered.

Mace unbuttoned his shirt and pulled it and his T-shirt over his head, setting them on the bed. Tag winced. Mace didn't have to look to know huge bruises had formed at the impact sites. The doctor dropped her gloves into a receptacle and donned another pair. Her white coat sleeve brushed against his skin as she palpated each injury in turn.

"There's no penetration into the skin," she said. "That's good. You're lucky this one didn't crack a rib. It's going to be tender for a few days, though. Ice both areas for about fifteen minutes off and on for a day or two to keep the swelling down. Make sure you put a towel between the ice and your skin. Try to rest. I'll give you something for the pain."

"No, thanks," he said, pulling his T-shirt back on. Rest? Not a flying snowball's chance in the Sahara. Not until Lark was safe. "I'll take some Tylenol if I need it. Are we done here?"

She nodded. "I'll get your discharge paperwork together."

"I fucked this up," Mace said. "How did they know where she would be today?"

"Not a stretch," Gabe said, shifting a crutch into a more comfortable position. "The lieutenant governor's son's marriage was all over Twitter. They clearly know who Lark is, know who her sister is, knew where to be."

He fingered the bandage over his ear. "If Palachka took her to Sokolov, she could be at his house. We should go get her. Grab the FBI and storm the place."

"If she's there," Alex said. "That's a big *if*."

"Did she have her cell phone?" Gabe asked.

"No pockets in her dress," Mace said, "but her purse went into the van with her."

Anxiety pressed against his breastbone, canceling out the discomfort of his injuries.

Jace put a hand on his shoulder. "I know you don't want to hear this, but we could go live at any time. At some point, you might have to let the FBI handle this."

"I know that," he gritted out through clenched teeth.

A nurse bustled in. "Discharge papers for Sergeant Beckett."

He stood, reaching for them. "Thanks."

"The doctor wants you to—"

"I got this. Thanks."

"You guys are all stubborn as mules." The nurse shrugged. "Come back if gangrene sets in."

Mace was in no mood for her humor. He strode to the door, dropping the discharge instructions into the trash can. "Let's get the hell out of here."

Chapter 18

Saturday, February 18. 5:30 p.m.
Lark's Home. Boston, Massachusetts.

VIKTOR SOKOLOV HAD insisted Iggy drive her home. She rode in sullen silence with arms folded across her chest.

"You gotta gimme the address sooner or later, sweets," Iggy said.

"Murderer. Let me out at the next corner."

He glowered at her before turning back to the road. "I got my orders. Mr. Sokolov says I drive you home, I drive you home."

"Fuck Sokolov. And fuck you." Fishing out her cell phone, she snapped a pic of his profile. After this was all over, she would report him to the police. He would pay for killing Mace.

"Address?" he prompted.

She stared out the window as she gave it to him. Grief washed through her anew. Right now, she had no choice but to find the unscrupulous hacker who'd laid a false trail leading back to her.

After, though . . . after, she would find a way to take down Iggy, Sokolov, and the whole damned mob, if she had to.

Not soon enough for her, he pulled into her drive. She refused to acknowledge him, shoving the door open and exiting without a word or backward glance, shivering in the bitter air. Her torn lace dress offered no warmth. The moon, just a shade off full, provided enough light for her to see as she strode to her front door and opened it. She paused inside, waiting while Iggy drummed his fingers on the steering wheel, looked around, and finally drove off.

She plopped onto her sofa and checked her phone for messages. She'd missed two calls from Trevor and five from a number she didn't recognize. Mace, she hoped.

First on her to-do list had to be to call her sister, who would be frantic. She dialed Kaley.

"Hello?"

"It's me."

"Lark! It's Lark," Kaley said, voice fading as she pulled her cell phone away from her mouth. "Where are you? Are you all right? What happened? We've been so worried!"

"I'll explain everything, I promise. Where are you?"

"We're at the police station. Where are you? Who were those men? How did you get away?"

"Kaley, slow down. Are you all right? That man walloped you pretty hard."

"Typical you're worried about me when you were the one dragged into a car and kidnapped. We're fine. We'll wait at the police station for you."

Lark hesitated. "I can't go there. Not right now. There's something I need to do first."

"You want to go see Mace first?" Kaley guessed, voice softening. "They took him away pretty fast."

"Do you know where? I'd like to pay my respects." Her voice wobbled, air trapped in her throat making it hard to breathe.

Kaley sucked in a breath. "Oh, Lark! You poor thing. You thought . . . honey, he's alive. They took him to the hospital to get checked out."

For a moment, Lark's world grayed and fuzzed around the edges. "A . . . alive? Are you . . . sure?"

Kaley snickered. "Oh, yeah. My high school French teacher didn't give us lessons in swear words, but from the context, he was cussing like a crazy drunk trucker."

She shook her head to get rid of the buzzing. "But I saw him. Get hit, go down. He was lying in a pool of blood. I *saw* it."

"Honey, he was wearing some sort of super suit. Bulletproof clothes. Who knew?"

Sudden urgency sharpened Lark's focus. She needed to see Mace. Right now.

"Lark, you have to file a report. You're a kidnap victim." Kaley paused. "How did you get away, anyway?"

She wasn't prepared to answer any questions. Not yet. No matter how well meaning. "Uh."

"Lark? What's going on?"

She ignored her sister. "This is all just a huge misunderstanding. No one kidnapped me. I just went to talk to someone, then came home."

"Who?" Suspicion darkened Kaley's voice. "What the hell is going on, Lark?"

Lark blew out a frustrated breath. "I can't tell you, Kay. Not right now. I just wanted you guys to know I was okay."

"Well, okay, I guess. If you really don't want to file assault charges against those men." Doubt rang in her voice. "I guess we're pretty much done here. We were just waiting to see if the cops could find the van, but they couldn't."

"Kaley, I'm so sorry I ruined your wedding." The words left her in a rush.

Her sister chuckled. "The press is having a field day speculating about why the wedding was canceled so abruptly. Apparently I got cold feet and bolted. Either that, or we decided to elope. Peter's going to hold a press conference tomorrow and make something up to explain all this."

Lark sighed heavily. "Mother's right about me. I'm just a big screw-up."

"Don't even go there, Lark," her sister snapped. "You're not a screw-up. How could you know what would happen? Even though you won't tell me what happened."

"I will, I promise. Just later, okay?"

"Humph. Fine."

"Did they tell you what hospital Mace is at?"

Paper crinkled in the background. "An Army hospital. But he was released hours ago. They gave the police the name of the hotel where he and his team are staying. One of those extended stay hotels." She read off an address.

Lark curled around one of her bright pillows, hugging it tightly as she squeezed her eyes closed. Mace was alive. He'd been shot trying to rescue her, but he'd survived Iggy's hail of bullets. He shimmered in her mind as a real-life knight in shining armor. Bulletproof clothes? She couldn't explain her necessity to see him, only that she had to check for herself that he still breathed. "Could you maybe drive me back to the hotel? My car's still there."

"Of course. I'll be there in fifteen minutes."

To keep from dwelling too heavily on the night's events, she took several deep breaths, calmed her mind, and began to mentally review the various hackers, crackers, and hactivists she'd gotten to know over the past nine years, groaning a little when she realized the number swelled quickly to well over a thousand.

Okay, let's eat this elephant one bite at a time.

She could ignore the script kiddies. They were nuisances who used other people's programs to cause mischief, like defacing websites or creating viruses. Sure, they could take advantage of security flaws to damage a company's infrastructure, but they also left huge footprints in their wake, making them easy to track down and prosecute. None of them had the necessary chops to do what her nemesis had done. Assuming sixty percent of the community of computer enthusiasts never rose above the level of script kiddie, that left her with roughly four hundred names.

She could also cross off nation-state cyberthreats. China, Russia, North Korea, Iran. Their motivations ranged from cyberespionage to theft of intellectual property to blind paranoia. To attacks against the US government, like the Office of Personnel Management and the Government Accountability Office. Economic espionage drove the destructive attacks against corporations like Westinghouse Electric Corporation and U.S. Steel. Both Germany and Turkey had been victims of cyberattacks that had caused massive damage to a steel mill and a gas pipeline.

She also dismissed those who launched denial of service attacks against business networks, which were designed to overwhelm and disrupt normal work operations. Further, she ruled out the hacktivists. They usually had political gripes or objections to commercial capitalism.

Okay, that left about three hundred and fifty.

She mentally eliminated those too young to be around when she was most heavily involved in the Darknet community. Ditto for those lacking the imagination and skills to diagnose not just the complexity of the tech but also the personality behind the code . . . her personality. That brought the number down to a hundred and seventy.

A honk outside sent her scrambling out the door. A dark red Ford Explorer idled in her driveway; Kaley leaned out the window and waved, then clicked the doors open. Lark climbed in, immediately noticing the butterfly bandages on Kaley's cheek.

"Fuckers."

"His ring cut me," she said. "And I got some scrapes on my knees and hands. It could have been worse. We could have all been shot, like Mace was."

"Mace was the only threat," Lark said. "No offense."

"No, you're right," her sister said. "So what exactly happened tonight? What happened to your face? Did one of those bastards hit you?"

Lark bit her lip. "Right now I barely know what's happening. I need to figure some stuff out. Then I'll tell you everything, I promise."

Kaley frowned. "Mother's worried."

"Really?"

"Yes, really. Armed men took her daughter at gunpoint. Naturally she's frantic."

Had her sister *met* Isla Larkspur? Lark rolled her eyes and punched in her mother's number. Mace would have to wait until her mother had been appeased.

"Hadley. Where on earth did you disappear to? The girls were babbling some nonsense about you being kidnapped. The police came."

"Yes, mother, I know. It was a misunderstanding. A man wanted to meet with me, and his employees got a little overzealous. But everything's fine."

"What a relief. I'm disappointed in you, Hadley. Trust you to ruin Kaley's wedding. Just like when you were six and gorged yourself on your sister's birthday cake. You vomited all over her presents, if you recall."

Lark gave an exaggerated sigh. "How can I not, when you remind me of it so often?"

"Don't get fresh with me, young lady. Do you know how many hours I spent organizing the wedding of the year? All that's wrecked now."

"Sorry," she muttered reflexively.

Her mother gave a disapproving sniff. "Peter's father is announcing his candidacy for Senate next month. The entire family is under scrutiny. Please do your best to stay out of trouble."

Familiar frustration bubbled up inside Lark. "I'll let Kaley know how worried you've been." She hit the end button with more force than necessary. The phone immediately vibrated, and the theme song to a video game started playing. She jammed the green button. "Trevor! Thank God!"

"What's wrong?" His deep voice immediately calmed her.

"Oh, the usual. Embarrassing my parents. What's that noise?" She could hear popping noises, and something that sounded like a car crash.

"Nothing important. Talk to me."

She heard a rush of air and a grunt. A voice in the background shouted something she couldn't understand. "Jesus H. Christ on a pogo stick. Are you in a freaking *firefight*?" Her voice rose two octaves.

Humor flowed through the receiver. "Only a little one. I'm a tad pressed for time, though. What's going on?"

"Um, it's complicated." How to condense the past ten hours into a few sentences? "When I called you, I was hoping for advice on how to interrogate a prisoner. Or come to London to hide out for a while. That's all been, how do you always put it, overcome by events?"

Trevor paused long enough that Lark checked to make sure they were still connected. "Trev?"

"I take it this isn't some big joke?"

"Wish it were. But my prisoner turned out to be a hero. He got shot trying to protect me, but he's okay. He was wearing bullet-proof clothes, if you can believe that."

"Your prisoner. Saved you."

"Well, sort of. I'm fine, though. But I'm really wondering how an Army soldier who works in logistics moonlights as a body-guard? I mean, why else have bulletproof clothes?"

"Lark. What is this soldier's name?" Trevor snapped off the words.

Lark's shoulders hunched. She'd been stupid about this entire situation. "Staff Sergeant Thomas Beckett. Code named Mace."

"Good. Happens I know him." Trevor chuckled. "Our units have worked together in the past. He's a good man. Quite the charmer with the ladies, though."

Lark let out the breath she hadn't known she'd been holding. "So he's Delta Force?"

Something crashed in the background, and Trevor grunted. The line went silent for a few seconds. "Bollocks."

"Trev? Are you . . . alive?"

He sounded out of breath. "Peachy. Anyroad, I can tell you Mace is well worth getting to know. Is it serious?"

Lark giggled. "I barely know him. Call me when you're not getting shot at."

"Will do. Cheers." The line went dead.

She snickered, snorted, then threw back her head, hooting with laughter. Kaley glanced at her uneasily. She couldn't stop, though. What rabbit hole had she fallen down? The entire evening took on a hazy, surreal air. Stolen millions, terrifying villains, threats of dismemberment, and her friend phoning her in the middle of combat.

"Lark, are you . . . okay?" her sister asked.

She hiccupped twice and sobered. "Not really, no. Somehow I don't think I'll ever be the same again."

Chapter 19

Saturday, February 18. 7:30 p.m.
Extended Stay Hotel. Boston, Massachusetts.

MORE THAN AN hour later, she parked her Jeep and trotted up to Mace's hotel suite. He might still be at the hospital, but she needed to see for herself that he was all right. Maybe she could hang out in the hallway until he got back? Maybe one of his teammates would let her inside. Gathering her courage, she raised her fist and knocked.

The door flung open so abruptly it banged against the inner wall. Mace braced a hand on the frame, breathing shallowly, eyes wild. He focused in on her like a laser for half a heartbeat, then grabbed her and hauled her into his arms. He squeezed her so tightly she could barely breathe, but she wrapped her arms around his waist and held on just as strongly.

"You didn't answer your phone," he muttered into her hair. "I didn't know . . . I thought . . . why didn't you answer your phone?"

She pushed a wad of his T-shirt out of her mouth with her

tongue. "I needed to see for myself that you were all right. I thought . . . I thought you were dead."

"I thought you were," he admitted. "God, you're freezing."

He pulled away from her abruptly. Grabbing her hand, he pulled her into his bedroom so quickly she barely registered the two other men in the living area.

"I've got her," he tossed over his shoulder, kicking the door closed with a foot. He lifted her onto the bed, and dropped down beside her, scooping her into his arms again. She laid her head against his chest, feeling his rapid heartbeat. He'd been worried. He wanted her here. His warmth surrounded her, unthawing her from the inside out.

"Was that your swim team?" She tried a chuckle, but it came out more of a soft whimper.

"Yeah. Want to tell me what—?"

"Wait."

She pulled away and sat up, taking in the bandage on his head. Reaching out with a tentative hand, she touched it, running her fingers back and forth. "Take off your T-shirt."

"I'm fine, Lark. I was worried about you."

"I'm fine, too. So we're both fine. Take off your T-shirt."

Instead of doing as she bid, he tunneled both hands through her hair, probing gently. He stroked a finger across the cheek where Viktor Sokolov had slapped her, making a pained noise deep in his throat.

"Who hit you?" His low growl both alarmed and thrilled her.

"Later. I want to see your injuries."

He moved his hands down her throat, hesitated at the tear on her dress, then continued down her shoulders and arms. He slid his palms around her waist, all with a touch so gentle she barely felt it. Her body reacted, though, skin tingling everywhere he'd brushed. When he dropped his eyes to her legs, she took the torn lace and tucked it out of sight.

"It looks worse than it is," she said. "They didn't hurt me. Not really. Now you. I want to see."

He shook his head, capturing her gaze with his own. "I thought I'd lost you. Those men . . . how did you get away?"

She wasn't ready yet to lay it all out. Instead, she gave in to the electric buzz being so close to him gave her. Her palm smoothed across his chest, following the ropes of muscle, then dropped to trace his six-pack abs with her fingers. The scrape of her nails against his heat sent shivers up her spine.

"I will. Tell you. Let me warm up first."

She curled her palm around his ribs, reveling in the feel of steel under his skin. When she looked up, she saw the heat flaring in his eyes. He cupped her cheeks in his large hands, tilting her head toward him. He gave her every chance to stop him as he dipped his head. She met him halfway, fusing their lips together, feeling a rush of desire from her scalp to her toes. When they finally broke apart, both were breathing heavily.

Mace rested his forehead against hers, then raised it to press a kiss onto her forehead. "Now's probably not the time. You've been through a trauma. Which you'll tell me about right now."

"Now's the perfect time." She twisted on his lap and flipped her leg over so she straddled him, balancing on her knees. "I'm a pretty tough cookie. Remind me to tell you later how I subdued a Mossad agent."

His laugh sounded strained. "Are you sure?"

She answered the question by cupping his chin and kissing him, angling her head to touch her tongue to his. His breath hitched and he sucked it deeper into his mouth, tangling them together, arms coming up to stroke across her back. She moaned at the sensations, which burned hotter as he began to undo the tiny buttons at the back of her dress. Each fingertip became a match, each tiny lick of flame igniting her body. She arched slightly to press her aching breasts against his chest. He shuddered, arms tightening to lock them together.

She'd never been shy about sex. She knew what she liked, and how to get it. Sometimes a man would be put off by her confidence, but somehow she knew Mace would not be. She tilted her pelvis forward, gulping as she rubbed her core against the bulge stretching his jeans to the breaking point.

"You have the most beautiful eyes I've ever seen," he said, cupping her face and brushing his thumbs back and forth across her cheeks. "Like new leaves refracted through crystals. Gorgeous."

A surprised giggle bubbled up her throat. "No one's ever described them like that before. Huge, yeah. Cat's eyes, yeah. And my lashes are so long people ask me if they're fake every fucking day of my life."

Mace traced a finger over her nose. "There's nothing fake about you, *belle nana*."

She rested her palms on his shoulders, rocking gently against his arousal. "Did you just call me a banana?"

He gave a wolfish grin, heated gaze dropping to her breasts. "More like hot chick." He ran his palms up her ribs to either side of her breasts and cupped them, then leaned forward to pull a nipple into his mouth through her dress. A bolt of pleasure shot straight to her core. "A ver' hot chick."

"More," she demanded, arching her breasts upward. She inhaled his clean male scent, running greedy fingers across his collarbone. They slid up the strong column of his neck of their own accord, delving into his hair. She ran her hands over the closely cropped sides and up into the longer blond hair atop his head. The strands felt unbelievably soft.

"God, that feels amazing," he said.

She reached between them and stroked his erection through his jeans. "Now, Mace. I want you inside of me."

"Not yet, *belle*." He slid his huge hands under her hips and lifted, twisting them around to set her on the mattress, then slid between her legs to kneel on the floor. Looking up her body, he sent her a wicked grin. "I've been dying to do this since we danced."

Her breath left her in a whoosh. "I'm all in favor . . ."

He pulled her bottom to the edge of the bed, opening her to him, and draped her legs over his shoulders.

". . . of the idea," she gasped.

Mace groaned. "Lawd have mercy. Red lace panties. You goan to kill me."

"I might have maybe thought about you when I put them on. Maybe." She hooked her fingers into the barely there lingerie and pushed. He helped her, pulling them down her legs and off. Settling her legs back onto his shoulders, she arched back, which thrust her breasts and her pelvis forward.

"I want to kiss you," he said hoarsely. "Taste you. Touch you."

She giggled. "All in favor, say aye. Aye."

"Aye," he whispered. He captured her gaze, holding eye contact right until the second his mouth met her warm, wet core. She shuddered as he kissed her, as he bestowed long, lingering licks and tiny nips that had her curling her ankles to pull him closer. Her breath came in uncontrolled pants as pleasure from his expert touch swirled and collided inside her. Her hands flailed and she finally gripped the comforter.

"Mace . . . Jesus . . ." she said, fighting for breath.

"Mmm-hmm?" He lifted his lids to watch her, not stopping, clearly enjoying himself.

"That's . . . oh, sweet lord . . . don't stop . . ."

"Not a chance, little bird."

He found her sensitive nub, laving it with his tongue and teeth until she shivered and writhed, unable to stem the cries of pleasure bursting from her. His fingers delved into her folds, and he slipped one, and then two, into her slick channel. And just like that, she was in free fall, clamping down on him as her body shook with release. He kept stroking her, prolonging her orgasm, until she finally pulled away, laughing, and let her legs slide from his shoulders. She went limp, flopping her arms onto the mattress.

"Holy, holy hell. You're like the world's best male human at that."

He laughed, rising up on his knees and placing his hands at the tops of her thighs, stroking his thumbs along her sensitized skin.

"You've experienced the best female human?" he teased. "Or any female human?"

She narrowed her eyes, looking into the hot gleam in his. "Are you shitting me? You just got turned on by the thought of two women together."

Without breaking eye contact, he brought his fingers up and sucked her juices from one, then the other. "Little bird, that is not why I'm turned on."

Her lips parted on a satisfied sigh. "I can help with that."

Chapter 20

MACE ROSE IN one smooth move, cupping her buttocks in his large hands. Lark wrapped her legs around his waist as he reversed their position, sitting on the edge of the bed with her straddling him. He could barely move with his jeans trying to strangle his erection. It felt like an ice pick skewering him, but he was too much of a he-man to whimper.

The room lay covered in shadows under the faint moonlight. Shadows were good. The gloom would obscure the worst of his bruises. He wanted Lark's full, undistracted attention. Her sweet scent surrounded him; he pressed his nose into the side of her neck and sucked her fragrance greedily into his lungs. She ran her tongue along the column of his throat and nipped at his chin as he unfastened the rest of those damned tiny buttons. Whoever designed those was a sadist.

"Just rip the whole thing off," Lark said. "It's not like I'm ever going to wear it again."

"True, but I wan' to take my time unwrapping my present."

He'd be damned if he'd rush this. He'd been walking around sporting wood ever since he met her.

Her eyes sparkled up at him. "Is it your birthday?"

"I'm saying it is." He skimmed his hands up under her skirt, catching the fabric on his fingertips and tugging it upward. He couldn't tear his gaze from the silky skin bared in tiny increments. "God, you're gorgeous."

She shifted restlessly against him, running her hands over his shoulders and chest. Gripping the bottom of his T-shirt, Lark lifted it to his chest, and, without thinking, he stripped it off the rest of the way.

"Holy God!"

Oh, shit.

"It looks worse than it is," he said, echoing her previous words.

"Like fuck it does," she said, tracing shaking fingers over the substantial bruises on his shoulder and ribs. "If you didn't have your supersuit on . . . God, Mace, you'd be dead right now."

"Shh," he murmured, stroking her hair. "I'm all right. Bruises fade, okay? I'm fine."

She snuffled, and his heart stuttered. "Please don' cry, *chér*."

"I can't help it. Because of me—"

"Because of them," he corrected.

She dropped her forehead to his shoulder, nodding. "Because of them. Fuckers."

For several minutes, they simply held one another. Mace had never been more contented. Then Lark moved, pressing down and wriggling her bottom. The sensation made him groan.

He grabbed her hips and held her still. "We should stop, little bird."

"Do you really want to?" Uncertainty put a wobble in her voice. "I mean, I'll stop if you don't want this."

"Lawd a'mercy. I don't know if I've ever wanted anything more."

"Good."

She shifted off him, her clever hands sliding his zipper down. He pushed his jeans to his hips, shuddering and jerking involuntarily as she stroked him through his boxer briefs. This woman knew exactly what she wanted, and he was glad as hell she wanted him.

Her tongue swept into his mouth. She tasted sweet and hot, much like Lark herself. With her taste still on his lips, he thought maybe he'd died and gone to heaven, but she proved him wrong when she pulled away from him, eyes glazed and mouth damp, and shimmied out of her dress. It pooled at her feet. She stood before him in nothing but her red lace bra and those sexy high heels. He swallowed audibly, nearly weeping at the sight of surprisingly full, perfect breasts. She might be small, but she had curves in all the right places.

Smiling like the vixen she was, she crawled onto the bed and knelt there, legs slightly apart, looking like sex on a stick. Capturing his gaze, she ran a hand down between her breasts to her navel. He was next to her before he even realized he'd moved, hauling her into his arms and kissing her like she was a banquet and he was starved.

"Pants off," she ordered, trying to push his jeans farther down his legs. He stood only as long as it took him to shuck his jeans and underwear, then rejoined her.

"Holy baby Moses. Pretty sure that's not going to fit."

He chuckled, running his palms up her silky legs. "Pretty sure it will."

She licked her lips, the minx. "Can't wait to find out."

Mace wrapped his arms around her, turning her onto her back. He followed her down until he nestled right where he ached to be. The sensation wrung a gasp from him and he hung his head, fighting the need to be inside her that very second. They fit together perfectly.

"Condom," she gasped.

He reached blindly for his jeans, yanking his wallet out and snatching a foil packet, tearing it open and rolling it on in a flash. Lark giggled.

"Okay," she said. "I'm ready to tell you what happened tonight."

Wait . . . what? He forced himself to stillness. "Now . . . ?"

She threw back her head and laughed. "Oh, my God. Your face!"

He had to force the words out through vocal cords that didn't want to work. "If that's what you want." Sit back, he ordered his body. But he couldn't move, still poised over her body.

"I'm kidding," she said. The look on her face was pure sex, a full-out I-want-you-right-now expression that nearly crippled him.

Relief washed through him. Holy freaking God. How did she have enough control to joke?

"Later," she said, letting her legs drop open in clear invitation. "Much later. Right now, I need you inside of me. Right fucking now."

Reason and logic left him in a rush. He positioned himself at her entrance and pushed home in one long thrust. The incredible caress nearly made him come right then and there. "God, you're so wet. So tight. So perfect."

"Ahh. Perfect. Yes. That's the word."

He withdrew almost all the way, then thrust home again. And

did it again, loving the way she writhed under him. He tried to slow down, but she wasn't having any of it, wrapping her sexy heels around his butt to pull him in more deeply.

"Ah! Yes!"

He gave up control then, stroking inside her fast and hard. The sighs and moans she uttered made him crazy. She rolled her hips in a slow circle that nearly blew his head off.

"Don't. I don't think I—"

She exploded beneath him, gasping his name over and over as she clamped down on him, trembling and convulsing. It sent him hard over the edge. He thrust deep and held himself there, moaning as he came right behind her, the sensations so intense the world grayed around him.

When he could finally move again, he rolled them both so her head rested on his chest. They were both still out of breath. He ran his fingers up and down her spine lazily as their bodies cooled.

She started to giggle, which made him smile.

"What is it?"

"You are built like a Greek god."

A soft laugh rumbled through his chest as he wrapped his arms around her. "And you're damned good for my ego."

"Wow," she murmured sleepily. "Just . . . wow."

Wow, indeed.

Chapter 21

Sunday, February 19. 8:48 a.m.
Extended Stay Hotel. Boston, Massachusetts.

LARK GROANED, BURROWING under the blankets to shut out the bright morning light. It was February, for God's sake. The sun should have better sense than to shine.

Her stomach growled. She reluctantly rolled over to look at her clock. Only it wasn't there. Nor was her Tardis table lamp. Sitting up, she yawned and stretched. Oh, yeah. She'd spent the night with Mace. A satisfied smirk curled her lips as she flopped back onto the pillows.

Voices drifted into the bedroom. Ugh. People meant she'd have to put on clothes. And the only thing she had to wear was her torn dress. In the end, her need for caffeine trumped her desire to stay in bed.

Climbing out from under Mace's sheets, she found her underthings and put them back on. Rooting through the bureau drawers netted her a pair of gym shorts that would work if she tied them tightly. She did so, then pulled on a clean olive-colored T-shirt. She peeked out the door; the voices came from the adjoining suite. She darted into the bathroom, took care of business, then brushed her teeth with toothpaste and her finger. She did what she could with her hair. It would have to do.

Creeping toward the connecting door made her feel like a teenager trying to sneak past her parents when she missed curfew. Who was there? The voices became clearer. So did a heavenly smell. Bacon?

". . . only a matter of time."

"We'll blow up that bridge when we get to it," Mace said.

"We have to know the threat level. Did she—"

"Good morning, sleepyhead," someone said behind her. She jumped, turning to see a man walking through the suite door juggling—*thank you, Caffeine Gods*—a drink carrier full of coffee cups.

"Is one of those for me?" she asked, hope in her voice. She could take him, she thought. Wrestle him to the ground. But then he might drop the caffeine.

The man, a blond-haired, blue-eyed country boy, lifted one of the cups and handed it to her. "Venti quad shot cinnamon dolce latte. Extra hot."

"Thank you thank you," she said, nearly snatching the cup from his hand. She inhaled the steam, then sipped. It burned her tongue and throat. "Perfect."

Mace stepped out of the adjoining suite. "Did I hear . . . ah, you're awake."

Lark's heart skipped a beat. At least, that's what it felt like. But damned if he didn't look yummy in the morning. He'd obviously showered and shaved, and wore clothes almost identical to the ones she'd borrowed. He looked magnificent.

He came over to her and wrapped an arm around her waist, bending to kiss her full on the mouth. "Good morning. My clothes never looked that good on me."

"Funny, I was just thinking the same thing," she said, raising her coffee out of reach. "Careful."

Mace released her and turned to the country boy. "This knucklehead is Alex Wood."

Alex stuck out a hand. "Pleasure, ma'am."

She groaned as she shook it. "You ma'am me again and I'll . . . I'll do something awful that I'll think of later when I've woken up properly."

Alex gave an aw-shucks grin.

"It's just Lark, if you value your life," Mace said. "Come in and meet everyone else."

Lark obediently followed him into the connecting suite. Conversation ceased, and she became the focus of all eyes.

Mace pulled her to his side. "The scowly one there is John McTaggert. The one on the crutches is Gabe Morgan, who couldn't land a simple night jump without breaking his ankle."

"Nice to meet you." White teeth flashed against tanned skin as Gabe grinned at her from across the extended-stay's full kitchen. With his shaggy golden hair, two-day beard, and cleft in a strong chin, he looked like a fallen angel.

Compared to Mace's gunmetal blue eyes, high cheekbones, and the dimple-like grooves along his jaw, Gabe simply disappeared. She leaned against Mace, her innards melting as his hand immediately slid around her waist.

She waved her coffee cup in their general direction. "Hi, guys."

John McTaggert merely nodded and turned back to the stove, where he scooped bread coated with egg onto a spatula and flipped it over.

"French toast?" she asked, already salivating. He was also scrambling some eggs, and bacon strips lay on paper towels to catch the grease.

Mace pointed to the small table, where plates had been set out, along with butter and syrup. She went to sit.

"What time is it?" she asked.

"Going on nine," Mace told her. "You were dead to the world when I got up."

"Which was when?" she asked, gulping some more coffee. Come on, brain. Wake up.

He glanced at the clock on the microwave. "Around five, I guess."

"That's not even a time. That's the middle of the night. What, do you hate sleep?"

Mace quirked an amused brow at her. "I needed to go for a run. The guys kept an eye on things while I was out."

John McTaggert came over and slid four pieces of French toast onto her plate, adding bacon and eggs. The other men sat down and were similarly served.

"Thank you, John," she said shyly. Who would have guessed that the big scary man could cook?

"You can just call me Tag," he said. "I'm not sure I'd remember to turn around if I heard someone call me John."

"Tag it is. What about you, Alex? What's your nickname?"

The farm boy moved a shoulder as though ridding himself of a fly. "I got called a lot of things growing up I'm glad never stuck."

Lark dug in to the food. "Yum. Do they teach you to cook like this at supersoldier school?" The sudden silence made her glance up and around. "I mean, logistics school? If there even is such a thing."

The men looked at one another uneasily.

"I know, I know," she groused. "Beans and bullets. Got it. But just in case you do something besides deliver toilet paper, thank you for your service to your country."

No one answered. She drained her coffee cup and pushed back her chair. "I gotta run. I need to go into the office."

"Lark." Mace caught her arm. "We need to talk."

"Later."

"Now." He gently but firmly pulled her back to the table. "What happened yesterday?"

Avoiding talking about it also meant she could ignore her fear. "Nothing. Well, a lot, but I'm not ready . . . I'm going to get into trouble if I don't get to work."

Mace frowned. "It's Sunday. It's best to get it out. And we need to know."

It seemed her reprieve was over.

"It's so surreal. Almost like it never happened at all." She sighed, sliding her plate out of the way and settling her forearms onto the table. "CliffsNotes version? Some guy named Viktor Sokolov accused me of stealing fifty million dollars from him. I have to find the real thief, or he's going to kill me."

A stunned silence greeted her bald statement. She looked around at these big, tough he-men, staring at her like she'd grown another head. "What?"

"What? *What?*" Mace nearly shouted. "What the hell, Lark? Why would a mobster think . . ." He stopped. Took a deep breath, then another. "Lark, you have exactly one opportunity here to tell us what you're involved in and why."

She narrowed her eyes. "I'm not *involved* in anything. And fuck you for thinking I would be. I'm being set up."

"Who by?" Alex asked.

Toying with her fork, she managed a careless shrug. "By someone who spread my signature all over a hack. I haven't seen the logs. I need to see the code if I'm going to have any hope of finding the real thief. Some dude named Elliott gave me a thumb drive."

"Do you have any idea why someone would want to hurt you that way?" In contrast to his low brows and seemingly permanent glower, Tag's voice was gentle.

"Besides getting away with fifty million dollars?"

"Yes," Gabe said. "Someone sophisticated enough to execute that kind of theft could very probably leave no trail at all. Why point it to you?"

"No idea." Lark pressed her palms into her eyes, but when she opened them, nothing had changed. Mace had retreated to the kitchen. She couldn't even look at him. How could he think she would steal a nickel, much less millions of dollars? He clearly did not know her at all.

"Take us through it. Please," Alex said, casting a chiding glance at Mace.

"Fine." Lark thought about what to say. "After I saw Mace get *shot*, I was thrown into the van. They put a bag over my head so I couldn't see where we were going. I don't know why they bothered, except to scare me. We drove to Mr. Sokolov's home. He served me tea and cookies. I left."

"Uh, maybe you want to expand on that a little?" Alex said.

Lark blew out an annoyed breath. "Okay, fine. I sat in a basement for *hours* before I got dragged up to his office. He hit me and threatened to chop off my finger. But even though he believed me about not stealing his fifty mil, he says I need to find it and get it back to him in less than a week."

Silence filled the room.

"Or what?" asked Tag.

"Or, you know, Palachka tears me to pieces." She looked at her plate rather than any of them. "Iggy, the guy who shot Mace, drove me home. End of story."

Mace came over and placed a hand on her shoulder. "I'm sorry. I shouldn't have said that."

"Yeah, well, men are idiots."

Tag laughed. "You got that right."

Lark stood, and Mace's hand slid away. "My laptop's still at the hotel. I need to grab it before I head in to work."

"Why don't you stay here instead?" Mace said. "Alex can check you out and you can work here."

She shook her head, not looking at him. "I need the FBI's computers."

Tag collected the plates and brought them to the sink. "Alex, you've got washing detail. We'll start back to Fort Devens after we clean up. We have training this morning at eleven hundred hours, don't forget."

"Shit. Do you think—"

"No. Don't even try it, Mace. We train no matter where we are. And it's the whole squadron."

Mace muttered a curse. "Lark, I'm driving you to work. No arguments, okay?"

Lark ducked her head, warmed by his concern. "It's not necessary. I'm safe for a few days. Sokolov needs me to find the money, remember? Tag, thanks for breakfast. It was delish."

"You're welcome," he said, frowning at Mace. "Okay, fine, we'll follow you in the rental, then pick you up and head west."

She grabbed her purse and waited by the door, glad to spend more time with Mace. He joined her, jingling his keys in his hands. Hands—and fingers, and tongue—which had brought her immense pleasure the previous night. But she wasn't ready to forgive him for thinking she might be involved in the theft of mob money.

They walked to her car in silence. He held the passenger door for her. She slid inside and buckled herself in, deliberately silent and a little sullen. Why she still held out hope that someone would just accept her for who she was—and trust her—was beyond her. It never happened, no matter how much she wanted it to.

He turned the key. It started up, and he backed out of the parking space and pulled onto the street.

"Do you need directions?" she finally asked.

"I remember where you are," he said. "Look, I'm really sorry for my reaction back there. It was uncalled for."

"Yes, it was." She watched the trees go by as they left the hotel behind.

Mace glanced over at her. "You used to be a hacker?"

She took in a lot of air, then blew it out noisily. "Yes. Okay? Yes, I used to do that. For fun, though. Not to steal anything, or even damage anything. It was empowering, if you must know. My parents . . . well, you met my mother. She's determined to make me a proper lady. A proper Larkspur. I went to Cotillion, for God's sake."

Mace began to laugh. "It's odd how things work out. So did I."

She stared at him, mouth open. "You did?"

"Yep. My mother insisted we have some culture in our lives. She was from N'Orleans. My da courted her, and she moved into the Bayou when they got married, but she didn't want us stigmatized by our roots. Her words, not mine."

Curious despite herself, she twisted to face him. "What stigma?"

"My da was a shrimper. I started working on that boat the day I turned twelve."

Lark wrinkled her brows. "I don't get it. That's a stigma?"

Mace chuckled. "Yah, for sure. Because of that, us kids were *mal pris.* Stuck in the Bayou with no hope of escape."

"There's nothing wrong with earning an honest living. At least your family produced something. Food that my parents ate at fancy parties with rich friends."

Mace dipped his chin once. "Yeah, but much as I love the Bayou, I didn't want to be a shrimper. I wanted to be a supersoldier." He cast a grin in her direction that she did not return.

"Is your family still there?" She couldn't seem to curb her curiosity.

"My brother and sister. Solomon runs the business, and Bonnie does the books. My older sister, Susanna, married one of the civil engineers who came after the Storm to help repair the levees and dams. She's in N'Orleans with him."

Lark detected a bitterness in his tone he probably wasn't even aware of. "What about everyone else? Your parents?"

Mace was silent.

"You don't have to tell me," she said. "I just wondered."

Mace shook his head. "I don't mind. The Storm took my da."

"Oh, no," she murmured. "Hurricane Katrina?"

He nodded curtly. "He sent my mother and sisters to my auntie in Arkansas, but we stayed. The Storm submerged our home almos' to the roof. Da's boat ended up quarter of a mile inland. But the worst part . . . a wave knocked Da off the roof. Solomon and I tried to find him, but we never did."

Tears of sympathy appeared in her eyes. "I'm so sorry. That's awful."

His hands tightened on the steering wheel, then relaxed. "Yeah, well, it was a long time ago."

She resisted the urge to reach out to him. What could she say? Compared to him, she'd never experienced hardship. Rebelling against her parents hardly counted.

He pulled into the parking lot. "I'll come up with you."

Lark didn't want their time together to end. "Okay."

They went up to her room in silence. Housekeeping had been by; her bed was made, and her clothes had been folded neatly and placed on top of the bureau. It looked unnatural. She opened her suitcase on the bed and threw all her stuff into it willy-nilly. Mace chuckled, putting a hand at the small of her back as he carried her suitcase down to the car.

"Where do you live?"

"Danvers. Head north."

She directed him to her townhouse on Newbury Street. The homes had all been built in the early eighties, and it showed. Her end unit sported pale yellow clapboard on top and ugly brick on the bottom. She liked the bright red shutters, though. She'd copied the color onto an accent wall inside, which, as usual, cheered her as she entered.

Mace looked around her small living room, taking in the royal blue sofa and loveseat covered with pillows ranging from lime green to bold geometric patterns to her favorite, a linen pillow covered with birds and flowers. The woven area rug under her simple coffee table had a muted turquoise pattern. He flicked a look at the multipanel art on one wall, depicting a magnificent sunset over a lake.

"It's very you."

She laughed. "I like it. Make yourself at home. I'll be as quick as I can."

She bounced up the stairs two at a time and entered her bedroom, just as colorful as the downstairs. Grabbing some clothing, she headed into the bathroom to shower. When she finally emerged, dressed, makeup in place, heels on, she saw that Mace had stretched out on her bed and was fast asleep.

Should she wake him? Join him? As tempting as that was, she needed to get to the office. The work on her plate had doubled, suddenly leaving her with too much to do and too little time. Not only did she need to start her search for her mystery hacker, she also had an actual project to complete.

"Mace," she whispered.

His eyes opened, finding her unerringly. Unlike herself when she awoke, he appeared immediately alert. He swung his shoes off the bedspread and stood, stretching mightily. "You ready?"

"Yeah."

"Give me your phone." He held out his hand.

She unlocked it and passed it over. He programmed in his number and handed it back. She immediately sent him a text with her number.

"Thank you," he said. "Let's roll. We can't be late for training."

Chapter 22

Sunday, February 19. 11:00 a.m.
Shooting House. Fort Devens, Massachusetts.

MACE SEATED HIMSELF on the battered artichoke-colored Naugahyde couch, wriggling a little to get comfortable. Ken Acolatse, the troop's senior NCO, stood by the window, the bright sunlight bouncing off his dark skin. Muscles rippled as he crossed his arms.

"We're on standby, Sir Lancelot. Word can come down at any time."

"I know that, sergeant major," he said. He breathed in through his nose, out through his mouth, using the meditation techniques he'd learned during Selection. His mind calmed, his need to protect Lark pushed down as he accepted his current reality. He looked around the room, consciously focusing on each object: front door to his left, dining room table with four chairs, round wooden table in the right corner with a nonworking lamp on it, coffee table in front of him with a braided rug beneath. Ugly collage on the wall above his head, featuring all of the characters from *The Simpsons*.

"We're moving to a former FBI safe house this afternoon. We'll use it as our base of operations until we go live," Ken said. "We all know you do this from time to time. It's admirable, but the unit comes first."

"I know that," he said again. "If any of you have the slightest doubt that I can operate at one hundred percent, tell me now."

Ken shook his head. "I don't doubt you. If I did, I'd have Jace sideline you in a hot second."

"I appreciate your vote of confidence. This girl. Lark. She's not like anybody—"

I've ever met, he meant to say. But the door burst inward, and a camouflaged figure hurtled through, throwing a canister toward the ceiling. Mace closed his eyes reflexively. The flash-bang detonated with a searingly bright light, accompanied by a boom that disoriented him. He opened his eyes, forcing himself to focus on what was happening. The man came at him, firing four rounds in rapid succession that whistled around his head. Mace didn't so much as twitch.

Two more figures swarmed inside, searching for targets. The first man passed in front of him and positioned himself in the right corner, weapon up. The second moved left, firing toward the dining room table. The third stayed by the door.

Silence settled over the room. Not more than four seconds had passed since initial entry. Smoke filled the room from the flash-bang grenade. Mace had to force himself not to cough.

"Hands on top of your head," the first man ordered. "Lace your fingers together. Do it now."

Mace complied, knowing the others did the same.

"Search," the first man said. He trained his weapon behind Mace. The one by the door strode over to the couch and did something Mace couldn't see, then turned to him. He patted Mace down, smoothing his hands under his arms, around his waist, and down his legs, relieving him of his sidearm and boot knife.

The first man gave the same command to the man in the left corner, who moved into the dining area, covered by the man at the door, then searched Ken and Gabe.

The first man looked at the three in turn, eyes serious. "I need you to stay calm and do exactly what we tell you to do," he said. "Are there any more terrorists in this room? Any danger you're aware of?"

Mace shook his head. "No."

"Then please follow me." The first man left the room, Mace, Gabe, and Ken following him out. They all stopped in the plain wooden hallway.

"Clear," the man called. "Stand down."

They trooped back into the room. Mace pulled his earplugs out. The three men slung their M4 carbines over their shoulders and stripped off their helmets. Gavin, Tag, and Alex inspected the room.

"All right. Let's debrief," Tag said.

Mace only half listened as the others walked through the room-clearing exercise step-by-step, each operator detailing where he'd stepped, shot, decided.

Mace turned to look behind the couch, at the two target silhouettes of terrorists holding rifles that had been pointed at his head. Just below the hideous *Simpsons* collage, two holes sprouted between the eyes of each target. "Goddammit, Tag. Couldn't you have shot up that damned picture?"

Ken walked over to finger the single shot in the head of the target seated at the table. "Alex, two shots."

Alex frowned. "But I had him, sergeant major. He was down."

He'd been recruited from the 75th Ranger Regiment and was an experienced operator, but despite having been a member of Jace's A-Team for two years, was still considered the new guy.

Ken stiffened, lips tightening and chin jutting forward. He stalked over to Alex. His displeasure was a palpable thing that intelligent people avoided whenever possible. He was a scary good marksman—and sometimes just plain scary—commanding respect across the squadron and beyond. "Always, Sergeant Wood. No exceptions. No grandstanding. Got me?"

"Yes, sergeant major." To his credit, Alex took the reprimand meekly. "It won't happen again."

They'd been training in the live-fire Shooting House for three hours, practicing various scenarios for room-clearing. The smack of boots against the wooden hallway had all six straightening and turning. Only one man walked that way. Bo Granville, Delta Squadron's commander, appeared in the doorway.

"Done?"

"Yes, sir," Ken Acolatse said.

"Good. Time for the main event. Let's go outside."

They joined the other members of Delta Squadron. Mace wasn't surprised to see Heather Langstrom-Reed standing next to her husband, Jace, nor Stephanie Tams, their research specialist. Both were invaluable members of their team. Two strangers stood off to one side.

From the outside, the Kill House building looked like an enormous, oddly shaped warehouse. The multilevel building could be configured in a variety of ways, to simulate houses, offices, churches, and schools. Various special units used it to train in urban warfare—building-clearing, infiltration techniques, hostage rescue. The trick was, it was an indoor shooting range. Every exercise conducted inside utilized live ammunition. The exercises required perfect coordination, precision, and accuracy. There was no room for error.

Colonel Granville appeared, rolling his unlit cigar from one side of his mouth to the other. His closely cropped hair didn't conceal the ring of gray on his balding head, but anyone who couldn't see past his bulldog face and build to his sharp intelligence wasn't paying attention. He was a dedicated and hard-core career soldier, and one of the best tacticians Mace had ever come across. He held up his hands. Every operator fell silent.

"All right, you fuckers, listen up!"

Alex, who couldn't be trusted to behave at the best of times, pulled his ears away from his head like Dumbo. Granville ignored him.

"It's confirmed. The damned Russkies got the suitcase bomb into Boston. Delta Squadron has been assigned as the rapid reaction force to augment the Homeland/FBI joint task force," he boomed. The man's voice could carry the length of a parade field. "We have dedicated support once we confirm the location of the nuke. This is our government's top priority, and they've opened up the purse strings. Anything you need, tell me and I'll make it happen."

Mace found himself once again grateful to be part of the 1st Special Forces Operational Detachment-Delta. The red tape the rest of the military dealt with disappeared for them. Plus, since they recruited from all branches of service, they rarely wore uniforms or adhered to accepted military grooming standards. Or, frankly, bothered with the rules and regulations governing others.

A relaxed atmosphere and informality between the operators and support staff allowed a camaraderie unmatched in other units.

"All right. Now for the particulars. Stephanie, the floor's yours."

The newly promoted buck sergeant stepped to the front. Of all of them, only she and the squadron commander wore camouflaged field uniforms.

"Our combined intelligence assets are pulling every thread we can think of to find the suitcase bomb," she said. "One of those threads involves the Sokolov crime family here in New England. It's a tenuous connection at best, but we can't afford to ignore any lead."

Heather began passing out sheets of paper. Mace looked his over. It consisted of two photos and several paragraphs of text.

"For those who don't know, the head of the family, Viktor Sokolov, brought an FBI cybersecurity analyst unwillingly to his home last night and accused her of a hacking theft of millions of dollars of mob money."

Mace scrutinized the photo of the bastard who had terrorized Lark.

"We know from Ms. Larkspur's debriefing that Sokolov needs that money available to him in less than a week. While we have no concrete information on why, we do know that the Russians intend to sell the bomb to the highest bidder. Obviously figuring out who, where, and when is our top priority." She glanced at the notes in her hand. "A suitcase nuke could go for anything from thirty to sixty million dollars; his fifty mil falls right into that sweet spot, making him a person of interest."

Mutters and curses broke out among the Delta operators. Mace's gut clenched as he thought again how much danger Lark had really been in.

"The second photo on your intelligence report is Mikhail Kerghakov, an accountant with long-standing ties to Sokolov. Fifty-four years old, second generation Russian immigrant. I've listed known associates and prior employment. Unfortunately, both Sokolov and his principal accountant are very careful, and no federal charges have ever stuck. Still, he might be another thread we can pull, if we can get him to talk. You'll work alongside the FBI on this." She gestured to the two strangers, who moved forward.

Mace scanned the names included on the piece of paper. Lark wasn't listed; but then again, she wasn't an agent. Still, it speared an empty place inside him. "Will the FBI provide other support? The computer people, for instance?"

Beside him, Alex snorted. "I know where your mind just went, dickhead. You're working. And so is she."

"I know, I know."

"Come on," Jace said. "We have a room set up inside where we can talk."

For the next hour, the nine Delta Squadron members and two FBI special agents kicked around ideas on how to approach the crime family's chief accountant.

"Obviously he's not likely to cooperate," one agent said. "He's been under scrutiny for years. He's never given up one iota of usable intelligence."

"We need a way to get inside his decision cycle," Jace said.

Mace leaned back in his chair, arms crossed over his chest. "Everyone has an Achilles' heel. How come you guys never found his?"

The agent bristled. "We know what motivates him, and it's not just loyalty to Sokolov. He's fanatically protective of his family. They're all on the level, though. Honest and hardworking folks.

And we have a little thing called the Constitution that keeps us from harassing them."

"Sure. Protect and defend." Mace smirked. "We, on the other hand, have a few tricks up our sleeves that you don't."

"I won't countenance anything illegal. That's not what we do." The agent tried to stare him down. Mace looked back impassively, giving the other man maybe ten seconds before he folded. Sure enough, the agent looked away.

"We uphold the same Constitution you do," Jace said reassuringly. "No worries on that score. On the other hand, we have specialized training to handle these kinds of situations."

The agent sneered. "Torture, you mean. No way."

Mace laughed, straightening the pages of information about their target in front of him. "Our best weapon is our brain. We leave the thuggery to others."

"So what are you suggesting?" the agent asked.

"That you two take a lunch break," Jace said at once. "Let us handle this. I give you my word we will not unlawfully detain him or use extreme measures. But our way covers your asses and gives you plausible deniability. We'll get what you need."

The other agent got up. "I'm good with this. Let's go."

The man rubbed the back of his neck, hesitated, glared, and finally joined his partner near the door. "We'll be waiting."

Jace looked around the table. "All right, team. Let's get this done."

Chapter 23

Sunday, February 19. 11:00 a.m.
FBI Field Office. Boston, Massachusetts.

THE CORRIDORS AND offices pulsed with an unnatural stillness, making Lark feel like she should tiptoe through them. She made a beeline for the SCIF, where a few other employees worked at terminals.

Today she would dive into who'd used her hacker handle to steal fifty million dollars for the mob. Oh, and to analyze the malicious code's behavior.

She might as well run the code while she did some thinking. Opening the folder containing the program, she pointed it toward a safe, contained area on the server, and allowed it to run.

The dual monitors fed her information about various aspects of the program as it executed. She watched as it tried to connect to another system, creating a temporary file and deleting it a few minutes later. Running another tool, she attempted to recover the contents of the transitory file.

While the tool ran, she returned to her assessment of her nemesis. The perpetrator of the massive theft of mob money obviously knew enough about her to know her signature hacks. She mentally sorted them into three columns: No Way, On the Fence, and Ratfinks. She immediately moved ChaosCowboy into the No Way column. Ditto for Zane Quimby, aka Hermitage. Sammi Stasis, a husband-and-wife team from Iceland, went into the On the Fence column. She added London-based Habib Amari to the No Way column, and moved Firecr@cker and Bear, both gray hat hackers, to On the Fence. She'd met them in the Darknet, but knew virtually nothing about their true identities.

Callie Wang in China went on the Ratfink list. She'd developed a sophisticated Trojan that encrypted the patient databases of hospitals around the world, demanding a ransom to decrypt the information. She was a criminal, pure and simple. Theft of millions of dollars might seem like an easy target for her. Ditto for IcedRailroadTr4ck, a group of cybercriminals operating mostly in Siberia. They'd stolen half a billion dollars over the course of three years by penetrating scores of banks in a dozen countries.

She didn't know where to put Asylum 40-bit. No one knew much about them, though they'd taken credit for a number of hacking coups over the past five years. They could be legit white hats, who just enjoyed the intellectual challenge of, and bragging rights for, exploiting functional vulnerabilities. More often than not, these types of hackers, including herself in her youth, informed the company or agency about the security flaws so they could be fixed. On the other hand, the group might have executed malicious hacks they did not make public, including virtual bank heists.

Sighing, she returned to the work at hand.

"You're glaring at the screen."

Lark looked up at Jocelyn. "It's being dumb. Or I am."

"I doubt that. Lots of speculation on the news about your sister's wedding being canceled. Either she got left at the altar, or he did. What happened?"

Lark hadn't even thought about the news crews. Fortunately, extra foundation and concealer hid her bruise. "They were both abducted by aliens and married on Mars."

The other woman pulled over a chair and sat down. "Fine, don't tell me. Family secrets, right?"

Lark gave a noncommittal shrug. "How come you're here on a Sunday?"

"We got tipped off about an active cyberattack . . ." Lark tuned her out as the older woman described the attack, still trying to figure out who might have framed her for the theft. When Jocelyn fell silent, Lark looked up to find her staring.

"You didn't hear a word I said."

Lark sighed. "Just have a lot on my mind. Sorry about that."

Jocelyn linked her hands together and inverted them as she arched her back and stretched her arms toward the ceiling. "Share."

"I really don't want to rehash it all right now, okay? Please?"

"Sure. Let's get some coffee."

"Let's go!" Lark retrieved her cell phone from the lockbox as they left and checked her messages. Her heart leaped when she saw a text from Mace.

Last night was amazing.

She couldn't stop the sappy smile spreading across her face. Jocelyn pounced on it at once.

"Aha! A text from a man. I recognize that look. Spill."

Lark hugged the phone to her chest, afraid Jocelyn might snatch it out of her hands. “Just someone I met Friday night at a nightclub, if you must know.”

“Oho! And spent the night with. You have no poker face, Lark. None at all.”

She shook her head, not ready to talk about anything that had happened this weekend. Let Jocelyn think the obvious. The truth was stranger by far.

“So who is he? Damn it all, if I’d been there Friday night, I could have met him.”

Lark power-walked to the other end of the building, forcing Jocelyn to stretch her legs to keep up. Her body still hummed from the potency of Mace’s touch. One night with him wasn’t enough. She wanted more of his magic.

Once they reached the break room, poured their coffee, and sat down, the other woman started up again.

“What’s his name? What does he do? Is he cute?”

Lark slanted her an exasperated look. “You’re like a dog with a bone. His name is Thomas. He’s a soldier in the Army. And yes, he’s drop-dead movie star *cute*.”

Jocelyn’s eyes sparkled. “And you like him.”

“I don’t even know him very well.” But that wasn’t strictly true. They’d shared a connection, one she couldn’t deny even if she wanted to. She thumbed her phone on.

Conceited much?

“Well, your night sounds like much more fun than mine.”

Lark set her phone on the table next to her coffee. “Anyone claim responsibility for the cyberattack?”

Jocelyn slouched back in her chair, one hand idly turning her cup around and around. "Not yet. The attack failed, so maybe no one will. But they got as far as they did because of freaking unpatched servers."

"We'll always get to be the heroes because IT departments fail to patch their servers."

Jocelyn shot her a sly, knowing look. "But we both know you used to be on the other side of the fence, don't we?"

Lark's smile faded as she examined Jocelyn's face. "What would even make you say that?"

"Don't worry, sunshine. You're not the only white hat hacker the FBI has snatched up. Hermitage is here, too. And maybe a few others."

Lark tapped her nails against the table, uneasy with the conversation. "Who else? You?"

Jocelyn rose, graceful as ever. "Maybe."

Lark drained her coffee cup. "I don't have time for games, Joss. I have some stuff I need to take care of. I have to find someone. I need to try, anyway."

The other woman examined Lark with shrewd eyes. "A blast from your past?"

Lark shrugged, avoiding her gaze. "An old friend. Gotta go."

Sometimes Jocelyn's questions made her uncomfortable. The older woman always seemed to know more about Lark than she should.

Admit it. You want to see me again.

Maybe. If I have time.

He sent her back a frowny face. She laughed out loud. Flirting with Mace was fun.

She made it back to her cubicle without seeing anyone else. Logging into her account, she brought up a terminal window and started typing. Within moments, she had special software running that allowed her into a dark network. She ran her authorization credentials, tapping her fingernails against the dove gray surface until a cursor appeared.

During her month-long incarceration after the jockey riding incident, her only contact with the outside world had been her computer. Restless and bored, she lurked in chatrooms, eventually finding a discussion board about hacking. Her interest piqued, she followed a trail of forums deeper and deeper into the dark web, learning as she went. Turned out she was a natural at it. She visualized programming languages like they were pictures. Finding a community where she fit in lit a fire inside her. She threw herself into learning everything she could about computer hardware, software, and exploitations of systems, loving the exhilaration of code exploitation. Eventually, she discovered a mentor in ChaosCowboy.

Following one of her established circuits, she activated a rendezvous point and typed in an encrypted message to ChaosCowboy. She did the same in several other places. Anxiety roiled inside her. She didn't even know if he still lived in that world, or still connected to this dark network. She also didn't know how, or even if, he could help her. But he'd been there in her time of need as a child, guiding her and teaching her the skills the FBI now wanted, and she itched for his advice. There was little else she could do, though.

He would either contact her, or he wouldn't.

Chapter 24

Sunday, February 19. 12:00 p.m.
Otis Fitch's Property. Ducard, Massachusetts.

"WE'RE MEETING FITCH at noon," Fyodor said. "Could you stop primping so we can go?"

Fatianova set down her finishing brush, checking her reflection carefully. "I need to look my best for this meeting. I have a bad feeling about this place."

Fyodor laughed. "You're just a snob."

They'd driven out together to the Berkshires, following increasingly smaller roads until they reached Otis Fitch's farm, turning in past a guard shack sporting a sign declaring the property to be the home of Citizens for a Free America. White folks only.

Snow blanketed the trees and buildings, which focused the property in a better light, she thought, covering the corrugated metal roof and aging wooden siding of the first building they passed, the function of which she couldn't even guess. Other structures seemed to be homes, but it all seemed haphazard to her. They drove past two flagpoles, one flying the American flag, the other hoisting a Confederate flag.

A very pregnant woman greeted them as they pulled up to the only proper-looking house on the lot. Instead of entering it, though, they'd crunched across hard-packed snow to a wooden-slatted structure nearby, with a garage door on one end and stacks and stacks of firewood tucked under an overhang. The interior smelled musty and consisted of shabby living room furniture and a tiny room with a bed and dresser. A naked bulb was the only source of lighting.

She rose from the vanity, smoothing her blouse into her flared trousers and slipping on her fur coat. "Let's go."

"You look very nice." Fyodor slipped an arm around her waist and moved in to kiss her. At the last moment, she tilted her head so his wet lips landed on her cheek instead. He didn't seem to notice. He stroked her cheek with one cold finger and winked. "After we close this deal, we can celebrate."

"We'll see," she said.

The path to the main house had been cleared, so she didn't slip in her stylish suede boots. Fyodor knocked on the door. The same pregnant woman opened it and ushered them inside, pointing toward the office and vanishing without a word.

Fatianova stepped into the room and almost gasped aloud.

Otis Fitch sat behind a desk that looked like it belonged in a kitchen decorated with chickens, dressed in plain denim shirt and pants. He held himself ramrod-straight. His sharp face and narrow eyes sat below buzz-cut hair; a stubbly mustache and beard didn't hide his thin lips. Add sloping shoulders and a crooked nose, and he appeared rough and uncouth to her. She could tell he was not a tall man, but imagined his whipcord physique made up for his lack of height.

All of that paled in comparison to the tattoos.

Two SS bolts directly under his chin ran from the top of his neck to his collarbone. A hand grenade on one side and a skull wearing a red, white, and blue bandana surrounded the Nazi symbols. She could see some sort of spider web crawling up just above the opening of his shirt. A small 88 had been inked in at the outer corner of his left eye.

He was a horror.

She swallowed and approached the desk. He eyed her coolly, but didn't rise.

"Good evening, Mr. Fitch," she said, removing her coat and sitting uninvited in one of the folding metal chairs in front of the desk. Fyodor took the other. "I'm Fatianova Uvarov, and this is my colleague, Fyodor Petrov. I will be translating for him."

A sneer curled one corner of his nose. "So you made it here."

He hadn't even looked at her body. She frowned, confused. "You have a . . . lovely farmstead here. Very private."

His direct stare was unnerving. "It's been in my family for five generations."

"What's he saying?" Fyodor snapped.

She switched to Russian. "We're just making small talk."

"Well, get on with it. He brought our package into the States. He has it here. Tell him we want it."

She kept her expression neutral. Fyodor had the finesse of a wild Ukrainian pig. On the other hand, if something went wrong with these people, he made a good patsy. "Fyodor says it's nice to finally meet you in person, and expresses his thanks for transporting our medical equipment from the Yukon."

Otis Fitch scratched the stubble on his cheek. "Yeah, no problem. I sent my best men."

"Are you sure you can trust them?"

He laughed, a harsh, unamused sound. "Lady, if I don't trust 'em, they sure as hell ain't part of my crew."

"I apologize. I meant no disrespect, Mr. Fitch."

"Chrissakes, lady, call me Otis. Ain't no Mr. Fitch here."

Fyodor tapped her arm to get her attention. "What's he saying? What's going on?"

This conversation would go much more quickly without the constant interruptions, but Fatianova reminded herself that she needed her colleague, however temporarily. "The bomb is here."

"Maybe he's dumb enough to give it to us without getting his final payment."

"I seriously doubt that. Anyway, I'm not going to risk it." She switched back to English. "Fyodor says we're ready to give you your final payment of eighteen thousand dollars, as agreed."

Otis gave another humorless laugh. "Tell Foo-dor that won't even cover gas. We'll be renegotiating my fee."

The blood drained from her face. "Excuse me?"

"You hired me to bring some experimental science thing in from Canada. Stolen, obviously. Tell me what it really is."

"What . . . what makes you think it's anything but what Fyodor said?"

"Tell me anyway."

She'd been afraid of this. Clearly the man wasn't as stupid as he looked. She glanced across at Fyodor and switched to Russian.

"He thinks we stole an experimental scientific device from the Canadians. What should I tell him?"

He tapped his fingertips against his leg. To Fatianova, his anxiety felt palpable. Surely the separatist could see it, as well. "Tell him he's right. Tell him it has to be installed in a controlled lab in order to work. That way, he won't be tempted to open it."

Well, that was a surprise. He'd actually come up with a good answer. She tried to remember a recent scientific breakthrough that could help her now. Certainly this man would not have read current scientific journals.

"Fyodor says there's an international research facility in Whitehorse, Canada," she said to Otis. "Very hush-hush. Fyodor worked in a lab there for the past three years. His team is experimenting with—"

She stopped, unable to find the right words in English to explain nanoelectric scaffolds. Raising both hands in the international sign for "I don't know," she thought about how to explain it so it sounded exotic and mysterious. It didn't even matter if she got the details wrong.

"Erm, the scientists there developed a very advanced device that can be injected directly into the brain with a special needle. Fyodor says the new device will revolutionize the way scientists study the brain. He says it can be used to treat heart conditions and even possibly brain disorders."

When she finished her fabrication, Otis's eyes had glazed over. "So what? You had my men go fetch a needle?"

This man had no interest in science. He epitomized the naïvely arrogant American assumption that the world revolved around them and their needs. Keeping a tight grip on her patience, she took a breath and kept lying.

"Not just the needle. The entire device, and all the research associated with it. Fyodor says American companies will be falling over themselves to buy it."

Interest finally sparked in those wily eyes. "So Foo-dor stole it right out from under their noses, huh? Clever bastard."

Fyodor rapped on her arm. "What's going on? You're here to translate. So translate."

She patted his hand. The constant switching of languages started an ache in her head. "I'm just telling him what you told me to say. English takes twice as many words to convey a simple idea."

Otis scratched his nose. "So how much is this thing worth? I'm guessing ten times what you agreed to pay me."

Much more than that, but she would keep that information to herself. He was fishing around to see how valuable the device was, guessing at what she could get for it on the black market.

"Perhaps that much, but I doubt it. I don't really know yet. But you must understand that this equipment is very delicate. It can only operate in a special laboratory called a clean room. No dust, no dirt. Do you understand? It can't be opened out here. Everything would be ruined."

"Yeah, I get it. So it stays in its crate. And I get an additional thirty thou, or you don't ever see it."

She felt her eyes harden. "Fyodor doesn't have that much. You agreed to thirty-five thousand total, half up front. He paid you that. We kept our end of the bargain. I'd strongly suggest you do the same."

He glanced at Fyodor and back at her, eyes amused. "Or what? You don't get your shit until I get my dough."

"Very well, then. After he sells it—"

"Nuh-uh. Cash on the barrelhead, or it don't happen. What, you think I'm some dumb redneck dope you can clown?"

Fatianova's brows wrinkled as she tried and failed to follow his colloquialisms. "I'm sorry. What does this mean? Dope . . . a clown? I assure you, we're not transporting illegal drugs."

"No, I . . ." Otis finally smiled, baring yellow-stained teeth. "I mean your science machine is worth a hell of a lot more than you're saying. So my price just went up to thirty thou."

She thought it over. How greedy would the man be? Fatianova couldn't blame him for wanting cash up front. He had no idea how rich her device would make her. She could afford a measly few million rubles. The entry fees alone would cover his payment and more. "Twenty-five. Otherwise, there's no profit in it for me. Erm, Fyodor."

"Sure, all right. I'll settle for twenty-five." Otis smiled, the smug, self-satisfied look of a man who thought he'd bested her. She hated that expression. It made her want to carve him into small pieces. "When do I get my money?"

"I'll arrange it tomorrow. Then your men will help us load it onto our truck, and we'll part ways. Agreed?"

"Sure thing. Nice doing business with . . . Foo-dor."

As they left the house to return to their hovel, she exhaled in relief. This would all work out. Her auction would still go forward.

"Did you see those tattoos?"

How could anyone miss them? "He's a dangerous man."

"I agree." Fyodor fidgeted. "Can we trust him?"

No. Only greed would make Otis keep his word to a foreigner. "We have no choice."

"He'll come through. I know it." Fyodor reached for her, his false bravado not fooling her for an instant. "Let's celebrate."

Fatianova shook him off. “Go get drunk, then sleep it off on the couch.”

He grumbled, but left her in peace as she mentally catalogued the things she still needed to do to make her auction a success.

And wondered, once again, when she could kill him.

Chapter 25

Sunday, February 19. 9:20 p.m.
Little Italy. Boston, Massachusetts.

Elliott watched the willowy redhead glide across the floor, her green silk dress molded to her killer body and tight ass. The short length and ridiculously high heels made her legs seem to go on forever. He couldn't keep his eyes off her. Neither could any other man in the room.

As the hostess led the way straight toward them, he glanced across at Mikhail Kerghakov, whose gaze had locked onto the swell of her breasts. The pale man's salt-and-pepper hair had been clipped short on the sides, but long enough on top so that strands covered part of his forehead. A crisp white shirt and black tie under an expensive suit partially hid his turkey neck. His ears stuck out, but his shrewd eyes countered any comical effect. No one with half a brain would underestimate him.

This time of night, the lights had been turned low and cast blue shadows across the room, creating an intimate ambience.

The restaurant had been divided into distinct sections: a long bar area; casual family dining; and a much more exclusive section, separated from the main room by a long, looping shoulder-high cushioned wall. Small tables on one side of the barrier gave way to semicircular booths on the other, enclosed on three sides for maximum privacy.

As the woman approached, Kerghakov turned his face away, picking up his wineglass and swirling the pale liquid. His body-guards, one on each side of the booth, snapped into high alert, hands dipping inside their jackets. Each stepped forward to block her approach.

Like Kerghakov's guard dogs, her two bodyguards wore dark suits with the coats unbuttoned for easy access to their hardware, and sunglasses. What, was there some rule in the Bodyguard Handbook that said they had to blind themselves indoors?

The woman glided to a stop, arching her brows and letting her eyes droop in haughty boredom. Her lip curled slightly as she said something he couldn't hear. One of the guards turned his head to the booth.

"She'd like a word, sir. Should I send her away?"

Kerghakov set his wineglass back onto the table without tasting it. "Let her through."

The two bodyguards immediately dropped their hands and stepped away. One of her dogs tried to stay by her side, but the bigger of Kerghakov's guards held out an arm to stop him. The man's face hardened. Heather glanced at him, flicking a negligent finger in a "go away" gesture. He didn't like it, but backed off.

"I'm Heather Langstrom-Reed," the woman said in nearly accentless Russian. "I'm so pleased to meet you, Mr. Kerghakov."

He looked her up and down, gaze lingering at the juncture of her thighs. "I already have a date tonight, thanks. Maybe tomorrow night?"

The guard dog bristled, but settled when she threw a frown his way. Were they doing the nasty on the side? He was good-looking enough, all chiseled cheekbones and six-pack abs.

"We have business to discuss," she said.

"This is hardly the place or time for a meeting. Make an appointment with my secretary. I'll see if I can work you in next week."

"I'm afraid this really can't wait."

"I don't see how that's possible," Kerghakov replied, sipping his white wine. "I don't know you."

Elliott watched the interplay with curiosity. He knew how cagey Kerghakov could be. Would Heather be able to match him in what was clearly a battle of wits?

Heather cocked her head and looked down at him. "Nevertheless."

He sighed. "What is so urgent you must interrupt my dinner?"

Her long hair hung in sweet curls over her shoulders and down her back, the perfect foil for the forest green dress. He'd bet his left nut she was a tigress in bed. Elliott's gaze shifted to the possessive bodyguard, and found him glaring his way. He threw the guard an insolent smirk.

"Our business is private," Heather said. She looked pointedly at him and Kerghakov's latest slut, a hand settling onto her hip as she cocked a leg.

Kerghakov shrugged, voice soft as he told the girl to go wait at the bar. She scowled, shot Heather a murderous look, and slid reluctantly out of the booth, hovering there until Kerghakov narrowed his eyes in warning. She stalked away toward the bar.

Kerghakov flicked his fingers, and his bodyguards moved out of earshot. So did hers.

"Elliott stays," Kerghakov said.

He hid his surprise by taking deep swallows of his beer. Why? Maybe Kerghakov trusted him.

Wishful thinking.

Heather took her place across from Kerghakov, moving aside the nearly full plate of spaghetti and resting her forearms on the table. "It's true we've never met, but I'm given to understand we might have a common business interest."

"I have many business interests."

"I heard a rumor, though, that you may know something about a particular item, one that's made its way into Boston from your mother country."

Kerghakov halted in the middle of bringing a prawn to his mouth. He set his fork aside, a forefinger idly nudging the handle along the edge of his plate as he regarded Heather.

"Then your rumor sent you on a wild goose chase."

"Your body language suggests otherwise."

"Fuck my body language. I have nothing to say to you."

Elliot ate his lasagna in small bites, ready to speak if needed. What would the woman do now?

She leaned forward, giving Kerghakov an eyeful down her dress. His eyes dropped, but to his credit, he met her gaze again.

"Let's not beat around the bush, Mikhail," she said. "I know you have an interest in this item. So does the organization I represent. My boss would like to talk to you. Now, you have two choices. You voluntarily walk out of here and have a pleasant conversation, or you decide to be stubborn and die tonight."

Kerghakov laughed, his soft voice making the sound ghoulish.

"I'm not afraid of your threats. Look around you. Would your boss really risk my men opening fire in this very crowded restaurant?"

Heather pursed her lips and nodded, as though he'd said something clever. "You could go that route, certainly. And, most certainly, you would be caught in the crossfire; I can make sure of that. Or, I can ensure your safe passage, and your family's safety. If you're straight with us, I can guarantee your family will not be arrested, or hassled in any way. I will also guarantee you won't be detained, arrested, or prosecuted. We want information; nothing more."

Kerghakov looked down at his barely eaten spaghetti, then took a healthy swallow of his wine. He sat back, one hand resting on the table and the other in his lap. Elliott could see the gears moving in his head. At long last, he snagged a clean wineglass and poured from the bottle sitting between them. He handed it to her.

She swirled the liquid in the wineglass before sipping. "This is an excellent Chablis."

"Who do you work for that you so idly threaten my life?"

Heather sipped again before setting the glass down. "I'm here as an intermediary for the FBI."

Elliott started, surprised, though he kept his face expressionless. It was a gutsy move, coming right out and saying it.

Kerghakov twirled some pasta onto his fork and ate it. "Unlikely. Federal agents wouldn't authorize a murder."

She gave a gentle smile. "The FBI surrounded this restaurant before I came in. My task is to convince you to exit peacefully."

He scratched his earlobe, eyes puzzled. "You're honest. That's refreshing for a Fed."

"I said I'm an intermediary. Come on. Leave these people to their meals. Come talk to us."

"No. Why should I?"

Heather shrugged and crossed her legs. "Because if you don't, you'll be arrested and held as an enemy of the state, and disappear into the military prison at Guantanamo Bay."

A small smile crossed his lips and vanished. "You think you can make any charge stick? I've done absolutely nothing illegal."

"Also, your family would be brought in for questioning, and would be publicly charged with a variety of crimes. We would make their lives very difficult."

Kerghakov's brows snapped down and his eyes grew icy. "That's a dangerous threat to make. You better be damned sure of your position."

"I don't mean to make more threats. I'm just telling you what the FBI plans to do if they can't get your voluntary cooperation. I don't want to go that route. As I said, I'm hoping we can just talk."

Kerghakov exhaled through his nose and looked up at the ceiling. "Just talk? Nothing more?"

"Just information."

"And immunity?"

She laughed. "For anything you say tonight, yes. Not for anything you've done in the past or may do in the future."

"I thought I might catch you out on that one. Do you really have the authority for this?"

"Yes, I really do."

He ran his thumb and forefinger over his chin. "If you arrest me, I'll deny it all. If you harm any member of my family, I will bury you."

"I understand."

"Everything I say is off the record?"

"Everything. You have my word."

He nodded, making his turkey neck wobble. "Ask your questions, then."

Heather leaned back against the padded semicircle. "I'd prefer you to talk with my boss. I'm just a messenger who happens to speak Russian."

"No. It's you or no one. Now, or never."

Heather smoothed her dress along her thighs and recrossed her legs. Elliott recognized the nervous gesture. He did the same with his jeans.

"I have your word you'll answer honestly?"

Kerghakov stabbed a prawn. "It's beyond me why I'm even giving you the time of day. By all rights, I should have my men kill you here and now. But," he added quickly, holding up a hand as fire flashed through her eyes. "I don't want to ruin my dinner. And you remind me of my daughter. She, too, is bold. Daring. And very outspoken. She does not, however, threaten to kill me."

Heather looked him squarely in the eye. "I'm sorry for that. I knew I had only moments to make my case. I needed to get your attention."

He patted his lips with a napkin, then dropped it back into his lap. "You have it."

"I'm glad to hear it. This item—is it in Boston already?"

"You think I'm selling it?"

"Or you know who is."

Kerghakov rubbed a hand under his chin. "I believe it's here, yes."

"All right. Are you the seller?"

He shook his head. "No. An interested buyer."

Her lips parted just the tiniest bit. "Do you know who the seller is?"

Kerghakov shrugged a shoulder. "Not precisely. I have a contact. A broker."

"Broker?"

"A middleman. It keeps us all protected."

Heather nodded her understanding, leaning forward and resting her forearms on the table. "You said you wanted it. For yourself? An organization? A cause? What do you intend to do with it?"

He chuckled. "That's a lot of questions all at once."

She smiled, her eyes lighting in amusement. "I don't want to wear out my welcome. Also, if I don't come out soon, the cavalry will ride to the rescue."

"Then, by all means, let's be quick. I want to get back to my dinner before it gets cold." He glanced down. "Although I think it might be too late."

Heather chuckled. "I'm sure the kitchen will reheat it for you."

He looked at her in horror.

She reached for her wineglass, but didn't drink. "So why do you want it?"

"I'm entering the auction on behalf of a client."

Heather cocked her head. "And who would that be?"

"No one to concern the FBI." He ate another prawn. "Ahh. Still warm."

"Mikhail—"

"No. I won't compromise him. Your promise of immunity doesn't extend to him."

Heather blinked, leaning away from him. "Are you a lawyer as well as an accountant?"

He breathed an eerie laugh. "No. Just a lowly, unimportant bean counter."

"I thought you agreed to be truthful," she said in reproach.

"You have a legitimate CPA firm, yes. But your average accountant isn't in the market for a bomb of this particular nature."

His shrewd gaze roved over her face. "I told you—I'm just a proxy. What do you intend to do with this information?"

"Well, find the bomb and stop the sale," she said. "Obviously."

He smiled. "Obviously. But I meant, will the FBI enter the auction to stop any of the rest of us from getting it?"

"I don't know what their plan is at the moment. I'd imagine they'll want to get it off the market any way they can. What does your client want with a nuclear bomb, Mikhail?"

"I don't know what his plan is at the moment."

"I said immunity," Heather said. "All this is off the record. And no one will mention your involvement. Period."

Kerghakov sighed. "You wouldn't believe me if I told you. Anyway, I can't discuss anything my client will do or not do. Now I have a question for you. Who gave you my name?"

Heather shook her head. "I don't know."

His eyes narrowed to slits, displeasure flashing through them. "Don't lie to me. It's obvious I have a leak somewhere."

"Maybe. But I truly don't know. They didn't tell me."

Kerghakov thrust his plate aside. "Well. This has been interesting. Are we through?"

"Almost. Mikhail, who is your contact?"

He reached across the table to snag his slut's unused napkin. Pulling a ballpoint pen from the inner pocket of his suit coat, he wrote something in block letters across it. Handing it back to her, he said, "Would you send my friend back over on your way out?"

Heather stood. "Thank you for your time, Mikhail. I apologize for interrupting your dinner."

Heather looked just as stunning walking away. Elliot couldn't tear his gaze from her ass. As she and her guard dogs reached the bar, the good-looking one saw the slut and jerked his head back toward Kerghakov. She scowled, but slid off the stool and carried her drink back toward the booth.

"Do you know why you're here?" Kerghakov asked. Elliott jerked his attention back to the booth.

"Not really, no," he admitted.

Kerghakov grimaced and gestured toward the departing party. "I'm on their radar. I'm sure I'm under surveillance, and they probably have a wiretap on my phone. I can't meet with Mr. Sokolov, and I certainly can't go to his home. There can be no link between us, do you understand?"

The lightbulb popped on over his head. "You want me to tell him what you talked about tonight."

Kerghakov nodded. "Wait until a large party leaves the restaurant, preferably one with children. Mingle with them, talk to them. The FBI won't pay any attention to a family with kids. Get into a taxi. Go to someplace crowded, like the House of Blues or, better yet, the Machine Nightclub."

Elliott blanched. "That's a gay club."

"So? It'll be crowded, and that's the point. Get lost in the crowd. Wait at least two hours. If anyone's following you, they'll be bored by then. Pick someone up and leave with them."

He knew better than to argue further. "What about my car?"

"Leave it. Pick it up tomorrow."

"What are you going to do? Slip out the back?"

Kerghakov dropped his napkin onto the table and stood, holding out a hand to the slut, who had finally reached the booth. "Me? I'm walking straight out the front door. Make sure you brief Mr. Sokolov tonight."

Chapter 26

Monday, February 20. 10:00 a.m.
FBI Field Office. Boston, Massachusetts.

"Boss wants us."

Lark looked up at Jocelyn. "I just saw him. He's being nice to me. It creeps me out."

Jocelyn laughed. "Not Melvin. Doug."

She closed out her email and locked her computer onto a screensaver showing various scenes of zebras running, playing, and in general looking cute.

"What's with the zebras?"

Lark giggled. "They're impossibly adorable."

Jocelyn cast a sideways glance at her. "Back in 2009, someone hacked into the power grid of the nuclear power plant outside of Greensboro, Massachusetts. The systems sustained no damage, but the first thing users saw when they logged on was the rear end of a zebra."

"Really?" Lark dropped her eyes, afraid her friend would see the guilt in her eyes. "I guess someone else likes zebras, too. Anyway, I'm sure that person just meant to help the company improve their systems security."

"Sure. That must be it. Doesn't everyone like zebras? Here, we're in the big conference room."

"We? We who?"

Lark followed Jocelyn inside and stopped, startled. People filled the room almost to capacity. Some had seated themselves at the conference table, but it held only twelve, leaving many to stand or lean against the walls. What was going on? As she looked around, Lark realized she knew a lot of them. She saw the five section chiefs, as well as senior agents from the satellite offices. With a jolt of surprise, she spotted John McTaggert and Alex Wood.

And Mace.

He smiled warmly at her. Her brow knitted, bewildered, but she returned the smile, instantly feeling better for seeing him. It didn't, however, alleviate her confusion. What was he doing here? What were any of them doing here? Much as she wanted to go to his side, Jocelyn pulled her to an unoccupied patch of wall instead.

Doug entered the room. He took his place at the head of the boat-shaped dark wooden table. The room quieted.

"What's going on?" Lark whispered. Jocelyn shook her head, putting a finger to her lips.

"First, thank you all for coming at such short notice. I appreciate it. For anyone who doesn't know me, I'm Doug Huckabee. I run things here in Boston." He scanned the room. "I'd like to personally welcome our Homeland Security investigators and our special operations partners. This will be a joint FBI-Homeland-military effort. Glad to have you on board, gentlemen."

Murmurs echoed around the room as the three groups acknowledged one another.

"You can all get acquainted later. All right. Most of you know why we're here. For the rest of you, we have a time-critical situation unfolding rapidly. We've received credible intel that a small nuclear device, also called a suitcase bomb, is here in Massachusetts."

Gasps peppered the room. Lark almost hit herself on the forehead. Of course. The hunt for the nuke.

"Now's the time to get everyone up to speed. I want a free flow of information from everyone. We're going with full disclosure here. I don't think I need to emphasize how serious a situation this is. Wanda, if you would?"

A heavy-set older woman straightened the already-straight laptop in front of her. "I'm Special Agent Wanda Forth from the Weapons of Mass Destruction Directorate."

Lark smothered an irreverent laugh. Wander Forth? She suppressed the urge to ask the woman if she were, indeed, a wandering world traveler.

Wanda tapped a button on the laptop, and a map of the Bering Strait appeared on the monitor mounted on the wall. She activated a laser pointer and guided the red light to the left side of the strait. "We believe whoever stole this device smuggled it through Kamchatka, which is this peninsula here, at the far edge of Russia. From there, it traveled through St. Lawrence Island, just west of mainland Alaska, and was flown to here." As she spoke, she moved the pointer to each location. "A town called Whitehorse, in the Yukon Territory of western Canada."

"We lost it from there," Doug said. Wanda shot him an annoyed look. "Using signals intelligence and imagery analysis, as well as every source on the ground we could muster, we believe a neo-Nazi militia here in Massachusetts smuggled it across the border. One of the first things we need to do now is set up surveillance on their farm to verify whether or not the nuke is on their property."

Wanda poked at her laptop. The monitor flashed to a photo of an open suitcase with silver canisters, switches, and wires inside. "This is a mock-up of what you're looking for. It might not be in a suitcase, per se. It could also fit into a large backpack."

"So it's a dirty bomb?" one of the section chiefs asked.

"No." Wanda had the long-suffering look of someone who'd answered this question a thousand times before. "A dirty bomb mixes traditional explosives with irradiated matter. The explosion pollutes the area when it discharges the radioactive material, yes, but most of the damage comes from the explosion itself, not the radiation. What we're talking about here is an actual nuclear bomb."

"What magnitude are we talking?" the same man asked.

"Five kilotons; that's about a quarter of the yield of Hiroshima."

Doug tapped the table to get her attention. "Physical damage, or radiation poisoning?"

"Primarily radiation, although there would certainly be physical damage as well."

"The CDC is prepping for the possibility this thing actually goes off, right, Wanda?" Doug asked.

"Absolutely, sir. They're standing by with decontamination equipment and medical personnel."

Anxious mutters crisscrossed the room. Lark's gut clenched.

The anathema of someone deliberately setting off a nuclear bomb chilled her.

Doug let the noise die down before he turned to a stocky, grim-faced man with a buzz cut, dressed in a green military uniform with a silver oak leaf pinned to his epaulets. Rows and rows of ribbons and badges crammed the left side of the uniform. Topping the ribbons was a rectangular badge showing a rifle against a blue background, encircled with some sort of ivy wreath. It looked important. The man looked important.

"Colonel Granville, if you would?"

The military officer rose and stepped over to the monitor mounted on the wall. He nodded to a woman wearing a similar green uniform. She had three stripes on her sleeve, and only a few ribbons. Lark wondered what it meant. The woman tapped on her tablet, and a photo popped up on the monitor. The man in the photo appeared to be in his fifties, with mostly gray hair, a sagging chin, and protruding ears.

"This is Mikhail Kerghakov. He works as a mob accountant for Viktor Sokolov, the head of the Sokolov crime family here in New England. We think he's one of the bidders for the nuke, acting on behalf of someone, most probably Sokolov himself. We haven't discovered the names of other potential buyers, but we believe there are at least three other interested parties."

Lark's world tipped sideways. Mr. Sokolov? Bidding on a nuclear bomb? Well, at least now she knew what the fifty million was for. Before she could stop herself, she blurted out, "But what would be his objective? Why would the mob want a mini-nuke?"

"It doesn't make sense, actually," one of the section chiefs said. "The mob thrives because it exploits existing business enterprises. Racketeering, extortion, loan sharking. Also, the corruption of elected officials and labor leaders. Stock manipulation. Destroying those infrastructures would only hurt them."

"Maybe they intend to eliminate their competition?" someone asked.

A woman sitting beside Mace answered. "There are much easier ways to eliminate competition. The murder of key figures, for example. Either the organization collapses from the inside, or they fall into line."

"All right," Doug said. "We'll work on that. Meanwhile, Kerghakov gave us this woman, Fatianova Uvarov."

The new photo showed an unsmiling blonde, classically beautiful and impeccably groomed.

"She's a Russian national here on a B-1 visa, purportedly to attend the International Symposium on Nuclear Safety next week. According to Kerghakov, she's the one brokering the auction for the bomb."

"Do we know where she is?" Mace asked.

Doug grimaced. "We know she checked out of her Boston hotel and rented a truck, but we can't confirmation where she went. In fact, the only contact we have for her is an Outlook.com account. Unfortunately, when we contacted her, we realized she sent her email through a proxy server."

One of the Homeland Security representatives raised his hand. "A proxy server hides her IP address, right?"

"Yes," Melvin said. "We can't track her location."

"Technology has gotten much more sophisticated," Doug said, giving a wry smile. "People don't want the government snooping into their private business."

Lark clasped her hands together. Should she speak up? Contradict Melvin in front of his boss and everyone in the room? If she did, it would cement Melvin's hatred of her. But this was just too important to kowtow to his miserable ego. As she opened her mouth to speak, Melvin shot her a warning look.

"Ms. Larkspur? Do you have something to add?"

She started at Mace's voice, which echoed through the room. She looked across at him. He'd obviously witnessed their silent exchange.

She hesitated, but when he nodded encouragingly, she took a deep breath.

"What Melvin is saying is true," she said directly to Doug, "but not always. Outlook.com is really nothing more than a website, even though it acts as an email server. It's entirely possible she just changed her browser's proxy settings, instead of using an actual proxy server like AnonyMizer or Vtunnel. That's good enough for most people. But Outlook.com keeps IP logs, same as all email services do. With a court order, we could make them turn over those logs."

Doug Huckabee zeroed in on her. "What would that give us?"

"Well, the complete message source. Including the IP address of the original sender."

"It's not as simple as she's making it out to be," Melvin said, puffing out his linebacker-sized chest. His lowered eyebrows, jutting jaw, and huge frame leant him an impressive air. Too bad other people couldn't see the big bully inside.

"No," she said. "Of course it's not. I've made it seem simple so you'd understand, but Melvin's a hundred percent right. There's no guarantee it will work. It depends on how sophisticated she is." *There. That should make the asswipe feel better. Who says I can't play nice?*

"I'll get the court order," Doug said. "Meanwhile, Lark, here, had an interesting encounter with the mob. I've opened a formal investigation. Lark, want to fill us in?"

Full disclosure, Doug had said. He therefore wanted her to be as honest and open as possible. Fine. She could do that.

"I was kidnapped last Saturday. It was actually the second attempt," she said, stepping forward. "The first time, one of our special operations partners—" she deliberately parroted Doug's term "—saved me. The second time, my kidnappers delivered me to Mr. Sokolov."

She waited for the flurry of whispers to subside.

"Someone is framing me for the theft of fifty million dollars of mob money," she said baldly. "The theft was accomplished through electronic means, which I'm still tracking down."

"How do we know you're being framed?" Melvin asked, voice aggressive. Almost accusing, damn him. "Why would the mob think that unless there's some truth to it? It wouldn't be the first time a hacker's gone rogue."

Her eyes flashed. How dare he impugn her integrity? Before she could speak, though, Doug held up a hand.

"Melvin, we've verified that she isn't involved in this except as an innocent bystander. Lark, take us through what happened."

Still huffy, she glared at Melvin. "Most of the great hackers leave tags in their hacks for bragging rights. Something that says 'Look at me! I did this!' Or, sometimes hackers aren't careful enough, and leave tiny footprints behind that can be tracked."

"Someone used your tags," Doug said. "Right?"

She nodded. "Way back when, I might have played around in some systems where I technically shouldn't have been. I never compromised systems safety, and I never stole information for material gain."

Melvin made a scoffing noise. Her eyes narrowed to daggers. Too bad she couldn't incinerate him with her laser vision.

"My signature included the words *fix yer shit* and my handle, SPURious. Both of those were embedded in the code fragments Mr. Sokolov gave me. Also, the hacker renamed a root access file SPURious, and also created a user profile with that name. It's overkill. Like signing your name four times in a row. But someone who knows me used my past against me."

Doug nodded. "Finding that money trail is your only priority starting now."

"Gotcha."

The Homeland Security representative set down his travel mug with a bang. "You can't possibly be considering returning the money to the mob. Clearly it's earmarked for the suitcase bomb. We can't allow that nuke into anyone's hands except ours. We need to keep that money."

Doug raised his hands to calm the rumblings echoing throughout the room. "First we need to *find* that money. At the moment, it could be anywhere, in anyone's hands."

Mace poked the man sitting in front of him and whispered into his ear. The man cast him an exasperated look, but knocked on the table.

"Jace Reed, heading the Rapid Reaction Force. Doug, I'm sure you'll agree that Lark needs to be put into protective custody."

So that was Mace's boss. She looked him over curiously. Dark curly hair cut short, straight nose, strong chin. Broad shoulders and muscles straining against his plain black T-shirt. Eyes that returned her gaze with a directness that startled her. She looked away.

"Absolutely. Sokolov gave her a week, which expires in roughly two days." Doug turned to address Lark directly. "While you're probably safe until Sunday, I'm taking no chances with your life. And after that, we have to assume you're in imminent danger."

Mace stood directly behind his boss. "I'll head the protection detail, if that's acceptable."

"Fine." Uh-oh. Jace sounded annoyed. "We'll coordinate with you, Doug, for additional assets. Are you good with that?"

Doug looked from her to Mace and back again, a grin tugging at his mouth. "Would it do me any good to say no? I take it you two know one another."

Lark felt herself turn beet red. A couple of people laughed. So much for keeping their budding relationship under the radar.

"Do it, then," Doug said in resignation. "Run your plans past me, all right?"

"I will," Jace said. "And when the Rapid Reaction Force is in play, we'll make sure she's safely inside this building."

"Good. Does anyone else have anything to add? No? Then we're adjourned."

Chapter 27

LARK HUNG BACK in the room, waving Jocelyn to go on ahead, hovering until Mace disengaged himself and came over. Her smile seemed wan and apologetic. He forced himself to keep a professional distance.

"I didn't mean to embarrass you," he said.

"You didn't. Not really, anyway. You just surprised me. I'm going to take a bunch of shit from my co-workers, though."

"I'm sorry. I just want to make sure you stay safe."

She gave a more genuine smile, and the knot in his stomach unclenched. "I kind of want that, too."

Jace appeared beside them before Mace could respond. He'd missed her, more than he'd been prepared for.

"All right, Sir Galahad," Jace said, voice a deep rumble. "Write me up a calc protection plan. We're official now, so bring me what you need—within reason—and I'll make sure you get it."

"I appreciate your—"

"Like you gave me a choice, asshole. Make sure you plan for

when they pull the trigger on the Rapid Reaction Force. At that point, you're purely operational."

"Yes, sir." He deserved an ass-chewing for speaking over Jace in the meeting, essentially backing him into a corner. His boss understood him, understood all of the men under his command. But when it came to a mission directive, he expected his teammates to perform at one hundred percent.

"We'll keep you safe, Lark," Jace said directly to her. "Sokolov won't be getting his hands on you again."

"Thanks. But it's not something we need to worry about for a few days, at least."

The special operators gathered around Mace, looking Lark over curiously. He couldn't blame them. They either knew or suspected his relationship with her, and they intended to put their lives on the line for her.

"Meet the rest of the team," he said. "You know Alex, Tag, and Gabe. These knuckleheads are Ken Acolatse, Gavin Selle, and Scott Griffin. Jace is my team leader and his wife Heather is our intel analyst. The gruff bear talking to Huckabee is our squadron commander, LTC Granville, and the woman in uniform with him is Sergeant Tams, our researcher."

"Nice to meet you all. I'm sorry to drag you into my mess."

"Actually, you're our most direct link to the nuke. That makes you the most important person here." He couldn't have her thinking she was a burden.

"If you say so," she said, wrinkling her nose at him. "I got work to do, though. And so do you all. You can skedaddle now."

"Actually, I'm sticking to you like white on rice," he told her unapologetically. "Until I have a solid plan in place, I'm your shadow."

She turned to Jace, who nodded agreement. "It's the best move." He glanced around and saw Stephanie, who immediately made her way to his side. "Steph, would you email our clearances over here? We'll need access to the SCIF."

"Sure thing. I'll do it now." The woman could work miracles with nothing but a tablet.

Lark gave him an irritated look. "Fine. But you have to be an über-silent bowl of rice. I need to concentrate. I can't do that with you looking over my shoulder."

He couldn't help himself. He smiled down at her, his tender feelings on display for anyone who was looking. She glared back at him.

"Come on, shadow. I have my orders." She stalked toward the door, and he followed.

Doug excused himself from LTC Granville and intercepted her. "Do you need anything? People? Processing power? Coffee?"

Clearly he knew his employee. Mace stifled a grin.

"Nothing right now. Well, except for the coffee. I need a vat of coffee. I'll swing by the break room."

"You think of anything, come to me."

"All righty. Thanks."

Lark power-walked out of the conference room and down the carpeted hallway. He hustled to keep up. She made a sharp left turn into a small kitchenette. The brunette who'd been standing next to her during the briefing stared into the refrigerator. When she rose and turned with a yogurt in her hand, he was treated to an eyeful down her white silk blouse.

"Well, hello, handsome," she purred. Glossy red lips parted in a sensuous smile. "Let me be the first to welcome you to our little party. I'm Jocelyn Katsaros."

Her hips swayed as she crossed the room and offered her hand. He took it, the feel of her fingers sliding across his palm an annoyance. He tried a polite nod.

"Mace."

She didn't take the hint, scooping his arm in hers and leaning toward him conspiratorially. "We'd all better be on our toes on this one. This will either make or break ol' Dougie's career. And probably ours, too."

Lark stomped to the counter and filled a Styrofoam cup to the brim, her back to him. Deliberately, he thought. He disengaged himself from Jocelyn's grip, ignoring the pout on her face.

"Why don't we focus on the damage a nuclear bomb detonated on US soil could do, instead of on careers being made or broken?" he said, maybe a little more sharply than he'd intended.

She grinned at him, unabashed, and he realized she'd been teasing him. It didn't endear her to him. Neither did the calculation that sharpened her face.

"Well, didn't that put me in my place?"

Lark stalked past them without a single glance. Mace followed her, intending to clear the air, but then realized Jocelyn brought up the rear of their impromptu train. The three of them wound their way silently through a cube farm, ending up midway down a row of identical cubicles.

All similarity ended with the cube he saw there. Lark had tacked up yellow-and-red wallpaper in the space between her desk and the overhead storage cabinet. A pink Himalayan salt lamp rested near the telephone. A large leafy thing that reminded him of the man-eating plant from *Little Shop of Horrors* took up most of the left side of the L-shaped desk. A row of plush Avengers toys lined the wall near the lamp. Her computer mouse had zebra stripes.

And a bowl with a goldfish sat next to her keyboard.

He started to laugh. She whipped her head around to glare daggers at him, but he couldn't stop.

"What?" she asked belligerently.

"Nothing," he croaked through another chuckle. "It's just so uniquely you."

Her narrowed eyes assessed him, then slid to Jocelyn, who'd dragged in two rolling chairs from other cubicles. "I'm me. Nothing more, nothing less. I'm sorry if you don't like it."

He'd wanted to speak with her privately, but fuck it. Jocelyn didn't seem to be going anywhere; too bad if she witnessed this. He settled his hands on her shoulders and hauled her up against him. She tensed, pulling away, eyes flashing. He ignored her temper, resting his forehead against hers until she looked at him. *Really* looked at him. Her lips parted just a tiny bit as confusion flickered through her eyes.

His heart thumped as he lowered his gaze to her mouth. Her sweet, fiery, intriguingly perfect mouth. The tip of her tongue touched her top lip, causing an unexpected rush of heat to his groin. He swallowed his groan as he settled his mouth on hers, stroking them together. She made a tiny mewling noise that fired his blood. He'd intended it to be a gentle, reassuring kiss. As soon as her lips softened under his, though, he licked into her mouth, tangling their tongues together. She tasted of sunshine and flowers, and he laughed at himself for his sappy thoughts.

"Ahem."

He let his eyes drift open, seeing Lark's glazed expression. She gave a tiny giggle.

"Do you understand now?" he whispered.

She nodded, then eased out of his arms.

"Ahem," Jocelyn said, louder this time. "Clearly you're the man Lark spent the weekend with. I thought you said his name was Thomas?"

"Mace is a nickname."

Jocelyn slanted Lark a look of tolerance. "Can we get to work, now that we have that settled?"

They both looked at her. A huge smile spread over Lark's face. "Sure thingy, bossy lady."

"I'm your boss," came a gruff voice from the cubicle's entryway. "You report to me, not her."

Lark's face closed down. Mace looked at the man who'd tacitly told Lark to keep her mouth closed during the briefing. He forced himself to remain open and relaxed. Lark wouldn't appreciate him going he-man all over her boss.

"Duh, Melvin. It's just an expression."

Melvin looked him over. Mace returned a bland smile. Lark's *only* boss dismissed him with a very slight wrinkling of his nose. "You're one of the military guys, right? Lark has work to do. She doesn't need any distractions. And I assure you she's perfectly safe. We're in an FBI building, for God's sake. Security's tight here."

Mace didn't bother to mention he and his teammates had identified three potentially vulnerable points of entry. The contract guards carried weapons, but most likely had only a few hours of training. They would be simple to subdue. He was taking no chances with her safety given the threat. Still, it would take big brass balls to try to acquire Lark inside the FBI building.

"Do you have a computer I can borrow? I can work my protection plan and be out of Lark's hair. How about that desk?" He pointed to the empty cubby across from Lark's.

"That's perfect," Jocelyn said. "He's on vacation till next week."

Melvin scowled, but finally nodded. "Have IT set him up with guest access."

"Sure thingy, bossy boss," Lark said. "Oh, Jocelyn, I keep forgetting to ask you. That program you found on the server with the clocking anomaly. What did it do?"

"Program?" Jocelyn wrinkled her brow. "What program?"

Lark gave an exaggerated sigh. "The clocking anomaly on the infected server. Melvin said you were running it down."

"Got no idea what you're talking about, chickadee. Sorry."

Lark looked at Melvin. A muscle ticked near his jaw, and he wouldn't meet her eyes. He knew exactly to what Lark referred.

"I took it off her plate and did it myself. It turned out to be nothing."

"Nothing? How can it be nothing? Someone deliberately installed it—"

"I'm telling you it wasn't important," Melvin said. "You've got real work to do. That's where you put your focus, not on some harmless clocking discrepancy. Understand?"

"Anomalies give me hives."

"Find the mob's money," Melvin said. "Focus, Lark. Don't go down rabbit holes."

"Fine. For fuck's sake. I will."

Melvin walked away, which was good, because Mace didn't like how he treated Lark. Not one bit.

"Finally," Jocelyn said. "We don't need to wait for IT. I have root access. I'll set you up."

Lark gave an impish grin. Mace suspected that she, too, had access she shouldn't have. Jocelyn crossed to the other cubicle and sat down.

"You, too?" he asked Lark.

Her eyes widened. "Certainly not. That would be a clear violation of policy and procedure. And I'm pretty sure what you heard Jocelyn say is that she would contact IT to set up a temporary account for you."

He grinned. "Yup. That's what I heard, too."

They shared a smile, then Lark slipped into her chair. "Okay. Let's see if anyone nibbled at the cheese."

LARK LOGGED BACK into the darknet. Had ChaosCowboy received her message? Had anyone followed her breadcrumbs?

A reply to her encrypted message flashed on her screen. ChaosCowboy! She clicked it open, and found directions to a private chat room. Following the link, she entered the room, praying he would answer her.

U there?

Howdy, SPURious. It's been a right long spell.

A whoosh of relief escaped her. He would be able to help her, if only to settle her nerves. She hated feeling out of control.

Five years. Last she'd heard, he'd been caught and charged under the federal computer crime statutes. How long did they keep u?

For a fair piece. The vittles sucked a rat's patoot.

She typed in a frowny face. Sorry.

Pshaw. Ain't nuthin' but a thing. U been raisin' hell?

I went legit. But I need ur help with something.

Not a surprise. You were always too ethical.

How to explain it? Remember the hack of the Bangladesh Bank last March? This is like that. Except that someone used my handle to frame me for it.

Bet ur fit to be tied. Whatcha need?

He hadn't asked the amount of the theft. Lark found that a little strange. It would be her first question.

You heard about it?

Yup. Bunch of yellow-bellied scalawags out there. I was waitin' fer yer call.

She needed to find out who'd told him, but first things first.

She typed in a smiling face. I have data from the injured party. I need to backtrace the theft and find the cash, and I only have a few days.

Send me the data. I'll see what I can do.

Her innards relaxed. ChaosCowboy had taught her nearly everything she knew about advanced cracking techniques, taking her far beyond the level of script kiddie.

Suddenly, a new screen popped up on her monitor, showing an aerial view of her parents' mansion in Nantucket; the wide expanses of manicured lawn, the mansion itself, and Polpis Harbor.

What the hell? This wasn't email; someone had instant-messaged the image directly to her.

She brought up a terminal window and ran an IP locator on the sender. It took her to a free proxy service. Before she could dig further, another photo appeared, this time a close-up of Kaley and Peter, lounging by the pool.

Why would someone be spying on her family?

U there, SPURious?

A third photo joined the others. She stared at it, horror raising the hairs at the back of her neck and churning her stomach. This last photo showed their home security alarm panel . . . from the inside. To the right of the front door of her parents' home. Someone had broken in, and wanted her to know it.

The threat blew her mind. Stop your investigation, or we'll hurt your family. Fuck. Fuck fuck fuck.

Gotta vamoose, babe. U change ur mind?

Rattled, Lark grabbed the thumb drive Elliott had given her and forced her shaking hand to insert it into the USB slot. She copied the data and pasted it into the private chat window.

See what u can do with it. I'll work it on my end.

Meet here l8r?

Give me a couple hours. Meet at 5?

Sounds good. Thx.

She disconnected from the dark net and sat back, chin dropping to her chest. The pictures immediately vanished. She closed her eyes. If she returned the mob's money to Mr. Sokolov, her family might be harmed. That was unacceptable.

"What's wrong?"

Mace's calm voice steadied her even before she opened her eyes. He stood over her, concern creasing his face. "You look like someone died."

The unfortunate choice of words caused her anxiety to come roaring back. "Someone just threatened my family."

Mace's brows snapped down and his body became rigid. He pinned Lark with a gaze so intense she almost flinched. "Tell me."

She did. He listened in earnest, gaze roving over her face as though to glean every nuance.

"And you have no idea who might be behind the threat?"

"Well, other than it's very probably from the thieves who stole the mob money. I need to warn Kaley. They need to go into hiding or to Europe or something."

Mace gripped her shoulder reassuringly. "I'll take care of that. Doug won't have any problem either sending a protection detail to them, or taking them somewhere safe."

"My parents, too?"

"Absolutely."

Relief flooded her. "Thank you. I . . . thank you."

"Family is everything," he said.

Grateful for his understanding, she jumped up and hugged him. He wrapped his arms around her, and something inside her relaxed.

"I was hoping I'd see you last night," he murmured.

"Your hotel room is too crowded," she said. "And you're conceited. What makes you think I want to sleep with you again?"

The heat in his eyes nearly scalded her. A rush of sensation vibrated through her in response. "I'm dying for a repeat. If you felt just half as much as I did—"

She forced herself to pull away. "I'm not looking for another hookup."

"I'm not, either," he said. His mouth turned down and he ran a hand down his face. "Listen, we'll get this all figured out. We'll find the suitcase bomb. We'll get whoever's threatening you and your family. And then . . ."

"And then nothing," she said, but she couldn't help wishing things could be different. "I mean, yes, I'd love to spend about thirty-six hours in bed with you. Okay? Jeez. I admit it, okay?"

"But?" He didn't look happy.

"But people aren't who they say they are. Either they lie about who they are, or they change into the exact thing they say they hate. Either way, it makes for a lousy relationship."

Mace looked down at her for several long moments. "Who hurt you, Lark?"

"No one. Stay on target, supersoldier. We both have jobs to do."

He touched a gentle hand to her cheek. "True. But this conversation isn't over."

"Mace, I can't let the bad guys win. I just can't," she said in a rush, worry for her family flooding back. "But I'm no closer to figuring it out than I was this morning. I need to step it up."

"Or take it down a notch." Mace immediately shook his head. "No, of course you can't do that. You'd still be in danger. Sokolov would be after you, and I won't be with you all the time."

"All righty, then. Time to find the real thieves."

Chapter 28

It didn't take Mace long to put together a twenty-four hour rotating guard schedule for Lark, and another one for her family. Developing a contingency plan for when the Rapid Reaction Force deployed took him longer. Finally, he went in search of Jace, finding him sitting with a couple of team members and some strangers. One he recognized from the briefing earlier looked up and nodded a greeting.

"You one of Jace's? I'm Noah Jennings, DHS."

Mace shook his hand. "Mace Beckett."

"These guys are with me. We were just deciding who will join your protection detail."

Jace annotated the list in front of him, looked up, and winked. Mace couldn't suppress the relief rippling through the back of his skull. "I shouldn't be surprised."

"Damned straight you shouldn't. Noah is lending us three bodies. Will that do?"

"For Lark, yes. But we have another problem."

Jace groaned. "We don't have enough of those already?"

"Someone broke into Lark's parents' house and sent her pictures meant to threaten her." He relayed what had happened. "We need to get them into protective custody right away."

Noah Jennings rose. "Give me the details. I'll get that going."

Mace handed him the protection plan he'd just written up. "Family names, addresses, contact data. In case I missed anything, Lark's cell phone number is at the bottom."

"Nice work," Noah said. "I'm on it."

When he returned to his borrowed cubicle, he was disappointed not to see Lark.

"She went to the SCIF," someone said. He turned his head to see a whip-thin blond man in nerdy glasses and a face pockmarked with acne scars. Some stray hairs on his chin were probably supposed to be a beard.

"Where is it?"

"Other end of the building. Go past the fire stairs, last door on the right. But you can't get in without a—"

"Thanks."

Mace found the SCIF without issue. He presented his military ID to the guard on duty, who checked his computer and handed him a red visitor's badge. "You'll have to be escorted while you're inside, Sergeant."

The SCIF housed various types of top secret information, compartmented into different areas and computer systems. Just because he had access to some data didn't mean he could access all of it. Need to know, and all that. He could have pushed the issue, but it wasn't worth it.

"I'll escort him," a silky voice said from behind him. He turned to see Jocelyn. "Lock your cell phone and wristwatch into one of those lockboxes and take the key with you."

He did so. Jocelyn pressed numbers on the cypher lock, pulled open the door, and gestured him inside.

It looked like any other SCIF; he'd been in enough of them to know. Thick walls with maps and other information tacked to them, computer workstations, separate areas for different classifications of data. Radio frequency shielding and acoustical dampening. Intrusion detection system and special metal file cabinets.

He saw Lark halfway down the right side of the large room. Jocelyn led the way to her workstation. She looked up and smiled.

"Hey, there."

"Hey, yourself. How're things going? Hot on the money trail?"

Jocelyn grabbed two nearby chairs and dragged them over, practically pushing him into one. He settled in next to Lark. Jocelyn sat on her other side.

"I'm using the account data Elliott gave me to follow the pennies until it leads me to the dollars."

"What have you learned?" Jocelyn asked.

"I traced the mob money from where it exited one of their bank accounts to a shell corporation in the Caymans."

"So it's an illegal account? Can we seize it?" Mace asked.

"No, and no. Quick lesson in financial transactions, kiddies. Shell companies aren't illegal. They just don't have any assets and they produce squat. They're there purely to process transactions, which is what happened here. As far as the Cayman Islands, even though it's a known tax haven, it's still not illegal to have an account there."

She paused to make sure they understood. "Anywho, the shell corporation is owned by Sosa-Vega Participações Financeiras," she said, stumbling over the pronunciation. "Which is Portuguese for Sosa-Vega Financial Holdings, headquartered in Sao Paulo, Brazil."

It seemed like Jocelyn intended to interrupt, but Mace held up a hand. "Where did it go from there?"

"It's not like there's a road map with convenient red arrows." She snatched a sheet of paper from the desk and started writing. "According to their website, Sosa-Vega brought in eighty-two point five billion-with-a-*b* in US dollars last year. A hundred and fifty thousand employees serving millions of customers, institutions, small businesses, and the government."

Jocelyn slumped back in her chair, shoulders and face relaxing. "Damn. It's a dead end, then."

"Who're you talking to?" Lark scoffed. "My master's is in digital forensics."

Mace watched her. She clearly loved the challenge of the puzzle she was unraveling. "You found something?"

"I'm counting on a little help from some of those hundred and fifty thousand employees."

Jocelyn laughed, though it sounded a little forced to Mace. "You're showing me up, Larkspur. Won't be long before you steal my job. You did a little social engineering, I take it?"

She beamed, dancing a little in her chair. "You bet. And no way I'm letting you go anywhere, Joss. I need you."

"Not for long." The other woman sounded sad.

A *ding* announced a new email, which Lark quickly opened. "Yes! Let's hear it for spear-phishing!"

Jocelyn raised her brows. "What did you do?"

"Accessed Sosa-Vega's organizational structure. Weird what the FBI keeps track of. Anyway, I sent a very official-looking internal memo asking all the network engineers to fill out a short form."

Several more *dings* had her pumping her fist in triumph. "And the cavalry rides over the hill."

Mace scratched his head. “You’ve lost me completely.”

Lark laughed. “Any unsuspecting dweebs who filled out my form received a sweet bit of malware in return. Thanks to them, I own their system, or part of it. Now watch me work my magic.”

Mace could only stare. “You’re a menace, little bird. I’m glad you’re on our side.”

She smirked. “Don’t forget it, supersoldier.”

He lounged back in the chair, content just to watch her. She kept up a running commentary as she worked, with Jocelyn making suggestions on the side. As time passed, his eyelids began to droop.

“I did it!” Lark crowed, waking Mace from his half doze. He stretched, glancing at his watch. It was nearly four-thirty in the afternoon.

“Tell me,” he invited.

“I’ve been trolling from system to system, and I just hit their financial database.” Her fingers flew over the keyboard. “I’m running an algorithm right now to match dollar amounts with dates and destinations.”

“That large an amount shouldn’t be hard for you to spot, right?” Mace asked.

“Jeez. Believe it or not, the mob money isn’t the only fifty-million-dollar transaction. Seriously?” She peered at the screen, humming to herself as she clicked from screen to screen.

“What are you doing now?” Jocelyn asked.

“I’m following the deposits and withdrawals. Sosa-Vega uses the Caymans shell corporation to move large . . . wait, here we go.”

Mace leaned forward to look over her shoulder, but the lines and lines of numbers meant little to him. Lark bent back, rubbing her cheek against his hair. He immediately turned his head to skim his lips over her ear.

"Ahem," Jocelyn said. "Money?"

She jerked upright, returning her attention to the screen. "Spoilsport. Okay. The money was deposited into . . ."

She froze in place, a hand half-raised to point at the screen.

"Lark?" Her unnatural stillness alarmed him. "Lark, talk to us."

She let out her breath in a rush, probably not even aware she'd been holding it. "Elliot was right. He told me where to look. Check your own nine-to-five, he said. I didn't want to assume, so I tracked the money from point to point, just like I'm supposed to. But he was right all along."

"What are you talking about?" Jocelyn asked.

"I know where the money is," she whispered, voice bleak.

"Where?"

Her lips drooped and she dropped her hand into her lap.

"Where's the mob's money, Lark?" Mace asked.

"Here."

Mace shook his head, not understanding. "What do you mean, here? The United States? Massachusetts? Boston?"

She sighed, shoulders slumping, and squeezed her hands together. "No. Here. One Center Plaza."

Jocelyn jackknifed up in her chair. "What?"

Chills slithered down Mace's spine and raised the hairs on his arms.

Jocelyn sounded no less shocked than Mace felt. "Are you seriously saying that the *FBI* stole mob money?"

Chapter 29

Lark jumped from her chair and began to pace, the enormity of her findings making it impossible to sit still. Tracking down the money trail had been a thrilling adventure, no matter how serious the personal consequences if she failed. Why? Because she'd never intended to fail.

Her conclusions, however, opened the biggest can of worms in the history of worm cans. She didn't know what she was supposed to do now. She stopped in front of Mace, crossing her arms to hide her shivers.

"Are you okay?" he asked.

She let out an unladylike snort, channeling all her anxiety into anger, just as she'd done as a child, and aiming it at him. "Of course I'm not okay. Are you the dumbest person on the planet? I guess I really didn't believe Elliott, but it's true. Someone at the FBI stole fifty million dollars from the mob and framed me for it. I'm about as far from *okay* as it's possible to get. What a dumb question."

To her surprise, he chuckled and reached for her, gripping her wrists lightly and pulling her gently to him. Her shivers eased as she let him, drawing comfort from his solid, calm presence. "You're not going to pick a fight by insulting me. You're scared. I get it; I'm scared, too. This just ballooned from dangerous crisis to calculated shitstorm."

She leaned against him. "What do we do?" she whispered.

Mace stood, keeping hold of her hands. "First things first. We brief our bosses and kick around our options."

Jocelyn rolled her chair away from the workstation. "Congratulations, sunshine. Very few people could have found that money so fast. Go brief Doug. I'll stay here."

Lark scrubbed her palms over her upper arms, barely registering Jocelyn's sour tone. "Okay. If you think that's best."

They left the SCIF and picked up their electronics. Mace dialed his phone one-handed. "Need you in Doug's office pronto. Yeah. Heading there now."

Jace waited for them outside the special agent in charge's office, half sitting on the receptionist's desk. "He's in a meeting. What's the urgency?"

"Unless it's the president, he's interruptible. Lark found the money."

Jace's eyes narrowed just the slightest bit, but he rose and strode to the office door without hesitation. Wow. What would it be like to have someone trust you so much they'd interrupt a meeting with the Big Boss without asking a single question?

Jace pushed the door ajar and stuck his head in. "Doug? We have a priority development."

Lark couldn't see inside, but she heard Doug say, "We'll continue this later, gentlemen. Give us the room, please." Chairs scraped back, and half a dozen agents filed out, looking curiously at the three of them.

"Come on in, Jace."

The three trooped in. Doug sat at his small conference table, shuffling through maps and reports. He looked up at them and shoved the papers aside.

"What's so urgent?" he asked.

The two supersoldiers sat at the table, and Doug gestured for her to do the same. She did so, assailed by doubts. What if Doug knew about the money transfer? Worse, what if he had orchestrated it? She fidgeted. The odds were against his involvement, but still. Whom could she trust?

Mace. She trusted Mace. And he thought briefing the Big Bosses was the way to go.

"So what's the new development?"

She realized with a start that all three men were looking at her. "Ah, um . . . well, I found the fifty mil."

A smile spread across Doug's face. "Outstanding. I knew if anyone could, it would be you. Where did it end up? Ukraine? Bangladesh?"

Well, the news wasn't going to get any more palatable if she pussyfooted around it. She took a deep breath and spit it out. "Sir . . . the money traces right back. Here. This building. Us."

He laughed. "Okay. Funny. Now tell me what really happened. I've got half a dozen agencies to coordinate, and no time to do it."

Lark rubbed a nervous hand across her mouth. Until this moment, she hadn't even considered that he might not believe her.

Jace stared hard at her. "Sir, she's not kidding. She believes it's the truth. Lay it out for us, Lark."

She did. "Obviously the money isn't sitting in someone's desk. But it is in an account this field office owns and uses. The bank downstairs, to be specific."

When she finished, the four of them sat in tense silence.

"This information does not leave this room," Doug said finally.

"Yes, sir." If she'd thought she was out of her depth holding a man hostage after a kidnapping attempt, it was nothing compared to her bewilderment at the prospect of an FBI plot and cover-up.

Doug scrubbed a hard hand across the back of his neck. "This scenario just keeps getting better and better. How do we find the person or persons responsible for the theft?"

Lark brushed a hand across a pile of papers near her, wanting to either straighten them up or fling them across the room. "I have an idea about that."

He nodded, tacitly inviting her to continue.

"The thumb drive Elliott gave me contained their banking info, sure, but it also had part of the code that the thief used. It's kind of a long shot, but if the thief executed the hack here in the building, I might be able to find that code buried somewhere in one of our networks."

Doug gulped from the coffee cup at his elbow. Lark stared longingly at it. She would kill for some caffeine right about now.

"Our networks are all segmented, secured, and locked down," she continued. "No one person can touch every network as a security precaution."

"Okay," Doug said. "What do you need from me?"

She looked at him blankly. Wasn't it obvious? "Access. I need access."

"To what?" Jace asked.

Why could no one follow her trains of thought? Life would be so much easier if people could read minds. She glanced at Mace. Maybe not. She didn't want anyone else knowing how delicious she found him.

"She needs root access to every single one of your network segments," Mace said.

Something inside her relaxed. Mace had no trouble keeping up with the twists and turns of her brain. And he seemed to like her anyway. She beamed at him.

"I need someone in charge of granting computer access to give me blanket clearance to look at everything," she clarified, "on all servers, at any level of clearance."

Doug's thin lips tightened even further. He looked as grim as she'd ever seen him. He rose and strode to his desk, slipping out of his suit coat and draping it over the back of his executive chair. Pulling his laptop from his desk, he brought it back to them and opened up a document showing a line-and-block diagram of the IT division, complete with photographs of each employee. He studied it. Lark tried to view it upside down without success.

Doug spun the laptop around so she could see it. "Do you know them well?" he asked, pointing to the three assigned to Identity & Access Management.

She thought about it. "Actually, no. I don't know that one at all. The other two, Georgie and Oliver, hang around Jocelyn a lot, but a lot of the drooling idiots do. I mean, the very professional and respected men in this field office."

Doug chuckled tiredly. "Yeah, but that's a problem for another day. All right. I'll call Georgie. He's too new to be involved in this, whatever 'this' is. You'll have access by the time you get back to your desk."

"Thanks."

"Keep me posted. And don't talk about this with anyone outside this room."

"Of course not."

"I know, but it had to be said. Gentlemen, would you stay behind for a moment?"

Lark slipped from the room. As if on cue, her stomach growled. Now that she thought about it, she'd missed lunch. She swung by her desk to grab her purse, then headed to the elevators. There was a bagel place just outside the One Center Plaza entrance. Should she wait for Mace? Her stomach rumbled again. Nah. He was busy plotting supersoldier stuff. She could slip in and out again without anyone the wiser.

Half a dozen people waited in line, but she didn't mind. The walk, however brief, cleared her head and readied her for her next challenge. When she reached the counter, she gave her order, then waited impatiently while a slow-as-shit teenager prepared it. How long could it possibly take to spread some peanut butter on a pumpernickel bagel? She nearly snatched the bag from him, turning to go just as her cell phone rang.

"Center of the universe; God speaking." She unwrapped her bagel one-handed, pressing the phone to her ear with the other.

"Hey. It's, uh, Elliott."

Lark took a huge bite, mumbling around the peanut butter. "Hey ho. Wasn't expecting to hear from you."

"I, uh, wanted to know if you've traced the IP addresses yet."

She ducked off to one side and leaned against a bike rack, licking peanut butter from her thumb. "Why? It hasn't even been two days."

"Maybe you need some help? I could do something to help."

Her brows wrinkled, dread starting to curl in her gut. She

dropped the bagel back into the bag. "What's going on, Elliott? Is . . . is he asking for an update? Is that what this call is about?"

"Well . . . yeah."

"Shit. He gave me more time. What's wrong?"

"I don't know. He wanted me to call you; I don't know why. It doesn't pay to ask a lot of questions."

"He's your father?"

"My uncle."

"I'm so sorry," Lark said, sympathy tugging at her. "Sometimes families just blow chunks of pig's feet. Elliott, you seem like a nice guy. How come you don't just bail?"

Elliott's bitterness poured through her ear. "I've done things. I work for him. He owns me, Hadley."

"Just Lark, please. And why? Just because he's your uncle? What would he do if you just left? Like, just disappeared."

Elliott's voice dropped to a whisper. "He'd send Palachka after me."

Lark recoiled, gulped, and reflexively checked her finger to make sure it was still attached. "He doesn't even seem to like you very much."

"Yeah, I'm not his favorite. But I'm family, and he promised my mom he'd take care of me. So we're trapped together in this suckfest."

"I'm really sorry."

"The code?" he said again. "How far have you gotten?"

She started to blurt out that she'd found Sokolov's missing money, but some instinct made her hesitate. "I'm on it," she said instead. "I'll make his deadline."

"Really?" His voice lifted in surprise. "I thought, well, I mean . . . I thought you'd have it figured out, or at least be close?"

Lark settled her backside more firmly against the bike rack, shifting a leg to rest behind her on a metal rung. "Let's lay it on the line, Elliott. You knew from the start what I would find. How?"

"Um, well, I really didn't . . ."

"Elliott, you all but told me the FBI framed me for the theft. Come on. I'm not stupid. You'd already traced the money. You knew exactly what I'd find. Why the subterfuge? Why not just tell me and save us both some time?"

He hesitated so long she checked to see if they were still connected. "Well?"

"The theft happened on one of my accounts. He was so pissed, I just couldn't—" His voice broke. "I try my best, but . . . he's a monster."

Lark felt a burn of fury, her voice rising several octaves. "So you set me up? You knew what he might do, you son of a bitch!"

"I'm sorry," he said. "I'm really, really . . ."

"Thanks for calling." She thumbed her phone off, all sympathy for Elliott erased. She dropped her half-eaten bagel into the trash, making a mental note to relay the conversation to Mace.

She'd stopped shaking with anger by the time she reached her cubicle. Mace was pacing back and forth in front of it. When he saw her, his face cleared in relief, then darkened with ire. *Uh-oh.*

"Where did you go?" he asked, obviously struggling to keep his voice level. "I couldn't find you."

She edged around him and tucked her purse into the bottom drawer. "I grabbed a bagel."

"Outside?"

"Well, yes. That's where they sell bagels."

He moved closer, settling his hands onto her shoulders. "Lark, I can't protect you if I'm not with you. You worried me."

"I'm safe enough, Mace. I found his money. Also, I had a chat with the asshat who gave me the thumb drive." She laid it out for him. "The only explanation is that they have someone inside who's been feeding them info."

Unsurprisingly, he was pissed. When he started swearing in Cajun, she laughed, feeling better. "You're pretty good at that cussing thing."

"Lots of practice. What's next on your agenda?"

"Search for the code the hacker who framed me used. And I might as well finish up the malware project."

Mace released her, but slipped his hand into hers as they walked down to the SCIF. Something bumped in her chest. Good grief. Had her heart really just skipped a beat? She twined her fingers around his, feeling suddenly cheerful.

"Are you going to sit and watch me again?" she asked, setting her phone into the lockbox.

"Not this time, enjoyable as it is. I need to go meet Jace and the team. But I'll be back in an hour or so."

"Okie doke." She entered the SCIF and stopped, leaning back against the door. She enjoyed being with him. Sure, she wanted to jump him, but beyond her hormones, the truth was that she liked him.

Familiar doubt tugged at her. Her former fiancé, Ralph Pearson, had soured her on the idea of anything permanent with a man. He had tried to change her, just as her parents had, into a useless, pampered poodle whose sole job was to see and be seen. No, thanks.

Mace seemed different. He followed her convoluted thought process, had accepted all her weirdness, and had missed her when she stepped out to buy a bagel.

Someone pushed open the SCIF's door, bumping it against her back. Muttering an apology, she power-walked down to her workstation and plopped into the chair.

All right. Time to work.

True to his word, Doug had given her complete access to the field office's networks. She set up a search string using the code Elliott had provided.

"Go forth and find my nemesis," she said to the screen.

Since the search could take hours, she turned her attention to her original assignment, figuring out what the malware program had been designed to do. Within moments, she became absorbed in examining the various windows popping up all over the monitor, some of which continuously scrolled data. She poked and prodded at the data, parsing it out in different ways, following where it led until she found what she sought.

"Hmm." She traced the lines of code with a finger on the screen. It looked like a VPN tunnel, a secure link between two computers. But the infected server managed a slew of virtual machines. Why would someone bury a virtual private network on a server designed to run virtual private networks?

The government and businesses used VPNs all the time. It allowed employees to connect securely to their work computers as though they sat at their desks. Employees who worked remotely or traveled a lot relied on them for continued productivity while away from the office. Creating a separate tunnel within the server, though, hid its existence entirely.

The twenty-four-thousand-dollar question was, where did the VPN tunnel into?

Lark moved her finger down the code and stopped a few lines later. Her brows knitted as she studied the unique string of characters identifying the piece of hardware at the other end of the tunnel. It took her only moments to check the network diagram and find the information she needed.

She sat back, swiveled her chair, and looked at the locked and barred gate to the secure server room that ran the network for the SCIF. Her brain fuzzed gray as her body chilled and numbed, her limbs suddenly as heavy as cement. Her mind grappled unsuccessfully to process what she'd just learned. No way. Absolutely no way.

She needed to find Mace.

No, Doug first. As loathe as she was to add to his troubles, this could not wait. She headed for the front of the SCIF and grabbed one of the secure telephones.

"Huckabee."

She unstuck her tongue from the roof of her dry mouth. "Sir, it's Lark. I, uh, need you to come to the SCIF."

"Can't it wait? I'm up to my ass in alligators."

She swallowed hard. "I don't think so. It's pretty important."

His sigh echoed down the line. "All right. Give me ten minutes."

Lark spent the time pacing back and forth in the enclosed space, earning her covert glances from the other employees working there. When he finally appeared, Mace walked at his side, and tears sprang to her eyes with relief at seeing him. She pounced on them and very nearly dragged Doug back to her workstation.

"Okay, okay," Doug said, disengaging his arm. He looked worn out. "I'm here. What's the latest emergency?"

"I know it's not the nuke, sir, but I found what seems to be an intentional data leak inside the SCIF." She spoke so fast her words ran together.

Huckabee stared at her blankly. "Excuse me?"

She shifted from foot to foot, hating her unwelcome news. "I think someone is transmitting classified information out of the SCIF," she clarified. "Using a piece of unauthorized equipment."

Mace's gaze snapped around to her face, staring hard at her.

"The hell you say." Doug sat down hard. "The hits just keep coming. What the hell is going on? Is Saturn in retrograde and no one told me?"

"I thought you should know right away."

"I'll have a heart attack before this is all over. Bring me up to speed."

Lark clasped her hands together. "Remember you assigned me to deconstruct a piece of malware that a security scan detected? The infected server wasn't located here in the SCIF. It was just a regular, average server running virtual machines. No big deal."

"Virtual machines?"

"Like, when you log onto your desktop computer. You put in your user ID and password, right? But when you do that and your desktop appears, it's not actually in your office. It's on one of these servers in the datacenter. It's set up that way so the systems administrators don't have to physically install hardware or software on each and every computer in this building, which would require like a hundred more SysAds and cost a bazillion more dollars. But to you, it looks and acts exactly like your own desktop."

"Got it."

"So the malware program opened up a portal linking the virtual server to a second server. That second server is behind that door." She nodded to the locked room.

Huckabee stared at the gate across the door. "No data can leave here via computer. The SCIF has a standalone network."

"I know." Lark took a deep, fortifying breath. "SCIF servers don't have any way to connect to any computer outside of this room." Lark couldn't stop her head from shaking from side to side, denying what she was about to say, as though not speaking the words made the whole shebang untrue. "What I'm saying is that someone physically accessed this server room and installed an illegal router."

"Terrific." Huckabee grimaced. "Son of a *bitch*."

"Maybe Saturn has a big brother that's also in retrograde," she said. Her joke fell flat. Looking at the floor, she said, "I'm sorry, Doug. Based on the evidence I uncovered by deconstructing this piece of malware, I think someone—or maybe more than one person—is stealing classified information from our top secret facility."

"Are you sure—and I mean, absolutely certain—that what you're saying is accurate? Is there a way it could be anything else? *Anything* else?"

"No, sir. I know what I'm saying. I'm talking about espionage."

Chapter 30

Monday, February 20. 3:00 p.m.
Otis Fitch's Property. Ducard, Massachusetts.

FATIANOVA HURLED HER whiskey glass across the room. It hit the wall and shattered, shards of glass splintering in all directions. Liquid trickled down the fake paneling.

"Goddamned Americans," she hissed. "You can't trust a one of them. How did these cheating bastards ever manage to win the Cold War?"

Fyodor paced, wringing his hands. "How could you be so stupid? That skinhead played you. I knew we couldn't count on him."

She whirled on him, fury pouring from her like a living force. He took a step back. "Me? You found him in the first place. You negotiated with him, remember?"

She'd transferred twenty-five thousand dollars into his bank account, as agreed. But Otis Fitch hadn't brought her the package.

Instead, he'd been conveniently unavailable all morning, out hunting with his men. She'd arranged for the auction to take place in three days, aboard a yacht she'd chartered back in Boston. If she had nothing to sell, all her plans would come to naught.

She stomped across the driveway to the main house, bursting in without knocking. The pregnant woman jerked back, startled, and dropped her broom and dustpan. Fatianova brushed past her, stalking to the office door and jerking it open, her fingers shaking with anger. As expected, Otis had not gone hunting. He looked up from a ledger and set down his pen, leaning back to gaze at them.

"Oh, it's you." He sounded anything but welcoming. "What do you want?"

"Mr. Fitch, we're ready to drive back to Boston," she said through gritted teeth. "Please load my crate onto the truck so we can leave."

Otis shrugged. "Ain't no one here to carry it. My men are out hunting—"

"Cut the bullshit," she interrupted. "We had a bargain. I paid you; now you bring me what you promised."

Otis's eyes turned glacial. "All right. No bullshit. Seems you lied to me, honey. And I don't take well to being clowned."

Fatianova flashed hot, then cold. He couldn't have opened the crate. Could he? "I didn't lie. The device is very sensitive."

"Well, then," he drawled, "that would be the only thing you told the truth about. See, you met my price way too easy. Got me thinking. I'm figuring that thing—which ain't any medical equipment—is worth a whole lot more greenbacks than I first thought."

She rubbed her temples, feeling a raging headache starting. "I'm willing to renegotiate your fee."

"Ain't no need. I got my own science guy. He took a peek under the hood, and guess what he found? An itty-bitty nuclear bomb. How about that?"

"Look, Mr. Fitch. Otis. That device is useless to you. How about if I cut you in on the profit when I sell it? Ten percent, perhaps?"

He smiled, though to Fatianova it looked more like baring his teeth. "Yeah, that's a fuckton of bills. I bet that thing would go for ten, fifteen mil easy."

More like thirty million, but she didn't correct him. "So your cut would be a million dollars, at a minimum. With that kind of capital, you could go anywhere, be anything you want. Buy a yacht and go fishing every day. Travel the world. Retire."

He twitched a shoulder, as though ridding himself of a fly. "See, that ain't in the cards. 'Cause I got me another idea. We got land here, 'bout sixty acres. Belonged to my pappy, and to his before that. And as more folks see the light, my crew's gettin' bigger. The kind of money you're talking about could buy me more land, and all the guns and ammo I need to defend it. No one would fuck with us."

"Then what's the problem?"

He cracked his neck, then exposed his teeth again. "No one would fuck with us even more if we was a nuclear power."

She stared at him, shocked. "You can't be serious."

"As a heart attack, honey. Keep the government wolves from my door. Might even secede. Be our own autonomous country."

Fatianova couldn't wrap her head around his revelation. "Why on earth would you want that? You live in a democratic republic. Your rights come from your Constitution. You're already free."

"I said autonomous. We could run our own damned lives. We could stop the corrupt government from stealing our money through taxes, from trying to take our guns away, from so many regulations nothing ever gets done. The nation going to hell."

She pressed her fingertips to her forehead and massaged there.

"You've got to be kidding me. This is about your reckless political agenda? You're stealing my property because you hate your government?"

"Seems you stole it first, honey."

Arguing with him about his radical ideology would waste time she didn't have. So would begging him. Otis Fitch had somehow deluded himself into believing the government wouldn't storm his walls en masse to retrieve a stolen nuclear weapon.

"When you come to your senses and realize you'll destroy everything you've built if you go down this path, call me," she said. "Your government will never let you to keep it. They'll crush you."

"Buh-bye."

She had no choice but to depart, fuming, the tires spinning in the snow as she stomped on the accelerator. As she and Fyodor drove back to civilization, she searched desperately for a way to salvage the situation. Get her money so she could retire in luxury. Proceed with the auction, and take her bidders for all she could.

For a product she no longer had.

Chapter 31

Monday, February 20. 2:35 p.m.
FBI Field Office. Boston, Massachusetts.

"ESPIONAGE," LARK SAID again. "That's what I'm talking about. The Big *E*. The *do-not-pass-Go, go-directly-to-jail Big E*."

What the hell? Mace folded his arms across his chest, listening with the same intensity as Doug Huckabee.

Lark jabbed a finger at one of the open windows on the monitor. "Think of a server as just a computer that can do complicated stuff. The malware connects the two servers, so you can look at information on either one just like opening up any old window. And this bit here tells the connection to shut down and erase itself from the logs after three minutes. So whatever information or documents are being stolen, when the log gets erased, there's no record of the transfer ever happening."

"Okay," Doug said in a resigned tone. "How was it done?"

Lark's shoulders drooped, eyes closing in misery. "There's only one way. Bypass the SCIF's firewall. And the only way to do that is to physically install a router inside the SCIF's server room."

He followed her gaze to the server room. "Who has the combination? We need to get in there."

She tugged at an earlobe, shoulders tensing as she rose. "It'll say on the door."

The three of them trooped over to the cypher-locked gate. Sure enough, a small frame mounted beside the entrance held a printed piece of paper with several names and phone numbers.

"I'll call IT and tell them to send down whoever has that goddamned combination." Doug headed toward the front of the room and the telephones.

"Who has both the knowledge and the access to do something like this?" Mace asked.

Lark looked doubtfully at the server room. "A network architect could do it. Servers need love, same as any computer."

"Who else?"

Lark's eyes lit up. "I have an idea. I retrieved some text from the binary file . . . oh, forget it. Come with me."

She led the way back to the infected server, and sat down in the driver's seat. The cleaned-up text still showed on the monitor.

"The malware program only ran when told to," she said, fingers flying over the keyboard as she typed in commands, "and then erased all records of having established the link between the two servers. What I'm doing is looking to see who was logged onto the infected server during the times the malware ran, so I can cross-reference the two."

Mace sat down close to her and put a steadying hand on her knee. "How long will it take to do that?"

"Zero-point-zero seconds. I have it."

He chuckled. "Damn, you're good."

The compliment warmed her. "I found a bogus account. Leonard Rose."

"What did poor Leonard ever do to you?"

She grinned. "I'll bet you a million dollars there's no employee by that name."

"Why not?" Mace asked.

"Because Leonard Rose is a famous hacker from the '80s, the Einstein behind a group called the Legion of Doom," Lark said. "I mean, I could be wrong. But I'm not."

"So someone created a false identity?"

"Yes. And that answers another question. When I first looked at the malware, I noticed a clocking anomaly; the server's clock was off by thirty minutes. It was a deliberate time-sync error."

"English, please?" Mace said.

Lark craned her neck around to peer at him. "Every computer, every server, every router on a network pings a centralized spot to get the right time. Like back when dinosaurs roamed the earth, you could call a number and it would tell you, 'the time is now four o'clock. *Beep*.' This server, this infected server, thinks the time is thirty minutes into the future. When he steals the classified documents, the server logs an incorrect time of access, giving him an alibi. Clever. I have the bogus account, but not who's really behind the thefts."

"Okay. Deliberate time-sync error. Got it."

Doug and a young man she didn't recognize walked back to the gated server room, so she and Mace joined them.

"Go ahead and open the room up, son," Doug said. The man

entered a code on the cypher pad, and the gate swung open. As he made to step inside, Huckabee raised two fingers. "That's all we needed. You can head on back upstairs now. Thanks a bunch."

The three of them trooped inside the server room, dwarfing the small space. Four metal shelves in the middle of the floor housed eight stacked servers each. Dozens of blue cables had been plugged into the backs of the servers.

"We're looking for a small rectangle with flashing lights," Lark said.

Without further ado, they spread out, searching.

"Got it," Mace said, his height giving him a perspective she lacked.

"Careful," Doug barked. "We'll need any fingerprints intact."

Mace carefully disentangled the black Cisco router, holding it by the corners. Doug came over, shaking out a handkerchief and using it as he unplugged the power cord and disconnected the Ethernet cable.

"I'm officially taking possession of this device," he said. "I'll store it in my safe until the investigative team arrives. Good work, guys."

Lark blew out a relieved breath as they left the server room. Even though they didn't know who the spy was, they had at least stopped him cold.

Mace followed Lark as she logged off the workstation and headed to the other end of the building to grab her purse. She couldn't remember a time she'd been so glad to leave work. The whole day had been one big roller coaster ride, and her brain had turned to mush.

"We're calling it a day," he said into his phone. "Be down in five. Meet us in front, all right?" He wrapped an arm around Lark's shoulders as they entered the elevator. "Rough day at the office, huh?"

Laughter bubbled up from her throat and spilled forth. "You could say that, yeah. It was a shitfest filled to the brim with endless puddles of shit."

They pushed through the revolving doors, both scanning the area around them. Lark didn't see anything unusual. The team's rental idled at the curb, Alex behind the wheel.

"Everything's been quiet," Tag said, opening the back door for Lark.

A dark green Ford Explorer pulled in beside the rental, effectively pinning Alex inside. Mace whipped his handgun out and aimed across the roof before Lark became aware he'd moved.

"Get down," Tag snapped, shoving Lark hard between the shoulder blades. She sprawled across the backseat, fear spiking through her system. He placed himself between her and the threat as Alex scrambled over the center console and out the passenger door, crouching behind the engine block as they, too, drew guns.

Iggy and the other man who'd taken her to see Viktor Sokolov jumped out of the SUV. Iggy lifted the muzzle of a shotgun, pumping it and leveling it at Tag. The other slapped a formidable-looking rifle against his shoulder, finger on the trigger.

All five shooters froze, trapped in a Mexican standoff.

Chapter 32

LARK CROUCHED INSIDE the car, heart thundering in her chest as the two groups squared off with one another. At least no one was shooting yet.

"Put down your weapons," Mace ordered, voice tight with tension. "And get the fuck out of here."

She peeked out the window. A stretch limousine eased in behind the truck. A thickset man with the bulbous nose and cheeks ruddy from alcohol abuse strolled over. She recognized Roman Vetrov, known as Palachka, from Mr. Sokolov's home office. He ignored all of the firepower, leaning down to squint into the rental sedan's back seat, then rapped on the window.

"Who the fuck are you?" Mace snarled. "Get away from her."

Palachka watched her with his creepy flat stare, then knocked again. She eased across the backseat and lowered the window.

"Mr. Sokolov would like a word," he said, jerking his head toward the limousine.

"She's not going anywhere with you," Tag growled.

The tension, already high, ratcheted up a few notches. Someone would start shooting, and she couldn't bear to see Mace, or any of them, shot because of her.

"Wait," she said, struggling back across the seat. She pushed against Tag's legs to get him to move aside, but he didn't budge. "Everyone, calm down. He just wants to talk. Right?"

Palachka shifted his cold eyes around, seemingly taking in the tableau for the first time. He flicked a finger. His two henchmen lowered their weapons a fraction. None of the others so much as twitched.

"Tag, please."

He still didn't move. Lark finally resorted to climbing over the seat and exiting through the front passenger door. Mace held out a hand, preventing her from going any farther.

"No way," he said.

"Will you guarantee my safety?" she asked Palachka.

He rested his reptile gaze on her. "Mr. Sokolov wants to talk to you. That's all. You won't be harmed. At this time."

She took a deep breath. "All right. I'll talk to him."

Palachka swept a hand toward the limousine. "He's waiting."

She took a step away from Mace. He grabbed her shoulder, stopping her.

"You're not going in there alone."

Lark managed a wan smile. "I'm not sure we really have much choice."

"I'm going with her," Mace said directly to Palachka. "Otherwise, this doesn't happen."

Palachka shrugged. "Leave your weapons. The rest of you stay here with my men."

Mace shared a look with Alex and Tag. Some sort of understanding passed between them. He set his gun on the hood of the car, then followed Palachka down to the limousine, keeping Lark behind him. The driver hopped out and opened the back door. Lark hesitated, remembering Sokolov's casual cruelty, but if she didn't speak with him, violence would follow. She stepped inside.

"Holy shit!" The limo was straight out of a Hollywood movie. Two bars illuminated by purple lighting lined each side of the interior. The ten feet of the limo's length separated posh leather seats front and back. Two flat screen televisions and a skylight completed the decor. "You could live in this thing."

Viktor Sokolov sat in the rear, a laptop and file folders on the seat next to him. Today he wore a custom-tailored navy suit with a steel blue–striped tie. He took off his reading glasses and set aside an overflowing binder. "It suits my needs. We need to talk."

She and Mace seated themselves side by side. Tension radiated from him through the arm touching hers.

"All right." Her mouth was as dry as the moon, stomach quivering. "You could've just called me. With all the shit you know about me, I'm sure you have my cell number."

"I find face-to-face meetings more productive. What progress have you made?"

"I still have more time."

He just looked at her. "I'll ask you again. Where's my money?"

Chills swept through her body, raising goose bumps on her arms. "You know? How do you know? I didn't tell Elliot that."

He ignored her question. "You found my money."

"Yeah. But how do you know that?"

A brief frown crossed his features. "Elliott seemed to feel you'd made more progress than you let on. Guess even a broken watch is right twice a day. Why haven't you transferred the funds back to my account?"

Until that very moment, she hadn't known what she intended to do. She worked some moisture into her mouth. Even then, she had to force the words from her parched throat.

"I'm not giving it back."

Anger tightened his eyes and flattened his mouth. "What did you say?"

Mace froze beside her. She felt his tension, his worry for her. He didn't say a word, though, thank God.

Mustering every ounce of courage she possessed, she repeated her death sentence. "I won't give you the money back."

The threat to her mattered little compared to the threat to the population if Sokolov got his hands on the nuclear bomb, no matter how small it was compared to its grown-up cousins.

"Why the fuck not?" Mr. Sokolov's eyes had gone glacier cold. "Are you really this stupid? Do I need to remind you what will happen if you don't?"

She swallowed so hard it hurt. "I know what you're planning to do with it. You're bidding on a suitcase bomb. A nuke. I won't risk American lives. I just won't."

She'd surprised him; she could tell by the very stillness of his face. He scrutinized her from head to toe, taking her measure. She forced herself not to squirm.

"I got a bedtime story for you, little girl," he said at last. Her breath escaped in an audible whoosh. At least he hadn't whipped out a gun and shot them right then and there. Still, she knew she'd put herself and Mace in very real danger.

"You know who Lucky Luciano was?"

"Sure. He was a mobster. Everyone knows that."

Mr. Sokolov fingered the bridge of his crooked nose. "He took the small gangs of New York and created one organized mob. He controlled them because they were afraid of him."

Lark shivered. "You made your point last time, Mr. Sokolov. You don't need to threaten me."

"Then why are we talking here?" He glared at her. "Lucky Luciano was prosecuted and jailed in the midthirties, but he still ran his businesses from inside prison."

"You mean he bribed people to help him."

"I *mean*," Sokolov said, "that he kept control of the New York families."

"So what are you saying? That even if you're sent to prison, you can still have me killed?"

"Yes. But that's not my point. Shut up and listen before I decide you're not worth my time."

"Okie doke." She wished she felt as confident as she sounded. Where was he going with all this, if not to threaten her?

"World War II broke out while Luciano was inside. The Japs attacked Pearl Harbor, then the USS *Lafayette* caught fire on a New York dock, supposedly sabotaged by German spies. The Navy feared more spies would get in through the docks, which were controlled by mob-organized unions. They approached Luciano and asked him to protect the docks from our enemies."

Interested despite herself, Lark said, "He agreed?"

Mr. Sokolov nodded. "He said yes, not only to providing security at the docks, but he also promised there wouldn't be any union strikes as long as the war lasted. Then he went even further; he provided intelligence to the US government."

"How? Why? What did he get out of it? Did the government pay him?"

"No, he wasn't paid. When World War II ended, he was released from prison and went home to Sicily. That's all. That was it. That was the deal."

"So he did it out of self-interest. For a Get Out of Jail Free card."

Mr. Sokolov undid the top button of his shirt and tugged his tie loose. "Christ. You're a goddamned mouthy bitch, you know that? You remind me of my fucking useless nephew."

Lark flinched, a hand rising to touch the cheek where he'd hit her, reminded of the similar bruise on Elliott's face. "Sorry. I'll be quiet."

"You do that. What I'm trying to tell you is that Luciano was an American. He loved his country as much as anyone else. Why wouldn't he pull whatever strings he could to help win the war?"

Lark laughed, forgetting she'd just promised to shut up. "Are you seriously trying to tell me that a man who made his living screwing over the government would suddenly start working for them?"

Mr. Sokolov didn't smile. "Why can't a mobster be a patriot?"

The thought stopped her cold. Was he seriously saying . . . ?

Mace shifted restlessly beside her. She put a hand on his knee. He stilled.

"Are you trying to tell me you're a patriot?" She couldn't help the sarcastic tinge to her voice. "Am I supposed to swallow that crock of shit?"

"I don't give a fuck either way. Yes, I intend to bid on the nuke. And I intend to win. And when it's safely in my hands, I can personally ensure it's never used on American soil."

"Seriously?"

He smiled faintly. "As a heart attack."

Lark scrubbed both hands down her face before dropping

them back into her lap. "Okay. Let's say I believe you. Which I don't. Maybe. I mean, you have to admit it sounds pretty far-fetched, right?"

"Your opinion means shit to me, mouthy girl. But that's the way it is."

Unable to help herself, Lark twisted her head to look at Mace. "What do you think?"

"I think he's a criminal who threatened to kill you. I wouldn't trust him to tell me rain is wet."

"Well, yeah, there's that."

Sokolov ignored Mace. "Elliott tells me the girl who hacked a nuclear power plant just to help them tighten their security has principles. You've shown me here you have a strong moral compass and a lot of courage. I respect those things."

Lark crossed her arms and legs. "Even if I wanted to help you, I don't think I can. I used FBI resources to track down your fifty mil. The FBI has control of it now. I seriously doubt they'll give it back just 'cause I ask nicely."

"Find a way."

She pressed her lips together and relaxed them. "What if the government just seizes it? I think that's a lot more likely to happen."

"They have no justification to do that."

"Um. So, say you buy the nuke. You say you won't use it; but what will you do with it?"

He didn't hesitate. "I'll sell it. To Iran or Syria or back to Russia. I don't care, as long as it's not used in the United States."

"No. Not acceptable. How do you know they won't just smuggle it right back in?"

"It's unlikely."

"But possible." She thought for a minute. "What about this.

Lucky Luciano helped out during World War II, you said, by handing over information about German spies. You want to help now by stopping the nuke from being used. So do we. Why don't we team up?"

His brows knit. "What do you have in mind?"

"Well, you're one of the bidders, right? So let the FBI or whoever go to the auction with you. We get everyone in one room and arrest them all. Except you, of course. The government seizes the nuke and dismantles it. That way, no one can use it."

Mr. Sokolov leaned forward and took a bottle of water from the bar. "One way or another, my money will be returned to me."

Lark saw another bottle near her. She snagged it and twisted off the cap, taking several long gulps. "I just saved you fifty mil. Pretty cool, huh?"

Sokolov gave her a quizzical look. "You're . . . unique, aren't you?"

She looked down at her lap. Was that a compliment? "I have no authority to make any deals with you; you know that, right?"

He nodded. "You're a junior cyber scientist with barely five months with the FBI. If you'd told me you could, I'd've killed you."

Mace tensed, and she had the sense he was about to fling himself across the limousine and choke Sokolov. Lark put her hand on his arm, trying to make him sit back. He didn't budge, muscles gathered to leap. Sokolov reached into his suit jacket and brought out a small revolver.

"Sit. Stay," he snapped.

Lark took several careful breaths. The tension in the small space had skyrocketed. "Mace. Stop. Please."

Mace rubbed a hand over his jaw, then slowly, too slowly, settled back in the seat.

"It's fine," she lied. Everyone in the limo knew she lied. The smallest misstep would still get them killed, and she felt so far out of her depth she might drown. "Everything's fine."

"Put away your peashooter, or this conversation is over," Mace growled.

Sokolov sneered, but slipped the revolver back inside his jacket. "Muzzle your dog, mouthy girl."

Lark decided the best option was to ignore the confrontation. "Mr. Sokolov, what if you give us what you know about the bidders? Like, who, and where you're meeting, or how the auction's going to be handled. Is it anonymously online? Face-to-face auction? What?"

"And in return?"

"I do my level best to get the FBI to return your money. No promises, but I'll give it my best shot. We arrest everyone and sort it out later."

Sokolov stretched out his legs. "In my experience, the government is real good at fucking up operations like this. I can't take that chance."

"You won't back out of the auction, you mean?"

"Yeah. Here's my deal," he said. "Take it or leave it. I'll tell you who, when and where. On condition of complete immunity from prosecution. I want it all in writing."

Who would even have the authority to make this deal? Someone probably higher up the food chain than Doug Huckabee. "I'll find someone."

"You do that. One more thing. You'll be coming with me, mouthy girl. As insurance in case something goes wrong."

"Um." Lark's mind went blank. "What? No. I'm not an agent or anything. I'm just a computer scientist."

"Take it or leave it," he said again. He plucked a business card from his breast pocket and held it out to her. "Once you have everything in order, contact me directly."

She leaned forward to take the card. "I'm all over this."

"Then get the hell out of my car."

Chapter 33

MACE TURNED TO help Lark out of the limousine, glad to leave Sokolov's forceful presence. A mobster who was a loyal patriot? Who only wanted the nuke to keep other criminals from using it?

Give me a break.

No one outside had moved, but he hadn't expected them to. His men wouldn't leave Lark unprotected, no matter the cost. The heavyset man with the dead eyes and ruddy cheeks who'd tapped on Lark's window still stood by the limousine, hands in his pockets. When he saw them, he snapped his fingers toward his two goons.

"Let's go."

The two men backed away from Alex and Tag. When they reached the truck, they lowered their weapons. Everyone climbed into their respective vehicles and pulled away.

Alex and Tag holstered their semiautomatics. Alex brought Mace's Browning to him.

"What happened?" Tag asked.

"I think Lark just made a deal with the devil," Mace said.

Lark turned to him. "Thank you."

"For what?" He looked down at her, knowing she could see the worry in his eyes.

"For not, you know. Being all macho and shit. Not trying to talk over me or take over. Except for that last bit, you were great."

A smile flickered and vanished. "You were handling it."

"Most alpha males wouldn't have been able to help being sexist jerks." She touched his forearm, stroking down until she held his hand. "I think I just fell in love with you a little bit."

The smile returned, this time making his eyes twinkle and his heart beat harder. "Just a little?"

"Ugh! Men." She released his palm and punched him in the arm instead. "I'm trying to say thank you, you jerk."

Alex laughed. "So what's the deal? And who's the devil?"

Mace filled them in. Alex gave a slow whistle.

"You can all go home," Lark said. "I need to go brief Doug. Again."

"We'll stay," Tag said at once. Alex nodded.

"No need," she said. "I'm in no danger from Mr. Sokolov."

"We'll wait," Mace said, using his firm "I'm-not-budging" tone.

"For fuck's sake. Fine. But you're wasting time with me when you could be polishing your guns or something." She walked to the revolving door and reentered One Center Plaza.

Mace turned to his teammates. "She's right that there's no immediate threat from Sokolov. I need to brief all of you on some developments, though. We should all meet—"

His phone chirped. Two seconds later, Tag and Alex's rang as well.

"Shit," he said. "I think we just went operational."

He put his phone on speaker. "Jace, you got me, Tag, and Alex."

"No, we're not operational yet," Jace said immediately. "However, unless there's a critical need for you at the FBI, the joint task force is meeting at our new base of operations." He rattled off an address, which Alex wrote on his hand. "Best if you can meet us here while we sort through our options."

He hated leaving Lark alone. She was still in danger from whoever engineered the mob theft in the first place, but he was a special operator, and it was time for him to do his job.

"Alex, you drive," he ordered, jumping into the passenger seat. Tag climbed into the back. Mace thumbed to the right app and typed a message to Lark.

Duty calls.

He fidgeted as he waited for her response.

B careful.

Bank on it, little bird.

"Fill us in. What developments?" Tag asked.

As they drove, he filled them in on the infected server, the suspected espionage, and the rogue router. When he finished, his friends stayed dead quiet. Unexpectedly, Alex began to crack up. In fact, he laughed so hard he convulsed and the car swerved. He corrected his course, but continued to snicker. It pulled a reluctant smile from Mace.

"What the fuck's so funny, dickhead?" Tag asked. "This is serious shit."

Alex guffawed. "Do you remember why we came to Massachusetts in the first place? Anyone? To find a nuke. Remember that?"

Mace cast him an exasperated look. "So what?"

"Nothing. If looking for a nuclear bomb leads to spying, FBI cover-ups, stolen millions and a pissed-off mob boss, hell, I'm all in. It's just another Tuesday, right?"

"I guess you've got a point. This got complicated fast."

"She'll be fine," Tag said, reading his expression. "She's smart. She'll be careful."

"Yeah."

All too soon, they pulled into a split-level clapboard and red brick house in the Boston suburb of Melrose. The bay window at the bottom didn't offset the plain white boards or insipid blue shutters. An American flag hung tiredly atop the garage. The houses to either side were much larger, nicer, and separated from them by mature trees, which would at least give them some privacy from nosy neighbors.

Alex parked on the street since four cars already choked the drive. Jace opened the front door before they even reached it, glancing up and down the street as he gestured them inside.

"You made good time," he said. "We're still setting up."

"What is this place?" Alex asked.

"Former FBI safe house. Our base of operations until we recover Fatianova Uvarov." He shut the door behind them and locked it.

Mace looked around. The house had an open floor plan; instead of doors, simple arches separated one area from another. From the front door, he had a clear view up the stairs in front of him, into the living room on his left, and the kitchen and dining rooms straight ahead.

"Your gear's stowed in the third bedroom upstairs," Jace said, jerking a thumb at the stairs. "The one with the black-and-white bedspread. We're all tripled up, so don't expect any privacy till this thing's done."

"Hope you packed a toothbrush, Mace," Alex said. "Your morning breath could be weaponized."

"Ha fucking ha. So can your farts."

The suburban house swarmed with warm bodies, between his own teammates, the FBI and DHS agents manning a line of computers on the dining room table, and the FBI SWAT agents cleaning weapons in the living room.

Shouting from a smaller room off the living room piqued his curiosity; he walked past the impressive array of artillery lying on the coffee table, floor, and across the two armless upholstered chairs, nodding a greeting to the agents.

"Welcome to the circus," one said, sliding a bore brush through the barrel of a disassembled M4 Carbine. "Ready for some fun?"

"Always." He took the step down that put him inside the TV room. Gavin Selle, Gabe, and Scott "Sandman" Griffin sat practically on top of one another on a couch. Gavin had a controller in his hands, gyrating it madly in a flat semicircle.

"Slow down! You're spilling it," Gabe said. He reached for the controller, which Gavin held out of reach. "You gotta get a good rhythm down."

The Sandman kicked Gavin's leg. "Let me. I watched my mother do it all the time."

"Hand it over, loser." Gabe lunged for the controller, using his body weight to pin Gavin in place and snatching it from his hands. The other two let out howls of protest. "Let an expert do it."

Mace glanced at the TV, then did a double take. A cartoon girl with huge manga eyes and a pink chef's hat clapped her hands to her face, round mouth opened in horror. The word *FAILED* was plastered across her yellow apron.

"What in God's name are you knuckleheads doing?"

Gabe pressed one of the triggers to restart . . . something. The cartoon girl's mouth tipped up in a beatific smile as she gave a thumbs-up. "You can do it!" she encouraged him.

"Making cupcakes," Gabe said. "Gavin keeps spilling the batter."

Mace stared at the TV, where Gabe carefully cracked three eggs and added them to a bowl. "Cupcakes."

Gavin snorted in disgust, using two hands to shove the Sandman. The other man barely shifted. "Only because you friggin' kept kicking me. Keep your goddamned feet on your own side of the cushions."

Gabe leaned forward, making the same back-and-forth semicircle Gavin had. On the screen, a floating spoon spun in a bowl, creating a smooth yellow batter.

"Even better than Mama!" crowed the cartoon girl, hearts shining in her eyes.

"Ha!" He sat back, tossing the controller into Gavin's lap. "Owned, you sons of bitches."

Mace walked to the TV, where the empty video game case finally solved the mystery. "Cooking Mama. You're playing Cooking Mama?"

"Hey, you're blocking the TV." Gavin made a shooing gesture. "Outta my line of sight. I'm going to decorate the shit out of these cupcakes."

Shaking his head, Mace wandered into the kitchen, joining

Jace, Ken Acolatse, and Alex. Ken stirred a pot of delicious-smelling—and real—sauce.

"Spaghetti in twenty," he said. "Fifteen people will be hard to keep fed. We'll need to rotate kitchen duty."

"I counted twenty," Mace said. "Five SWAT, the DHS guy, four special agents, and us."

"SWAT's staying, but none of the other agents are," Jace said. "They're getting us intel."

The kitchen table was full, so Mace leaned against the refrigerator. All of the Delta Force operators knew how to cook; some were just better than others. He himself couldn't handle much more than the basics. However, he could concoct a kick-ass field stew made from nothing but edible and medicinal plants he found in whatever environment his team operated. Usually they tasted better with some rabbit or snake added.

"What do we have so far?" he asked.

Alex tipped his chair back on two legs and set a size twelve shoe on the table, crossing his other ankle over his knee. "This woman, Fatianova Uvarov—say that three times fast—is a no-shit nuclear physicist. Wicked smart. She works at the Kuznetsov Institute of Applied Nuclear Physics in Moscow, as the head of the team developing predictive analysis for core meltdowns."

Jace reached over and shoved Alex's foot off the table. "We're practicing our big boy manners today, young Padawan. People eat off this table."

The chair hit all four legs with a bang. Alex scrambled to uncross his legs. Completely unfazed, he continued talking. "What that means is that they plan for different reactor accident scenarios where the nuclear core overheats or is damaged. Like Three

Mile Island is about to blow again. How much radiation will be released, how far will it travel, and how badly will people be affected?"

"Okay, so she presumably has the knowledge to handle nuclear material. Do we know if she had access to nukes?" Mace asked.

"Stephanie believes she did, and I concur. Signals Intelligence tracked communications between her and another scientist by the name of Fyodor Petrov," Jace said. "They've been calling and texting regularly for the past eight months. He lives in Smolensk, Russia. Fatianova traveled there about five months ago, then went back again last month."

"What did they talk about?" Mace asked.

"It was all coded," Jace said. "SIGINT didn't prioritize it at the time, so we don't know. But—and this is a big but—turns out there's a nuclear graveyard outside of Lyubinsk, an hour by car from Moscow."

Alex stretched and stood, walking to the stove and grabbing the stirring spoon. "The FBI thinks that's where the mini-nuke came from."

Ken stopped measuring out pasta. "That spoon hits your lips, you hit the floor."

Alex grumbled, but set the spoon aside. He turned, resting his backside against the counter. "I'm starving. I haven't eaten in a week. Longer. I'm about to pass out from malnourishment."

"Quit yer whining," Ken said. "You ate lunch, same as the rest of us."

"I'm not sure Lazy Larry's Burgers qualifies as food."

Mace ignored them, moving away from the refrigerator to allow Ken to grab two potholders from atop it. "What makes the

FBI think the nuke came from this graveyard? Russia has, what, thirty? Forty of them?"

"A couple of things," Jace said. "Fatianova lives in Moscow, so it's close. Also, Stephanie dug up a news story in the *Moscow Times* about a couple bodies turning up dead on the installation last month. No one is admitting anything was stolen, though."

"Were they identified?"

"Yeah. They're just petty thieves. It's not a huge stretch to think Fatianova and Fyodor hatched this plan themselves, then eliminated the witnesses."

"So Fatianova somehow steals a suitcase nuke, smuggles it into the States, and is now auctioning it off? Is that about right?"

Ken used the mitts to pull a pan of meatballs from the oven. The rich scent made Mace's stomach rumble. "I think it's probably a lot more complicated than that."

"So last I heard, the only contact we had for her was an Outlook.com account. Where did all this new intel come from?"

Ken added the meatballs to the sauce while the pasta simmered. "The Special Agent in Charge of the Boston Field Office filed a warrant to get Microsoft to turn over their IP logs to the FBI. Then they hand-walked it over to the Outlook.com data center and stood on someone's desk until they got the files. That started a roll of information, most of which only came through in the past ninety minutes."

"Well, I can add a few details. Not about Fatianova, but about the bidders. I'm expecting some information from our friendly neighborhood mob boss."

Jace laughed. "Seriously? How'd you swing that?"

"Lark did. Assuming the FBI grants Viktor Sokolov immunity,

he'll give us the location of the auction, and whatever he knows about the other bidders."

The other operators stared at him in incredulity.

"This is the same guy who threatened to kill her, right?" Jace asked.

"Yeah."

"Remind me never to underestimate her."

Chapter 34

Tuesday, February 21. 10:00 a.m.
FBI Field Office. Boston, Massachusetts.

FROM HER WORKSTATION inside the SCIF, Lark fidgeted with her bracelet as she watched Doug talk with someone at the Department of Justice. She really needed to get back to her laptop to meet ChaosCowboy. Could she safely leave the SCIF?

"What's up?" Jocelyn asked.

"I'm not sure, but I have to go take care of something. Will you stay to see if Doug needs me for anything?"

"After this, everyone will know your name."

"I'm nothing special," Lark said, touching her throat in surprise at Jocelyn's sour tone. "Just another cog in the wheel."

Jocelyn shook her head, resentment flashing through her eyes. "Lark, you're working directly with the SAIC. The fucking Special Agent in Charge. In ten years, I've never done that. You, on the other hand, have in the space of four months worked on projects involving spying, nuclear bombs, and the theft of millions of dollars in mob money. Your career's made."

Lark cringed a little. "I didn't ask for any of this, I swear."

"I know. If anything, that makes it worse. Look," she said, "I came to the FBI the same way you did. I'm no rocket scientist, but I'm damned good at my job. Thanks to Melvin, I've never been recognized for any of it. If I'd been assigned the malware project, maybe I'd finally have gotten some acknowledgment. Maybe even a little appreciation."

Lark sat still as a stone, stunned. "I didn't know you felt that way."

"Yeah, well, you wouldn't. You're like a cross between Miss Mary Sunshine and a foulmouthed trucker. You see the good in everyone and everything. You always have, even when your life was damned near intolerable."

Lark tried to swallow the lump in her throat, chagrined and confused. "What do you even know about my life? You hint about things all the time you can't know anything about. What's with that?"

Jocelyn drummed her fingers against the desk, then pushed her chair back so she was even with Lark. "Because I do know, that's why."

"You looked in my file?" Indignation flared inside her. "What the fuck, Joss?"

The older woman sighed, flipping her waterfall of hair behind her shoulders with a practiced flick. "No. I didn't need to. I do know you, no matter what you may think. Look, right now you're supposed to meet someone in the darknet, right?"

Lark's mouth dropped open. "How do you know that?"

"Lark, when I say I came to the FBI the same way you did,

I mean exactly that. You got an immunity deal for putting your skills to use for the government. So did I."

"I had no idea," Lark said, biting her lip. "You were a white hat hacker, too?"

Jocelyn crossed her arms, shoulders so tight Lark thought they might shatter any minute. "More or less. I learned from Zane Quimby, if you want to know the truth. He taught me the ins and outs of systems exploitation."

Lark didn't know what to say. "Um, I bet he was a great teacher. He has mad skills."

"He's forgotten more than I'll ever know," Jocelyn said, staring down at her clasped hands. "And I, in turn, showed newbies around the computer underground."

"Okay," she said slowly. "I'm not sure where you're going with this, Joss."

Jocelyn took a deep breath. "They caught me, arrested me, ten years ago. Instead of prosecuting me, though, they made me the same offer they made you. Go legit, or go to jail. You remember when. After we hacked the Greensboro nuclear plant."

"What?" Lark shook her head to dispel the weird buzzing in her ears. She knew Jocelyn was speaking English, but she couldn't seem to absorb her meaning.

"Why don't we skip the darknet chat and just talk here."

Lark felt a jolt of unreality. "What are you saying?"

Jocelyn cast her an impatient look. "You know what I'm saying."

"No." Lark jumped from the chair and began to pace in a tight circle. "No. I know ChaosCowboy. I've known him since I was fourteen years old. He's the reason I know anything about anything. He saved my sanity."

"I saved you."

"You can't be him. You just can't."

"Why?" Jocelyn pushed herself to her feet and blocked Lark's attempts to stomp around. For a moment, the two women just stared at one another. "I was swimming in the darknet while you were still running away from home in Nantucket."

Lark's hands came up in a subconscious effort to ward Jocelyn off. "I was eight. I told ChaosCowboy that story."

Jocelyn gave a jerky nod, sudden moisture in her eyes making them glisten. "You hid from the search parties for three days, but you got so hungry you broke into the caretaker's cottage for food. He caught you half-buried in his refrigerator and called your parents."

"Oh, my God," Lark said, her brain finally knitting the pieces together. "Oh, my good fucking God. You're really him."

Jocelyn opened her arms, and Lark dove into them, clutching her friend around the waist as Jocelyn squeezed her around the shoulders.

"I can't believe it. I can't believe I'm finally meeting you in person, after all these years." Emotion clogged Lark's throat. ChaosCowboy had been more than her mentor and friend. He'd—she'd—been her lifeline in an otherwise excruciating existence. She owed Jocelyn more than she could ever give in return.

"What the hell are you two doing? Do you really think that's appropriate behavior for this office?"

Melvin.

Pinheaded blowhard. Lark clamped her lips closed before the words escaped as she pulled away from Jocelyn. Both turned to their boss.

"I don't think hugging is against any policy," Jocelyn said coolly. "What can we do for you, Melvin?"

He planted his feet wide, arms crossed over his bulky chest, chin thrust forward. Ignoring Jocelyn, he pinned Lark with a scowl. "I hear you cracked the malware, even though I doubt you really figured out anything at all. So you've got time to do some real work. I've got identity fraud cases backing up on my desk. Report to my office to pick up the files."

"But I'm still working with Doug on the joint task force." She tried to stem her burst of animosity. Melvin was, after all, her boss. He could recommend she be fired. She loved her job, despite the fact that her boss's face would be next to *jerk* in the dictionary.

"Doug doesn't need you full time, and you work for me."

Lark rolled her eyes. On the other hand, enough was enough. Being fired was better than putting up with his bullying one more second. "Come on, Melvin, I'm not in the mood. We all work for Doug."

Jocelyn stepped forward, standing toe-to-toe with Melvin. "Are you sure you want to have this conversation right now?"

He tried to stare her down, but Jocelyn met him glare for glare. And then the unbelievable happened—Melvin backed down, both literally and figuratively, taking a step back from her and glancing away. "I have a meeting in five minutes. I don't have the time for this."

He turned on his heel and marched away, tension radiating from his body. The two women looked at once another.

"What the hell just happened?" Lark asked.

Jocelyn dropped into a chair. "Let's talk about the hacking code you sent me in the darknet."

"The one Elliott gave me on the thumb drive. Did you find something in it that could tell you exactly who framed me?" Lark craned her neck to watch Melvin's retreating form, still astonished by his reaction.

Jocelyn looked pointedly toward him. "Yes. The theft was carried out by a supposed FBI employee named Leonard Rose. We both know that's bogus."

"Yeah, I found that fake account in the malware." Lark whipped her head around, mouth dropping open as she realized what she'd just said. "Wait—you're saying that the person who stole the mob's money is also the one selling classified secrets?"

Jocelyn's eyes widened. She shifted in the chair, crossing her legs and uncrossing them. "You . . . cracked the malware? I didn't realize."

"Uh, yeah," she mumbled, realizing in hindsight she should have kept her mouth shut. Doug would fire her if he realized she'd so casually revealed the existence of a spy in their midst.

"Good job," Jocelyn said. "Have you told Doug yet?"

"Yeah. So who created that user account?" she asked, trying to distract the other woman.

"Melvin."

"What?" she gasped. "Are you serious?"

"Everything okay?" Doug asked, appearing beside them. Lark jerked in surprise. "Melvin didn't look too happy."

"He just wanted an update," Jocelyn said. "No big deal."

Lark cast her a doubtful look. No big deal? It was huge. Why on earth didn't Jocelyn want to toot her own horn and report their odious boss?

Doug raised his brows. "I'm glad to hear it. My plate is about as full as it's going to get. Lark, do you have a moment?"

"You bet." Lark followed Doug toward the front of the SCIF, pausing to glance back at Jocelyn as she went through the door.

The woman lifted her hand. Lark did the same, then let the heavy metal contraption swing closed behind her. They collected their cell phones, then walked toward Doug's office. It felt strange to watch everyone step aside to let them through.

"I thought I'd give you an update," he said. "I called in a Cyber Action Team from Washington, DC. They'll be here tomorrow morning to start the espionage investigation."

"Okay, good," she said. "I, uh, might have something for them when they get here."

"No, it's their baby now. We can't touch anything if we hope to get convictions out of it." Doug placed both hands at the small of his back, stretching as they walked. "The attorney general agreed that in exchange for material information on the whereabouts of the mini-nuke, Viktor Sokolov will be granted immunity for his role in procuring the bomb."

"Wonder of wonders; someone over there showed common sense. I have his business card. Do they talk to him? Do you? Should I give his card to you?"

Doug stopped and turned to her, forcing her to halt, as well. "While it would normally be the job of a supervisory special agent to liaise with members of the public who are helping with an on-going operation, in this case I think it makes more sense for you to continue to deal with him directly. He seems to like you, and we need to keep on his good side."

"I'm pretty sure he doesn't like me at all. He threatened to chop off my finger." Lark swallowed, hands fisting at her sides. "I don't think that's a good idea. He's scary."

He ducked his head to meet her gaze soberly. "And dangerous. Believe me, I know what I'm asking of you. Computer scientists don't have any field training; you're supposed to be strictly support staff. And if you don't feel you can do it, tell me now. No harm, no foul. It won't be held against you."

"But it would help you." She pressed her palms into her eyes, rubbing furiously. Could she walk back into the lion's den? Put herself into Palachka's crosshairs again? Sure, maybe Sokolov liked her. That would not, however, save her. "Okay. All right. I can do this. I will do this."

"I'll give you every support. You won't be out there on your own. Thank you, Lark. I owe you."

She shook her head. "Am I a member of the FBI or not? I can do dangerous."

He put a hand on her shoulder and squeezed. "You're as brave as they come."

She laughed. No, she wasn't. She was the biggest scaredy cat in the world. "What about returning his money? Are we returning his money? What did they say about that?"

"I didn't ask them." Rubbing the back of his neck, he cast her a sideways glance and a tired smile. "One of my computer scientists tracked the illegal theft of money belonging to a private individual against whom no charges are pending. I have no reason or desire to illegally withhold those funds from him. I had Finance give you temporary access to our bank account downstairs. Arrange the transfer back to him, will you?"

A whoosh of air left her lungs as she sagged in relief. "Yes. I will. I'll do that right now. Oh, he wanted the deal in writing."

Doug started walking again. "The attorney general's working that right now. He'll have it to me before close of business today. You can reassure Sokolov it's on the way."

"Okay." She sighed, contemplating her new role as mob liaison. Shit.

They reached Doug's office. "Let me know if you need anything from me."

"I'm good for now." Lark left Doug talking with his assistant and strode back to her cubicle. She needed to talk to Jocelyn about her findings, but not until Lark did her own verification. Her phone buzzed.

"Center—"

"Lark, it's me. Elliott."

"Hey ho." She opened a small green container and sprinkled tiny flakes into the goldfish bowl. Goldie darted to the top to swallow the food. "Have you decided to escape? Be free?"

Elliott laughed, but it sounded forced and sad to Lark. "I dream that every single night. Listen, he wanted me to call you."

Lark rubbed her pinkie against her palm. "Your timing is perfect. You can tell him he'll have his immunity agreement by the end of the day, and his money pretty much as soon as we hang up."

"That should make him less surly. I'll call again when he knows when and where the auction will be."

"Elliott—"

"Gotta go." Elliott hung up.

Lark dropped her head into her hands. She could easily have turned out like Elliott, trapped and unhappy. Thanks to ChaosCowboy, she'd landed on the right side of the law. Maybe she couldn't save him, but it made her even more grateful for her own position.

Using her new banking access, she logged into the FBI account housing Sokolov's fifty million dollars, and transferred it back to the account number Elliott had given her. Done and done.

Chapter 35

Saturday, February 25. 7:00 p.m.
Chartered Yacht. Massachusetts Bay.

MACE TUCKED LARK close to his side as she fidgeted with her chunky bracelets for the umpteenth time. He felt her anxiety pulse along his own nerves. He squeezed her shoulder to bolster her confidence.

The state department had delivered Sokolov's immunity agreement as promised, stipulating that it would reimburse him for whatever the nuke cost him. None of them wanted to raise suspicion by trying to inject a last-minute bidder. If Mace had his way, Lark would be a thousand miles away and safe, but Sokolov remained insistent that Lark join him, and Doug had asked her to go along as some sort of FBI liaison. And since Mace wouldn't permit her to board the yacht alone, here he was, dressed in a suit and tie. A regular suit, since his had been damaged.

"Only one bodyguard can be armed, and that's Palachka. You'll have to leave your weapons behind," Sokolov said.

Mace nodded his understanding, even though he didn't like it one bit. He glanced down at Lark, who looked delicious in her green dress.

The past week with her had been amazing. Even though the members of the joint task force had trained together for countless hours, practicing scenario after scenario, he'd had free time to spend with her. They'd gone sightseeing, cuddled on the sofa watching movies, and made love in her colorful bedroom.

"I'm out of a job," she'd said days ago, as they lay in bed. "The Cyber Action Team from Washington, DC took everything. The server, the router, even my own freaking laptop. I'm not allowed within a hundred miles of any of it."

He'd hugged her, loving the scent of her skin.

"Are you sniffing me, Mace Beckett?"

"Mmm." He nuzzled into her neck. "You bet your ass I am."

In fact, she'd groused about it all week. Something drove her unease about the investigation, but he'd been unable to pry it out of her.

"If you know something, are you really not supposed to tell?" she'd asked. "Just wait for the dimwits to catch up, or maybe even miss it entirely?"

When he'd pressed her, she'd slid on top of him, and he promptly forgot what he'd been about to say.

"They move like stagnant pond water," she'd grumbled a few hours ago. "I mean, I get how an investigation works. But do they really need to spend days and days examining every period and semicolon? If they'd just let me show them, we'd be done tomorrow."

Her phone had buzzed. She hit the speaker button.

"Center—"

"It's me, Elliott."

"Hey ho. Whatcha got for me?"

"My uncle says the auction will be tonight on a rented yacht out of Massachusetts Bay called the *Lazy Bee.* It sails at 7:00 p.m. sharp. He wants you there by six thirty."

Her heart sank, but she'd given Doug her word. "They won't let me go alone."

"Yeah, he figured that. You can bring the guy who was with you in the limo. Oh, wear something fancy. I guess this will be some sort of floating cocktail party."

"Okie doke. Will I see you there?"

"Me?" Elliott's voice lifted in surprise. "No way. I don't rate. Kerghakov will be there, though."

"Thanks for the heads-up." She thumbed her phone off and turned to Mace. "Way to wait till the very last second."

"I'm positive that's the auctioneer's doing," he reassured her. "Fatianova Uvarov, not Sokolov."

Now, Sokolov's party strolled down the pier to the impressive five-story, two-hundred-foot yacht awaiting them. A festive atmosphere permeated the dock. No one seemed to mind the metal detection wand, laughing when their excessive jewelry or Rolex watches set it off. Sokolov endured the wand with aplomb, then gestured to Palachka, who was admitted without being checked. Lark leaned over the gangplank as they ascended, looking into the deep water. Mace tightened his hold on her.

"Don't fall in, little bird."

She tossed him a mock look of disdain. "I swim like a fish, not a bird."

The FBI/DHS/Delta task force had spent the past few hours planning and coordinating a shipboard assault. His palms itched.

No strategy ever survived more than a minute or two after the go order, then everything became free-flowing. That's when accidents happened. Would he be able to stow Lark away in a safe place?

Probably not.

As they stepped aboard, a crewman offered champagne. Women in flawless makeup and fancy cocktail dresses accompanied self-assured, self-important men. Mace mentally catalogued them, but at this point he couldn't classify them. His mission to identify the bidders required vigilance and attention to the smallest details.

Lark accepted the glass of bubbly, holding the widemouthed wineglass by the stem and swirling the liquid gently before sipping. "Holy cow. This is good stuff. Krug Grande Cuvée, if I'm not mistaken. Runs about two hundred a bottle."

Mace took a glass for himself and sniffed it, as he saw others doing. "I thought you served champagne in flutes."

Lark gave a lopsided smile. "The experts will tell you that flutes prevent enough oxygen from reaching the liquid to bring out the aroma properly. One must not limit the flavor of a high-end champagne."

"Naturally," he said, mentally shaking his head. Give him a Pilsner or a stout any day. "A few years ago, we helped train a couple of German Army units at a place in the Bad Kissingen district called Wildflecken." He pronounced it *Veel-flick-en*. "It's called Top of the Rock. At the end of the week, if the training went well, the commanders would organize a six-kilometer run to Kloster Kreuzberg at the top of the mountain. Beautiful old monastery with a fantastic view, and it's still a working brewery supervised by monks. You haven't lived until you've had a big ol' mug of German lager."

"That's a long way to run just to drink beer."

He looked down at her in surprise. "It's less than four miles. I do that just to warm up in the morning. Although, to be fair, it's all uphill, and pretty steep at the end. Still. Worth it. I'll take you sometime."

He felt her freeze beside him. Shit. Why had he said that? He wanted to get to know her better, but she was skittish as a colt. He had patience in spades, though, and she was worth the wait.

"I would like that," she whispered.

His heart bumped crazily. Before he said something to make her withdraw again, he forced himself to be silent and simply hugged her to his side. After a moment, she returned the pressure.

They joined the rest of Sokolov's party as they made their way to the roof of the yacht, where other laughing, chattering groups mingled. Altogether, more than two hundred guests milled about, admiring the view as the yacht raised anchor and pulled away from the dock. He needed to check out the other guests on the ship.

"Will you be all right on your own for a bit?" he asked.

She nodded, fingers tightening on his waist before she pulled away. "Be careful."

"Bank on it, little bird."

He spent an hour roaming through the decks, passing cliques on all levels. Several huddled in small sitting areas. Covertly watching their body language, he marked in each group the person to whom the others deferred. Peeking into the bridge, he waved to the pilot, who gave him a friendly smile.

"Want to see how she operates?" he asked.

"You bet." Mace entered the bridge.

The pilot began explaining the various computer screens.

Mace barely listened. He knew how to pilot a ship, even one this size. Instead, he checked their heading.

"We're heading out of Massachusetts Bay?"

"Yep. Right out into the Atlantic Ocean. The stars will be brighter than you can imagine."

Mace grimaced. "Let me guess. Twelve miles out?"

The pilot checked his log book. "Closer to fifteen, but yes."

"Into international waters."

He shrugged, looking uneasy. "I've been doing this a long time. I do what the client wants me to do. I don't ask questions."

Twelve miles from shore, US laws became hard to enforce. Still, Title 18 of the US Code stipulated that crimes committed in international waters could still be prosecuted if the vessel itself was registered in the United States and the crime involved illegal nuclear material. Even if the auction itself took place offshore, the participants could still be prosecuted. Fatianova apparently didn't realize that.

He left the bridge and found a quiet corner, pulling out his cell phone. Jace answered on the first ring.

"Whatcha got?"

"We're heading into the Atlantic, past the twelve-mile mark." He gave Jace their heading and course. "The yacht is laid out exactly as the plans showed—thank you, Majesty Yacht Charter—except that they removed the long dining table on the observation deck to accommodate the guests. Also, they modified the saloon on the aft lower deck into a kick-ass movie theatre. The television has got to be a hundred inches."

Jace laughed. "Bet the sound system is unreal."

"Yeah. I'm virtually certain the auction will take place there. It's big enough, and there're pads of paper and pens near the seats."

"Okay. Any way you can vanish into a corner?"

"No way in hell. The other problem is they closed off the escape hatch. The one on the starboard side is operational, though."

"Anything else?"

Mace gave a quick look to ensure no one had come into hearing distance. "I've identified three of the bidders. One from the Asia, maybe North Korean. One from the Middle East. I'm guessing Iranian. The third looks South American. Venezuelan, no doubt. They're known to want nuclear weapons."

His team leader blew out a breath. "Wish we knew how many bidders there are. When she actually starts the auction, do you think Sokolov will tell us?"

Mace considered it. "He says he will. He's as invested as we are in stopping this thing, if I believe him. Anyway, he did give us the yacht, so for now I'll give him the benefit of the doubt. Where are you?"

"About three miles behind you on a coast guard cutter. We're prepped to close with you and blow the hull when you give the signal."

He stared up at the ceiling, thinking. "Total personnel on board is two fifteen, plus or minus five. Fatianova turned this into a major party. Tag will have to reduce the charge on the limpet mine."

"Not a problem. Have you ever known Tag to miss his mark?"

Never. Tag worked magic with explosives. "I'll call when I have more."

He made his way back to the observation deck. A steward offered him a tray of smoked oysters on a half shell. He waved the man away and found Lark.

"Having fun?" he asked, slipping his arm around her waist.

"Tons," she said. "It's a terrific party."

He laughed at her sardonic tone. She didn't want to be here any more than he wanted her in danger.

Viktor Sokolov joined them. "I didn't have the chance to thank you earlier for taking care of our little issue."

Returning his fifty millions dollars, he meant.

"Easy peasy." She peered at him. "So which one of these high society bitches is in charge of this shindig?"

Sokolov looked around. "She's already gone below. That's what I came to tell you. The auction is about to begin."

Chapter 36

Saturday, February 25. 8:00 p.m.
Chartered Yacht. Atlantic Ocean.

FATIANOVA SURVEYED THE group gathered in the saloon with the enormous television. The only compartment on the yacht large enough to hold all of them, it was still crowded with eighteen bidders, two interpreters, and Fyodor. All men. She controlled a sneer. Men tended to be much easier to control than women.

As soon as they'd passed the twelve-mile mark, she'd given the signal. In ones and twos, they ambled below and found seats.

"Gentlemen. Is everyone settled?" She stood in front of the television. It dwarfed her. Barely waiting for the nods of assent, she said, "This will be a closed bidding. You'll find pens, paper, and envelopes near you. Please enter your bid and seal it. I'll announce the highest bidder, and you'll have the opportunity to increase your bid, if you so choose. If you decide not to continue on, you'll return to your guests on the upper decks. Is everyone clear on how this will work?"

"I want to see the merchandise," the Iranian bidder said. The others murmured agreement. "I insist on examining it myself."

She'd been afraid of that. She played a dangerous game, auctioning off a bomb she no longer possessed. She'd come up with an equally dangerous solution. Forcing herself not to fidget, she nodded.

"The winner of the auction will examine it prior to payment," she said. "And can then choose to take it with him when he debarks; or for a small fee, arrange to have it delivered to the address of his choice."

The mutters of displeasure irked her. "Gentlemen, please be reasonable. The item is in the ship's hold. We can't all be seen traipsing down there. It would arouse suspicion, don't you think?"

"Then let us begin." The arrogant Iranian took the paper and scrawled on it. His condescending attitude nettled her. She hated control being taken from her, even on such a small scale as this. He wouldn't win, she decided.

"Gentlemen, you may enter your first bid."

One by one, the others sealed their envelopes. Fyodor collected them, opening them and handing them to her. She scanned them. The high bid came in at a measly five million. Unacceptable.

"The high bid stands at five million," she announced calmly.

Two of the bidders got up and walked out. Imbeciles. Did they really think they were going to buy a nuclear weapon for so little? The second and third rounds brought the bid to eleven million. Four more bidders left in defeat. The field shrank with every round.

At last, only five remained. The bid stood at a respectable thirty-three million. What would happen now? The New Irish Republican Army should have bowed out already; how could they have the kind of money required here? Venezuela was desperate to become a nuclear power and probably wanted to reverse-engineer the device, but she doubted they had much more in the coffers than had already been offered. The Iranian had the advantage of Middle Eastern oil money, but the drug cartel raked in billions every year in profits. She couldn't even guess why the American mobster wanted to buy a mini-nuke, but that wasn't her problem. Time to finish this.

"Gentlemen, this will be the final round. The bidding stands at thirty-three million. Put your best and final bid in the envelope. The high bidder wins the merchandise."

Her fingers shook as she took each slip of paper from Fyodor. Now came the most dangerous part of her plan. She held up the winning bid, higher than his closest competitor by ten million dollars. "The device goes to the American gentleman for fifty million dollars."

A muted *whoomp* shook the floor under her feet.

Chapter 37

Saturday, February 25. 9:15 p.m.
Chartered Yacht. Atlantic Ocean.

LARK GRABBED THE nearest thing—which turned out to be Mace—as the reverberations from the explosion vibrated against the soles of her feet. He ended his brief phone call and widened his stance for balance, holding her tightly as the yacht began to list to starboard. The lighting system flickered, died, and came back on. Crystal flower vases, wineglasses, and plates crashed to the deck and shattered. Trays of canapés tumbled, spilling food onto the polished wood. Chairs slid across the deck and hit the railing. She ignored the cries and screams of the guests as they tumbled to the deck or latched onto whatever stable thing was closest to keep themselves upright. Her heart pounded as fear rushed through her. Had the engines exploded?

"What happened?" she asked him, struggling for calm. "Are we sinking? We're sinking, aren't we?"

He turned her face up to his with a gentle finger under her chin.

"Everything's fine, Lark. I signaled Tag to blow a small breach in the hull. Tag's the best there is with explosives. We're not going to sink. The pilot will be forced to head back to land."

A crewman rushed to the staircase and disappeared below deck. The two stewards looked no less terrified than the passengers. One slipped on an oyster, his foot flying up as he landed hard on his butt. The yacht shivered and shifted more, starting another round of screaming. She rolled her eyes. Like that would help.

"I need to get below deck," Mace said, standing. "I want you to go to the bridge and stay there, okay? I'll come get you."

She had no idea where the bridge was located. "Can't I come with you?"

He put a hand on each shoulder and smiled down at her. "Normally, I'd be thrilled you want to stay with me. Right now, though, I need to meet up with the team before we get underway again."

"Your swim team." She returned his smile, unsurprised that the supersoldiers were poised to board the yacht. She cupped his cheeks and pressing a quick kiss to his mouth. "More of that later."

"A whole lot more, I hope." His eyes twinkled as he backed away, then turned and sprinted to the staircase.

She looked around for a crewman. Several passed her, so she hastened after them. Down the stairs, through the passageway, heading to the bow of the ship. Most of the crew crowded the area. She slipped between them until she could see the captain, who had a microphone to his mouth.

"Attention, all passengers and crew. This is the captain speaking. We've experienced a minor fire in the engine room, taking one of our engines offline. There is absolutely no cause for alarm. The ship might continue to list slightly, but will remain afloat. Repeat. There is no cause for alarm. All passengers should remain calm, and obey the crew's orders as we sail back to port."

Liar, liar, pants on fire. The ship would be taking on water. He had to know his ship's hull had been breached, even if he didn't yet know why. Still, telling frightened people a hole had opened in the bottom of the ship would only incite panic.

"How close are we to shore?" she asked.

The captain spared her a quick glance. "We're about ten miles out. I've dropped our speed to five knots. Should take two hours to get back to the pier. I'm just being overly cautious here. There's no cause for alarm."

She heard it before she saw it, a shift in the sound of the ocean against the hull of the yacht. The coast guard cutter appeared before them like a specter, coming alongside and activating a spotlight so powerful it blinded her.

"Ship ahoy! This is the coast guard cutter *Leviathan*. Cut your engine and prepare to be boarded."

The captain cursed. "I knew I should have skipped this trip. Killing the engine."

Lark pushed forward to the bridge window so she could see. A helicopter came into view, hovering thirty-five feet above the bow. Four ropes dropped onto the deck, dark shapes sliding down them until they hit the deck. They unclipped themselves from the ropes, then swarmed port and starboard, running full tilt without using the life rails. The helicopter lifted up and headed to the stern.

Two of those dark shapes burst into the bridge, assault rifles aimed and steady.

"Hands up where I can see them," one ordered. "No one move a muscle."

Lark squeaked, flinging her arms up and freezing in place until she realized that under the Army helmets and uniforms they wore, she recognized them.

"Jace!" she blurted out.

He didn't so much as glance at her as he covered Alex, who systematically searched the captain and crew. "It's all right, Lark. We're securing the ship. Has anyone given you anything to hold? A package, or anything you're not sure what it is?"

"Not a thing."

"Are you aware of any danger in this room or elsewhere?"

"No. Well, the bodyguards have guns."

"We're aware. Thank you."

"Where's Mace?"

"He's with the team securing the auction room. All of you, please follow me to the main deck." He lowered his rifle across his chest, watchful and wary as he led the captain and crew toward the main deck. Alex brought up the rear, equally alert.

From amidships, they all heard the gunshots, rapid exchanges that sounded like an entire army to her. The group staggered to a stop.

"Please keep moving up to the main deck," Alex said. The normally laid-back farm boy's tone brooked no disobedience. "We need to secure the boat."

"Is that Mace? Mace is down there, isn't he?"

Jace shot her a warning look. "Lark, please help me get these people to safety."

"Okay," she said in a small voice. "Listen up, everyone. This is the cavalry. You'll all be safe on deck. No, don't push and shove. It's okay."

Despite their jackets, the captain and crew shivered in the

frigid air, joining the frightened throngs of partygoers. Several of them passed their jackets to guests, who slid into them gratefully. She saw other black-clad figures, soldiers, systematically moving down the boat, searching passengers and sending them to the bow. Men in blue uniforms and hats identifying them as coast guardsmen began to interview the guests, asking for identification.

Where was Mace? In the middle of that firefight? The shooting had stopped. If he'd been hurt, Jace would know about it, right?

Jace pressed a small device in his right ear. "Bow secured. Roger, Sandman. Heading down there now."

"Where are you going?" Lark asked, taking a few steps after him. "Are we secure? Secured?"

"We have positive control of the boat, yes." He leaned down to murmur into her ear, "We need to find the nuke. I'm heading down to the hold to meet the rest of the team."

"No one got shot?"

"None of the good guys." He gave her a nod and strode away.

Curiosity gnawed at her. What did a nuclear weapon look like? A shiny missile, or a tangle of cords in a big suitcase? Jace said the ship was safe now. Surely it wouldn't hurt anything if she took a peek? Without getting caught, of course. She eased away from the group, then trotted to the stairs that would take her to Mace.

The hold had to be at the bottom of the yacht, right? She kept heading down the stairs until she came to a corridor with a ladder. Climbing down in her heels turned out to be more awkward than she'd anticipated, but she managed. She hustled down the passageway to the entrance of the cargo hold and peeped through the hatch.

Just inside, Alex swung the muzzle of his rifle away from her. His eyes narrowed. "Lark, you shouldn't be down here."

So much for remaining undetected. "I just wanted to see."

She tried to peer past him, but he put out an arm, blocking her way. "You need to be up on the main deck with the others. Look, I'll find someone to escort you."

She plonked her fists onto her hips. "Are you going to shoot me?"

He gaped at her, appalled. "Of course not."

"Then I want to see."

He curled his fingers in indecision, then dropped his arm with a sigh. "Fine. Get me in trouble. Mace'll have my head."

"I'll stay up here, okay? I don't want to cause problems."

She tried to make herself inconspicuous beside the ladder leading into the cargo hold, which seemed bigger than it ought to be, and much more crowded than she'd imagined. Behind the ladder, furniture had been strapped down, probably in case anything above broke. About halfway down the hold area, she saw an enormous walk-in refrigerator. Two tall metal shelves had been bolted into the floor, one filled with sealed boxes of tea and coffee, palettes of bottled water and sodas, and crates of champagne. The second was crammed with cleaning supplies and toilet paper. Lots and lots of toilet paper.

Half a dozen men, both Delta Force and coast guard, stood in a loose semicircle around a large crate. She found Mace unerringly, as though an invisible force locked her onto him. He stood with his legs apart, arms folded across his chest and an assault rifle slung over his shoulder. His face might have been chiseled from stone; he seemed hard, focused, and deadly. A ripple of lust hit her. This was not her gentle lover. This was a battle-hardened warrior. She smiled.

Someone had pried the front of the crate off, setting a crowbar across one edge of it. Four others carefully lifted out a black suitcase. Not one of those fabric ones, either. This one had hard sides and was the biggest case she'd ever seen. The men set it carefully atop the crate.

"We got it," one of the coast guardsmen crowed. Several others high-fived, looking satisfied. But she watched Mace and the other Delta Force special operators. They shared uneasy glances. Why? What was wrong?

Mace and the one she remembered as the Sandman thumbed open the latches and raised the lid bit by bit.

"Careful," a tall man barked.

The Sandman cast him an irritated look. "How many hours do you have training on nuclear weaponry? None? Then shut the hell up and let us have a look."

Lark craned her neck to see.

They eased the lid back so it lay on the crate, anger and frustration flashing across their faces. She jumped as Mace slammed a hand onto the suitcase, swearing in Cajun French. It impressed her even as her heart sank. He turned to the others.

"It's empty," Mace said.

Chapter 38

Sunday, February 26. 9:00 a.m.
FBI Field Office. Boston, Massachusetts.

FATIANOVA TWISTED HER fingers around and around, taking slow, even breaths. She didn't need the presence of her interrogators to know how much trouble she was in. If she were deported back to Russia, she would face up to twenty years in prison for treason. Twenty years of concertina wire, a ten-by-ten box for two with bars for walls, and tasteless food cooked in vats.

Surely the United States treated its prisoners better? She hadn't actually sold a nuclear bomb to anyone. And maybe they couldn't prove she brought it into the country in the first place. No one needed to know Otis Fitch had double-crossed her. They would have to let her go.

But they could still deport her.

The interrogation room had two-tone gray walls and a large mirror on one side. Two-way, she assumed. Who else was back there? A functional fluorescent light shone on the rectangular Formica table and the video camera pointed her way. A tall, distinguished-looking man with gray hair wearing a cheap suit, and a fine-boned, beautiful woman with red hair sat on the other side of the table in the generic stackable chairs. The hard seat hurt Fatianova's backside. She shifted, crossing her legs in an effort to get more comfortable. The gray-haired man reached forward and pressed a button on the video camera.

"First interview with Fatianova Uvarov," he said. "Started at 9:00 a.m. on February twenty-sixth, conducted by Douglas Huckabee, Special Agent in Charge of the Boston Field Office of the Federal Bureau of Investigation. Also in attendance is Heather Langstrom-Reed as Russian interpreter. Interview begins now."

The woman leaned forward, resting her forearms on the table. "Ms. Uvarov," she said in Russian. "I'm here in case you need an interpreter. I know you speak excellent English, but if at any point during this conversation you find you need help with certain words or terms, please don't hesitate to utilize me, all right?"

Fatianova inclined her head. "I understand."

"We all set?" the gray-haired man asked Heather in English. At her nod, he turned to Fatianova. "Ms. Uvarov, my name is Douglas Huckabee, and I'll be conducting this interview. Before we start, is there anything you need? Coffee? Water? A soda?"

"No." A full bladder would weaken her resolve. They were clever, these Americans, but Russians had mastered the art of interrogation hundreds of years before the United States even existed.

"Then would you please state your full name and address for the record?"

"Fatianova Vladimirovna Uvarov." She gave her Moscow address. *Pretend to cooperate. Reveal nothing incriminating.*

"Thank you. And when did you arrive in the United States?"

Act unconcerned. Breathe normally. It became her mantra.

"I came here with other members of the Kuznetsov Institute of Applied Nuclear Physics for the International Symposium on Nuclear Safety. The symposium took place last week."

Douglas Huckabee opened the folder in front of him and flipped up the first page. "On a B-1 visa, I see. It says here you're a nuclear engineer?"

"*Da.* Yes."

He flicked a finger against the paper. "And yet you didn't arrive on the same flight as the rest of your group. Neither you nor your associate, Fyodor Petrov, show up on the manifest for that flight. Can you explain that?"

"We decided to come a few days early to sightsee, that's all. Nothing nefarious."

His gaze snapped up to hers and stayed there. "Yes. That's the crux of things, isn't it? Your nefarious activities. Did you know we have Mr. Petrov in another room? He's been very helpful in filling in some gaps. In fact, we can't get him to shut up." He grimaced. "Ms. Uvarov . . . may I call you Fatianova?"

She uncrossed and recrossed her legs. They'd given her an insipid set of scrubs to wear, along with an ill-fitting pair of tennis shoes, taking possession of all her belongings. The fabric scratched against her skin. "If you like."

"Fine. Good. So, Fatianova, can you account for your whereabouts since you arrived in our country? I'll need specific details of where and when, please."

She pretended to think. "Well, we drove around the city quite a bit. I don't know if I remember every place we stopped to see."

"Try."

For the next few minutes, she rambled on, naming places she knew from photographs. Faneuil Hall, Boston Commons, the statue of Paul Revere. She stopped only when the interrogation room door opened and another man entered.

"You're needed out front," he said to Doug Huckabee, who hesitated, nodded, and rose, taking the brown folder with him.

"I'll be right back, Fatianova. Can I bring you anything when I return?"

She shook her head, looking over the new arrival. In his sixties, he immediately reminded her of a weasel. Small and thin, with the kind of hipless body that caused his pants to hang loosely and his shirt to come untucked. His beard hid sunken cheeks, and his glasses rested on the top of his balding head.

"Ms. Uvarov," he said in a croaky, smoke-roughened voice. "You're an educated woman. You keep up on world politics, yes?"

The question threw her off guard. Where was this going? "Yes, as much as anyone else, I suppose."

He pulled a pack of cigarettes from his breast pocket, looked at it, and dropped it onto the table with a sigh. "So tell me. How many detainees do you think the United States is holding on suspicion of terrorism right now?"

"I'm sure I have no idea." The man made her nervous.

"Well, Guantanamo claims we have about fifty prisoners left there." He peered at the pack of cigarettes as he twirled it around and around, then finally took one out and stuck it between his lips. "The number is closer to seven hundred and fifty. And while I can't confirm the existence of cooperative agreements with nations whose human rights laws may be more, uh, lax than ours, there are rumors."

"You can't frighten me."

"In fact," he said, ignoring her, "rumor has it that some citizens from your own country, missing and presumed dead, are in fact very much alive. Wishing, maybe, that they were dead."

He pulled out a cheap plastic lighter and lit the cigarette, taking a deep draw before blowing the smoke toward the ceiling.

"You can't smoke in here." She pointed to the sign on the door, not knowing what else to say.

"Ms. Uvarov, you're responsible for bringing a Russian nuclear weapon onto US soil. Do you really think your government is going to care if you suddenly disappear off the face of the earth?"

"I've done no such thing. I'm completely innocent in this."

"Is that your last word?"

"What does that mean?" She felt a chill snake down her spine. The man talked like a KGB agent.

"I think it's time for you to disappear." He got up and walked out, followed closely by Heather Langstrom-Reed.

For the next three hours, Fatianova in turns sweated and chilled. She sat, then paced, then sat again. Could the man really make her disappear? Did Americans do that sort of thing? Who watched from behind the two-way mirror?

By the time the door rattled and opened, Fatianova felt like screaming her rage and disappointment. Nothing about her scheme had worked as expected.

Doug Huckabee came back in, followed by the translator. They sat across from her as they had before. Neither looked friendly. Neither spoke for a long time.

"You have exactly one bargaining chip," Huckabee said abruptly. "One. Are you listening, Fatianova?"

Swallowing convulsively, she whispered, "Yes."

"Your value proposition to me, right now, is to truthfully answer the question that I'm going to ask you. The first time."

She opened her mouth, but he held up an imperious hand, so she subsided.

"The next time you open your mouth, when I ask you this question, you can proclaim your bullshit innocence to me if you want. Which, incidentally, annoys me, because I've got a baby girl on the way, and you're threatening her life as well. So this will be the first and last time I ask you this question. I get the truth and DHS goes away. Happy to put you in a federal penitentiary and lock you away until my daughter graduates college. You continue to proclaim your innocence, and we already know you're not, then I turn you over to DHS, we continue the hunt without you, and you conveniently disappear. So. Should I ask you the question?"

She wrapped her arms around her middle, feeling cold. Maybe she could still salvage something from this debacle. "If I cooperate, will I get immunity?"

Doug Huckabee stared at her for so long she had to force herself not to squirm.

"I bet you fool people, don't you?" he said finally. "I'll bet people take one look at you, and see a beautiful, geeky scientist. And miss the ice that runs through your veins and the steel that runs through your spine. People look at me, they see a good ol' boy." He leaned in close. "Now look deeper. I fight for the American way of life. Do you really think I wouldn't do anything—*any*thing—to keep my countrymen safe from terrorists?"

She swallowed. No. No, she didn't.

"Now. Do you really want to fuck with me?"

"Ask your question."

Chapter 39

Wednesday, March 1. 6:30 a.m.
Otis Fitch's Property. Ducard, Massachusetts.

THE DELTA FORCE operators jogged up the ten-mile dirt trail leading from the highway up to Otis Fitch's property, home to Citizens for a Free America. Jace pushed the pace hard. Around them, the Berkshires rose majestically; the terrain was rocky, wooded, and rough going.

The entire team had resorted to hard physical training to combat the frustration of days of confabs between the bigwigs, jurisdictional pissing contests, equipment delays, and the current standoff with the white separatists. The longer this dragged on, the more time Otis Fitch and his cronies had to prepare for the inevitable assault on his compound.

Fitch's acreage squatted fifteen miles northwest of the tiny hamlet of Ducard. Portions of the Hoosic River meandered through his land. Between the fresh water, ample hunting on his fifty acres, and their probable stockpile of weapons, they could withstand a long-term siege. Nobody wanted another Waco or Ruby Ridge, but leaving a nuclear bomb in the hands of a group on the terrorist watch list spelled an even greater disaster.

Fatianova Uvarov had laid out the entire fiasco, admitting to the theft of the Russian suitcase bomb, the pilot who delivered the package to Whitehorse, Canada, and the failure of a hired mercenary to smuggle it into Boston. Her reluctant partnership with the white supremacists. The botched deal with Citizens for a Free America. After her signed confession, she'd asked to be tried in the United States, rather than be deported back to Russia. The attorney general had been only too happy to oblige.

The team exited the tree line and hit the staging area, running past the two helicopters, the section of the clearing designated as the parking lot, and the rows of tents that had been erected to house the numerous agencies who wanted a piece of the action. Between local law enforcement, Department of Homeland Security, the ATF, and the FBI's SWAT, the uniforms blurred together into one sea of green camouflage. The Massachusetts state governor had even activated one of the National Guard's field artillery platoons, providing a 155 mm self-propelled Howitzer and the crew to operate it, and the deputy assistant secretary for the Bureau of International Security and Nonproliferation had visited.

In a few hours, the news vans would drive up to the staging area, and bored newscasters would report that nothing had changed.

The team reached their own tent.

"All right, guys. Hit the showers," Jace said. "Breakfast in twenty."

The shower tent only accommodated four at a time, so the team rotated through the stalls to the sinks to shave. In less than twenty minutes, they were dressed and seated in the mess tent, where a local restaurant provided three squares a day and prepackaged sandwiches and snacks.

Mace wolfed down his eggs, fried potatoes, corn beef hash, bacon, sausage, and toast. They'd expended a lot of calories during their morning workout, so he and his teammates stuffed themselves. The food was certainly a step up from their usual field chow. Before the rest finished, he grabbed a Styrofoam cup of coffee and headed away from the camp, where other groups started emerging from their tents, yawning and scratching. He dialed the phone as he walked.

"Center of the universe; God speaking."

"Shouldn't it be goddess?"

Lark chuckled. "You say that every time. Besides, we don't want to confuse the natives on the extent of my powers."

"True." He pictured her at her desk, stirring the water in the fishbowl with the end of a pen while she squinted at her computer screen. "Are you still pink?"

"Nah. I figured you'd be getting blue balls out there, so I went blue in sympathy."

"Ya got that right. Send me a pic."

"Hang on." She returned to the line at the same time that Mace's phone beeped to let him know he had a new text message. He took the time to click on the photo she'd sent. Sure enough, her hair was now a lightish sky blue, streaked with darker peacock highlights. His dick approved, perking right up.

"It's sexy as hell. All I can think about right now is that hair brushing against my—"

"Hey, now," she interrupted. "I'm at work. Behave."

He didn't want to. He wanted to savor and share his fantasy with her. "Grr. In that case, how's the weather?"

She laughed at his sour tone. "Been raining ever since you left. How's your day going so far?"

"Two hours of PT and breakfast. Nothing's changed up here."

She gasped. "Two hours? Like, you exercised for two hours?"

He didn't tell her the physical training hadn't even been a full workout. They had yet to get weights up here. They made do, though, by benching logs felled to clear their perimeter.

"It's not like we have anything else to do until diplomacy fails and we're given the go-ahead."

The line went quiet for a moment.

"You're sure it will?" Lark asked. "Maybe you're wrong."

"Maybe. I hope so. Talk dirty to me."

"Not when I can't do anything about it," she said. "Call me later tonight, and it'll be a different story."

He sighed heavily, his dick happy about their planned date, pressing against the buttons of his combat pants. Unlike the ATF and SWAT units, his team's uniforms lacked name tags, branch insignia, or markings of any sort, in deference to the covert nature of their missions.

"Deal. So how are you saving the world today?"

She chuckled. "I should be asking you that, supersoldier. Although—"

"What?"

"Well . . . I found out more about the money theft. It bugged me I couldn't track it further than the FBI bank account."

"You figured out who?"

"The trail leads directly to my crapjacker peckerhead boss."

"Melvin?" he asked. "Melvin Dewey? The big guy who cut you off in the briefing?"

"Yeah. Him."

He heard the soft hesitation in her voice. "Why do you doubt what you found?"

"Well . . . here's the thing. He's a jerk. But . . . that doesn't necessarily make him a traitor."

Mace thought about it. "You think it was too easy? Finding the trail leading to him?"

"Yes. That's it exactly."

"So . . . you think the person who stole the mob's money is also the one leaking classified information out of the SCIF?"

Lark huffed out a breath. "Yes."

"I agree."

"So here's what I think. When Doug Huckabee assigned me to investigate the malware, whoever is responsible for it realized it was only a matter of time before I figured out what he's been doing. So he—or she—framed me for stealing mob money."

Mace swore to himself. Lark was still in danger, and he wasn't there to protect her. "And the other threats? The video of your parents' house?"

"A last-ditch warning. Joss and I started investigating Melvin. Now that we have the right data, everything points to him. But everything pointed to me, too."

Mace's phone chirped in his ear, letting him know he had a text message. He pulled the phone from his ear long enough to check it.

Command tent now.

"Shit. I gotta go. Something might be shaking loose finally." He started jogging back toward camp. "Please be careful, Lark. Right now, Doug and I are the only people you know you can trust."

"Be safe." She sounded distressed. "Call me tonight?"

"Count on it. Love you."

Dead silence.

Shit. Why had he said that? It'd just slipped out. Maybe if he just hung up? Nope, not his style.

"So how badly are you freaking out right now?"

She exhaled a breath; she'd probably been holding it. "Gotta go. People to do. Work to see."

The line cut off. He cursed. Would she even answer his call tonight? Talking to her had become the highlight of his day these past two weeks. He would hate it if she bolted out of nervousness.

Alex and Gavin entered the huge central tent on his heels. Jace gestured for them to join him near the serviceable metal conference table in the center. A mess of satellite images, aerial photographs, and maps littered the tabletop. The local sheriff and the heads of the ATF, SWAT, and Homeland Security elements watched them approach. The National Guard's field artillery platoon leader, a shiny new second lieutenant, narrowed his eyes. No doubt he'd been told they were some sort of shit-hot no-name unit and wanted to take their measure. Mace snorted to himself.

Javier Castellanos from the FBI's Weapons of Mass Destruction Directorate sat at the head of the table. He raised his hands, and the tent immediately quieted.

"As you all know, we've been trying to find a diplomatic solution to this standoff. I failed. The FBI hostage negotiator failed. The governor failed. They've refused to release the nuke into our custody. They've refused to throw down their arms and surrender."

One of the SWAT officers asked, "What about releasing the women and children from the compound?"

"Also a no, with a fuck-you tacked on for good measure," Castellanos said in a resigned voice. "The president's given the go-ahead for our joint task force to enact more aggressive action, since negotiations are clearly not producing any results."

Finally! Mace felt the same surge of anticipation from his teammates, though none of them so much as twitched or changed expressions.

"I'll retain operational command," he continued, "but the on-the-ground tactical officer will be Clive Driscoll from SWAT. Also, the HMRU helicopter arrives back here today. For anyone not familiar," he glanced at the field artillery lieutenant, a relatively new addition to their ever-growing assemblage, "the Hazardous Materials Response Unit will neutralize the bomb once we find it, and gather forensic evidence so we can prosecute these fuckers." He looked over at the special operators. "They'll be taking video, so anyone not wanting to have their picture taken should be aware."

Jace nodded. Message received. Don't be around when the HAZMAT team did its thing.

"How many of them will there be?" Clive Driscoll asked.

"Six," Castellanos said. "Three FBI special agents, two forensic scientists, and someone who will know how to transport the damned thing out of here."

Driscoll leaned across the table to pick up a photograph showing the property. Infrared thermal imaging lit up nineteen warm bodies in varying sizes, plus a number of smaller shapes. They knew from surveillance that the white supremacists allowed half a dozen dogs free run of the property, while caging the chickens and pigs. They even kept two goats.

"From visual observation, we think there are seven men, five women, and eight children, ranging in age from an infant up to three older teens."

The local sheriff pushed another photo toward Jace with one fat finger. "I know these folks. A nasty bunch, women and kids included. Otis thinks he's some sort of revolutionary. We already know he has no intention of ending this peacefully."

Driscoll shuffled a dozen photos and laid them out on the table in a spiral. "This is the latest from the helicopter flyover, taken earlier today. We need to know this area as well as they do. Find a discreet way in. Find and neutralize any booby traps. Even physically put eyes on the nuke, if possible."

"Sir, I'd like to take my team out and do exactly that," Jace said.

Castellanos nodded. "I'll take you up on that."

"I'll coordinate for any resources you need," Noah Jennings said. The Department of Homeland Security had assigned him as the federal security officer; his function was to coordinate communications between the agencies involved in recovering the suitcase bomb. "We got the tactical headsets I asked for. Everyone will be able to talk to everyone else when this goes down."

Clive Driscoll nodded his thanks. "We'll get you a list in a few hours. Jace, I'd like a couple of my men to go scouts-out with you. I have a former SEAL and an Army Ranger. Both can hang."

Jace pursed his lips. "Give us first shot, Clive, okay? My team's worked together for years. Once we get a feel for what's out there, we'll add whoever you want. Is that acceptable?"

"Yeah. That's 'bout what I expected." Driscoll looked neither surprised nor bothered by the answer. "When do you want to start?"

"Now. We'll go tonight, too, but this way we won't be surprised if they have thermal imaging capability."

"Night vision goggles?" one of the SWAT team members asked. "You really think these dumb hicks have something like that?"

The sheriff raised both eyebrows. "These dumb hicks aren't as dumb as you think they are. Don't underestimate Otis Fitch. He's a wily old bastard."

Castellanos held up a hand. "Assume they have both thermal imaging cameras and NVGs. Any way to mask your body heat?"

"To some extent," Jace said. "We wear a special synthetic fabric that diffuses our heat signatures during night ops. The technology's not perfect, but it's light years better than anything commercially available."

Driscoll rearranged two of the photographs. "Ghost suit development was all the rage what? Five or six years ago? I thought no one could make it work."

Humor lit Jace's eyes as his mouth twitched into a slight smile. "It's true none of the companies could produce a viable prototype at the time. It's a little-known fact that the CIA runs one of the best R&D labs in the world. They bought out the patents. Now the technology is used exclusively by the military."

Castellanos stood. "Any questions for me before I turn this over to Clive? No? All right, then. I'll leave you to work out the tactics. Clive, brief me when you've got a solid plan in place."

The final tactical assault plan would be based on the exploratory plans they'd made days ago, each iteration modified as more intelligence became available. Each man at the table stayed focused, knowing they rapidly approached zero hour.

Virtually everyone at the staging area, including the press, realized an assault on Otis Fitch's collection of houses was unavoidable. As the leader of the Citizens for a Free America, his demands during their attempted negotiations were both simple and impossible: Declare his land an independent nation and a nuclear power. Release two of his followers from federal prison.

Cease the tyrannical federal control of the two nearby national forests and return the stolen lands back to mill operators and farmers. Stop taxing them, oppressing them, or trying to arrest them. Leave them the hell alone to do whatever it was they did on a daily basis, which seemed to have a lot more in common with drinking moonshine while fishing, drinking moonshine while barbecuing, and drinking moonshine while sitting around a campfire than any actual work.

The independent nation of Bubbafied Whitesonlyland would never happen. The only ones who didn't seem to realize that were the skinheads themselves.

"I'm breaking you into four teams," Clive Driscoll said. He read off the names of each team leader and team members. A mix of FBI, ATF, and DHS agents made up Teams One and Two. Mace was glad to see he'd chosen to leave the Delta Force team intact as Team Three. Local law enforcement made up Team Four. "Obviously this plan will be tweaked based on what Jace's team scouts out, but you can pretty well plan on us moving under cover of darkness and starting the assault at dawn. Catch them in bed, asleep or hung over. Either one's good."

Driscoll flipped on the projector attached to his laptop. An aerial shot of the buildings appeared on the tripod projection screen. "Let me quickly run through the buildings we've identified. From east to west, we have the main house, with Otis, his wife, and three children. The barn-slash-workshop-slash-equipment shed is this center building, and we know that's where the nuke is; the HMRU helicopter's been doing regular flyovers. West of that are three dormitory-style bunkhouses; one for the five women, one for the four men, and one for the five children. We can see that they're clearing land and building homes nearby, but those aren't finished yet, so we have them all contained in this one area for now."

Mace pointed to the screen. "Have you identified the other two buildings?"

"This thing between the male bunkhouse and the one for the children is just a big pole tent. They use it for communal dining. The one next to the women's dormitory seems to be a canning room, but we think they've also dug a root cellar in it. We've seen them bring out jars of peaches and pickled beets, and they store their garden vegetables there."

Mace nodded his thanks.

"Their boat is to the northwest, at the Hoosic River. It's on a trailer, but the truck's up at the main house, so there will be no easy escape that way. Also, the guard shack fronts the road up to the main house and is manned 24/7, so we won't be coming straight in on the road. Everyone good so far?"

Driscoll waited for several heartbeats. When no one said anything, he gave a sharp nod.

"Good. Everyone will carry two weapons. You have your choice of an M-16 rifle or a shotgun, loaded with rubber bullets and bean bag shells respectively. You'll also carry a sidearm, which will carry lethal rounds. Our objective is to arrest all nineteen of them with zero injuries or deaths on either side. The press has been calling this another Ruby Ridge for days. Let's prove them wrong."

Mace nodded along with the others, even though he knew beyond a shadow of a doubt the white supremacists wouldn't give in easily, and some injuries seemed inevitable.

"The house and the bunkhouses are the main threats," Driscoll said. "We're going to surround them and hit them from all sides simultaneously. Team One, the five of you will hit the main house.

Keep in mind there are women and children in there, but don't discount the possibility that some of them may also be armed. Fitch's kids are nine and twelve; more than old enough to have been both brainwashed and taught how to shoot.

"Team Two, you'll hit the men's and women's barracks. Disarm and contain them, then two of you secure the children in their barracks. Keep them contained inside." He gave a wry smile. "We don't need a news helicopter getting a shot of us terrorizing kids."

"We know if there are weapons in the kids' bunkhouse?" the team leader asked.

"Assume there are," Driscoll said. "These are zealots, so expect armed resistance. Yes, we're hitting them at dawn. Yes, we know where the roving patrols and guards are. Still, better safe than sorry."

"Gotcha."

"Team Three, you'll approach from the high ground to the northwest," Driscoll said, nodding to Jace. "There's no cover closer than a hundred yards on the north edge of the property, so your approach needs to be under cover of darkness. Your objective is the barn where the nuke is, since you all have training in nuclear weaponry. And obviously we don't want anyone getting the idea to set it off."

Mace felt a rush of relief. Driscoll was making sound tactical decisions, making the best use of his motley crew of law enforcement and special operators.

"Team Four, you're smoke and overwatch. Anyone who tries to escape off the back end of the property, pop smoke grenades and take 'em down."

Nods all around ensured the professionals understood their objectives.

"The Hazardous Materials Response Unit's helicopter will assist us with tracking anyone who tries to rabbit," Driscoll went on. "Once we've made the arrests, they'll land and take possession of the nuke. Any questions?"

"Yes, sir. What will my guys be doing?" the field artillery platoon leader asked.

"You'll be ready to drop either explosive, illuminating, or smoke cartridges on my mark. You're a last resort. I'm hoping we'll be in, out, and done before any news outlets get wind of what we're doing; but in case they show up, I'd rather the world doesn't see us bombing homes."

"Yes, sir. My guys will be ready."

"Sheriff, I'd sure appreciate it if you and your men would keep our staging area secure while the main assault takes place," Clive Driscoll said.

"Yeah, no problem."

"Any other questions?"

No one else said anything.

Jace stood. "Clive, I'll need some of those headsets. Give us an hour, and we'll go snoop around."

The team fell in on their leader as he left, grinning and giving each other discreet low fives.

Chapter 40

Thursday, March 2. 3:00 a.m.
Otis Fitch's Property. Ducard, Massachusetts.

MACE PATTED HIS horse's sweaty neck, trying to get the damned thing to stop skittering sideways. He looked from the narrow track they followed to the steep drop on his right, and nudged the horse's side with his boot. It snorted and shook its head.

"She can smell your fear," Alex offered. "Loosen up your grip on the reins. And quit hanging on to the saddle horn like she's going to buck you off."

Mace tried to relax, but he'd been butting heads with the stubborn mare for miles. "How do you know she won't?"

"Cripes, Mace. She's the gentlest horse I could find in the stable."

Mace prodded the horse's side again, and she finally eased away from the edge. "We don't have horses in the Bayou. Are you sure this isn't a mule?"

Alex laughed. "I'm sure. Give her her head. She knows what she's doing."

For the past ten hours, the team had skied, snowshoed, and crawled all over the landscape in and around Otis Fitch's property. Leaving visible trails through the snow and trees seemed less risky than allowing an unfamiliarity with the terrain. In such a short time, no way could they know the area as well as men who'd probably lived here for generations. Still, they'd lined up good overwatch and sniper positions, marked two tripwires and four landmines, and neutralized a roadside bomb from the dirt road leading up to the compound.

Gabe, peeved to be left behind, now monitored their progress, ready to update them on any changes on the fly. He chuckled into Mace's tactical headset.

"Did Alex mention he used to do the rodeo circuit? Rode bulls."

"I won, too," Alex bragged.

The horses walked in single file up the steep, icy track. Recent warmer temperatures had half melted the snow, but tonight the temperature hovered at a balmy twenty-four degrees, and snow had started falling around them.

While their two snipers worked their way into position, he and the rest of the team rode the tree line four miles above and behind the compound. From there, they would descend to the edge of Otis Fitch's property and wait for the go-ahead.

"We're here," Mace said. The mare jogged sideways again. A hoof slipped on loose rocks. His mouth flattened as he looked down the steep descent. "Mule, imma 'bout to hurt you."

Despite his words, he stroked a hand down her neck and

rubbed between her ears. She shook her head, making the leather and metal bridle jingle, and followed the other horses off the track into a small clearing. The six of them dismounted.

A deputy sheriff roped the horses together while Mace, Alex, Tag, Jace, and The Sandman pulled their gear off the pack horse. When they were set, the deputy nodded farewell and began the trek back down the mountain, the horses following docilely in a line behind him. Mace patted his mare as she passed.

"Thanks for not bucking me off, mule."

She whickered in response, perfectly calm now that he no longer rode her, and swished her tail as she followed the horse in front of her.

The five of them already wore specially made gray-and-white headgear that matched their winter camouflage clothing, but now they pulled the protective scarves up over their noses and set the attached night vision goggles. They donned their MOLLE backpacks, then each operator checked the other to ensure everything was locked down tight. Pistols strapped to their thighs and rifles cradled in their arms, they waited for Jace to give the signal to move out.

"Heads on a swivel, guys," he said. "Let's assume at least some of these folks have military training. We know they're not above setting booby traps and mines, so we'll go in slow and silent. Alex, you set with the capture gun?"

Alex patted the air rifle strapped to his pack. "I have eight tranquilizing darts. Any of the pooches that decide to come our way will get a nice little nap."

"All right, then. Let's roll."

The descent down the mountainside and across the icy river

took them almost two hours. Both Mace and Tag took tumbles, sliding on patches of ice and mud on the steep slope until stopped by a rocky outcrop. Despite that, they settled just inside the tree line at the north end of the property, giving the mine a wide berth, at five in the morning.

Alex set the tranquilizer gun next to him on a snowdrift. They'd seen the dogs roaming near the house on multiple occasions, but had stayed upwind so as not to be detected. Now they did not have that luxury.

The collection of buildings were a hundred yards across the tract of high, snow-covered grass. Given the cover of darkness and a great deal of stealth, the operators could cross to the barn-like structure, which the white supremacists also used as a workshop and nuclear storage facility. Mace marked the rusted-out truck and abandoned refrigerator near the barn, the stacked bales of frozen straw midway in the field, and a giant orange tractor-looking piece of farm equipment squatting nearby.

"What is it?" he asked Alex.

"Corn harvester," the farm boy said. "It's a self-propelled combine. It should be in the barn. Guess they ran out of room, what with the nuke and all."

"We're at the north edge of the property," Jace murmured into his headset. "Disarming the tripwire now."

Mace and Tag eased forward to the booby trap, slithering on their bellies because it was virtually invisible in the darkness. If they hadn't already marked its location, they never would have seen it. Mace pinched the wire between thumb and forefinger, preventing it from tightening as Tag separated it from the trigger, rendering the explosive at the other end inert.

"Clear."

With help from the helicopter's searchlight, they had already marked the position of the two thermal imaging cameras. Now, they began the dangerous crossing to the barn.

"Hold."

Everyone froze at Jace's soft order.

"Roving guard at ten o'clock. One of those mutts is with him," the team leader said. "Let's see if they move on."

Mace forced himself to patience as the white supremacist trudged from the men's barracks to the barn and circled it. He continued west past the main house, then turned down the road leading to the guard shack.

"Clear. Moving forward."

The special operators half crouched, weapons up and ready as they crunched across the meadow. Halfway to their target, the mutt accompanying the roving guard trotted back into view, coming up the track toward the main house. It hesitated, turning in their direction, and gave a questioning woof.

"Alex, you're up," Jace said.

The mutt, some sort of Rottweiler mix, loped toward them, its growl clearly carrying across the frigid air. Just as it began to bark, Alex fired the tranquilizer dart. The dog wobbled to a halt, then sagged to the ground. He checked the dog as they passed.

"It's breathing easy."

The team continued on, passing some sort of yard storage shed, complete with a painted swastika on its roof.

"Charming people," Alex muttered.

At last, they reached the northwest corner of the mammoth barn.

"Command, this is Team Three. We're in position," Jace said.

"Roger," Clive Driscoll said. "Everyone's set. On my mark."

Mace welcomed the fresh surge of adrenaline. "Let's get this show on the road."

"Three . . . two . . . one . . . go go go!"

Chapter 41

Thursday, March 2. 5:30 a.m.
Otis Fitch's Property. Ducard, Massachusetts.

MACE BURST THROUGH the barn door half a step behind Alex. He barely had time to register six warm bodies when someone flipped on the overhead lights. His night vision goggles bloomed out, blinding him with a solid greenish-white haze as the photons pouring in overwhelmed the amplification plate.

Cursing, he tore them off, blinking furiously to adjust to the brightness, already searching for cover. Shots rang out—the *chnk chnk* of an MP5, bursts from an M-16 assault rifle, the echoing boom of a shotgun. A long, L-shaped workbench, wooden top over brick, ran the width of the barn. Mace fired blindly and dove behind a table saw, Alex sliding in next to him and rolling behind a metal lathe. Neither piece of equipment provided much protection.

"Goddammit," Driscoll swore. "It's an ambush. They knew we were coming."

Yeah, no shit.

He heard the sound of gunfire from outside the barn. Ten feet away, The Sandman crouched behind six black barrels on a pallet. Tag plastered himself to a support beam, risking several peeks around it.

"Three active shooters in the loft," he reported tersely. "Nine o'clock high. One inside a stall at two o'clock. I can't see the others. Damnit!"

Jace rolled from behind a wood chipper and ran, bent over, to a tractor parked at the other end of the work bench, next to several animal pens. Puffs of dirt rose around him as bullets plowed into the floor. "Part of the loft is enclosed; I see a door with a shooter."

Mace became aware of the terrified screams of horses at the other end of the barn and the bleating and squealing of animals near Jace. He pressed his back along the legs of the table saw, rifle held upright in both hands, and pushed himself up far enough to eyeball the loft. A spray of automatic gunfire slammed into the metal and the work bench around him, causing him to flinch as a shard of wood embedded itself in his neck. He reached up and yanked it out with an oath.

Tag popped out from behind the support beam, firing into the loft. Jace targeted the shooter in the enclosed doorway, hitting him squarely in the chest with a double shot of rubber bullets. The man fell backward into the straw.

The Sandman, crazy bastard that he was, started to laugh. "I'm hiding behind barrels of freaking diesel fuel. Outstanding."

Christ.

They were sitting ducks where they were. Mace leaped to his feet, running full tilt along the left wall of the barn, beneath the hay loft. Holes appeared above him as someone started shooting through the floor; that gave him the edge he needed as he half glimpsed a shadow above him and fired. His target grunted and staggered away from the bullet holes. Mace continued to fire, emptying his magazine and swapping it out for a fresh one without slackening his forward progress. Behind him, the others leapfrogged forward, firing at half-seen targets.

"Look out!"

Alex careened into Mace, knocking him into the wall. A bullet tore a chunk out of the wooden wall where his head had been.

Somehow, he twisted around, righting himself and bringing his rifle to bear. The blast of Alex's shotgun nearly deafened him. It hit the man who'd popped out of an empty horse stall, their fifth shooter, straight in the face, and he cursed and doubled over, clawing at his eyes. Alex leaped across the intervening space and tackled him, flipping him onto his stomach and zip-tying his wrists behind his back before the man could rally.

Mace followed closely behind, turning his rifle upward to guard Alex's back. This wasn't going to work. Live rounds from semiautomatic assault weapons beat rubber bullets and beanbag shells every time.

"Weapons free!" bellowed Jace, who had evidently come to the same conclusion.

Breathing a sigh of relief, he dropped the rifle and drew his sidearm, firing almost instantly at one of the shooters in the loft. The man clutched his stomach, pitched forward, and fell onto the dirt floor.

"Shooter down," Jace shouted, "from the enclosed part of the loft."

"Shooter down in the loft proper," Mace added. "And third shooter secured in the first stall."

Tag appeared underneath the loft.

"Six o'clock high," Mace called to him, having the better visual angle.

Without hesitation, Tag swung around, firing five rounds in rapid succession into the hay loft. Someone screamed.

"Dad!" The voice rose in horror. "Dad!"

Mace could hear someone scramble through the hay and drop to his knees. Shit. A kid. "You in the loft. Throw down your weapon and surrender."

"Fuck you!"

The five of them moved to the center of the barn, each turned outward in a loose perimeter.

"Do you want to die, kid?"

Jace, Alex, and Tag started shooting almost in tandem. Mace turned in time to see the sixth shooter shove open an occupied horse stall, level his MP5, and fall before he could get a single shot off. The horse squealed and reared in fright, barely missing the man's prone body. Covered by the others, Alex approached it, arms up, speaking soothingly. The horse shied, but finally calmed enough for him to grab its halter. Alex stroked its neck as he led it back into the stall and secured the door.

"Throw down your weapons," Jace called to the kid in the loft, his voice brooking no disobedience. "Your pals are dead or dying. Do you really want to join them?"

A blond head appeared at the edge of the loft. The boy's face, streaked with tears, shone with defiance and fear. He couldn't be more than sixteen.

"All right," he said, a quaver in his voice. "I'll come down. Please . . . please don't hurt me."

"No one will—"

The *whoomp whoomp* of rotor blades chopping at the air as the HMRU helicopter arrived drowned out the rest of Jace's words. The boy whipped up an M-16, finger depressing the trigger as he sprayed rounds indiscriminately in their direction, screaming obscenities.

Mace didn't know who fired the kill shot. At least ten rounds pierced the boy's chest and head. He was dead before he hit the floor.

"Fuck it all," Jace swore. "Goddammit to hell."

Sickened, Mace stumbled toward the door. "Son of a *bitch*!"

Alex appeared next to him, gripping his elbow. He pulled free.

"You didn't have a choice," Alex said. "None of us did."

"I know that." Mace stopped, breathing deeply to control the rush of emotions.

"Motherfuckers brainwashed this poor kid," Tag said. "Made him believe he couldn't surrender. They're as responsible for this as we are."

Jace scrubbed a hand down his face. "Command, Team Three. Barn is secure. Commencing search for the package."

"Roger, Team Three," Driscoll said.

They found it in the last horse stall. The fifth shooter still wriggled to get free of the zip ties, glaring up at The Sandman, who had his heavy boot pressed against the man's collarbone. Mace couldn't blame him. It was a small enough expression of their shared rage over the forced killing of the boy.

A heavy green tarpaulin covered a banded wooden shipping crate in one corner; Mace and Tag tugged it off and to one side. Jace took the crowbar from a hook on the wall.

"We need to make sure," he said. They carefully pried the lid off and removed the industrial packing material, revealing an oversized red-and-silver suitcase. Mace and Alex loosened the straps and eased open the lid.

There it lay, beautiful and deadly. Two silver neutron-generating canisters surrounding an arming switch, nestled on either side of a red case containing high explosives. A circuit board with wires connecting the various pieces completed the nuclear bomb.

Jace keyed his mike. "Command, Team Three. Package is secure."

"Roger, Team Three. Team Two is taking fire. Can you maintain a protective posture where you are?"

Could they guard the nuke against reacquisition by the white supremacists? Damned right they could, and would.

"Affirmative, Command. We'll hold steady here," Jace said. "Sandman, stay here with the nuke. Tag, there's an open portal in the loft. See what you can do to help Team Two. Mace, Alex, we'll take the front door. No one gets in."

"Roger that."

"Got it, boss."

They scattered to their assigned positions.

The human-sized entrance through which they'd entered, as opposed to the huge, closed double doors at the other end of the barn, showed both the white supremacists and the friendly forces hunkered down in a firefight. The HMRU helicopter circled five hundred feet above them. The copilot had flipped on the searchlight.

They all heard the muted *whoomph*, saw the streak of dark gray smoke twisting into the air from the direction of the guard shack. Mace barely had time to breathe "Oh, shit!" before the RPG exploded against the helicopter's tail boom. He watched with horror as pieces of the tail rotor blew apart in the ball of fire, thrown in all directions as the helicopter spun to the left and dropped. A figure in a crewman's flight suit gripped both sides of the open door, but the helicopter bucked and he pitched headfirst out the door. The pilot dropped the collective and autorotated, then flared it to grab the air, working desperately to bring it to the ground without crashing.

"Losing altitude," he said, voice calm in their earpieces. "Brace for impact."

Time seemed to stop until the helicopter slammed into the ground, glass shattering as most of the windows burst. One of the struts collapsed as the main rotor hit the grass and buckled. They heard the cries and groans of the passengers through the pilot's headset.

"Status report," Driscoll said. "Pilot, respond."

No one answered.

"Helo, please acknowledge. Anyone available, respond. Shit. Can anyone see them?"

From his position, Mace could see shapes moving around. "Roger, Command. I see activity. Looks like the pilot's down, though, and I don't see the copilot."

"Hello? Hello, is anyone out there?" A woman's voice shrieked through the headset, so high-pitched it hurt his ears. "We need medical help right away."

"Identify yourself," Driscoll said. "Can you tell me the status of those on board? How badly are you hurt?"

"I'm one of the forensic scientists," she said, sounding slightly calmer. "We have three injured. My leg is broken. Manny's unconscious. One of the FBI agents has broken ribs, I think, and he's coughing up blood. He's not looking so good. I think the pilot is dead. The copilot was thrown out of the cockpit and isn't moving. Neither is the crewman who fell."

"I need to get out there," Mace said. "Evaluate the situation and stabilize them, if I can."

"Team Three, stand by," Driscoll said. "Control, we need those ambulances down here stat."

"Roger, Command," Javier Castellanos said. "Sending them down now, but I won't put them in the middle of a firefight. Can you secure the helicopter?"

Mace saw figures running through the dawn mist. Two armed women ran toward the children's dormitory, but the others headed directly for the helicopter. "Contact, ten o'clock west. Four men, all armed."

"Oh, my God," the woman shrilled. "They're coming right for us."

"Team Three, intercept. Protect that helo," Driscoll commanded.

"Roger that," Jace said. "Sandman, take this door. Mace, Alex, with me. Let's move."

The three operators sprinted toward the downed aircraft, zigzagging across the open field. The skinheads saw them and raised their rifles, firing as they ran. Mace felt the whine of a bullet pass by his head and kicked it harder. He returned fire, hearing the others do the same, glad they'd switched to their sidearms and live ammunition.

The separatists scattered, taking refuge behind the refrigerator and old farm truck.

Mace dove behind the combine alongside Jace. Alex crouched behind the bales of straw, rising to return fire. One of the separatists tumbled to the ground.

"Cover me," Mace called, pushing away from the huge front tire. Trusting his teammates to cover his six, he leaped over the combine's blades and ran flat out toward the helicopter. The crewman who'd fallen lay to his left; he dropped to slide in beside him, pressing his fingers to the man's carotid artery. No pulse.

He rolled to his feet. A bullet plowed into the ground near his boot, and he felt something slap against his pack. Keeping a low profile, he sprinted the rest of the way to the helicopter, firing a few wild rounds to keep the separatists back.

"Friendly coming aboard," he shouted, leaping onto the strut and into the main cabin. A man wearing a flight suit, on his belly at the far door, crabbed around into a half sit-up and pointed his semiautomatic toward Mace, finger on the trigger.

"Friend," Mace barked. "Stand down, crewman. What's your status?"

The crewman relaxed. "I'm good. Just bumps and bruises."

Mace could see blood dripping down the side of his face, but he seemed both mobile and able, so he turned to the other occupants in the confined space.

One of the FBI agents crouched to the side of the far cabin door, sidearm in his hand. They nodded to one another, immediately refocusing on their primary objectives. The woman who'd called for help sat awkwardly behind the copilot's seat, her leg bent at an unnatural angle, cradling a man's unconscious head in her lap. Another member of the HMRU team crouched near her, the whites of his eyes showing as he swallowed over and over again. When he saw Mace, hope flared on his face.

"I'm coming in," Alex bellowed, jumping into the cabin. He immediately turned, firing out the door. "Got your back, bro."

The second FBI special agent pressed a towel against the third's chest, blood coating his hands. Mace wasted no time dropping his pack and pulling off his medical bag, briefly fingering the bullet hole piercing it. Fuckers had missed. "What happened?"

"One of the pieces of our equipment broke free and slammed into him. He's having a hard time breathing."

Bullets pinged against the outer skin of the helicopter. Alex and the FBI agent popped off round after round, keeping the separatists back. The forensic scientist cowered, hands pressed to her ears, her hair in wild disarray.

Mace listened to the radio chatter as he checked the man's pupils. He shivered with shock and pain. Lifting the towel, Mace cut away the man's shirt and examined the injury. He pulled gauze and a wound seal kit from his pack, cleaned the area as best he could, then pressed the seal over the area, preventing air from entering his chest and collapsing a lung. Finally, he spread an emergency blanket over him.

"Watch him, okay?" he said to the other agent. "If he loses consciousness, sound off."

"I will. Could you check on the pilot?"

"Yeah." He made his way into the cockpit. The pilot was slumped over the cyclic, eyes closed. His helmeted head rested against an instrument panel, face covered in blood. Mace pressed three fingers to his neck.

"Pilot's alive," he reported, "but unconscious. We'll need a back board for him."

"Tango approaching on your twelve o'clock, Mace," Tag shouted from the barn loft. "I don't have the right angle."

Shots echoed through the cabin. The woman screamed. Mace scrambled out of the cockpit in time to see the FBI agent go down. One of the separatists climbed in, aiming at the hurt crewman. Mace shot him twice in the chest; his body jerked, and he fell backward to the ground.

The slide of his handgun locked back. Shit. He was out of ammo.

"What's going on out there?" he asked, going to check on the agent. He'd been shot in the head. Mace scooped up his sidearm, pulling him out of the way and taking his place.

"Everyone converged on the helo," Jace said. "But we got it under control. We're mopping up now."

"I'm out of ammo," the crewman said.

"It's almost over," Mace said. "You're good."

The gunfire ceased. Mace heard shouts for the skinheads to surrender. He hopped down onto the skid, immediately spotting a teenager careening his way, heading for the trees. He snapped the handgun up, tracking the boy with his finger hovering at the trigger.

No.

Of its own volition, his arm dropped. Not another kid. Not today.

Instead, he holstered the gun and jumped off the strut, took three running steps, and tackled the boy, riding him down hard. Mace flipped him over, knee at the small of his back, and fastened the flex cuffs to his wrists.

He caught movement from of the corner of his eye. Like a flash-frame movie, he saw a woman round the end of the blown-off tail rotor. He had every chance to note denim overalls over a red flannel shirt, the camouflaged baseball cap crammed atop her blonde head, and the jumble of black tattoos spidering down her arms. The American-made Barrett REC7 aimed at his head. Time slowed and stretched as Mace slowly, too damned slowly, drew his sidearm and aimed.

"Mace, look out!"

A body slammed into him, knocking him sideways. Time snapped back into the here-and-now. He felt the bullet tear into his shoulder, experienced the instant flare of agony. He and Alex hit the ground together, and for a moment both lay stunned.

Wracking nausea blew through him. He shifted from his side to his stomach and vomited, then forced himself to sit up and cast about for the shooter. She lay on her stomach in handcuffs, the barrels of five weapons pointed at her head, glaring from an eye rapidly swelling shut.

Bitch.

He turned to Alex, who groaned but had not moved. "Thanks, buddy. I guess I'm getting slow in my old age."

Alex's back was still to him, blood smeared along his side. Something in Mace's gut froze and congealed as Alex groaned again.

"Alex. Shit. *Alex*!"

"Quit yelling in my ear. I can hear you just fine."

Mace chuffed out a relieved breath. "Thank Christ. Is that my blood? I caught a round in the shoulder. Which, thanks to you, is just a minor ding."

"Good." Alex coughed. "Saving your ass is becoming a habit."

"That was some nice tackle," Mace said. Why wasn't he jumping to his feet and laughing like the knucklehead he was? Shit. Somehow he must have been hit, as well. "You want to turn over and let me take a look?"

"Nah, I'm good. Just gonna rest for a few."

He barely noticed his teammates gathering around them. Gently, reluctantly, he eased Alex onto his back, supporting his head so it didn't hit the ground, then unbuckled his tactical vest and eased it from his body. Probed the hole near his armpit. Found the entry wound, which soaked his hands with his friend's blood. Found the exit wound on his upper back, allowing the single bullet to pass through Alex and enter Mace's shoulder. *Fuck.*

"My medic bag—" he started.

"Here." Jace shoved it into his hands.

Someone yelled for the EMTs, but Mace barely heard it over the roaring in his ears. He leaned over until he could see Alex's eyes. His pupils were dilated and his face had leached of all color, save for the blood flecked around his mouth.

Mace squeezed his arm. "You got a little scratch there. I'm going to put a Band-Aid on it, okay?"

Alex managed a faint nod. "Gimme a sec to catch my breath, and we'll all go get some beers."

"You got it, kid. First round's on me."

He cut Alex's uniform away, revealing the mangled skin and tissue above his ribs. Suppressing his own nausea and pain, he grabbed a fistful of gauze, wiping away the blood, trying to assess the extent of the damage. The thin material became saturated in an instant, and his heart sank. Even applying a wound seal didn't fully stop the flow of blood.

"Okay, kid. You've earned yourself a ride in a cool bird." He glanced at Jace, who was already on his radio calling for a Life Flight helicopter. "We'll get you all patched up, okay?"

"Sounds good. We won, right?"

"You bet your ass we did. We stopped these motherfuckers and have the nuke safely under our control. You did it, kid."

Someone shoved a liquid bag and tubing into his hands, and he wasted no time inserting the needle into Alex's arm and starting a saline drip. His hand settled onto the farm boy's forehead, his gut roiling at the clammy skin and shallow breaths. A fit of coughing exhausted Alex, more blood speckling his mouth.

Mace turned his head. "Get those goddamned ambulances down here. Now!"

"I could go for that beer now, dude," Alex said, voice feeble. "I'm so thirsty."

"I'll personally bring you one, Alex," Mace said, gripping his hand hard. "Just hang on a bit longer, okay? Keep your eyes on me."

"You're not that pretty. Where's Lark? I could . . . stare into her eyes . . ."

Tears pressed against the back of Mace's eyes as the churn in his gut grew worse. Alex's injuries were critical. If he didn't get to a hospital fast . . . Mace shut the thought from his mind. Alex wouldn't die today. Not on his watch.

He needed to keep the kid conscious. "Talk to me. Tell me . . . tell me about your farm. The sunsets. You're always going on about the sunsets."

A corner of Alex's mouth tipped up. "Nothing sweeter than the sun going down in Iowa. You can sit behind the windmill. Brilliant reds . . . and yellows. It's like God paints . . . the sky."

He shivered, starting to go into shock. Mace tore off his jacket, but his teammates were faster, tucking their coats around his limbs and under his head.

"So who watches it with you? Your family. Tell me about your little sister. She's fifteen, right?"

Alex tried to tighten his fingers. Mace brought his other hand around and clasped them both around Alex's, trying to squeeze all his own strength into Alex through sheer force of will.

"Annie," Alex wheezed. "She turned sixteen last month. Got

her driver's license, even though she's been driving the . . . tractor since she was . . . ten." His eyes fluttered closed.

"Hey! Alex! Stay awake. Open your eyes."

Alex raised his lids with difficulty. "So tired."

The wail of sirens penetrated the air. Three ambulances roared into the clearing, EMTs jumping out and running toward them before the vehicles came to a stop.

"Hang on, Alex. Help is here."

Alex mumbled something, gaze unfocused as he started to close his eyes again.

Mace grabbed him by the shoulder and shook him, putting all his fear and desperation into the one motion. "Goddammit, Alex, you open your goddamned eyes, do you hear me? Fight it. You're a fighter . . . fucking fight!"

Alex rolled his head toward Mace. "Just let me—"

"No. You keep your fucking eyes on me. On me!"

Alex's hand relaxed in Mace's grasp as his head lolled back. Mace sagged, cradling Alex's head in his lap while the light died out of his eyes.

Chapter 42

Thursday, March 2. 7:05 a.m.
Otis Fitch's Property. Ducard, Massachusetts.

MACE BECAME AWARE of the EMTs pushing him out of the way, checking Alex's pulse and shining a light into his eyes. Someone jostled his shoulder, and he realized another paramedic had torn his uniform top, trying to see his bullet wound. He yanked away, standing to stalk toward the woman who'd shot Alex, now upright and being dragged to an FBI cruiser. He didn't even know what he intended, riding a wave of fury and grief and the need to tear her apart. Hands gripped him, pulling him to a stop, and he fought them, until his teammates finally just wrapped their arms around him and held on. They stood together with heads bowed, sharing their grief as they shared everything else.

"Command, a Life Flight is four minutes out for the two criticals," Javier Castellanos said. "I'm sending down police transport for our prisoners, and another HMRU team is on its way."

Mace stepped away from his teammates, anguish and guilt

tearing through him like knives. He walked back to Alex, aware of his team flanking him. Mace knelt next to him, placing a hand on his chest and bowing his head.

"It's my fault," he muttered, emotion clogging his throat. "It's my fault."

"You know better than that," Jace said. "You did everything you could. We all saw that."

Tag gently closed Alex's eyes and folded his hands over his stomach. "It was just a freak thing. A one in a thousand shot that the bullet would hit above his tactical vest."

"I tried. But I couldn't save him." Mace fisted his hands. "Who's going to tell Annie her big brother's never coming home? Who's going to watch over her to make sure boys don't take advantage?"

"I'll make the call to his family," Jace said.

"No." His gaze snapped up. "I will. It needs to be me."

Tag laid a gentle hand on his shoulder. "You didn't fail, Mace. No one could have . . ."

"I should have."

"Don't be stupid," Tag said. "You're not Superman, no matter what you think."

"Let's get that shoulder looked at," a paramedic said, setting his trauma kit near Alex's legs. He squatted next to Mace and reached for his shoulder, not even glancing at the obviously dead man.

"Get the fuck off me," Mace snarled, jerking upright. His chest tightened as rage swamped him. "Get the fuck away from us. From him." He grabbed the trauma kit and hurled it as far as he could. It bounced against the ground, undamaged.

"Hey, man," the paramedic said, raising his hands. "I'm just trying to help."

Mace advanced on him, not even knowing what he intended.

"You can't help. Don't you get it?" His voice wobbled. "You're too late."

He stumbled, lightheaded from blood loss. Jace and Tag were right there, supporting him on either side. The Sandman bellowed for a stretcher. The paramedic came forward again, eyeing Mace as though he were a dangerous animal.

As his adrenaline levels dropped, though, Mace became aware of the throbbing pain and the steady drip of blood down his arm. The paramedic cleaned around the wound and put on a dressing, then wrapped an emergency blanket over him. Tag pushed on his shoulders, so he allowed himself to sit, then lie, on the stretcher. In the background, he heard arguing, but the voices drifted away, getting fainter.

"We're staying with him," Jace finally barked. "End of discussion."

Relieved, he closed his eyes, but immediately opened them again as Alex's empty, staring face swam to the fore. Tag sat next to him, head in his hands, staring at nothing as the ambulance wailed its way to the emergency room.

He was barely conscious as he went into surgery to have the bullet removed. Afterward, he lay in the recovery room, wishing that Lark, not Jace, had tipped back a plastic chair and gone to sleep.

As though he'd conjured her from thin air, Lark inched open the door and peered in, eyes wide and worried, mouth pinched with anxiety. When she saw him awake, a brilliant smile spread across her face, and everything inside him relaxed.

"Hi," she whispered, coming right over to his bed. He lifted a hand, which she immediately grasped, squeezing so tightly he thought a finger or two might pop off.

"Hey, yourself."

She looked at Jace, who settled the chair onto all four legs and brought it over to her. "Thanks for calling me."

"My pleasure," he said. "I'll be in the waiting room."

"Oh, don't let me chase you—"

"See ya," Mace said over her.

Jace managed a wan smile and left.

"So," she said, sitting down on the hard plastic. "The bullet. Clean entry, but it missed your clavicle and scapula. It caused only tissue damage."

Mace forced a smile. "You sound like you've been a doctor for years."

"I'm just repeating what the surgeon told me. You'll need physical therapy, but you'll heal good as new."

"Whew."

"Mace." Her face grew sad. "I'm really, truly sorry about Alex."

He nodded, throat tightening. "Thanks. He was . . . one of the good ones."

"He was brave and true."

"He saved me," Mace managed.

Lark peered into his face, but he didn't know what she was looking for. "And you would have done the same for him. I know that. Everyone knows it, Mace. Don't beat yourself up."

He just shook his head, unable to speak.

"And I just want you to know that I'm here for you. When you're ready to talk about it, I'm ready to listen."

He nodded again, ashamed of the tears suddenly pressing behind his eyes. How had she known he needed time to process what had happened?

"Listen, I have an idea."

"Yes?"

"Why don't you all come up to my parents' place in Nantucket this week? Today. Or tomorrow. Get some R&R."

His brows lifted in surprise. "What does your mother say?"

She grinned, pumping a hand in the air in triumph. "That's the best part. She and my father are away until next week. So we'd all have five whole days with the place to ourselves."

He gently pried her fingers loose from his hand, which had lost all feeling. "I think that's a very generous offer. I'll talk to Jace about it."

She cleared her throat, shifting around in the chair, looking everywhere but at him. "Um, I might have already talked to him. He might have said some leave after this mission is in order, and he's clearing it with Colonel . . . Granite?"

Mace chuckled, delighted with her spontaneity. "Granville."

"So, you'll come?"

"Bet on it, little bird."

Chapter 43

Friday, March 3. 3:00 p.m.
Larkspur Mansion. Nantucket, Massachusetts.

"THANKS FOR LETTING me come up here with you."

Lark glanced uneasily at Jocelyn. "You didn't actually give me much of a choice, Joss. I've never seen you so stressed. Now that we're almost there, can you tell me why you needed to get away from the office so desperately?"

She turned to stare out the window. "I just did."

"Man trouble?" But Lark thought she already knew why Jocelyn was running away from Boston. The Cyber Action Team from Washington, DC must have finished its investigation into the malware, and the results didn't look good for her.

"I suppose you could look at it that way."

Lark mentally willed Jocelyn to face her, but she wouldn't turn from the window. "Joss, you're going to have to talk to me sooner or later. Wouldn't you rather do this in private?"

Jocelyn finally looked at her, hostility pinching her face. "Do what? What needs to be talked about?" she barked. "Your loyalty should be to me. To me!"

Taken aback, Lark took a hand off the wheel, patting the air in a calm-down gesture. "Easy, Joss," she said, hoping to soothe the other woman. "I only found out you were ChaosCowboy last week. How have I been disloyal to you?"

She crossed her arms and refused to answer. All the brainpower in the world wasn't going to help Lark understand Jocelyn's antagonism if she refused to talk about it.

"How?" she insisted.

Jocelyn flopped back in her seat morosely, plucking at the seat belt. "Who got you this job, anyway? Me. Not Melvin. Not Doug. Me."

"Ooookay," she said, drawing out the word. "Let's try this another way. Why didn't you tell me when I started working at the field office that you were ChaosCowboy?"

"I wanted to wait for the right moment, I guess," Jocelyn said, sounding calmer, thank God. "Didn't you ever wonder how you got assigned to Boston right out of Quantico? Most new computer scientists get sent to small offices to get experience before they're ever even considered for a bigger assignment."

"You recommended me?" Lark asked, certain the answer would be yes. No coincidence would place the two of them in the same office.

"I pushed hard for you. Went around Melvin to Doug. I told him he'd be missing out on a stellar asset if he didn't ask for you by name."

She didn't know what to say to that. Jocelyn had opened her eyes to a whole new world. "But you never contacted me again after you were arrested years ago."

"I was protecting you. I didn't want you implicated. They didn't know who SPURious was, and I wouldn't tell them."

Lark thunked her head against the seat back, hands gripping the steering wheel with stiff fingers. *Hell, just go for it.*

"Here's the thing, Joss. Remember when you found the Leonard Rose account in Elliott's code string? And we said whoever created the bogus account framed me for the theft of Sokolov's money?"

"Of course. Melvin did it."

"Here's the thing, though. When I accidentally let it slip that the spy stealing classified secrets used the same fake account, you weren't surprised. You already knew that."

"I had no idea at all," Jocelyn said, shifting in her seat. "It shocked me, same as you."

"No," Lark said sadly. "It didn't. You didn't even ask me about the espionage. You asked me if I cracked the malware. You knew the malware was designed for spying."

The enmity returned. "So what? I've always been a better hacker than you, Lark. I'd already looked at the malware before Doug assigned it to you."

Lark felt something inside her wither and die. ChaosCowboy had been her lifeline. Her friend, mentor, and protector. This woman—Jocelyn—she didn't know at all. Her head dropped to her chest. "Was it all a lie?"

"We're here!" Jocelyn said, turning completely away from Lark. "Holy Mother Mary. That's not a house. That's a mansion."

The main house stood only two stories, but spread out over four separate wings. The facade mimicked a rustic farmhouse, with shingled siding and white trim. The center wing even had a barn-shaped roof. But no farmhouse possessed a five-car garage, three chimneys, or eight bedrooms. There was a barn, sure, in addition to the stables, guest house, trainer's bungalow, housekeeper's quarters, and the caretaker's cottage. The cook, daily cleaning staff, grooms and stable hands, exercise riders, and jockeys came in daily.

The whole thing was immense, sitting close enough to Nantucket Sound to see the white sailboats littering crystal blue water.

Lark parked near the garage. The two vans pulled in beside her, and everyone piled out. Jocelyn lifted her suitcase from the trunk, refusing to acknowledge her. Heart heavy, Lark spotted Mace with the larger group shouldering duffle bags. His left arm hung in a sling, but she reminded herself that he would regain full use of the arm. At six-three, he stood taller than all but the huge, black, extremely senior sergeant, Ken Something-That-Started-With-An-A. He saw her first, nodding and turning his head to say something to Mace, who immediately came to intercept her.

"What's wrong?"

Ken must have seen something in her body language. "I'm fine. I'm better now that we're here and can all relax."

Mace looked unconvinced, so she smiled brightly, grabbing her suitcase and rolling it to the side so she wouldn't bounce it over his toes.

Even though a tiny part of her wanted to do just that. One problem at a time. She and Jocelyn would have to have a meeting of minds at some point. But right now, what was she going to do about Mace and his 'love you'?" As much as it thrilled her to hear him say it, it equally terrified her. In her experience, men were either controlling, unreliable, or weak. Mace was none of those things. Maybe.

He put his arms around her and hugged her, warming her instantly. "Tell me, little bird. What's wrong?"

Lark shook her head, throat closing up. "I'll tell you, but later, okay? Let's get all of you settled first."

He frowned, clearly wanting to push the issue. "All right."

"Lark!" called Jace. "Would you come up here for a moment, please? Your mother thinks we're an advancing horde of Mongols."

Oh, shit. Fuck. Shit fuck. Her parents were in residence. Why? Why why why?

Chances were her mother had used those exact words, too. Lark hurried to the front door, where her mother stood with her arms folded imperiously across her chest, barring the entryway. Lark's vision of a few carefree days shriveled into dust.

"Hadley," her mother said. "This is a surprise. Why aren't you still in Boston?"

"Why aren't you still in Scottsdale?" Damn it. Her hostility was reflexive. She tried to modify her tone. "I mean, it's nice to see you. I just didn't expect you to be home."

Her mother's chin lifted. "Evidently. Who are all these people?"

"They're Army soldiers, Mother, stationed at Fort Bragg in North Carolina. They make sure soldiers fighting in Afghanistan and Iraq have all the ammunition they need to kill people." She felt honor-bound to protect their true identities, but she deliberately needled her haughty mother. Though why she cared enough to push her mother's buttons confused her. Shouldn't she have matured past that by now?

Mace appeared at her side and slipped an arm around her waist. She felt more than saw the rest of the team array themselves behind her, offering tacit support. It warmed her.

Her mother pinned Mace with a pointed look. "I know you. You're responsible for the mayhem that ruined my daughter's wedding."

"Not exactly, ma'am, though I am the man responsible for saving your daughter's life."

Lark smothered a laugh at her mother's uncomprehending frown. "Everyone, this is my mother, Isla Larkspur."

"Nice to meet you, ma'am," Mace said, echoed by similar sentiments from the others. Lark wasn't fooled, though. Mace's indignation matched her mother's aloofness.

Who offered a chilly nod. "Always a pleasure to meet Hadley's friends. Were you all planning on staying here?"

How did her mother manage to sound so disapproving?

"If it wouldn't be an inconvenience, ma'am," Jace said.

They all turned to stare at her mother. She gave a minute shrug, turned, and went back inside.

Lark turned to Jocelyn, Heather, Stephanie, and the cluster of men. "Well. See? We're all perfectly welcome."

They laughed, some with less amusement than others.

Lark led the way through the door. Inside, the room opened up into a two-story open living area, set with imposing striped chairs and a square rotating coffee table. She knew from experience the chairs were stiff and uncomfortable; her mother used them with guests she did not want to linger. A Berber rug separated the area from the entryway, and a curved staircase led to a balcony on the upper floor. To the right, a hallway led to other areas of the house. Unlike the exterior of the mansion, there was nothing rustic about the inside. It screamed wealth and privilege.

A comfortably overweight woman rushed down the stairs and enveloped Lark in a warm embrace.

"Lark, my sweet girl! At last, at last. You stayed away too long."

She returned her hug. "So good to see you, Mrs. G."

"Heaven's sake, honey. You're all grown up. Call me Peggy."

Lark laughed. "Not that grown up. You'll always be Mrs. G to me."

The woman turned to the group overflowing the entryway. "I'm Peggy Galati, the housekeeper here. My goodness, look at you all. Big, strapping men. And lovely, lovely ladies. All right, all right, let's get you sorted out."

She eyed the group, rubbing her hands together with brisk efficiency, and saw Heather and Jace holding hands. She pointed to them. "You two, I'll put you in the Rose Suite. Ladies, I have three rooms on the second floor that will do nicely for you. I think I'll have to split you men between here and the guest house. Lark, honey, your room is just as you left it."

Lark peeped up at Mace, who still stood by her side. "Would you mind helping me with my luggage?"

He glanced down at her small carry-on bag and then into her eyes, heat flaring, and snatched up the bag with his right hand. "It looks pretty heavy. How about if I take it up for you?"

"I'll show you where to put it."

Whoops and cat calls followed them up the stairs. Lark's face heated. Mace nuzzled her hair as they climbed.

"Ignore those idiots. I do."

"They mean well." Laughter bubbled up in her throat. "I'm in the next wing at the end. As far from my parents' room as humanly possible."

"Her choice, or yours?" he asked sourly. "Isla seems very critical of you."

"Mutual agreement, I think." As she stepped inside her bedroom, she realized that Mrs. G hadn't exaggerated. Her room looked just as it had when she'd left for college.

Mace put his hands on his hips as he looked around. Light yellow paint turned the room golden in the afternoon sunlight. Her built-in cupboard, bookshelf, and window seat were white and her spindly little desk under the second window echoed the yellow of the walls, but the bedrest pillow on the window seat was frog green. Teenage Mutant Ninja Turtles covered her curtains. She'd tacked posters of *The Matrix*, Brad Pitt from *Interview with the Vampire*, and Storm from the *X-Men* to her walls, and she'd draped the simple wooden bedstead with a pink-and-purple geometric spread that blasted bright color through the room. The whole thing swirled and clashed like a circus tent.

"Oh, for fuck's sake. This is just embarrassing."

Mace laughed, head thrown back. "It's authentically you."

She turned to look at him. He, too, was authentically himself. He wore a plain black polo shirt and khakis. He could wear a sack and still look delicious. Or better yet, nothing at all. "Uh, you can put my bag on the bed."

He did so. "Where do you suppose my bedroom will be? I didn't think to ask."

She pressed her hands against her thighs, looking at her twin bed. Down, girl.

"I'll ask Mrs. G. Um, dinner won't be until six. So we have some free time."

He swallowed, naked desire in his eyes. "I'm dying to kiss you."

"I don't want you dying," she said, "so I guess you'd better get on that."

For long moments, they just stood there, staring at one another. Then she moved. One step. Two. His masculine scent teased her nostrils. She reached out a hand, and he watched, apparently fascinated, as it flattened against his chest and began a slow glide south.

"Holy God," he muttered.

He reached for her, enveloping her, crowding her backward until she hit the wall. His mouth found hers and it felt like he would devour her. She opened to him, sucking his tongue into her mouth, sighing with pleasure as their tongues dueled and she ran her fingers through his hair.

"God, that feels great," he groaned. He shifted restlessly, trying to slide his left hand around her waist.

"Be careful," she said. "Don't hurt your shoulder."

"My shoulder's fine." As if to prove it, he shrugged out of the sling, then scooped both hands under her rear, lifting her up.

She helped by wrapping her legs around his waist, back pressed against the wall, fingers busily pulling his shirt out from the waistband of his pants. His hands slid along her calves, catching the fabric of her dress and pushing it up her thighs until he reached . . . he stopped, a quizzical look on his face, then bunched the sundress around her waist and looked down.

"Denim shorts?"

"Uh . . . I ran out of clean underwear?"

He pressed his forehead to hers as he laughed. "Denim shorts never looked so sexy."

"Yeah, but I bet they look better on the floor."

She dropped her legs. He wasted no time stripping the dress off her and unbuttoning her shorts, pushing them down her legs and groaning as it became obvious she wore no underwear.

"Never stop wearing them," he said. "I always want to imagine you just like this."

She unbuckled his belt and caressed him through his khakis. He shuddered in pleasure, but then grabbed her hand, kissing each finger as he somehow got his pants and shoes off.

She hummed in approval as he sprang free. "Let me touch you. I'm dying to touch you."

"Later. Right now, I need to be inside you. Right now."

She giggled, kicking her shorts off, then moaned as he picked her up again. His hands gripped her thighs, and he ground his hips against her heated core as he kissed her. She couldn't help her mewls of pleasure, bucking against him, then grinding her hips in a slow circle in the way she already knew he liked.

"Did I mention right now?" he gasped. He spread her legs apart, which opened her to him. His magical tongue traced her lips and nipped at them as he found her wet opening and nudged inside.

"Nuh-uh. None of that gentle crap." She pushed herself down, crying out as he thrust upward, seating himself fully inside her. She slid both hands behind his neck, arching back to deepen the penetration. He actually gasped and closed his eyes. "You like?"

"I love," he muttered, burying his face in her neck.

There was that word again. Love. Before it distracted her, though, he thrust again, harder this time.

"Oh, yes," she panted, right there with him. "More."

He chuckled and grunted at the same time, which made her laugh. And then she moaned as he licked her nipple into his mouth, sucking and nibbling. She writhed on top of him.

"Bed," she gasped.

"Here."

His hands clamped her hips, his mouth rough as he sucked her tongue into his mouth, as he drove himself up into her again and again. She grabbed his shoulders, trying to hold on as her world spun out of control.

"Mace . . . Mace . . . harder . . . oh, God, yes . . ."

He yanked both her wrists above her head and locked them

against the wall, interlacing their fingers, trapping her there, completely open to him. Vulnerable. And she came, clamping on to him tightly as her body shook, as he bucked into her wildly, as she reveled in the orgasm ripping through her so strongly she shuddered and splintered apart. He came with her, shouting her name, hugging her tightly to him as they floated and reformed.

And there they stood, both panting hard, her forehead dropped onto his shoulder and his against the wall. She wanted to stay like this, just like this, for the next four hours.

Someone pounded against the door.

"Go away," Mace growled.

How did he even have the energy to speak?

"I need you both downstairs right now," Tag called out. "We've got a crisis brewing."

Chapter 44

Friday, March 3. 4:25 p.m.
Larkspur Mansion. Nantucket, Massachusetts.

As soon as he stepped onto the staircase, Mace knew trouble had found them. Melvin Dewey stood just inside the door, gripping Mrs. G's arm tightly.

"I said, I want to fucking talk to Jocelyn Katsaros. I know she's here."

Mace turned to order Lark to go back upstairs, but Melvin saw her first.

"Get your ass down here, Lark," he snarled.

Mace put out a hand to stop her from moving past him. "Not going to happen. Let go of the woman, Dewey."

Jace, Gabe, and Tag stood by the collection of chairs. The remains of coffee and sandwiches littered the table.

"Not until Jocelyn gets her lying bitch ass in here."

Dewey stood slightly taller than Mace, which put him at six-four easily. His bulky shoulders were tight, his chin thrust forward belligerently. Mace mentally calculated where he would have to hit him to put him down.

Lark put her hand on Mace's arm, trying to push it out of the way. He didn't budge. "What on earth are you doing here, Melvin?"

Melvin jerked a frightened Mrs. G closer. "I followed you up here. You set me up. You and Jocelyn. Set me up to take the fall."

Mace took a slow step down. Tag eased toward Dewey from the other side.

"Either of you takes another step, I'll break her neck. I swear I will."

Both operators stopped. Breaking someone's neck was far more difficult than movies portrayed, but neither of them could take the chance Melvin knew what he was doing.

"Melvin, let her go," Jocelyn said, coming from the room next to the stairs. "For God's sake. What do you think you're doing?"

She'd obviously just come from the shower. Her chestnut hair lay damply across her neck and shoulders, droplets moistening her blouse. One arm was raised as she prodded Gavin into the room ahead of her.

"Over there," she said. "Get with the others."

She had a revolver. Pointed at Gavin's head.

Who caught his eye before he moved toward the chairs. He looked pissed. Mace read his expression easily. Should he try to disarm her? Mace shook his head minutely. Jocelyn's finger rested on the trigger. If Gavin moved to take the weapon from her, it might discharge and hit someone else. Besides, the odds were good they could talk her down. She wasn't a killer.

"Jocelyn, what the hell are you even doing with a gun?" Lark shrieked. "Put it down. You're scaring everyone. Why do you even have a gun?"

She tried to duck under Mace's arm, but he caught her by the back of her shirt, stepping in front of her again. Which turned out to be a good thing, because Melvin reached under his pants and pulled out a Springfield 1911, pressing it to Mrs. G's head. The situation shifted from talk to immediate danger.

Mace shifted his shoulders, trying to assess his own physical condition. Making love to Lark had split some of his stitches, but he could do whatever was needed. Hopefully no one could see the seeping blood.

"Thanks to you, the FBI—my own fucking office—tried to arrest me this morning. I barely got away. This is all your fault."

What?

"Oh, shit," Lark said.

Mace twisted around to look at her. "What's going on?"

"Short version? Melvin might have been selling secrets to the Russian mob, and probably other interested parties, too."

Jocelyn raised a dramatic arm—the one not holding the revolver—and pointed it at Dewey. "He's guilty as sin."

"How about the long version, Lark? We're a little confused here," Jace called up to her.

Lark resorted to peering around Mace's shoulder to see down the stairs. "It's a little complicated. Before the nuke became a thing, the intrusion detection system at my office detected a malware program, and I was assigned to figure out what it did. Well, I did that."

"And?" Tag prompted.

"The malware caused a time-sync error . . . uh, the program made the computer think it was a different time, so that when classified documents were stolen out of the SCIF, the intrusion detection system wouldn't notice. And I traced the theft of the classified data to Melvin."

"See?" Jocelyn cried. "You know he's guilty."

Lark all but hid her face against his arm. What had triggered so much anguish? She had no love for her boss, but she'd had doubts about his guilt. Had she discovered that Melvin really had been framed, as she had been?

"Lark?" he murmured. "You okay?"

She nodded and straightened. "He's guilty, yes. But so are you, Jocelyn."

Oh, shit. No wonder Lark was so torn up.

Two criminals, both with everything to lose. Both carrying guns, both threatening the lives of everyone he loved. He'd be damned if another teammate, or, God forbid, Lark, was harmed on his watch. His blood began to burn with combat readiness, his muscles coiled to react if given even half a chance. No one would die today.

"That's not true," Jocelyn cried. "I did nothing but tell Doug what he did. Like you should have, Lark."

She turned to look at Jocelyn. "Yes. I should have. But that loyalty you were complaining I didn't have? I fucking didn't want to turn you in!"

Jocelyn glared at her, waving the muzzle of the revolver back and forth in the air. Her finger still rested on the trigger, damn it.

Lark stepped from behind him to his side. He renewed his grip on the back of her shirt, poised to yank her back if needed.

"Based on my findings," she said, "my boss called in a special investigative unit called a Cyber Action Team. They confiscated everything and started their own investigation, starting from ground zero and inching their way like snails to the top. I'm guessing they came to the same conclusion I did days ago, based on them trying to arrest you, Melvin. And you, Joss, for using me to escape before you could be arrested."

"Not me," Jocelyn said, voice shrill. "He sold secrets to the Russians. He made his own bed."

"Don't play Miss Innocent with me," Melvin shot back. "You're lying in it right there with me."

Jocelyn snorted a disdainful laugh, looking around at the others. "He's the perfect fall guy, don't you see that? Everyone hates him already. No one would be surprised to hear he sold out his own government."

Melvin tightened his grip on Mrs. G, who cried out in pain. "And what about you, you bitch? Selling classified documents was your idea in the first place. I'm not going down for this alone."

Lark wrapped her hands around Mace's bicep. For comfort, he thought. He gently lifted them away, patting them before freeing himself for battle.

"Why, Joss? I just need to know why you did it." She sounded on the verge of tears, but he couldn't console her while the threat remained.

Jocelyn shrugged, a calculating expression on her face. "You're hopelessly naïve, Lark. You assume that because you won't lie or steal, no one around you would."

"But selling classified information? You did that . . . for money?"

"No." For a moment, Jocelyn looked lost. Her hands shifted restlessly, causing the muzzle of the revolver to waver. "Not for money. Just . . . I used to be one of the best hackers out there. Hell, I trained you, didn't I? I was free."

"Joss, we might have been white hats, but what we did was illegal. The FBI gave us a chance to go legit."

Jocelyn gave a bitter laugh. "Legit. Right. Ten years of legitimacy, Lark. Walls and rules and writing up monotonous case reports. I couldn't take it another minute. I did it to save my sanity."

Lark sniffled. "You chose to be a criminal because you were bored?"

"Lark, I'm dying in that office. A little piece of me dies, every single day." Jocelyn rested her backside against the wall, lowering the revolver as though it had become too heavy. "You're taking to it like a duck to water. I'm happy for you, I truly am. We're too different, I guess. I thought if I had you in the office, it might be enough. It's not."

Tag and Gavin eased apart millimeter by millimeter, shifting almost imperceptibly toward Melvin. To keep his attention off them, Mace jabbed a finger at him. "What about you, asshole?"

Melvin's laugh was nasty. "Of course it's about the money. Who the hell can retire on a government salary?"

Mace imagined his hands around Melvin's neck. Given half a chance, he'd happily beat the crap out of the contemptible man.

Lark stamped her foot, anger coursing through her face and small body. "But you, Melvin, you're the asshole who framed me for stealing Sokolov's mob money. You could have gotten me killed, you bastard."

"So what? Either way, you'd be off the malware project. But no. You had to be the hero and figure it all out."

Fury slithered down Mace's spine. One way or another, Melvin was taking a beat-down.

"How do you know that, Lark?" Gabe asked. Good man, keeping Melvin's attention focused. Tag and Gavin had shifted closer to him. Another few seconds . . .

She turned her attention to Gabe, as well. "Doug assigned me the malware project over Melvin's objections. I thought Melvin just didn't like me. Turns out he objected because he knew I'd figure it out. Jocelyn created a fake account that Melvin used to steal classified secrets. When I got too close, he framed me for the mob theft. The Cyber Action Team must have finally figured it out, too." She took a breath. "What secrets did you sell, Melvin? Who did you put in danger because of your greed?"

"What difference does it make now? The fucking intrusion detection system finally found the malware." He loosened his grip on his hostage. She stayed still and small, trying not to attract notice.

"Humor me."

Jocelyn straightened, the revolver dropping to her side. "He kept the Russian mob in the loop over the years. One step ahead of the FBI. That's how Sokolov knew about the suitcase bomb in the first place. We didn't realize the fifty mil was to buy the nuke. Why the hell would a mobster want a nuclear weapon, for God's sake? But Melvin pointed the Russians right at Lark, and a pissed-off Sokolov is dangerous." Her look seemed apologetic, but Mace wasn't buying it.

Tag reached a position where he could reach Melvin, if needed.

Once she decided to open up, Jocelyn couldn't seem to stem the flood of words pouring from her. Confession was good for the soul, apparently.

"He found a report listing all the nuclear storage facilities in Russian and Ukraine," she said. "Then he hinted around to a bunch of nuclear scientists that he could get them a nuke if they paid him enough. Fatianova Uvarov jumped at it."

Melvin glared at her. "But you wrote the program to disable the security grid at the nuclear dump in Lyubinsk. What you did was worse than what I did."

Lark whirled on Melvin, face contorted in fury. "You're a criminal. A cowardly, vile felon."

"I can't stand your fucking smartass attitude," Melvin said. "Your weird hair and your unprofessionalism. But I didn't think of threatening you to get you to back off. That was all her."

"Joss, tell me you didn't." Lark's voice rose. "You tried to frighten me? Threatened my family? My *sister*?"

Jocelyn frowned. "I'd never hurt you, Lark. But I needed you to stop before you found out what we were doing. But you didn't stop. You're like a dog with a bone."

Melvin jerked Mrs. G closer, using her as a human shield as he whipped the handgun around to point at Tag. "One more step, asshole. Take just one more step."

Tag stilled.

"Get down here, Lark," Melvin barked. "Get over there with the others. I don't have any qualms at all about shooting you. You have ten seconds. Then I'll shoot this woman first, then your boyfriend, then you. Are you understanding me, Lark?"

He didn't want to . . . but Mace came the rest of the way down the stairs, keeping Lark behind him.

Melvin raised the gun, pointing it at him. "I said—"

Jocelyn shot him.

Even as Melvin fell, Mace leaped to her side, snaking his arm under her neck in a choke hold and trying for the weapon in her hand. She twisted her wrist, dropping the handgun, and he missed the grab. To his shock, she stepped back into his choke hold, pressed her fingers against the back of his hand, twisted, and threw him into the ground. He rolled out of the throw and jumped to his feet.

Lark screamed in rage, lunging at Jocelyn, grabbing her hair and yanking down furiously. Jocelyn ducked low and turned toward Lark, slamming her knee into her gut. Lark choked, the wind knocked out of her, and dropped to the floor, clutching her middle.

Mace saw red. No one hurt Lark. He gave his best death glare, feeling as feral as he probably looked. Seeing his expression, Jocelyn's face whitened.

Her martial arts knowledge had taken him by surprise, and he cursed himself for not anticipating it. She crouched low, hands open. As a smaller woman, she probably favored taking the fight to the ground, where the advantage would be hers.

"Just let me walk out of here," she said. "I can disappear."

"Not a chance," he growled. "You're going to jail for your crimes."

He came at her fast, throwing a wide looping punch to draw her in. As expected, she parried the punch, grabbed his wrist, and moved in close to his body, setting him up for a shoulder throw. Before she could thrust her hips back, he twisted his arm free, stepped out, and drove the heel of his foot into her knee.

She screamed as her patella shattered, falling to one hip. She grabbed her ruined knee, rocking in agony.

Mace saw her handgun by her head the same time she did. As she rolled for it, Tag scooped Melvin's Springfield off the floor.

"Mace!"

Tag launched it across the room. Mace snatched it out of the air one-handed, turning back to Jocelyn. Who had her revolver pointed at his heart.

Mace pulled the trigger.

The two shots hit Jocelyn once in the chest and once in the head. She collapsed like a marionette with her strings cut.

Lark screamed, scrambling on all fours to her side, gathering Jocelyn's head into her lap and sobbing over her body. Jocelyn's blood soaked into Lark's clothing. Mace dropped his gun hand to his side, heart shredding, torn between wanting to comfort her and understanding that Lark would blame him for her oldest friend's death. He stood awkwardly, unsure of what to do.

"You didn't have a choice," Tag said. "It was her or Lark."

Mace nodded. "I know that. But Jesus, Tag. What if she can't see it? What if she can't forgive me?"

Tag put a hand on his shoulder and squeezed. "Easy, there, Mace. She's a smart cookie. It might take her a while, but she'll get there."

"I hope so," he muttered. What if she didn't, though? He could lose her for good.

"So much for rest and relaxation," Jace said. "Your shoulder's bleeding again."

"It's fine." Mace couldn't tear his gaze from Lark, hurting for her.

"This will take a while to sort through," Jace said. "And then Mrs. Larkspur will no doubt invite us to depart."

As if on cue, police cars screamed to a stop in front of the house.

Mace set the handgun on a stair and squatted next to Lark, who was still crying like her heart was breaking. "Honey, I'm so sorry. She didn't give me any choice. I didn't want to shoot her, believe me." He reached out a tentative hand to stroke her hair, expecting to be rebuffed.

Instead, Lark pressed her head closer to him. His heart leaped in his chest.

"I know," she whispered. "She was going to kill you, Mace. I can't believe she would do something like that, but she's not the same person I used to know. Or maybe I'm just fooling myself, and I never knew the true ChaosCowboy at all."

He curved himself protectively around her. "Shh. Plenty of time to dwell on that stuff later."

Tag checked on Melvin. "Single shot to his head. He's dead."

The police streamed inside. Everyone started talking at once.

"Quiet," one of the cops shouted. He keyed his shoulder mike. "We need a bus down here, pronto."

It took several hours to clear everything up. The police took witness statements and gathered up the evidence. The coroner bundled Melvin and Jocelyn away in body bags.

At last, only the special operators and the Larkspurs remained.

"You bring chaos with you wherever you go, Hadley," her mother said, mouth pinched tight and her arms crossed over her chest. "Why can't you be more like Kaley?"

Mace bristled, wishing he could slap the sour expression right off her snooty face. Lark brought color and joy with her, and anyone who couldn't see that wasn't worthy of her regard. He rubbed an irritated hand along the back of his neck. Goddammit.

Lark stiffened her spine and marched right up to her mother. "I am not like Kaley and I will never be like Kaley," she said loudly. "I'm sorry you think I'm less than, but I'm not. I'm sorry you can't see me for who I am, but that's your problem, Mother, not mine. I'm a good person and I deserve your respect. Now. My friends and I are going to relax here at the mansion for at least a week. We'll swim and sail and be loud and obnoxious. We'll run around naked if we want to. You're welcome to stay, if you want, but that's what's going to happen."

Isla Larkspur drew her head back, looking Lark over from head to toe, a curious expression on her face. Finally, she uncrossed her arms, letting them hang loosely at her sides. "Well, then. I'll head back to Scottsdale with your father. Take care of Peggy, please. She's had a shock."

The entire group watched her mount the stairs and enter the mansion.

Lark's breath caught in her throat, both hands rising to cover her mouth. "Oh, my God," she whispered. "I did it."

Mace looked down at Lark, and found her staring back at him, a wondering expression on her face. "What is it?" he asked, feeling his eyes warm with tenderness.

"You let me fight my own battle," she said, mouth round with surprise. "Like you did in Mr. Sokolov's limousine. You didn't try to jump in and take control away from me."

He chuckled. "You were handling it."

"Oh my God oh my God. You're like the world's best amazing person."

He burst out laughing. The phrasing was so uniquely Lark.

He grinned, grasping both her hands between his, bringing them to his mouth to kiss her knuckles before placing them against his heart. "I'm so proud of you."

A bright smile lit her face. "And you. Don't think you're escaping my grasp. You . . . you're my person," she whispered.

He grinned. "Do you realize how much I love you, little bird?"

She looked into his face and beamed.

"I do."

Don't miss the other thrilling Duty & Honor novels . . .

NIGHT HUSH

BAIT

DEEP COVER

Available now in print and e-book!

About the Author

LESLIE JONES was an Army Intelligence officer for many years and she brings her firsthand experience to the pages of her work. She resides in Phoenix, Arizona, and is currently hard at work on her next book. Her debut novel, *Night Hush*, was nominated for the Best First Novel RITA® Award.

Discover great authors, exclusive offers, and more at hc.com.